I0788420

FALLEN FROM THE STARS

THE KRAKEN #6

TIFFANY ROBERTS

FALLEN FROM THE STARS

Vasil has spent his life serving the needs of his people, denying his own desires — until a star falls from the sky. He follows its fiery trail and finds the unexpected: a mysterious human female. She is his chance at having the mate, the family for which he's longed. But when he discovers her connection to the organization that created and enslaved his ancestors, he must decide if claiming his happiness is worth the risk of exposing the kraken.

Stranded on an unknown planet, Theodora Velenti has limited supplies and no way to call for help. Hopeless, the arrival of a half-man, half-octopus alien doesn't seem like an improvement. But despite his differences, Theo finds herself drawn to him. Giving in to Vasil's advances means accepting that the life she knew is gone forever. Can she give up a chance of rescue or is what she and Vasil feel for each other real?

May your stars always shine bright.

CHAPTER 1

FIRE HAD FALLEN from the sky.

Vasil gave chase; he sped through restless waters, sweeping his arms to the sides, flaring his tentacles wide and snapping them together. He lifted his head above the surface as often as possible to keep the fiery object's trail in sight without sacrificing speed, but he was not quick enough — the smoke overhead grew wispier and more indistinct with each passing moment, hastened by the strengthening wind. It would dissipate entirely before long, and he would lose his only chance to locate the mysterious object.

He'd kept his den on land for nearly two years, and in that time, he'd never seen anything like what he'd experienced on the beach — a streak of orange fire blasting overhead that had briefly illuminated the sand as though it were a warm, sunny afternoon and seemed to set the water ablaze for a few heated moments. His knowledge of the surface world was limited, but fire did not fall from above. Wind came from the sky, and water when it rained, but *not* fire.

What was it? Had a star fallen from the night sky? He could recall one of the humans explaining to Arkon that the stars were distant balls of fire, but Vasil had not been directly involved in the conversation. *Could* a star plummet from its place overhead?

If so, what did it mean?

He *needed* to know what the thing was despite his misgivings; taking to open water after nightfall alone was foolish, but curiosity had overpowered his good sense.

Sea swells rose and fell around him, creating ever-changing peaks and valleys that only grew more pronounced as Vasil left land farther behind. The unease in his gut intensified and seeped into his bones. It solidified into cold, heavy dread as the sea became choppier and the smoke further faded.

Vasil rode a swell to its peak and scanned his surroundings. The sea was dark gray beneath an inky black sky, barely reflecting the twinkling starlight overhead. Water stretched to the horizon in all directions save one — dark clouds blotted out the sky to his left, creating the illusion that the water was clawing its way skyward to swallow the heavens. Flashes of lightning pulsed through the distant clouds, highlighting the enormity of the coming storm. Thunder followed a few heartbeats later, its rumbling vibrating through him to resonate with the icy dread harbored at his core.

The collapsing swell plunged him into a shadowy valley, limiting his view to the surrounding walls of water, the stars overhead, and a lingering span of the smoke trail.

He couldn't guess how long he'd been swimming; Vasil knew only that land was far behind him. He'd not reach The Watch before the storm struck even if he turned around now. Whether the fiery object awaited just beyond the next swell or somewhere beyond the horizon, he'd have no choice but to seek shelter on the ocean floor tonight until the weather subsided and the sea calmed.

His body ached from the exertion of his frantic pursuit, but he would not allow his efforts to be wasted.

Gritting his teeth, he pushed forward. The ocean tossed him up and down with increasing agitation and force, a precursor of what was to come, but he clung to his determination. He would use every available moment before he was forced to abandon his hunt.

The one occasion upon which he'd favored curiosity over caution had quickly become a dangerous situation. He was sure the humans had a word or a colorful expression for what he was experiencing; this seemed like a bad joke, made in poor taste and at Vasil's expense, but that word didn't feel right.

Fresh thunder boomed over the ocean, so deep and powerful it seemed it would crack open the sky and pour all the remaining stars onto Halora in a rain of silver fire. Instinct demanded Vasil seek shelter, but he had time to push a little farther.

He adjusted the rhythm of his tentacles to keep his head above water as he rode the next swell toward its peak. The smoke trail was at its thinnest thus far; stars shone through its ghostly form, which was only a shade or two lighter than the darkness beyond.

Howling wind whipped stinging moisture into his face. As he reached the apex of the swell, he swept his gaze over the tumultuous sea, searching for even the smallest sign of something in the water. Storm clouds loomed on the edge of his vision, closer than before. Disconcerting energy charged the air, crackling across his exposed skin.

Something flashed in the water — a brief reflection of starlight, even more fleeting than a lightning strike.

The water fell, obscuring Vasil's view of the object. Whatever it was, it had been relatively close, but that could change rapidly in these conditions. Vasil was at the mercy of wind and sea. Even with him swimming his hardest, it was possible the sea would only carry the object farther and farther away. He could chase it through the night and never draw nearer if the sea chose to toy with him.

He pushed onward, demanding more from his strained muscles. He'd come this far. He would not surrender.

Each time he crested a swell, he sought the object, and he was rewarded with occasional flickers of reflected starlight or glimpses of something paler than the surrounding water. He adjusted his course upon each sighting, battling powerful, conflicting currents to draw a little closer, one body length at a time.

With each beat of his hearts, the storm also drew closer.

As he sank into the next valley, the object descended an opposing swell directly ahead.

A flash of lightning covered the object in hard light for an instant. It was rounded and oblong with a reflective circle near the front. The object floated on the waves, ringed by dark, bulbous protrusions around its base — flotation sacs of some sort. The ghostly afterimage of its reflective surface lingered in his vision for several moments after darkness returned, drifting through his sight as the booming thunder reached into his chest and squeezed his hearts.

Rain began suddenly, falling in a relentless torrent that further limited his already obscured view.

Vasil did not allow his head to dip below the surface. He swam against the sea's pull with all his remaining strength and latched onto the object's flotation sacs with his tentacles once it was within reach.

The object itself was larger than him, well more than a body's length from one end to the other and almost half as tall — comparable in size to some of the middling fishing boats back in The Watch. Though he wasn't entirely sure about human measurements, he guessed this to be about five meters from front to back. It appeared entirely sealed above the water's surface. He pressed a hand to its side. If it was metal, it did not feel like any metal with which he was familiar; this seemed somehow smoother and denser.

More lightning flared in the sky, illuminating strange symbols on the object's side. They resembled the symbols used in human writing he'd seen at both The Watch and the Facility, but they were disrupted by dark marks that must've been caused by the fire.

The thunder's rumbling vibrated through the mysterious object.

This is beyond foolish. If it is metal, it is likely to be struck by lightning, and I will learn about fire from the inside out.

Just a quick look and he'd go below for shelter. A few more moments couldn't hurt — he'd not deny himself that after the struggle of locating this thing. He could not bring himself to abandon the pursuit of his curiosity despite the explicit danger.

Raindrops hammered the strange material, shattering and splashing to fill the air with stinging mist. With hands and tentacles, Vasil hauled himself out of the water and climbed atop the object. His suction cups felt a narrow seam on the surface, but it was too small to see. He paid it little mind; the circular section of glass inlaid on the top front of the object claimed his full attention.

Vasil leaned over the glass and wiped away the droplets gathered upon it with one hand, but it was too dark to see inside. What did it contain? Though he had no idea what this thing was, it seemed humanmade; this was no fallen star, unless humans had made the stars just like they'd made the kraken.

Humans hadn't *made* the stars, they'd come *from* them ages ago. Hadn't they?

As the object bobbed on the churning water, sea and sky lashed against it with wind, waves, and rain. All three struck with biting force, hitting Vasil repeatedly as though possessing solid form. The sting permeated his skin. He needed to leave, needed to give up this stupidity and seek shelter from the storm's fury.

Instead, he found himself leaning closer to the glass, lighting the tiny points of bioluminescence on his stripes. Their glow reflected on the smooth surface, creating the brief illusion of a sky full of stars. Through the reflections, he could just make out a dark, shadow-shrouded shape, defined only by faint highlights along its edges.

Vasil dipped his face closer still. What was it? There was something familiar about it, but he could not assemble the pieces into a complete, coherent mental image — until lightning arced overhead.

Neither the sudden flash nor the immediate, deafening peal of thunder accompanying it startled him; his mind was too absorbed by what he saw. For the briefest instant — a fraction of a heartbeat — the object's interior was illuminated. Though bereft of color, the image was burned into his mind with vibrancy and clarity.

There was a human female inside, eyes closed and features relaxed.

Countless thoughts tumbled through his head, most of them questions. Had humans come to Halora by plummeting from the stars? Was each star a human encased in one of these egg-like...*things*?

He thrust all questions aside save for the most immediate — was this human alive?

If he went below to shelter himself from the storm, he would lose the object to the sea forever. He could not haul it under with the flotation sacs inflated, but if he destroyed them and the object sank, he also wasn't likely to get it back to the surface again.

Could this thing weather the storm?

Could *he*?

He'd wasted too much time already. No one else would help this human. No one else could.

Moving as carefully as possible despite the thrashing sea, Vasil dragged himself below the surface and clung to the underside of the object. The sound of water rushing all around dominated his hearing, but it was not enough to fully drown out the booming thunder from above.

His tentacles brushed over the object's otherwise smooth surface in search of better purchase only to find a damaged portion; the object's outer shell had either cracked or been torn off in a spot on its underside, leaving a jagged wound behind. He dared not probe the damage further; his limited study of human machinery and technology over the last year or two had taught him primarily that much of it was far too complicated to be repaired without sophisticated tools and specific, precisely-crafted parts.

He held tight as the storm raged and the sea continued its violent dance, as the strange object leapt and fell on the water, as waves and currents battered his body. Time held no meaning — the rapid thumping of his hearts was the only measure of its passage, interrupted often by unpredictable lightning flashes that pierced the blackness and roaring thunder that vibrated into him through the object. At some point, Vasil closed his eyes and poured all his focus into maintaining his desperate grip on the object, fighting the aches that had suffused his body down to his smallest suction cups.

Abrasive sand scraped along his back.

Opening his eyes, he scrambled to a new position on the side of the object, dragging his torso above the surface.

The sky remained dark, the wind strong, but the rain seemed to have eased. And there was something directly ahead — a strip of paler gray in the gloom.

A beach.

Vasil shifted to the rear of the object and pushed, ignoring the fiery protests in his weary arms, shoulders, and tentacles. He moved with an awkward combination of swimming and crawling, digging his front tentacles into the sand to force the object forward. The waves rolling toward the shore helped him along. Soon, the water was shallow enough that he didn't have to swim.

The water steadily grew shallower until there was no swimming involved.

His advance faltered when the object's underside finally struck sand. Vasil paused, chest heaving. His body craved rest; were he to collapse there, he would undoubtedly have fallen into a deep, exhausted slumber despite the surf flowing over and around him.

But the tide could not be trusted to safeguard either Vasil or the object. Even a slight rise in the water level would be enough to carry either of them back out to sea.

He spread his tentacles, lowered his head, clenched his jaw, and pushed.

The object was heavier than he'd expected now that it was partially on land, but the smooth curve of its underside — paired with the incoming tide — eased its journey just enough for him to gain ground. When the object tipped forward, he paused only long enough to lower his stance and adjust the positions of his hands before pushing again.

Slowly, he moved the object out of the water. He allowed himself not a moment's respite until he'd pushed it beyond the driftwood and debris that marked the high tide line. Growling against the pain in his overexerted muscles, he gave one final shove before collapsing to the ground.

As he caught his breath, rain fell on his back. Its rhythm seemed deliberate, as though it were part of a song primarily played by instruments he could not hear. He closed his eyes and let himself feel everything — the drumming rain, the wet, rough sand beneath him, the rasp of briny air in and out of his lungs, and the throbbing aches in his limbs.

He pushed himself up slowly and climbed atop the egg-like object. He slid his palms over its surface to locate the tiny seams he'd felt before, but they were too narrow to even slip a claw between, and he could identify no release mechanism nearby. Even the edges of the glass seemed to blend smoothly into the rest of the exterior, offering no purchase for the tips of his claws.

Vasil rolled onto his back and turned toward the sea. The roiling waves were black and foreboding, but the sky bore the faintest hint of gray — a whispered announcement of approaching dawn? It felt as though days had passed since he'd leapt into the water to chase the unknown object. Could it only have been *hours* since he'd been on the beach near his den, contemplating what relationship he might hope to build with his daughter now that her parentage had been confirmed?

He lowered himself from the object and moved onto the long grass bordering the beach, where he eased onto the ground. Fumbling around in the dark wasn't likely to release the woman, especially when he knew nothing about the object's purpose or functionality. But he couldn't just leave her locked inside. If she yet lived, there was no guarantee of her continued survival. What if her air supply was limited or somehow tainted?

What if she was already dead?

He swept trembling arms and tentacles over the ground in a feeble search. All he needed was a rock with enough weight and he could attempt to break the glass.

His eyelids drooped, and his head dipped unintentionally. He shook himself, clawing at alertness, but his mind remained oddly hazy.

Breaking the glass could do her harm, and Arkon...Aymee...they are not here to tend her if she is wounded...

His limbs gave out beneath him, and he sagged onto the grass.

No one to help her.

I *must help her.*

He raised his head to look at the object, but it was too heavy to hold up. Everything was too heavy.

Vasil sank into darkness; it washed over him like seawater at high tide.

CHAPTER 2

Theo gasped and jolted forward as her eyes snapped open. Her harness cut into her chest, stealing the breath from her lungs. She struggled against it, yanking at the straps, but it held fast. The air felt thin; despite her rapid, ragged breaths, she couldn't get enough oxygen.

"*You need to exit the pod,*" Kane said through their neural link. He'd been the familiar voice inside her head for years, and hearing him grounded her enough to ease her panic. If only a little.

"No shit," she rasped.

"*The pod's internal systems have been damaged. You will need to use the manual release for the hatch.*"

"And what am I going to find out there? Am I going to be able to breathe, or is the air going to kill me?"

"*Yes, you're going to die when you open it. It should be a slow and painful death, quite entertaining for me. Or you can just stay put and fall into a gentle sleep.*"

Her groping fingers finally found the harness's buckle. She

pressed the button, and the straps' restrictive pressure finally relented.

"Your sarcasm is so not helpful right now, Kane. Remind me to have you wiped and rebooted the next time I'm in for evaluation." Pulling her arms free, she swept her hair out of her face and leaned forward, extending her arms to twist and pull each of the four emergency releases around the hatch two at a time. There was a loud hiss.

"You'd never do that, Theo."

Breath ragged, Theo rolled her eyes. "Of course I wouldn't."

She placed her hands on the hatch and pushed. It didn't budge until she moved off the seat and bunched her legs beneath her, opening just a crack. Salty, chilly air flowed in through the gap. The hydraulics kicked in a moment later, and the hatch swung upward to its fully-open position.

Theo inhaled deeply as she stared up at a gray, overcast sky. The air was sweeter than anything she could remember — nothing like the heavily filtered, recycled air she'd been used to for most of her life.

"Well, I'm not dead yet," she said, straightening her legs to stand upright.

"*Yet*," Kane emphasized.

"Dick. Oh wait, you don't have one."

"Neither do you, but that didn't stop you from teaching me how to be one."

"I taught you no such thing." She surveyed the open stretch of sand and rock before her, which was met by rolling waves only fifteen or twenty meters away. The water was a deeper gray than the sky, broken by white crests and foam. She couldn't recall the last time she'd seen water like this — if she'd ever seen it in person to begin with — much less walked upon something other than the hard, artificial flooring of interstellar ships and space stations.

Theo frowned and rubbed the spot where the harness had

dug into her chest. "Wanna be helpful, Kane, and tell me where the hell we are?"

Kane offered her a few moments of silence. She might have enjoyed it if it wasn't so alarming; he usually had an answer ready without delay.

"Kane?"

"I don't know."

"What?" Sudden heat suffused her — the beginning of panic. "How the hell do you not know?"

"There are no satellites within my range, IDC or otherwise. I am unable to pinpoint our current location."

Theo dropped into her seat and swept a hand over the console. The holographic controls flickered for an instant before the projection solidified. Her frown deepened.

"What happened? Where is everyone else?" she asked as she manipulated the controls to access the emergency beacon.

"If I don't know where we are, Theo, why would I know where anyone else is?"

The display flashed and pulsed with static before presenting an error message.

"Error? The beacon should've been activated automatically, right?"

"Due to the circumstances of the incident, it was not activated."

"It's an *emergency* beacon for a reason." She slapped the console and scowled.

"The beacon wasn't activated because there was a strong chance of the incident having been caused by an enemy attack. The IDC does not wish to broadcast the whereabouts of surviving crewmen to nearby enemies."

"So you can't detect any other pods nearby? We're *alone* here?"

"There are no other escape pods within range of my sensors, and ours was damaged in the explosion. Its long-range communications are destroyed, its internal air supply has been almost fully depleted,

and according to the limited records I was able to obtain as we left the ship, we may have been thrown through a tear created by the malfunctioning warp drive."

Theo leaned back and glared out at the gray clouds. "Got any good news?"

"*We have each other.*"

"I said *good* news."

"*If I had a mouth, I would be frowning.*" He went silent once again, but she could almost *feel* him thinking. It had been so strange when Kane was installed in her back when she'd enlisted in the IDC; she'd felt like she would never have a moment of privacy, like her thoughts would never be her own again. But now it was more disconcerting to contemplate his absence. He was part of her.

Her best friend.

Theo sighed and ran a hand through her hair, tugging it back from her face. "You know I love you."

"*I wish I had more information to offer, Theo.*"

"I know."

Sitting forward, Theo manipulated the controls to navigate to the diagnostics menu, but she'd only made it through two options before hitting another blaring red error message. Before she could even ask for assistance, Kane inserted a projection of the escape pod into her vision through her retinal implant.

"*Fortunately, the field generator held despite the exterior damage,*" he said as the image turned to display red areas of damage on the rear underside of the pod. The image enlarged to show the damage in greater detail. "*It held long enough to keep us alive, but we landed in an ocean when we arrived on this planet. Exposure to water increased the damage to the internal systems.*"

"Damn," she muttered as she studied the damage display. "If we were still on the ship, I could fix this, but we don't have the right tools or any of the parts. Not even to fix the transmitter."

Pushing herself to her feet, Theo grasped the edges of the hatch opening and climbed out. Her boots sank into the sand below. The air was moist; whether it was due to ocean mist or the threat of a storm, she couldn't tell. What would rain feel like on her skin? She couldn't remember — she hadn't experienced it since her childhood on Old Earth.

She walked to the back of the pod and groaned. The exterior shell was dented and scorched black above and below the floatation ring, and the hole on the underside was clearly visible despite the angle and the shadows. There was no way she could repair that without the resources to do so.

She cursed. "Completely wrecked."

Wind tousled her hair as she scanned her surroundings. The beach gave way to vegetation not far behind the pod, beginning with long grass and thickening to full-blown jungle not much farther along. The plants were more shades of green and purple than she realized existed. She turned back toward the ocean.

The waves crashed against the shore, the strongest reaching a point perhaps ten meters away from the pod before receding. She glanced to the side, studying the stretch of sand to the pod's left; it was nothing but soft sand this far inland. No debris.

"You said we landed *in* the ocean, right?" she asked.

"Yes."

"How the hell did the pod get here, then?"

"You do *understand how shorelines work, don't you? I know you've spent most of your life in the bowels of various ships..."*

"Don't get smart with me. Look." She settled her gaze on the water line before dragging it to the bits of driftwood and broken shells farthest from the sea. "You see how far away that is from the pod?"

"We've hardly been here long enough to have accurate data on the tidal patterns of this planet...but you are correct."

"Wait, did I just hear you right? Did you...did you just say I'm *correct*? Did you record that?"

"No. I'm afraid I'm all out of storage space."

Theo snorted.

"That sound is most unbecoming of you." He highlighted something on the ground, guiding her eyes down. It was a deep, wide groove leading from the pod to the wet sand, where it faded. *"That is not the result of riding the surf."*

"No, it's not." She stared down, examining the other imprints in the sand — longer, undulating marks, like something had been repeatedly swept over the ground. "The pod was pushed out of the water, Kane."

"I pushed it out of the water," someone said in a deep voice behind her.

Theo whirled around, dropping her hand to her hip to draw her knife. She had it pointed at the newcomer before she realized what she was looking at. Her heart stopped, her eyes widened, and she sucked in a sharp breath.

"What the fuck is that?" she rasped, taking several steps back.

The creature was unlike anything she'd ever seen. Its upper half was humanoid, with broad, powerful shoulders that tapered to a lean waist, muscular arms, and large, long-fingered hands. But those fingers ended in *claws*, and the placating way it held up its hands stretched the delicate webbing between each finger. The creature's skin was light gray, with white stripes on its head, upper arms, and...

Tentacles.

However human-like its features appeared above the waist, it was entirely alien below. The creature was held itself upright on a set of long, thick tentacles that curled over the sand beneath it. She watched those tentacles slowly spread out, lowering the creature's torso as though it were trying to appear smaller and less threatening.

"Unknown lifeform," Kane said, sounding as stunned as Theo felt. *"There is a firearm with the pod's emergency supplies."*

"Doesn't help me now, does it?" she murmured, her gaze drifting back up the creature's body to stop on its face.

Its facial features were a blend of human and alien; the basic structures were similar, but it was entirely hairless, its nose was broader and less pronounced, and its pupils were horizontal and oddly rectangular, stark against the polished silver of its irises.

"You would prefer to have remained in the water?" the creature asked, brow furrowed.

"It's talking, Kane."

"I heard it, Theodora."

"But it's speaking *our* language."

"I may not have a body, but I am not deaf."

The creature's brow knitted further, and its full lips fell into a deep frown. "Have you suffered a head injury? You seem confused."

Theo continued to stare at the creature, stunned.

"I am here to help," it said as its tentacles slithered over the sand to drag itself a little closer. The creature's movement prodded her out of her startlement.

"Stop right there," Theo warned, tightening her fingers around her weapon and straightening her arm. "Don't come any closer."

The creature halted, raising its hands a little higher. "I do not mean you any harm, but you need to know that your knife will offer you little protection."

"Are you threatening me?"

Its brow lowered. "No. I meant *I* am not threatened by your weapon."

"I'm sure this knife can slit your throat as easily as it'd slice through mine, so stay the fuck back."

"You would have to get it close enough to my throat first, and that will not—" the creature snapped its mouth shut and shook its head as Theo narrowed her eyes. "I am making it worse, am I not?"

"And I thought you *were awkward in social interactions,"* Kane said, his voice filled with humor.

"Shove it," she replied.

"I did shove it," the creature said, gesturing to the pod, "so it was above the high tide line."

"I wasn't talking to you."

The creature regarded her in silence for a few moments, head tilted to one side. "From what I understand, speaking to oneself is often a sign of mental instability in humans. Are you sure your head was not wounded?"

Theodora gritted her teeth as Kane laughed in her mind. Of all the personality traits the AI could've developed, why did smugness have to be one?

"Kane, speak out loud," she said.

The implant in her wrist glowed as Kane projected his voice outward. "You spoil all my fun, Theodora."

Now it was the creature that backed away, brows falling low over suspicious eyes. "You are not wearing a suit."

Theo glanced down at her jumpsuit then looked back at the creature with an arched brow.

"A *diving* suit," the creature continued, gaze flicking from the light on her wrist back to her face. "You have a...a *Sam* inside you."

"What?"

"I believe he is insulting your sexual escapades. Wasn't Sam one of the—"

"Not now, Kane," she bit out.

"The diving suits the humans use have computers inside them called *Sam,"* the creature said.

"I have no idea what you're talking about," Theo said, frowning. "Are you—wait, you said *humans*. Are there other humans here?"

"Yes. They came from the stars hundreds of years ago, just as you did last night."

"How is that possible? Kane, you said you didn't know where we are. How could there be humans here but no satellites?"

"I don't have an answer for you, Theo," Kane replied. "Many worlds have been colonized by humans since they became capable of interstellar travel. The potential circumstances that brought humans here without any advanced communications equipment are too varied and numerous for me to speculate upon unless you want to spend the next several years going over them."

"No." Theo regarded the creature before her. "What are you?"

"A kraken."

"Well, I think all our questions have been answered," Kane said.

"You are lost and afraid," the creature said, "but I will not harm you."

"How can I trust that?" she asked, glancing at *his* claws. She was sure he was male — he looked masculine. Like, *really* masculine, if his size and musculature were anything to go by.

"I saved you from the sea."

"For all I know, you only saved me so you could eat me later."

He recoiled, his features contorted in a mix of horror and disgust.

"What?" she asked. "I see those teeth, those claws. I know a predator when I see one."

"Why would I have made my presence known to you if I meant to eat you?"

"I dunno." She swept her gaze over him from top to bottom and back again. After her initial shock had passed, it wasn't nearly as unsettling to look at him as she would've thought. "Maybe you like to play with your food."

"Hunting is not a game, and we do not hunt humans."

"So there are more of you?" Body tensing, she looked past him, scanning the jungle.

The creature tilted his head, expression wary.

"You expect me to trust you," Theo said, "but you won't tell me if you're alone?"

"You and I are the only ones here."

Theo clenched her teeth; he was being intentionally vague. But she forced her frustration aside. She was a stranger to him, too, and he had no more reason to trust her than she did to trust him. Releasing a soft sigh, she cocked her head to the side. "Do you have a name?"

He nodded. "Vasil."

"Okay, good. I'm—"

"Theodora."

She nodded, completely ignoring the shiver coursing through her as his deep voice seemed to caress her name. Not going there. Totally not going there. "Yeah. But *Theo* will do, okay?"

"But that is only part of your name."

"That's okay. The full thing is a mouthful."

"Just Theo, then."

Theo studied him again. His posture had relaxed, and while he still appeared on guard, he didn't look as though he were planning to tear her to shreds.

"Why are you here, Vasil?" she asked.

His gaze, suddenly heavier, swept over Theo, and she could almost feel him looking *into* her. Despite having had Kane in her head for years, it wasn't comfortable to have someone see inside her so easily.

"Because I followed a fallen star."

CHAPTER 3

THEO SAT IN THE POD, LEGS CROSSED AT THE ANKLE AND BOOTED feet propped on the edge of the console. Her left arm was settled over her stomach while her right hand played with her lower lip.

"*You do realize there are productive activities by which you could pass your time?*" Kane asked.

She glanced at the second seat, upon which she'd piled the stock of emergency rations from the rear storage space. Kane was right — the supplies wouldn't last forever. She'd need to find other sources of food and water soon, but she refused to give him the satisfaction of voicing her agreement.

"I *am* being productive. I'm thinking," she said.

"*Your commanding officer would have a different term for this, I think.*"

"Good thing my CO isn't here."

But there *was* someone else here. Vasil.

She lowered her hand to her lap, leaned forward, and looked outside. With the angle of the pod, the sea was to her front and left, and the jungle was just visible on the right edge of her vision. Vasil was nowhere to be seen, but she knew he was close by. He'd allowed her back into the pod without objection after their initial…introduction. That seemingly blind trust triggered further suspicions in her mind. Before doing anything else, she'd retrieved the pistol Kane had mentioned. When she'd turned to search out Vasil again, he was gone.

Keeping the weapon within easy reach, she'd opened up the panel to access the console's wiring and circuitry, checking for any means of coaxing the communications system to work. She just needed a second of functionality to send a signal — a *second* — but Kane's assessment of the damage had been right. She couldn't repair it with her current resources.

Turning her head to the right, she fixed her gaze on the dense jungle vegetation. "He said there are humans here, which means the water should be potable, and there's likely food out there."

"*You're making some immense assumptions, Theo.*"

"If it's safe for them, why wouldn't it be safe for me? Last I checked, I'm human too."

"*Barely,*" Kane grumbled. "*If there are other humans on this planet, we have no idea what processes they go through to purify their water supply—*"

"There are water filtration containers in the storage space, Kane. You could pour raw sewage into one of those, and it'd still give you clean drinking water when it was done."

"*Well, we still have no idea how they obtain their food, no idea if any of the native flora or fauna are safe for your consumption. I can monitor the air and water with my sensors, but I will not be able to do the same with food.*"

"So you're saying you're only half-useful," she said with a smirk.

"*Yes. I've assimilated many of my host's traits.*"

"Ouch. Guess I left myself open for that one." With a sigh, dropped her feet to the floor. "Guess I better do something productive before I get another scolding."

After checking that her knife was in place, she clipped the holstered pistol onto her belt. She scanned her surroundings as she climbed out of the pod. The dark clouds had parted an hour or two ago, allowing the bright midday sun to shine upon the golden sand. The temperature had risen, and though it wasn't unbearable, she wasn't accustomed to anything outside the dry, carefully controlled seventy degrees Fahrenheit of IDC ships. This heat and humidity would become uncomfortable soon enough.

"If that kraken were still around, I could probably ask him what's safe," she said as she walked toward the jungle, boots sinking into the soft sand with each step.

"Where in your survivalist training did they tell you to entrust your wellbeing to alien lifeforms?"

"I didn't say I trust him. And it's not like that training prepared me for *this*." She swept a hand out in front of her. "I'm a ship mechanic, Kane. That means bare minimum when it comes to training for field operations."

"It means bare minimum in budget, as well," he muttered. *"If you were a field operative, I would at least have scanners capable of profiling organics to determine their composition and safety. You should've aspired for more."*

Theo's brows lowered, and she scowled. "Are you saying I'm not good enough?"

"I'm saying I'm not good enough to help you as I should be able, Theo. If the IDC had put just a little more money into the hardware they installed in you..."

"Nothing to be done about it now." She stopped a few paces away from the grass. "I like you as you are. You're family to me, Kane."

"Aww, did we just have a moment?"

"They're bound to happen here and there, especially when you never seem to shut up."

"Is that not what human family is for?"

Frowning, Theo took in a steadying breath and strode into the vegetation. "I wouldn't know."

"Neither would I. The one time I hope to lean on your limited expertise, and you fail me."

She rolled her eyes as she entered the grass. "You know exactly why I have *limited expertise* in that field, you jerk. Now let's focus on the task at hand."

"Yes, sir." A small blue orb projected from her left wrist, hovering in the air over it. Kane's voice emanated from the orb when he spoke again. "I will monitor for signs of life, but my capabilities in that regard are limited. May I suggest you draw your weapon?"

Theo drew the pistol from its holster and continued forward.

The only jungles she'd ever seen had been holographic projections — a few in her childhood, mostly from Earth shops that tried to use such images to lure in customers, and again in her IDC basic training. Her instructors had covered several potential biomes in rapid succession but had never gone into much detail for any of them.

This was her first experience in a place like this. Her youth had been concrete, steel, and glass, most of it stained with age and centuries of graffiti. There weren't many forests left on Old Earth, and slum dwellers like Theo certainly didn't get to visit them.

The vegetation grew denser as she moved away from the sea, shifting from long, soft grass to thick clumps of broad-leafed plants before leading to trees. She was surrounded by countless shades of green, violet, and brown, occasionally broken by bright flashes of red, yellow, orange, pink, and blue — the petals of strange flowers and growths amidst the foliage. The leaves rustled in the gentle wind flowing off the sea.

The strong scents of vegetation and moist earth overpowered the briny aroma from the beach. Everything smelled so *rich*, so *alive*, so unlike the scents to which she was accustomed. The stale, recycled air of most interstellar ships had become so familiar to her that this natural air was almost too much to take in, its ever-shifting scents too complex for her nose.

She ran her fingertips over the velvety surface of a large leaf, collecting the dew drops gathered upon it. Kane bathed her hand in soft light when she lifted it to the floating orb.

"Safe," he said, "but that doesn't mean anything about the groundwater, if there is any to be found."

"I'm sure there is," she said, rubbing the moisture between her thumb and forefinger. The hairs on the back of her neck stood on end, and she tilted her head to one side, listening. "Are you mapping our route?"

"Do you take me for some sort of amateur, Theodora Velenti?"

Theo grinned and continued forward. "Bare minimum budget and all that."

"I suppose I left *myself* open for that one."

"That you did."

"*We are being stalked*," Kane said through their neural link.

"I know," she whispered.

"*You* also *know that you do not need to reply to me aloud, Theo. It isn't exactly discrete for you to be speaking to yourself all the time.*"

She clenched her jaw and pressed her lips together. Communicating with Kane in her mind required more concentration than speaking did.

Is it him? she sent through the link.

"*I believe so, but I cannot say for certain. He seems to have some sort of camouflage that is obscuring visual identification, and he is out of my scanner's range.*"

We'll wait and see what he does.

"*Is that a wise choice, Theo?*"

Just keep watching him. He hasn't done anything to hurt me yet, but that doesn't mean he won't.

· · ·

Vasil crept through the foliage, wondering how land animals made passing through it silently seem so simple a task. Though he kept the movements of his tentacles slow and deliberate, he couldn't avoid making some noise. He only hoped it matched the other jungle sounds well enough that Theo wouldn't notice.

His skin changed along with the surrounding plants, matching their coloration and mimicking their texture, but it seemed to matter little — despite her steady, cautious pace, Theo didn't look toward him at all. He supposed her constant conversation with Kane was a boon for him in this situation; the more they talked, the less likely she was to hear Vasil's clumsy attempts at stealth.

The uneven ground, littered with rotting leaves and poking sticks, wasn't kind to the relatively soft undersides of his tentacles. He tasted dirt, vegetation, and countless other flavors he had no desire to explore further through his suction cups. Though he'd accompanied the human, Randall, and several other kraken into the jungle near The Watch on a few occasions to hunt and forage, Vasil had never grown fully used to the feel of the jungle floor.

Theo came to a halt up ahead. Vasil pressed himself against a tree trunk and peered around it to watch her.

She *certainly* wasn't from Halora. As though falling out of the sky wasn't enough proof, everything about her was different from the other humans he'd met thus far. The way she pronounced words was just a touch *off*, she had a computer embedded inside her body, and her clothing...

The people of The Watch typically wore simple clothes, all hand-made and well-worn, much of it loose and seemingly comfortable. Theo's clothing resembled the diving suits from the Facility far more closely than anything the humans of

Halora wore on a regular basis. Her clothing seemed to be a single piece, made from a material he couldn't identify. Her torso and thighs were clad in white, while the fabric on her lower legs, arms, and shoulders was black with gray accents. Some sort of metal symbol was pinned on her chest, near the collar of her suit, and there were white numbers printed on each shoulder.

The more he looked at her clothing, the more certain he was that he'd seen *something* like it before, but he couldn't make the connection.

She suddenly bent forward, giving him a full view of her curved backside. Vasil's claws sank into the bark. Desire blazed through him as he stared at her, and his cock stirred. Startled, he dropped a hand to press over his slit. He hadn't felt arousal — hadn't felt much of *anything* — since before he'd been taken prisoner by the human hunters two years ago.

Why now? Why *her*?

He clenched his teeth as, unbidden, his eyes roamed down her legs and up to her backside again. He'd not mated with anyone in a long while, but he knew the anatomy of human females allowed positions that were impossible when two kraken came together. How would those positions change the experience? How would she *feel*?

His claws dug deeper into the wood as he willed his body to calm.

This is not the time. There are more pressing matters to attend.

But he couldn't deny the significance of what he felt. His desire for Theo had sparked the moment he'd seen her face through the window; even without the benefit of color, her beauty had struck him with all the power of the storm that had been raging around him. It would have been so easy to abandon her to her fate. To save himself and return to his responsibilities. Even now, it should've been a simple thing.

And yet...he *wanted* her.

I do not know her. How can I want her?

His only answer was his continuing desire for Theo, burning low in his belly.

She rose and tossed aside a flower she had picked. She said something Vasil couldn't quite hear before resuming her walk.

Keeping his jaw clenched, he carefully tugged his claws out of the bark, eased out from behind the tree, and followed her. His attention continually fell to her legs and backside as the material of her clothing stretched and molded over her curves, yet his arousal neither increased nor diminished — it simply lingered like a predator awaiting the right moment to strike its prey. The play of muscle as humans walked had always been intriguing to him, but there was much more to this. He couldn't look away from her.

He imagined she'd turn the gun on him and shoot if she'd known he was staring; there was a clear hardness in her. Vasil guessed she'd been shaped by unpleasant experiences in her past — she'd drawn strength from hardship.

Why hadn't he?

Theo slowed several times to examine various plants; fortunately, she made no move to eat any of them, allowing him to remain hidden.

Stalking her through the jungle is not likely to build trust between us...

She was wary of him, and she was armed — a dangerous combination — but she wasn't safe wandering alone. Watching over her from a distance was the best he could do until they developed some mutual trust. It was just as things had always been — Vasil observed other people from a distance, uncertain of how to get any closer.

How would Jax, Arkon, Dracchus, or even Kronus have handled this situation? Randall would've been able to talk his way through it, but Randall had the added advantage of being human. Based on Theo's initial reaction, she'd never heard of a kraken before, much less seen one. She would've responded much better to encountering a human when she emerged from the pod.

Of course, if Vasil were human, he wouldn't have been able to save her as he had…

He thrust aside those pointless wonderings and focused instead on the situation at hand. He was here to keep an eye on Theo, to ensure she wasn't harmed. That goal was difficult enough without unnecessary distractions.

Ignoring the smells and tastes his suction cups continually picked up, he shifted his focus to sight and sound. Theo continued to study the plants she passed, but Vasil had yet to see anything he knew was safe for human consumption.

She stopped and tilted her head, staring up at something in front of her — something blocked from Vasil's view by a thick tree trunk.

"That's one weird looking plant," Theo said.

"Indeed," her computer replied.

Vasil moved forward slowly, veering off her path to position himself for a better view. He unintentionally held his breath as he did so, cringing at every crunching of leaf, at every creaking branch.

"Are these things collecting dew?" Theo asked.

"No. I cannot identify its composition, but it seems to be some sort of nectar or sap."

Theo stepped closer and extended a hand just as the target of her focus came into Vasil's view.

His hearts stopped.

The plant in front of Theo was familiar to Vasil — it had been purposefully pointed out to him during his first journey into the jungle. Its long, thick stalk jutted from a clump of assorted vegetation that concealed the oversized, layered leaves at its base. Thorns as long as Vasil's hand protruded from the sides of the stalk, seemingly harmless while they were still.

Standing on her toes, Theo studied one of the four nectar-coated tendrils dangling from the end of the stalk.

The humans had a name for these plants, simple but apt — *snatcher*.

"Did that just…move a little?" she asked as the tendrils withdrew slightly.

"It could be a reflexive reaction triggered by environ—"

"Back away!" Vasil roared, darting forward. Vegetation — living and dead — crunched and snapped in his path.

"What the—?" Theo turned, taking a single step toward Vasil as she raised her gun toward him, gripping it in both hands.

That step was the only thing that saved her. The snatcher lashed forward with startling speed, slicing through the space Theo had occupied a moment before. Its thorns bent inward, piercing the foliage on the jungle floor. The air displaced by its movement caused Theo's pale golden hair to sway gently.

Vasil was staring down the barrel of Theo's gun, and her finger was on the trigger, but she knew the snatcher had taken a swipe at her. Whether she'd heard it, felt it, or Kane had alerted her did not matter. She spun on her heel and stumbled backward. The plant righted itself, twisting toward her for another strike.

Vasil pushed himself harder, ignoring the bite of branches and rocks on his tentacles. He'd left too much distance between them. He'd been *too* cautious in their interactions, and she was going to pay for it.

"Kane, what the *fuck* is—"

Vasil slammed into Theo, cutting off her words. She grunted as she hit the ground. He caught himself with hands and tentacles, preventing his body from crushing hers. For a moment, her scent — metal and flowers — washed over him, and her warmth eased into his skin.

Then she drove her elbow into his sternum.

He released a grunt of his own as some of the air burst from his lungs. The blow had been solid and well-aimed, but Vasil had faced worse from some of the creatures he'd hunted — and from other kraken. He wouldn't allow himself to be fazed by the pain.

A fresh jolt of agony sought to test his resolve a heartbeat later; piercing pressure in two tentacles. The snatcher's thorns had caught him.

Theo struggled beneath him. "Get off me!"

He caught her wrists in his hands before she could hit him again. Fortunately, she seemed to have lost hold of her gun. That gave Vasil a little more time to act, but not much — she undoubtedly knew now that she couldn't physically overcome him, and she'd seek her weapon at the first opportunity.

The snatcher tugged on his wounded tentacles. He twisted slightly to look behind. The plant was exerting pressure to drag him closer.

Any further delay by Vasil and it would've been Theo impaled by the thorns.

The pain in his tentacles had dulled to a distant tingling that spread slowly upward, sapping his sense of feeling as it traveled. He wasn't sure of how far it would spread, wasn't sure how strong its final effects would be, wasn't sure how long he had to act.

But he knew without a doubt it would've killed Theo.

Something within Vasil shattered. Fire sparked and blazed out of the break to roil through his veins and surge into his muscles. The snatcher would've taken her before Vasil had ever had a chance to have her, and he had only himself to blame. With the decision to act left solely upon his shoulders, his shortcomings had nearly cost Theo her life.

Conscious thought fled as a red haze descended over Vasil's vision.

He released his hold on Theo, pushed himself up, and swung around to face the snatcher. He grasped its stalk with hands and tentacles, avoiding the thorns only because they remained closed, and tugged upwards. The resistance from the base of the plant was strong but brief. Amidst wildly shaking foliage and clods of moist jungle dirt, the snatcher's base — a clump of massive, tapering leaves — emerged from the vegetation. Countless dirt-caked roots, resembling the legs of some bottom-feeding scavenger, writhed in the air — reaching for the ground, reaching for *Vasil*.

Tightening his grip, Vasil pulled with all his strength, moving his arms and tentacles in opposite directions. The stalk cracked and snapped, tearing into several pieces. Thick, green-brown ichor oozed over Vasil's skin. He shifted his hold to the intact portions of the stem and repeated the process. The thorns that had pierced his skin were ripped free. The snatcher's roots thrashed wildly, more flexible tendrils — for feeding on prey — joining the leg-like protrusions.

Grasping the stalk at its base, Vasil slammed the heavy remains against the nearby tree trunk. Ichor splattered the bark. The plant fell to the jungle floor and wobbled; the roots clawed beneath it and pushed the clump of leaves up off the ground.

"Oh, hell no," Theo growled.

Vasil swung his gaze toward her voice to find her on her feet, the pistol in her hands. He tensed; he didn't want to harm her, but gunshot wounds were serious despite a kraken's rapid healing. She was close enough that he had a chance to disarm her before she—

She squeezed the trigger, and the gun went off with a low, thrumming sound. Six more shots followed the first in rapid succession, but they weren't the panicked, desperate reaction he'd expected. The snatcher released a high-pitched shriek. Each shot hit its mark in what Randall and his sister Larkin called a *tight grouping*, blasting the snatcher's base apart and splattering ichor, shredded leaves, and chunks of a wood-like substance across the forest floor.

The roots slowed as the base sagged onto the jungle floor, and the snatcher's remains finally went still. Smoke curled from the remains, and in several places, glowing orange embers slowly faded from view.

Vasil's hearts thundered, making his entire body throb. The fire in his blood burned him from the inside. Part of him — a part usually kept deeply buried — demanded he somehow make the snatcher suffer more. It hadn't yet paid a high enough price for daring to threaten Theo's life.

"The IDC does *not* pay me enough for this shit," Theo said, glaring at the smoldering remains.

The flames within Vasil were suddenly extinguished. Icy cold spread through him in the heat's absence. "What did you say?"

She lowered her weapon and looked up at him. "What?"

His eyes dipped briefly to the pistol; he couldn't understand why she wasn't aiming at him. "You said IDC. You…you are part of the IDC?"

"Yeah, I work on board their interstellar ships as a mechanic." Her brow furrowed. "How do you know about the IDC? What *is* this place?"

He clenched his jaw and drew in a deep breath, willing his hearts to quiet. He couldn't be sure whether she was unaware of the IDC's history of Halora or only pretending to be, but how could he fully trust someone from the organization that had kept his ancestors as slaves?

"Why are you here?" he asked. "Why *here*?"

"First tell me where *here* is," she demanded, eyes narrowing.

Was she seeking confirmation or was she truly as lost as she claimed? Those old lessons — *never trust humans* — whispered in the back of his mind, but they didn't apply anymore.

Or do they? None of the humans in The Watch are part of the IDC. Those memories are as distant for them as they are for us...

"Kraken, I need answers, and I need them now," Theo said.

Vasil felt as though he were being pulled in opposing directions. He wanted Theo. He was illogically, undeniably drawn to her, but if she was part of the IDC...*wasn't* she his enemy? It didn't seem right, didn't *feel* right, but he had more than just himself to consider. All his people would be at risk if they were found by the IDC.

What decision would Dracchus have made in this situation?

Dracchus would choose the kraken. He would do whatever is necessary to keep our kind safe.

But even Dracchus had fallen for a human. Things were different now; the distinction between friend and enemy was no longer clear.

Vasil turned toward Theo fully and met her gaze. A bit of feeling had returned to his wounded tentacles — a hint of pulsing pain still too distant to be distracting — and his limbs were shaky with his fading bloodlust, but he refused to show weakness.

"This world is my home," he said, "and I will not betray it or my people. I mean you no harm, Theo. I think I have proven that to you now. I will do all I can to aid your survival, but until I know I can trust you, I will only offer information *I* deem safe to share."

She holstered her weapon and sighed. "Look, I'm not here to hurt you *or* your people. I'm not even here by choice. I just need to know where the hell I am."

"So you can send for the IDC?"

"The IDC or whoever can get me out of here." She released a puff of air and shook her head. "If I can even figure out how to get a signal sent off-planet."

Vasil tilted his head to the side, studying her expression. "What do you mean?"

"There are no satellites within range to amp any outbound signals, but that's not even the half of it. The pod took some damage, and the comm equipment is fried. I'd need a long-range transmitter and some kind of broadcast tower to get a message to *anyone.*"

"She left her spare tower in her other jumpsuit," Kane said, making the orb of light floating over Theo's wrist pulse.

Theo rolled her eyes. "Har har."

Vasil's brow fell; he'd never witnessed such an interaction between Sam and the humans who used the diving suits, nor between anyone and the Computer in the Facility. "Why does it speak to you that way?"

"Kane?" Theo asked, raising her wrist. "He's an advanced artificial intelligence, military grade. Meant to assist in my duties." She glared at the orb. "They aren't *supposed* to have such strong personalities, but I guess they gave me a defective unit. He's basically a person without a body."

"Theodora, that is the sweetest thing anyone's ever said about me," Kane said.

"Just my luck I got stuck with a sarcastic jerk."

Kane's light seemed to condense into something more solid, almost as though he were narrowing his eyes. "You know we are programmed to learn from our environment. *You* taught me everything I know about personality, Theo."

"Anyway..." She lowered her arm and met Vasil's gaze. "You gonna tell me where I am?"

"You truly have no means of contacting the IDC or anyone else out *there?*" Vasil asked, waving a hand toward the sky. He didn't doubt the records and holograms he'd seen regarding existence beyond Halora, but it remained a difficult concept to internalize; his world, already too large for any one kraken to explore in a hundred lifetimes, was so tiny and insignificant compared to the universe...

"I wouldn't be standing here asking if I did," she said. "The emergency beacon on the pod would've transmitted my location if anything was in range. I wouldn't have to tell them where I am."

Despite everything, Vasil didn't doubt her honesty. He'd always been good at reading others, despite his people having limited social interactions in the past, and that talent had translated surprisingly well to humans.

"This world is called Halora," he finally said.

"Kane?"

"I am relaying the information I have on file to your retinal feed," the computer replied.

Blue light shone in each of Theo's eyes, covering both her pupils and her pale green irises. Vasil furrowed his brow. What was happening?

"This can't be right," she said after a few moments. "The IDC classified this planet as uninhabitable and declared it a dead system."

"To be fair," Kane offered, "your rank allowed us access only to the most basic files. *Need-to-know* and all that rubbish."

"But there are *humans* here."

"According to this creature," Kane said.

Theo looked at Vasil and frowned. "How would he know of us otherwise?"

"Perhaps his species is the reason this planet was deemed unsafe for habitation? Maybe they *ate* the human settlers who came here after assimilating our language."

"I thought computers are supposed to be things of logic and reason," Vasil said. "We do not eat humans. They are our friends, our mates, and—"

Theo's eyes, rounded in shock, dropped to stare at his pelvis. "Whoa! Hold up. Did you say *mates*? You...you have *sex* with *humans*?"

Vasil's shaft stirred behind his slit. "*I do not,*" he said, raising his hands placatingly as her expression shifted to something akin to insult. Had he spoken incorrectly or used the wrong tone? "Not that I *would* not, as the human form is attractive, but—"

Theo held up her hand. "Let me stop you there. You've already made this weird enough." She rubbed her eyes with her forefinger and thumb.

"I am curious about this creature's anatomy," Kane said. "Where is his—"

"Kane!" she snapped, lowering her hand. "That's enough."

"He has characteristics that closely resemble cephalopods from Old Earth. I'm simply speculating as to whether one of his tentacles — the proper term is *arms*, but I suppose that would get confusing in his case — is his reproductive organ or—"

Theo's cheeks reddened. "Kane."

Vasil glanced down at his tentacles, two of which still oozed blood from open wounds. Why would one of them be his reproductive organ? That would be as strange as a human male having a cock for a finger.

"What?" Kane asked. "It's biology, Theodora. *Science.* A male octopus tears off the arm that bears his reproductive organ and offers it to the female, thus—"

"No more talking!"

Mouth agape, Vasil stared at Theo. "Tears off the— Is it a joke, Theo, or is he being truthful?"

"I can assure you of my absolute sincerity in this matter, if nothing else," Kane said.

Vasil's stomach sank, and he shuddered. Kane's words created an image too painful to contemplate. He thrust it aside as quickly as he could.

Theo pressed her lips together and stared down at the jungle floor for several seconds. Vasil noted she seemed very careful to keep her gaze away from his tentacles.

Finally, she cleared her throat. "Um…thanks, by the way. For what you did," she said, motioning toward the snatcher's scattered remains.

"Yes. I mean…it was…" Vasil released an exasperated breath through his nostrils. He'd observed so many conversations; why was it so difficult for him to partake in them, to figure out what to say? "As I said before, I do not wish you harm. I also do not wish to *see* you harmed. But I did not think you would hesitate in shooting me if you deemed me a threat."

Theo smirked. "Yeah, probably not." She straightened and waved him ahead. "Guide away. Maybe you can show me what I can eat around here, and what wants to eat me."

Vasil nodded. *Doing* something would be preferable to struggling through a conversation. He turned, swept aside a few bits of the snatcher that had littered the jungle floor, and started forward. His eyes scanned for signs of the food the humans normally foraged — and for the dangers he'd been taught about. Theo's soft footsteps followed behind him.

"It is not, by the way," he said over his shoulder after a short while.

"What's not?" Theo asked.

"One of my tentacles."

Her steps faltered, and Kane's unsettlingly human laughter echoed between the trees.

CHAPTER 4

Theo scooped the spongy meat out of a *naba* stalk and slipped into her mouth. The juicy sweetness wasn't as overwhelming as it had been during her first taste; now that she knew what to expect, she relished it. She'd been wary when Vasil had harvested the plant, eyeing the soft meat within the stalks skeptically after he'd split it open, but her first taste had dispelled her misgivings. It was *glorious*. Fresh fruit had always been a rarity in her life, even on Old Earth.

She tossed the empty stalk out of the pod. After grabbing a water-gel pouch from her emergency stash, she propped her bare foot up on the console and leaned back in her seat. She stared up at the night sky and listened to the endlessly crashing waves. It wasn't as consistent or subtle as the hum of machinery on an interstellar ship, but it was just as soothing — if not more so.

Twisting off the lid of the pouch, she brought it to her lips and squeezed the gel into her mouth. It immediately liquified. Though it was refreshing, the gel always had an unidentifiable aftertaste. She'd have to make a trip tomorrow to the stream she and Vasil had found to fill the filtration containers with real water.

The stars seemed so different from land, so distant and small, and though they'd surrounded Theo for most of her life, she'd never truly looked at them. They were nothing more than balls of hot gas, but from here on Halora, they were almost... magical. There hadn't been much magic or hope for her as a child. What good would stars have done for her? They sure as hell couldn't have fed her, kept her warm at night, or protected from harm. Wishing on fallen stars was dangerous — all it did was make people hope for things that could never be.

"Do you think the IDC was covering something up?" Theo asked quietly.

"*I'm sure the IDC covers many things up,*" Kane replied. "*As far as this place...it seems quite probable.*"

"But why? There's clean water, food, and *life*. It's a perfect world to colonize." She frowned. "If Vasil is telling the truth and there *are* humans here, this place *was* colonized. Why wouldn't there be any records? Why classify it as uninhabitable?"

"*Prior colonization is but one of the many possible explanations. There might have been a single ship that landed here and had enough interaction with the natives to pass on our language and a basic understanding of our way of life. Speculation won't be of much help to us.*"

Theo sighed heavily and tossed the empty water-gel pouch to the floor. "No, it won't. But I know who can give us some answers." She lifted her head and raised her voice. "Hey, Vasil, why don't you come join me?"

"*You're inviting him inside?*" Kane demanded.

"Why not? What's he going to do?"

"*Oh, no reason for alarm. He only pushed this pod across thirty meters of sand by himself and tore that plant creature apart like it was made of paper.*"

"Exactly," she whispered. "Both of those instances were to

help me. If he wanted to hurt me, he could have done so a hundred times over by now."

"Did you call me, Theo?" Vasil asked from outside the pod.

"Why don't you come up here? Let's have a chat."

"Would it not be more accommodating for you to come out here?"

Theo wiggled in the seat. "Nope. I'm quite comfortable. Get your ass up here, kraken."

He was silent for a moment; Theo pressed her lips together and listened but heard only the continued sighing of the nearby waves. Just as she was about to speak again, the pod wobbled and rocked. Vasil's shadowy form blotted out the stars.

"I am here."

"Kane, power up the console," Theo said.

The console came to life, its light chasing away the darkness and casting a blue and yellow glow on his gray skin. He narrowed his strange eyes briefly, and his pupils contracted from almost-circles to that odd rectangular shape.

Theo patted the seat next to her. "Come sit."

Vasil slowly swept his gaze over the interior of the pod and shook his head. "Here is fine."

She arched a brow. "Are you scared of me?"

He adjusted his stance, grasping the edge of the entry and offering full view of the long black claws on his fingers as he leaned a little closer. "No. Are you not scared of me?"

Theo dropped her foot to the floor and leaned forward, resting her elbows on her knees and letting her hands dangle between them. She held his gaze. "Should I be?"

"My point this whole time is that you should be," Kane muttered.

Vasil unwaveringly held her gaze. She wasn't sure how long it was before he spoke again; it could've been ten seconds or ten minutes. "I am comfortable here."

Theo shrugged. "Suit yourself."

"Did you need something?"

"I want you to tell me about yourself, your people, and the humans here."

Wariness tightened his features. "What exactly do you want to know?"

"I'm curious as to why IDC would deem this planet unfit for human habitation when it is not only safe, but already colonized."

He frowned and shook his head. "*Safe* is not the right word for Halora, Theo."

Theo tried to ignore the tingle that traveled through her each time her name rumbled up from his chest. It was a gentle but possessive caress. She shouldn't have felt anything of the sort, especially not because of him. He wasn't even human!

"What word would you use?" she asked.

"*Alive. Hungry.* Humans and kraken remain the apex predators, but the snatcher is only one of the things that would gladly kill and eat you on this world."

Theo tilted her head. "Are you trying to scare me, Vasil?"

"I am trying to keep you safe," he replied, expression grave. "Fear is an aspect of self-preservation. It is necessary."

"This planet is no different from the others that humans have occupied. There will always be creatures that are faster and stronger than we are, but as far as I know, we've never come across anything like you." She pushed herself to her feet and stepped closer to him.

"You *made* us."

Theo stilled.

"And what is that meant to imply?" Kane demanded out loud from the console speaker.

Theo was glad Kane was coherent enough to respond — *she* sure as hell wasn't. Did Vasil seriously mean that humans…*created* him?

Vasil's lip curled, flashing pointed teeth, and he averted his gaze.

"Oh, hell no. You don't get to turn away and stop talking after a statement like that," Theo said.

He released a soft grunt. "Halora was colonized by humans over three hundred and fifty years ago."

Theo narrowed her eyes. More than three hundred and fifty years? There was no way the IDC didn't know about this place. Halora should have been either a thriving colony or totally abandoned by now. It didn't make any sense.

"Kane, are you sure there is nothing on file about this?" she asked.

"Nothing," Kane said, sounding perplexed for once instead of smug.

"The IDC came first," Vasil said, "and while they were here, they created my kind. A few decades later, they left and never returned."

Theo raised her hands, palms out. "Hold up. So when you say they created you—"

"They had a lab where they combined characteristics from different creatures. They used...*octopus*, is what Arkon said. And human."

Human.

She stared at him, eyes wide, lips parted, and jaw slack.

He's part human, she sent through her neural link with Kane.

"Human DNA doesn't necessarily make him human," Kane replied, sounding oddly unconvinced.

He said his kind mated *with humans,* Theo replied.

"And...we don't know what the term means to him. It likely just means sexual intercourse. The likelihood of humans and these creatures being able to reproduce—"

"Can you have babies with humans?" Theo blurted out.

Vasil recoiled, eyes going wide. His mouth opened as though he meant to speak, but no sound emerged.

"That's a yes," Theo declared. "Holy fuck."

She spun away, running a hand through her hair. The IDC

had been modifying humans for a long time — they'd eradicated most disease, given people longer lifespans, and made everyone generally more resilient — but that was a far cry from *creating* a new species!

What had the IDC been *thinking*? It's like they'd been playing God!

"I did not say *yes!*" Vasil said.

"You didn't have to. It was written all over your face." Theo plopped back down on the seat. "Oh, man. They broke *so* many laws."

"Yes, they *did*," Kane said through the speaker, "which means you need to think about this very carefully, Theo."

"No shit. If this is why there's no information about this planet, that means they were trying to hide what they did."

"And now *we* are aware of it." Kane's words were punctuated by heavy silence.

"No," Theo said after a while. "No, they wouldn't do anything to us for that, Kane. This stuff happened hundreds of years ago."

"They must never know about this," Vasil said, leaning through the doorway. His eyes were wide, pupils dilated. "You were telling me the truth when you said you have no means of communicating with them, were you not?"

"Like I said, if we had the means, we'd be waiting to be picked up right now." She bent forward and rubbed the bridge of her nose. "Why? Why would they go through the trouble and risk of creating you and then just leave?"

He inhaled deeply. Her eyes dipped to his chest of their own accord, sliding over his large, sculpted muscles.

"Because there was a war. Out *there*," Vasil said, turning his head as though to indicate the sky — but not before she caught his gaze falter.

"Given his suggested time frame, it could've been the Fringe-world Rebellion," said Kane.

The Fringeworld Rebellion was ancient history, and she'd never attended school. All she knew about it was that a whole mess of planets on the edges of IDC territory had joined forces to rebel against the Interstellar Defense Coalition back in the early days. They'd lost. History wasn't a necessary subject when your only job was to make sure the ship's engine didn't explode.

"There's an *and*, isn't there, Vasil?" Theo asked.

Vasil nodded and met her eyes again. "And around the same time, my people rose up against the humans and killed many of them."

Theo dropped her left hand, holding it just over the pistol propped against the side of her seat. "You might want to expand upon that before I draw my own conclusions."

His gaze flicked briefly to the weapon. If he was afraid, it didn't show in his expression; the silver of his eyes was a hard, cold gray in this light, like the hull of an old battlecruiser. She knew he was fast, and though she was sure of her aim, he was close enough that she'd only get off a single shot if she was lucky.

Something told her that wouldn't be enough.

"I should not tell you any of this," he said, his tone measured and even. "You are one of *them*."

"And you just told me your people slaughtered a bunch of humans. If you were looking to gain my trust, that is *definitely* not the way to go."

"It is the truth. Can I trust *you* with the rest of it?"

Theo picked up the pistol and rested it in her lap without looking away from him. "You should be glad I haven't shot you yet."

"You have the gun, Theo, but you do not *have the advantage here,"* Kane said in her mind.

I know that, she sent through the neural link, *but he needs to know I'm not going to cower when he says shit like that. It's not like I have much of a choice, either. I'm just...setting some boundaries.*

Vasil's jaw muscles bulged, and his features tightened. Theo knew he was conflicted, but she guessed he wasn't concerned about the possibility of taking a gunshot; the stakes, at least to him, were greater than that. She'd seen that sort of look too often during her youth to fool herself into thinking he was afraid of her.

"My people were kept as slaves," he said through pointed teeth. Theo's eyes widened. "We were used as tools, as subjects for experiments, and our intelligence and free will were ignored. They designed us to be controlled both in action and number, but they underestimated us. Their cruelty and indifference sparked something in my ancestors that drove us to revolt."

"Oh." She stared at him, lips parted, shocked by what she'd just heard. The IDC had done that? They'd created a whole new species using human DNA just to be used as *slaves*? As horrible as it was to hear that his people had killed humans, she honestly couldn't blame them if what he'd just told her was true.

Who was she to judge, anyway? Theo wasn't innocent. There was blood on her hands, too.

She could easily recall the feelings of helplessness, fear, and rage from her youth.

"That...defies logic," Kane said through the console speaker. "Why violate interstellar laws and create a new species to use as slaves when the IDC had access to all sorts of equipment that could've done any necessary work? Even then, robotics were advanced enough to fulfill almost any role, and the IDC hasn't been opposed to using prisoners for labor in the past."

"That doesn't make it right, Kane," Theo said, frowning at the console.

"I didn't say it was *right*, only that I doubt its veracity."

"I do not know that word," Vasil said, brows falling low.

"He thinks you're lying," Theo said.

"My honesty is being questioned by a computer that lives like a parasite inside a human?"

"Kane is *not* a parasite." She glared at Vasil, pressing her lips together.

"Perhaps you *should* use that pistol," Kane said.

Vasil clamped his hands over the hatch frame and leaned close, teeth bared. A low, rumbling growl rose from his chest. The pod groaned; how much force was he exerting?

Heart fluttering, Theo raised the pistol and aimed at his chest, but he didn't so much as glance at it. For the first time, she was truly afraid of him. "You're really pushing the benefit of the doubt to its limits, kraken. *You* are the unknown entity, here. I've been with Kane a long time. I trust him."

"And *you*, human, are alive because of *me*," Vasil snarled. Theo's eyes rounded further as a red tint overcame his skin. "How long do you think you would survive this world without my help? I chose to help you at risk to myself without a second thought but sharing this information with you risks *everyone* I know and care about.

"Fire your gun. If you do not kill me with the first shot, I will end you. I do *not* want to harm you, Theodora. Do not make yourself my enemy."

Theo stared at him, skin tingling with fear, chest rising and falling rapidly with shallow breaths. She tightened her grip on the pistol but did not pull the trigger. A faint tremor ran through her arm.

"*I was wrong, Theo. Put it down,*" Kane whispered in her mind. She'd never heard fear in his voice before now.

Keeping her gaze locked with Vasil's, she slowly lowered her weapon and placed it on the floor. She raised her empty hands, showing the kraken her palms, before settling them in her lap.

"I didn't call you here to threaten you or your people," Theo said, struggling to keep her voice calm and steady. "I just want to understand. I'm stuck on an alien planet with no way to get back to the life I knew, and you're the only person who can give me any answers. I'm lost, Vasil. I'm just trying to find my footing and figure out whether or not I can trust you."

A strange sensation tightened her chest. Saying it out loud made her realize just how lost she was. She was stranded. Her life would never be the same again — not unless she found some way to get a message sent out into the cosmos and it happened to be received by friendly forces. The odds of that seemed abysmal at the moment.

"I have saved your life twice." Vasil's voice was low. "Is that not enough for a start?"

Well now, don't I just feel like a shitty person?

Cheeks heating, Theo ran her hand through her hair, tugging the loose strands to rest over her shoulder. "Yes, it is. And I've done a bad job thanking you for it." She inhaled deeply, and slowly released the breath. "Is there...any chance you can take me to see the humans?"

"I cannot."

Telling herself *cannot* was at least better than *will not*, Theo nodded.

Vasil stared into her eyes for a long while, neither advancing nor retreating. The pod seemed entirely too small, even without him fully inside it, and the air was unbearably thick with tension. Theo felt self-conscious, uncomfortable, *judged*. She was on the verge of asking him to leave so she could rest when he finally spoke.

"There is something on this world called *halorium*," he said. "The IDC wanted it. I think it served as some sort of never-ending power source. But it interferes with human devices and makes them fail. They created us because their machines could not work near halorium."

Theo was silent for a time, then inclined her head. "Thank you, Vasil. For telling us."

Vasil nodded.

Ahem. Kane? she pulsed through the link.

"I should not have jumped to conclusions before you shared more of your story," Kane said aloud. "Please accept my apologies. I did not mean to provoke you."

Yes, you did.

"*I am* trying *to do the right thing, Theodora. I'm swallowing my pride for you. If I had a throat, I'd be choking right now.*"

Theo frowned.

Vasil's lips fell into a frown to mirror hers.

Theo stood and closed the small space separating her from the kraken. Up close, it was impossible not to notice how large he was. She couldn't stop her eyes from straying over the muscles of his abdomen and chest before they finally met his gaze.

She swallowed and extended a hand. "It's late. Maybe we can start over tomorrow?"

He looked at her hand, his expression shifting to something unreadable.

She cleared her throat. "If you're not accustomed to the gesture, you—"

"I am familiar with it," he said hurriedly.

"Oh. Okay, then." Theo began lowering her hand.

Vasil reached forward and took her hand in his — his hand engulfed hers almost entirely, but it was surprisingly warm and gentle. She'd expected cold, slimy skin befitting a sea creature, not smooth velvet over firm muscle.

As she stared at their hands, something spread through her fingers and along her arm. Something…arousing. It heated her from the inside out, soon swirling low in her belly. The sensation was as tantalizing as it was shocking. It didn't seem to matter that he had claws that could rip her to shreds or teeth made for tearing into meat.

Theo snatched her hand back. She cleared her throat,

retreated a couple steps, and offered him a smile. "I suppose this is goodnight."

For a few moments, he held his hand in the air, turned slightly as he stared at his palm. Then he shook his head as though waking from a trance. He pulled his arm back and nodded. The tube-like growths where his ears should've been expanded and contracted. "Yes. Goodnight."

Before she could say anything else, he was gone, restoring her view of the dark, star-sprinkled sky.

CHAPTER 5

THE SOUND OF WAVES CRASHING AGAINST THE SHORE WAS THE first thing Theo was aware of when she woke. She shifted her head, and light struck her eyelids, staining the comfortable darkness of sleep bright red. When she slitted her eyes open, she was blinded by the harsh sunlight. Groaning, she covered her face with one hand. She wasn't sure she could get used to this; on an interstellar ship, there was no true day or night. There was only a tightly-maintained schedule. Lights went off, lights came on, shifts changed.

But even at their worst, the lights on a ship were never this uncomfortably bright.

Turning her face away from the pod's opening, she lifted her hand to shield her face. Her eyelids fluttered open, and her eyes adjusted slowly to the brightness.

"I'm in hell," she muttered.

"Now you know how I've felt all these years," Kane said through the neural link.

She dropped her hand to her side and glared at the open hatch. "If you're that miserable, maybe I should trade you for an AI who actually enjoys my company."

"You'd be lost without me, Theodora."

She snorted. "I'm already lost *with* you."

"That's beside the point."

Smirking, she slowly sat up, tugged the blanket off her lap, and draped it over the back of the seat. She stretched her legs, arms, and back as she stood and moved to the open hatch to look outside.

"Vasil?" she called. He made no reply, and she saw no sign of him. "Did he come by while I was sleeping?"

"It would appear so," Kane replied. He highlighted something at the edge of her field of view, and she turned her head to focus on it.

Several large leaves had been laid atop the sand only a few meters from the pod, each with a pile of alien fruit atop it.

"He brought breakfast," she said, surprised.

"Now we just need a long-range transmitter, and we can recommend him for a medal. He'll be hailed as a hero."

"You're in a mood this morning." She sat down and tugged on her boots.

Kane scoffed. *"I woke with a foul taste in my mouth. Apologizing does not agree with me."*

"You don't have a mouth."

"No one is more aware of that than I."

Theo stood up. "Though it definitely doesn't stop you from running it nonstop."

"What is our plan, Theodora? What are we going to do?"

"First," she said as she climbed out of the pod, "I am going to eat."

She dropped down into the sand and approached the fruit Vasil had left. Most of it looked at least somewhat familiar to her now — he had pointed out several edible varieties as they'd trekked through the jungle together following Theo's near-impalement by the thorns of a sentient stick. Plucking up one what he'd called *daruk nuts*, Theo popped it into her mouth and bit down. The crunchy morsel broke apart between her teeth, and its salty smoothness caressed her taste buds. She closed her eyes and hummed as she chewed.

"Maybe it's just because the food on IDC ships tastes like crap, but I could get used to this planet if everything tastes this good," she said.

"What's next? We haven't discussed it, Theo, but this is *a serious situation."*

Theo's brows fell. "You think I don't know that? Can't you let me enjoy a meal without bringing up the fact that I lost everything but my life over the course of a few minutes?"

"Sorry." The word was followed by a faint, static-like thrumming in her head.

"What the hell was that?" she demanded, rubbing her temples with a finger and thumb.

"I've exceeded my maximum number of apologies for the month. I fear I might be damaging my CPU."

Theo grunted and tossed a handful of nuts in her mouth. She brushed off her hands and started peeling the winefruits. "You don't have to be such a jerk all the time, you know."

"I don't try *to be,"* he said. *"I...I put you in danger yesterday, Theo, and I need you to know I never intended for that to happen. I am* sorry."

She stilled her hands for a moment, staring down at the purple stains on her fingers from the juice. "I know, Kane. I never once thought you did. You always have my back."

"Do you believe what Vasil told you? About this halorium?"

She tossed aside half the rind and held the remaining fruit in one hand. Its natural wedges reminded her of pictures of oranges she'd seen back on Old Earth. Pressing her lips together, she tilted her head and considered what Vasil had said, studying her memory of his expression in her mind's eye.

"Yeah. Yeah, I do," she replied. "He didn't have to tell us anything at all."

"No, he didn't." Kane was silent for a few moments. *"I'm IDC property, and I'm not technically supposed to feel anything, but I'm troubled by what he said."*

"Me too." She climbed back into the pod, careful to hold the exposed winefruit upright. "The IDC was covering up something, and I'm pretty sure it was the kraken. I just... I don't understand why they just left them. I mean, they had the manpower, and they could have come here and wiped the kraken out. Could've destroyed every trace of what they did here. Instead, they just...pretended it didn't happen."

"I guess we should be grateful for that, given our current situation."

"Yeah."

Vasil had done so much for her already — despite her distrust of him, despite the way she'd treated him. The fruit he'd left this morning was only the next item on a growing list.

She slipped a wedge of fruit into her mouth as she moved to the rear of the pod, pausing as the sweet juice flowed over her tongue. She tilted her head back. "Oh my god, Kane. I swear I don't know how I'll be able to go back to that artificial crap they serve on the ship."

"Not to be a downer, but...there's no ship to go back to, so I guess you don't have to worry about that."

Theo sighed as she unfastened the straps holding her toolbox in place and slid the metal container closer. She ran her fingertips over the name etched on the lid — *M. VELENTI.*

"There's always another ship," she said quietly. "I got away with the important things. My toolbox and you."

"How sentimental of you," Kane replied. *"You know that you are more important than either of those, don't you?"*

"Aww, Kane. I think that's the sweetest thing you've said to me in a long time." Theo grinned, opening the door of the storage space to which she'd returned the food. It also contained first aid supplies, various tools, spare universal power cells, and extra clothing. The supplies were enough to last her a few weeks if she was smart — even longer if she supplemented with foraged food.

"Don't get used to it."

Theo chuckled as she pulled out the pair of automatic-filtration water containers from the bottom of the storage space. "I won't. And to answer your question from earlier, the plan, for now, is just to survive. Not much more we can do."

"Fair enough," Kane replied. *"I take it we're going back to the stream?"*

"Yep," she said, closing the storage door and stepping back. She hurriedly finished the rest of the winefruit, clicked the holstered pistol into place at her hip, and felt for her knife before exiting the pod with the containers.

Setting the containers aside for a few moments, she gathered the fruit off the leaves and moved it into the pod for safe keeping.

Kane's orb projected from her wrist when she finally walked into the jungle. The scents of moist vegetation and rich earth quickly replaced the beach's salty breeze. She remained alert, unwilling to be caught unaware as she had the day before.

Who would've guessed a plant — a *plant* — would be so high on the *dangerous predator* list?

What other surprises awaited her on this world?

She was grateful for what Vasil had taught her thus far. He *had* earned some of her trust — much more than she'd given him. Yet part of her knew she needed to remain on-guard, that she had no reason to feel guilty for protecting herself.

"Do you want me to highlight the route back to the stream?" Kane asked aloud, his orb pulsing gently with his words.

"I think I remember, but...it's hard to be sure. Everything looks the same." She ran her gaze over the trees and the thick vegetation covering the jungle floor. "Am I at least on the right path?"

"Close enough. I'll inform you if you stray too far."

"Any sign of carnivorous plants?"

"I don't see anything within my limited range," he replied, "but who's to say what other dangers lurk out here? Just be alert."

She continued forward, twigs and plant stalks snapping beneath her boots. The hot, muggy air soon had sweat rolling down her back, trickling between her breasts, and beading on her forehead and neck. Even her hair dampened with perspiration. All at once, her jumpsuit felt too constricting. It clung to her skin uncomfortably and chaffed her most sensitive parts. She'd never encountered this problem in the controlled atmospheres of interstellar ships.

Theo paused when a new sound joined the jungle ambiance — running water. She pushed through leaves and vines until she finally broke into the clearing along the stream's bank.

"Finally." She sighed in relief, stepped to the edge of the water, and set one of the extra containers down beside her. The opening in the canopy allowed the sun to shine bright and hot atop her head, adding to her discomfort. "This planet is going to be the death of me."

"I refuse to be stuck in a rotting corpse until my backup power cells die," Kane said. "It would take *years*."

"You won't have much of a choice, will you? And do you really think my corpse would last? You'd likely wind up in the belly of a beast before getting shat out—"

"Fill up your damned bottles so we can get out of here, Theo."

Theo laughed as she opened the first container. "Did I cross your wires?"

"I'll not have you insult the sophistication of my components by suggesting I have anything as crude as *wires*, thank you," he grumbled.

"Boy, you *are* touchy today." She bent forward and dipped the container into the stream, holding it firmly so it wouldn't be carried off by the current. Once it was full, she lifted it out, replaced the cap, and pressed the button to begin the filtration process. She stared at the water as she filled the second container. "You see anything in there that I don't?"

"Looks clear," Kane replied, "not that it made any difference yesterday. Why?"

She sealed the second container and activated it, placing it beside the first. "'Cause I stink to high hell, and it's hot."

"Every time I become wistful and long for a physical form of my own, you remind me why it would be a terrible thing to possess. Thank you, Theodora."

"The human body is a disgusting thing." With a smirk, Theo stood and kicked off her boots. She unbuckled her belt and laid it, along with the pistol, beside her footwear. Raising a hand to her collar, she released her jumpsuit's seal. The material sagged as the front seam opened. She peeled the suit off her body, pulling her arms out of the sleeves before shoving the whole thing down her legs, leaving only the under suit she wore beneath her outer garments. The touch of air directly on the skin of back, arms, and legs brought immediate relief from the heat.

Sitting in the grass along the bank, she drew her knife from its belt sheath and pulled the jumpsuit into her lap. She carefully used the sharp blade to make a few alterations that would make the uniform more comfortable in this unforgiving climate.

"Where do you think Vasil went?" she asked as she cut off one of the sleeves.

"Maybe he was eaten by a plant," Kane said.

Theo shook her head, smirking. "You saw how easily he tore that other one apart. I doubt it."

"I will note that we've not witnessed him eating yet, and his...*dental* situation suggests a more protein-rich diet. Perhaps he's hunting?"

"Maybe we just haven't been around him long enough to see

him eat. He might've eaten some of the fruit he gathered for me, for all we know. But you're probably right." She caught her lower lip between her teeth and carefully sliced through the material around the jumpsuit's waist. "You don't think he'd just...leave, do you?"

"Honestly, Theo, I don't know."

The thought of Vasil leaving was strangely unsettling to Theo. She had Kane, but what did he know about this world? He'd kept her from losing her mind several times in the past when the silence and solitude had become too much, but to go the rest of her life without meeting *anyone* else seemed...frightening. Before Kane, she'd had Malcolm — her tutor, her protector, the man she wished had been her father from the start. It had been so many years since he died that she'd forgotten what it was like to have someone near. Someone she could look at, touch, *feel.*

She was alone here without Vasil. What did it matter if he was a kraken? He was still...*alive.*

There were always other people on IDC ships, but her time around them had always been fleeting. She'd never made any lasting friendships, especially after enlisting. What was the point? Most people only wound up betraying you eventually, and those who didn't always left sooner or later — IDC crewmen were constantly being reassigned and shuffled around the universe.

She thought back to the few times she'd attempted to get close to others, to get *intimate*; each experience had left a sour taste in her mouth. Theo had been nothing more than a conquest, an easy fuck. In her desperation for human contact, she'd allowed herself to be used, all under the delusion that she could have more than a physical connection. And she couldn't bring herself to be angry about any of it — none of those men were at fault for failing to meet her expectations, which had always been vague even to Theo.

After a short series of disappointments, she'd simply distanced herself from everyone.

Theo sighed. She set the separated pieces of her suit aside and leaned forward to sheathe her knife. Why did she have to be so fucked up? She hated letting people close, yet she craved intimacy like she needed air.

She stood up, removed her under suit, and kneeled at the stream's edge. She scrubbed her clothing to wash away the sweat and dirt before spreading them out in the sun to dry.

Tossing her long hair back, she walked into the water. Her bare feet traversed slick rocks and soft mud, a welcome relief from wearing boots all the time. The cool water was wonderfully refreshing against her heated flesh.

"Keep an eye out for giant, predatory fish, would ya?" she asked, wading forward until the water reached her waist.

"This is a stream, Theo," Kane replied, "not the ocean."

"Kane, I was almost eaten by a *plant* yesterday."

"Just do what you need to do so we can get back."

Theo shook her head and dipped down to submerge herself up to her shoulders. She spread her arms to the sides, relishing the feel of water flowing over her skin. "Don't rush me. I'm in no hurry to get back to the pod and stare blankly at the sky until bedtime. If you're bored, go to sleep."

"I can't go to sleep," he said, "because you want me to keep watch. Please, feel free to take your time. It's not like *I* can go anywhere."

"Why thank you," she snickered.

"My pleasure, madam."

VASIL ROSE from the water and dragged himself onto the beach. He felt replenished. He'd not been in the water since pushing Theo's pod ashore the night before last and had forgotten how strange his body felt after prolonged periods in open air. The humidity helped, but it would never be enough; kraken *needed* the sea.

He carried his catch — a pair of meaty, long-bodied fish — in one hand, fingers hooked beneath the fish's gills, as he moved toward the pod. The humans he'd lived alongside ate many plants, but they all included meat in their diets whether it came from land or sea. He doubted the odd, tube-like containers she sometimes ate from contained any sort of meat; hopefully, she'd enjoy fresh fish.

"Theo?" Vasil called.

She did not answer, and nothing moved within the pod. He called her name again. The gentle wind and rolling waves provided the only sound.

Ignoring the scratchy sand clinging to his tentacles, he swept his gaze around the immediate area. The soft ground around the pod was cut through by chaotic tracks created by feet and tentacles, too jumbled for him to make any sense of.

A boulder coalesced in his chest and sank into his gut.

He hurried to the pod and raised his torso on flexed tentacles to peer inside; Theo was not within. As he lowered himself and spun around, he noticed the leaves upon which he'd left food for her were bare. Vasil rushed over and ran his tentacles over them, seeking any unfamiliar tastes or smells. All he detected was sand, fruit, the leaves themselves, and the faintest hint of Theo.

His hearts thundered, and his mind raced. If some beast had attacked her, there would've been a lingering scent, would've been some sign of struggle — blood, torn cloth, unfamiliar prints in the sand. *Something.*

The signs, however few in number, pointed toward her having left of her own will. Had he pushed too far the night before? Had he done nothing but give her real reason to fear him?

I shouldn't have been so aggressive. I should have...

No, that was wrong. She needed to understand what was at stake for Vasil and his people. The kraken had spent generations expecting the IDC's return, and Vasil's interactions with Theo, though brief, had been enough to confirm what he'd long suspected — human technology had only become more advanced in the years since the IDC's departure. The kraken would not survive if the IDC choose to reignite that old conflict.

Whether she'd fled in fear or not, he had to find her. He had to know she was okay.

But where might she have gone?

He set the fish down, wrapped them with the leaves, and surveyed his surroundings. No fresh footprints led along the shore in either direction, meaning she'd likely gone into the jungle. Why? He'd left her fresh food, and she knew now how dangerous the jungle could be.

Vasil ran a palm over his scalp and looked to the sea.

Why go if not to escape him? She wasn't used to kraken; she likely saw him as a monster.

The morning had dawned clear and sunny, leaving the ocean a mix of vibrant turquoise and teal beneath an azure sky. Gentle waves rolled onto the beach in an endless back-and-forth, claiming an infinitesimal bit of land each time the retreated.

Water.

Even having seen the humans of The Watch drink more times than he could count, he still seemed to forget so easily. Humans needed to consume water to survive. She may well have gone to the stream they'd discovered the day before to obtain fresh water.

Swept onward by an unexpected surge of excitement and hopefulness, Vasil plunged into the jungle. If Theo had left evidence of her recent passage, he was not skilled enough to pick it out amidst the dense foliage and layers of decaying vegetation covering the jungle floor. He used the landscape as his guide back toward the stream. Though the jungle was little more than a living, chaotic mess of green, purple, and brown to him, he'd committed to memory a few of the more unique features along the path — a large fallen log propped against another tree, a trunk with a huge cluster of pale blue fungus growing on one side, a curtain of vines sprinkled with red-orange blossoms.

Theo likely would've used the same markers to find her way, and if that failed, she had Kane. Vasil didn't doubt Kane had the ability to map Theo's location and guide her along the right path, just as Sam could through the diving suits.

But none of that provided him much assurance. His hearts did not ease, and the weight in his gut did not diminish. His skin felt overly warm and itchy, sparking a primal, unsettling urge to claw it off for relief. He could not forget the snatcher, and his imagination suggested other dangers lurking in the greenery too numerous for him to fully comprehend.

Why should she be so important to me after barely two days when I have gone years without approaching the youngling I sired?

The answer that resonated in his mind was too quick, too confident, too final.

Because Theo is mine *and mine alone.*

Ahead, the vegetation thickened, and through it came the muffled sound of trickling water. The stream was close. Vasil cast away all other thoughts. Finding Theodora was the only matter of any importance, and the way he felt about her had no bearing on that task.

He shoved through the foliage and emerged on the bank of the stream. With no barriers to dull the sound, the stream's burbling was loud and clear, but it wasn't enough to drown out his thumping hearts. He swung his gaze from upstream to downstream and sucked in a relieved breath.

Theo was downstream, submerged up to her shoulders in

the widest, deepest part of the stream with her back to him. The tension in his chest faded as he moved toward her.

She tipped back her head. Her light blonde hair spread around her, floating on the water's surface, as she ran her fingers through it. When she was done, she stood up.

Vasil halted. For an instant, nothing moved within him — not even his hearts or lungs — and all the world's sounds vanished.

Theo was naked.

Rivulets of water cascaded over her pale skin, trickling along her spine, her flaring hips, and the tantalizing curve of her backside, the latter of which was just visible above the water line.

Without conscious thought, Vasil moved into the nearby foliage and eased closer to her. His skin altered its color to match his surroundings. He could not remove his eyes from her. There were stark differences between the human and kraken form, and while he found beauty in both, there was an undeniable allure in the sensuality of human females.

She turned, making her way back toward the shore, and Vasil inhaled sharply. His attention was called in a dozen different directions; the black markings covering her left arm and side would have consumed his curiosity in most other situations, but her body above her mid-thighs was bared to him now. His gaze went to her firm, rounded breasts and the hardened nubs of her pink nipples, upon which droplets of water glistened, before dipping along her stomach. More of the black markings — lines and circles, lacking any discernable pattern, that reminded him, somehow, of machinery — ran over her belly toward her pelvis.

He held his gaze there even as she entered shallower water and more of her graceful legs emerged. She was hairless save for atop her head, and that confused him. He'd heard that humans all had hair covering their sexes — not that Theo was like any human he'd met. The top of her slit was just visible between her thighs, and for a moment, Vasil envisioned her legs spreading to reveal the delicate petals of her sex, pink and glistening with want — for *him*.

His cock throbbed, straining against his slit. He held it back only by force of will — and that hold was tenuous at best. He clenched his hands into fists at his sides. The sting of his claws digging into his palms offered no distraction from the sight before him. Perhaps it was because he'd been without sex for so long, but his want for Theo was so immense at that moment it caused him physical pain.

She reached the grassy bank and stepped onto land. Tilting her head to the side, she gathered her hair into her hands and twisted it, wringing out excess water.

Suddenly, she stilled, her body tensing briefly. "Do all kraken spy on bathing women?"

Vasil's throat constricted, and his breath hitched. She hadn't even *looked* at him; how could she have known he was there? A lucky guess, or were her senses enhanced beyond his comprehension?

Had Kane had something to do with it?

Despite her acknowledgment of his presence, she made no move to cover herself. Her stance — arms up with hands behind her head — forced her back to arch, jutting her chest forward and accentuating her breasts. It was as though she were flaunting her body the same way a female kraken would while seeking a mate.

But human females didn't behave the same way as kraken... did they?

"Do all humans strut naked through the jungle?" he asked, immediately feeling foolish for his words. He *knew* they didn't, and she hadn't been strutting, she'd been bathing.

She turned her face in his direction, and the corner of her mouth quirked upward. "When we believe we're alone."

"You were aware of my presence," he replied. His mouth felt dry; how was that even possible? He'd come from the sea only minutes ago.

She dropped her arms to her sides, and her wet hair fell around her shoulders. She turned, giving him her back, and bent forward to collect her clothing.

The ache in his pelvis deepened as his gaze dropped to her backside, continued down her shapely thighs and calves, and drifted back up again. The cleft of her sex was visible between her legs; he clenched his jaw and battled the urge to go to her. However much he *wanted*, he couldn't forsake all his people's ways. Females chose. That remained an important truth.

But...*was* this a show of *her* interest? Her behavior was at once forward and subtle, and he wasn't certain how to interpret it. Was it a display of trust, of mutual desire, or simply of confidence and comfort?

She stepped into her underclothing and drew it up her legs. What would her skin feel like beneath his palms, brushed in such a gentle caress?

"Not for too long," she said, tugging the material over her hips, hiding the flesh of her backside from his view.

Now that he knew what lay beneath her clothing, he found himself only more drawn to the way it fit her form. What would it be like to take her from behind, to slide his hands along her hips, her ass, up her spine? To twine his fingers in her hair as he thrust into her?

The image nearly broke his control.

He moved out of the foliage and closer to the water, forcing his skin to its normal color. "You do seem unconcerned."

"As big as IDC cruisers are, they don't designate much space for crew quarters. When you live so close to other soldiers for so long, sharing bunks and showers, privacy just...ceases to exist. And eventually, you stop caring." She slipped her arms into the straps of her undergarment and looked over her shoulder at him. "Does it bother you?"

Vasil swallowed thickly. The way she looked at him poured fresh heat into his veins. He barely kept his cock restrained behind his slit.

He gestured down at his body. "*Modesty* is not an issue for my kind. But in my experience, it is for humans."

Her gaze trekked down his body. There was curiosity in her eyes, but something else sparkled along with it. Interest?

She faced away from him again before he could determine what that gleam was. "Do your women look like me? Like human women?"

"From the waist up, more or less."

"So half of me is nothing new, huh?" She bent forward again and tugged on her boots one at a time.

He followed the motion of her hands up toward her knee with his gaze, continuing beyond to her thigh. He'd watched the play of muscles in her legs as she walked, but he was equally interested in her soft curves. The thought of warm, yielding flesh held an appeal he'd never considered before and intensified his curiosity.

"Kraken females are not as soft."

She glared at him. "I seriously hope you're not saying I'm fat."

The orb of light at her wrist pulsed as Kane spoke up. "Let me remind you, Theo, of the altercation you had on the—"

"That guy had it coming to him!" She straightened and ran her hands over her midsection. "There's nothing wrong with having a little in the middle."

Vasil furrowed his brow and — well aware of the risk to his wellbeing — moved closer to her. His attention shifted from her belly to the black markings on her otherwise pale skin.

"I do not understand what has angered you," he said as he

came to a stop beside her and spread his tentacles to bring his head closer to her eye level.

Her eyes widened infinitesimally, and her body tensed, but she did not retreat. She glanced down at his tentacles and back up. "Umm…"

"Kraken females have slighter builds than males, but they are…solid." He touched the pads of his fingers to his abdomen, pressing against the hard muscle beneath his soft skin. "There is nothing wrong with human women. Nothing wrong with *you*."

Theo's cheeks reddened, the flush spreading down her neck to her chest. "That's…kind of…sweet?"

"It's not exactly a compliment," Kane said.

Vasil frowned, eyes flicking toward the orb. The humans who used the diving suits said Sam, the suits' computer, was helpful, and the voice of the Computer in the Facility had been a comforting, familiar part of Vasil's life for many years, but he couldn't imagine having one *inside* him all the time, always speaking.

"Do you ever get tired of hearing him?" he asked.

Theo snickered. "Pretty often."

"I've been taught that it is impolite to speak of someone as though they aren't present," said Kane.

"I can correct that," replied Theo with a smirk. "Since you've been so cranky today, maybe you need a nap?"

"Sometimes I wish with all my processing power that I had a face just so I could glare at you."

Her smirk widened into a grin. "I guess I'll just have to use my imagination."

Vasil tilted his head. It would have been easy to assume Theo's relationship with Kane was adversarial, but his time around humans over the last two years had taught him differently. Though Kane and Theodora seemed to repeatedly insult each other, there was a familiarity and odd good-naturedness to their exchanges that reminded Vasil of Randall, who always seemed to have a quick retort on hand. It had taken time to learn that Randall poked fun at people he was friendly with, and that his joking was usually gentle. That he seemed to leave himself open to the same treatment from those close to him had helped ease Vasil's realization.

"You are *friends* with your computer," Vasil said.

Theo glanced at him, sighed, and raised her left arm. Kane's orb moved with her wrist, maintaining a constant distance above it. "Kane...is my family." She smiled sheepishly and shrugged one of her shoulders. "He's the only thing that kept me sane most days. It's...scary how quiet things can get when you're alone a lot of the time."

Vasil understood how she felt; he'd spent much of his time alone, constantly aware of the vast, merciless sea surrounding him, aware of his own tenuous hold on survival and how fragile life could be. The kraken had never been particularly social beings, not until a human had come into their lives. He couldn't imagine going back to the old ways after experiencing the companionship, conversation, and laughter that had risen from his people's integration with the humans of The Watch.

He couldn't face that silence any longer.

And he wasn't sure how to express any of that to Theo. For all the words he knew, none seemed adequate.

His eyes shifted from the light at her wrist to the black markings surrounding it. Extending his arm, he gently touched the pad of a finger to one of the thin lines. "What are these?"

She flinched but didn't pull away. Tiny bumps rose along her arm.

"They're called tattoos." She gestured at the stripes on his shoulder with her right hand. "You look like you have something similar."

"All kraken have stripes, but I have never seen a human with *tattoos*." He slowly traced the black line, following it up her arm. She shivered. "Have you had them since birth?"

"No," she said breathlessly, staring at his hand, "we choose to get them. They're not a…a natural thing."

Her skin was soft, warm, and responsive beneath his touch. His chest tightened, and his blood heated anew. He wanted to do more than touch her arm — he wanted to tear off her undergarment and run his hands over her bared curves. Her scent settled over his consciousness, more feminine now than before.

Vasil attempted to shake off the distraction of his desires, to focus on the conversation. He was curious about her markings, but his curiosity was fast turning toward the rest of her body — how would it feel, how would it respond to his touch? How would she *taste*?

"I do not understand," he said, forcing his hand to still when it reached her upper arm.

"We're not born with them," Theo said, "but some people choose to have them done. It's like…decoration, I guess. It's a way to change how we look. We can't exactly change our skin at will like you can."

Vasil brushed his thumb along the underside of her arm. There was no difference in feeling between the *tattoos* and the rest of her flesh "It is *in* your skin?"

She nodded.

"How?" he asked.

"They have these big machines. You set up the design you want and step into the chamber, and all these little lasers turn on and basically burn it into your skin." She lifted her right hand and settled it on her left forearm, slowly sliding her palm down. "It's like a hundred thousand needles stabbing you all at once, and it hurts like a mother fucker while it's happening, but the pain mostly stops once it's done. It itches for a day or two, but you have a brand-new tattoo to show off."

"Is it worth the pain?"

She looked down at the markings. "Yeah, I guess so. I can't really remember the pain, but I'll always have this kick-ass tattoo." Her eyes met his again, and she smirked. "Anyway, I'm all finished here."

She stepped away from him, breaking their contact, and bent down to gather her belongings from the ground. Straightening briefly, she fastened her belt around her waist, pistol and knife already in place, and then collected her outer suit — or rather the *pieces* of her outer suit. He'd thought it a single garment, like the diving suits from the Facility, but she held at least four separate parts now.

He tilted his head as he noticed the frayed edge of one of her sleeves; realization came to him a moment later. She'd *cut* the suit into pieces.

With the suit tucked under one arm, she turned toward a pair of containers standing on the bank. Vasil hurried forward and grabbed them both. She reeled back at his sudden movement.

"I have plenty of limbs to help you," he said quickly. "I am here. I might as well share the load."

Theo smiled. "Thanks."

He turned and moved through the thick foliage bordering the stream bank, heading toward the beach. Theo's footsteps — the soft crunching of leaves and branches — sounded immediately behind him.

The liquid in the containers — water, undoubtedly — sloshed as he moved. He forced himself to keep his eyes on his surroundings, to remain vigilant, but the urge to twist around and look at her only strengthened as they traveled. The short journey shouldn't have been any different from any he'd made with kraken hunting parties in the past, during which he'd always needed to remain observant for everyone's safety. It wasn't so long ago that he'd relieved a distracted Kronus — who'd been interested in a woman of his own — from watch duty to ensure the job was adequately done.

Arkon's word for Vasil's current behavior would've been *hypocritical.*

Words leapt out of his mouth before he even realized his intention to speak. "Do you have a mate?"

"You mean like a life partner or a fuck buddy?" Theo asked.

Vasil halted and spun around to face her. Eyes wide, she jerked and skidded to a sudden stop, nearly colliding with him.

"A *what?*" he demanded.

Her brows lowered. "A…fuck buddy?"

"A *fuck buddy,*" he repeated.

"That's what she said," Kane interjected.

Theo cleared her throat. "Um, fucking is when—"

"I know what *fucking* is," Vasil said.

She frowned and scratched behind her ear before dropping her hands to her waist and holding them to either side, palms up. "Not sure what answer you're looking for, then."

"I do not understand what the term *fuck buddy* means. It is not used by the humans on this world. Explain."

"Oh. Well, it's when you have a friend that you casually have sex with. No strings attached."

His brow furrowed. "How would you have sex with strings?"

Theo laughed, shaking her head. "Boy, you really are sheltered out here, aren't you? Not *literal* strings. It means you have no other obligation or commitment to one another. It's just about mutual pleasure. You can move on whenever you want to or see someone else."

In some ways, the concept reminded him of the way kraken pairings had been — females selected males to mate with and kept them as long as they chose. Those *relationships* ended on a whim. In Vasil's experience, those pairings had been devoid of love or affection despite the physical attraction and mutual respect they often began with.

But kraken couplings weren't about pleasure. They had an explicit purpose — reproduction. Kraken came together for the survival of their species, and any male who wanted to keep a female made sure to provide for her as best he could.

"You did not answer my initial question," Vasil said.

She smirked. "You didn't answer mine either."

"Are you *fucking* anyone?"

Theo's eyes widened, and she glanced away.

"What a lesson in subtlety," Kane murmured.

"That is how you defined mating, is it not?" Vasil asked, confused by her reaction. Why would she speak so candidly about it a moment ago only to look horrified now?

"If you were a human, I'd tell you it wasn't any of your fucking business." She tilted her head back and looked over his body before meeting his gaze. "But you're not. It's just that the way you asked made it sound like you're interested in…well, you know. *Sex*. With me."

"I am."

Theo took a couple steps backward, shock overcoming her expression. She held her hands up, palms out, as though to keep him at bay. "Whoa! Okay. Umm…"

"I would like to know you better, first," he said. "That is the way humans usually enter relationships, correct?"

"A…*relationship?*"

"That's what he said," Kane chimed.

"Kane. Sleep mode," Theo growled. The orb at her wrist blinked out.

Vasil moved forward, closing the distance she'd created between them. Though she didn't back farther away, her expression remained wary, and she kept her hands up.

"I did not mean to upset you," said Vasil. "I have been told I sometimes tend toward *unnecessary bluntness*."

"That's an understatement."

He dipped his chin in acknowledgment; self-awareness hadn't made it any easier for him to change the habit.

"You are attractive, Theodora. I am drawn to you. But it is

your personality that intrigues me and keeps me interested." Vasil drew in a deep breath, swelling his chest. "I am a skilled hunter, a keen-eyed scout, and a reliable companion. And I am interested in what you humans call a *forever relationship*. We would complement each other well as mates."

Theo stared at him for several moments. The corners of her lips twitched, her brows lifted quirked up over the bridge of her nose, and she smiled before bursting into laughter. Vasil tilted his head as she clutched her middle and doubled over with her intensifying laughter.

He frowned. Had he said something unintentionally humorous, or was she laughing at *him*?

"Are you all right?" he asked.

She held up a hand. "I'm sorry! I'm sorry!" Her laughter finally tapered off, diminishing to a few chuckles before ceasing completely, but her grin remained. "There's something to be admired in directness, but when it comes to this stuff, you have to slow it down a little, Vasil."

"Is it not best to state my intentions up front so there are no misunderstandings?"

"Well, yes, but you should start at the beginning and take baby steps from there."

Still frowning, he gestured to his tentacles.

She followed his gesture with her eyes. "I'm not quite getting—Oh! You don't take steps. Okay, so maybe that was a poor word choice on my part. What I mean is you need to take things *slow*. I don't know how it's done with your people, but—"

"Males display their suitability as a mate through hunting and physical confrontations with one another until a female chooses one to take to her den and procreate."

"Well, okay then. That explains your forwardness."

Vasil released a slow breath, glancing at the jungle floor as he gathered his thoughts. "I know that is not how humans behave. I was attempting to do it the human way. I did not expect to have sex with you *today*."

Her eyes flared wide again, her brows rising high above them. "Yeah, okay, about that…"

"Do not worry, Theo. Our *pieces* will fit."

Her gaze dropped to his slit. Just having her attention upon it was enough to stir his arousal, but he didn't think his cock suddenly extruding would be the best way to smooth over this situation. Or would it? Would it put her at ease? He'd been gravely mistaken if he'd ever thought he understood how human minds worked.

"I could show you," he said, "if it would help—"

Her eyes shot up to meet his, cheeks bright red. "No! No, that's okay. I um, believe you. How about we keep our genitals… hidden and just head back to the pod? Sound good? Great!" She hurried past him, boots crunching over the jungle floor. "Hey Kane, wake up."

Vasil turned to watch her moving away, feeling oddly empty and numb. It wasn't the result of rejection, not exactly — she'd fled without *verbally* rejecting him — but rather of confusion.

He followed her before she was too far ahead and attempted, with only minor success, to turn his focus back to keeping watch. Part of his mind continued racing.

Somehow, her reaction had made him want her more. In the end, it was the female's choice — he would not deny Theo that right — but he was determined to make himself the *only* reasonable choice.

CHAPTER 6

Rising from her crouch slightly, she peered over the pod's hatch opening. Vasil was outside building a fire on the sand. She ducked down quickly.

"*I guess it's time for your daily reminder that you do* not *have to speak out loud, Theo,*" Kane said through their neural link.

"My mind is a little overwhelmed right now, you know, what with a kraken wanting to have *sex* with me," she hissed, leaning her back against the pod's inner wall. "He's got tentacles, Kane! *Tentacles!*"

"*All the better to love you with.*"

She could almost hear the smirk in Kane's voice.

"Are you kidding? *Please* tell me you're kidding." She ran her fingers through her hair and groaned as she recalled the feel of Vasil's fingers brushing over her arm and the sensation it had elicited. She'd been *turned on*. By a…an *alien!*

"*Don't pretend you haven't been checking him out, Theodora. You're not exactly subtle about it.*"

"What?"

"I see through your eyes, Theo," Kane said. *"I can tell when you're focusing on his chest and abs."*

"I was just curious! Nothing wrong with a little curiosity. It doesn't mean anything!"

"Is this *what you're hiding from?"* Kane asked. An image appeared on her retinal display — Vasil's chest, muscles stretching and flexing as Kane replayed the short video on a loop.

"I can't believe you right now!" Theo forced the image away with a mental command and squeezed her eyes shut, but it didn't help.

Her imagination picked up where Kane had left off, showing her the play of muscles in Vasil's body as he moved with his strange, uneven gait. The mental image soon focused on something she'd noticed only briefly in person — a small slit at his pelvis where his skin seemed to have parted slightly. She had a strong suspicion of what hid beneath that slit. The thought was at once horrifying and intriguing.

What did his cock look like? Pink and floppy, slimy and squirmy like an eel? She quickly shoved that thought out of her mind. Perhaps was it long, hard, and unyielding, the same gray as the rest of his skin? Would it be warm? Would it respond to her touch? Would it—

"Fuuuuuuck." Theo pressed her fingers against her eyelids as though that could erase the mental images she'd produced.

She couldn't tell over the sound of the nearby waves, not for sure, but she swore Kane was chuckling softly in her head.

"This is well beyond the intentions of my programming," he said through the link, *"but we can work this out, Theo. Why not make a list? Pros and Cons."*

"What are you talking about?" She dropped her hands and blinked as the dark spots swimming across her vision faded. "Pros and cons of *what,* Kane?"

"You know. Reasons why you should and should not have alien tentacle sex."

Theo gaped, eyes sweeping over the floor without focusing on anything.

"You're *serious*?" She threw up her hands and rolled her eyes. "Of course you're serious! Oh my God, I can't believe you. He's an *alien*, Kane! It hasn't even been two days, and he wants sex and a relationship with me. A *forever* relationship, I might add."

"If we are to take him at his word, his genetic makeup is quite human. Half-human, I believe you said. We're both wrong to call him an alien."

"Whose side are you on, anyway?" Theo asked. "So, what, am I supposed to jump his alien dick — whatever that looks like — and have his squiggly little babies? What about getting off this planet? Getting back to the fleet?"

"I can't tell you what to do in this situation. I don't even have a body. Silly for you to look to me for sexual advice."

"Kane, seriously. Please."

"I know, I know. Really, though, I can't tell you what to do. If it doesn't feel right, don't. The immunoboosters the IDC injected you with will kill off any squiggly diseases he might have, and you were signed up for a ten-year stint. IDC protocol means your implant is going to prevent you from getting pregnant for three more years — one month after the end of your service. As for getting out of here...you don't have the parts to repair the comm array in the pod. There are no satellites. The chances of getting any sort of message out there are so low they might as well be non-existent."

Theo closed her eyes and tilted her head back. She'd known this, but she hadn't wanted to admit defeat so soon. She'd only been here for two days; that didn't seem long enough to just give up.

What did she really have to back to, though? Solitude in the bowels of another ship, long stretches of silence broken only by the clank of tools and the steady hum of machinery, and bland, pasty food?

She dropped onto her backside with a sigh. "So...I guess this is it."

"Apart from the occasional carnivorous plant, this planet doesn't seem all that bad," Kane said gently. *"And Vasil says there are other humans. That means you're not going to be alone."*

"Worked my ass off for years and *this* is what I get." Theo opened her eyes and looked around her. If there were no functioning satellites in orbit, and the humans had colonized this planet hundreds of years ago, this escape pod was very likely the most advanced piece of technology in the world. Just how far behind were the inhabitants of Halora?

What the hell was Theo supposed to do? She knew next to nothing about surviving in the wilds.

"Theo?" Vasil called from outside the pod.

She groaned.

"You can't hide forever," Kane said in her mind.

"I'm not *hiding*," she said, shifting onto her knees. "I was just...taking a moment for myself."

That wasn't really a lie; she'd changed out of her under suit into the sleeveless shirt and pants she'd cut from her uniform.

"My mistake." If Kane oozed any more sarcasm, Theo would drown in it.

"Ass."

"Theo?" Vasil repeated.

"One sec!" she called.

"And you are a beautiful, intelligent, independent woman. Go to your octo-man."

"Oh my God, you're impossible!" she whisper-growled.

Theo grabbed one of the water containers and pushed herself onto her feet. Turning, she leaned against the edge of the opening and looked down at Vasil, who had twisted away from the fire to face her. Their gazes met. His eyes were beautiful, even from this distance — like liquid silver, so bright and clear that part of her mind insisted they couldn't be real. After a few moments, his attention dipped to take in her torso, and a flare of desire sparked in the depths of his eyes.

Her heartbeat quickened, and heat flooded her; she'd experienced the same sensations at the stream earlier.

Though she'd known Vasil had been on the bank, watching her as she emerged from the water, she hadn't bothered to cover herself. She'd done nothing to hide. Theo had *let* him look his fill, and she liked the aroused fires that had gleamed in his eyes. She couldn't remember another time when she'd felt so empowered, so sensual, so…*wanted*. It had sparked a longing inside her that had yet to diminish.

Kane's voice drifted to her through the neural link. *"Those are interesting vital readings for someone who's not interested…"*

She blasted a quick retort to him — *Shut. Up.*

Clenching her teeth, Theo tucked the water container beneath her arm, turned, and carefully climbed out of the pod. She dropped the short distance to the ground, her bare feet sinking in the soft sand. The sea-kissed breeze swept over her, woven with the aroma of cooking meat.

She swept her hair out of her face with her free hand and approached Vasil. She'd just pretend their earlier conversation hadn't happened.

Yep. Easy. Totally didn't happen.

"Whatcha cooking?" she asked nonchalantly.

Vasil glanced at her over his shoulder and smiled, displaying sharp teeth. He reached forward and picked up a stick, upon which was impaled a sizzling fillet. "Fish. Are you hungry?"

Her mouth watered at the sight of the meat. "Starving."

Adjusting his hold on the stick, he turned it and offered her the uncharred end.

"Thanks," she said, accepting his offering. She walked to the opposite side of the fire and sat down facing him, standing the water container beside her. All she could do was hope the fire would be enough of a barrier between them to prevent her thoughts from straying into unwelcome territory.

Vasil's gaze remained fixated upon her, following her movements. There was something strange about the way he looked at her — like he could see *into* her, but his eyes held no judgment.

"Are you feeling well?" he asked.

"Yeah, why? Do I look sick or something?" Raising the stick, she blew on the hot fillet.

"No. But you went into the pod the moment we returned and have been whispering to Kane ever since."

"And?" She tore off a chunk of fish off the stick with her teeth. The moment the flakey meat hit her tongue, she closed her eyes and moaned, chewing slowly.

"You seemed distressed."

Theo waited until she'd swallowed before answering. "Nope, totally fine."

"You crashed on an alien world, were nearly killed in the jungle, have a kraken who wants you as his mate, and have no way to leave, but you are fine?"

She glanced at him briefly before returning her attention to her food. "Already had my freak-outs. Now I'm just dealing with one problem at a time. No reason to worry about things I can't do anything about, right?" She took another large bite.

At the edge of her vision, she saw him staring at her. She felt naked under his scrutiny despite her clothing. Oddly, it wasn't a bad feeling.

"Should your response to my stated intentions be considered a *freak-out?*" he asked.

"Where are the rest of your people?" she countered.

Evade. Evade. Evade.

"Elsewhere."

She looked up at him. "Nearby elsewhere or far away elsewhere?"

Without breaking eye contact with her, he picked up the other stick, raised it to his mouth, and took a bite of the sizzling meat. If it burned him, he displayed no pain.

Theo arched a brow. "Well, kraken?"

He chewed slowly, deliberately, the muscles of his jaw flexing and relaxing. After he finally swallowed, his tongue slipped out and slid over his lips. Her eyes focused on it, and her hand clenched her stick as she imagined what his tongue would feel like against her skin.

What the fuck is wrong with me?

It's been way *too long. That's all it is.*

"I can't quite tell if you're about to die, or you're just horny," Kane whispered in her mind.

She sent a panicked reply through their link.

What do you mean die, *Kane?*

"I mean give your heart a break, or it's going to burst through your ribcage, Theo. Just fuck him and get it over with, please."

Do you want to sleep? Cause I'll totally put you to sleep.

"You know what? I'm putting myself *to sleep. Goodnight."*

Despite everything, Theo's lips curved into a grin, and she snickered.

"Is Kane speaking in your head?" Vasil asked, jarring her back to reality.

"He was, but he's sleeping now."

"I cannot tell you where anyone else is, Theo."

Theo frowned. "Why not? I thought we were past that."

His lips fell into a frown to mirror her own, and a crease appeared at the center of his brow. He dropped his gaze to the sand and shifted in place, tentacles curling restlessly. "Because I do not know where *here* is."

"Are you saying you're just as stranded as I am?"

"I found your pod just as a storm swept in. There was no land in sight to gauge our location. We rode the storm out, and this is where it took us."

Theo lowered her stick, which she'd already picked clean of meat, and propped it against the stone ring Vasil had built around the fire.

"But you have *those*," she said, motioning to his tentacles. "You could just swim out there, right? Find your way back? It's not like you're stuck on land."

Not like I am.

"I did not leave you in the sea, Theodora, and I will not abandon you here," he said firmly. "I explored a bit this morning when I went for the fish, and I plan to go farther tomorrow."

Hearing him say he wouldn't leave her here eased something inside her, a fear she hadn't realized she'd been harboring. Though she was good at tricking herself into believing her own capabilities, into believing she could survive if it came down to it, she was scared at heart. She didn't know what she was *doing*, much less what she was going to do.

And…she didn't want to be left alone.

She dug her toes into the sand. "So, until then…"

"It is only us."

"What do we do in the meantime? What can *I* do?"

"This area is essentially our den. We make the most of it," he said, twisting to look back over his shoulder at the pod. "We have prey to hunt and fruit to forage, and your pod will serve as adequate shelter." He faced her again. "Many of the humans I know enjoy the beach. Do you?"

Theo turned her head, looking past the fire to survey the beach's pale sand and the cerulean ocean beyond. "I've never been on one until now. This is the first time I've been on land for more than a few hours in…eighteen years."

Had it really been that long since she left Old Earth?

Vasil tilted his head back to look up at the open sky, which was darkening to gray-blue as evening deepened. "You were up *there* for all that time?" His voice brimmed with unmasked wonder.

"Yeah. You get used to it, you know? The more time passes, the less you realize what you're missing." She shrugged her shoulders. "I didn't have much to miss anyway. My experiences planet-side were…unpleasant."

"Planet-side?"

Theo removed the cap — which doubled as a cup — from the container beside her and poured herself some water. "Yeah. It's something IDC soldiers say. Just means on a world. We spend a lot of time in space, even the ones who do the fighting. Time on a planet feels almost like this mythological thing after a while, so it kinda needs its own designation to keep it separate."

Vasil returned his attention to her and leaned closer; she found herself both grateful for and resentful of the fire separating them.

"What unpleasant experiences did you have?" he asked.

Theo cradled the cup between her hands and watched the reflections on the water inside. "Shitty childhood."

Movement from the corner of her eye forced her attention up again. Her heart skipped a beat as Vasil used his tentacles to drag himself closer to her around the edge of the fire. When he stopped, there was less than a meter of distance between them, and two of his tentacles were stretched out toward Theo — one in front of her, one behind. Neither limb touched her, but they were *so* close.

"My understanding of what those words mean to humans is limited," he said. "The meanings they hold for me are shaped by my experiences, which were very different from yours. Will you tell me more, Theo?"

She studied his expression silently, searching his eyes. Desire lingered within them, but it was the interest in his gaze that caught her attention. He genuinely wanted to hear more. He wanted to *know* her. If Vasil were human, she would've had sex with him without a second thought — she could see the potential for a real relationship in his eyes, and it called to her, speaking to what she'd wanted for so long. But there were so many differences between the two of them…

Could she really overlook them? Could she just fuck him and get it over with, as Kane had suggested?

She'd had a few hookups over the many years she'd been off-planet, but none of them stood out in her mind. She could barely remember their faces, much less their names. None of them had bothered to get to know her. They hadn't cared. For a long time, she'd told herself she hadn't cared, either. She'd been just as guilty of using others to scratch an itch and move on, but those couplings had left her feeling unsettled. Naked. Vulnerable.

At least those feelings had been predictable. With Vasil…*could* she really get it over with? She feared there was no quick solution — he didn't want to merely satisfy a craving. And she had no idea how that would make her feel.

Theo looked away from Vasil and brought the cup to her lips, drinking slowly to stall; she wasn't sure how to begin.

"There's really not too much to tell," she said, lowering the cup and idly running her finger up and down its side. "I wasn't wanted, and I'm sure my mother tried everything short of killing herself to get rid of me after finding out she was pregnant. Guess I was as stubborn then as I am now, because I refused to go anywhere."

Vasil's skin darkened a few shades. He clenched his jaw, and the cords on his neck stood out. He shook his head a moment later, clearing away some of his visible tension, but when he spoke his nostrils flared, and his brows fell low. "Why would anyone try to…to *get rid* of a youngling?"

Theo shrugged. "Too much responsibility, another mouth to feed, the inability to feel anything toward another human being but resentment — take your pick. I'm sure there are a million other reasons."

He raised his hands and spread his fingers as though something would form in the air between his palms only to curl them into fists a few moments later. "Nothing you said is an adequate reason. Younglings are precious things. The most important things."

She snorted and set down her empty cup. "I don't know how things are here, but that's not the case in the rest of the universe."

Theo glared at the fire and tossed a handful of sand toward it. The flames sputtered, hissed, and flickered. "The only reason she kept me alive as a baby was so she could collect more funding from the system and keep herself high on relinquiem. Otherwise, she would've thrown me in the garbage."

"Is everything all right, Theo?" Kane asked in her mind. *"Your vitals roused me—"*

I'm fine.

She inhaled deeply, shoving away her surge of anger. No matter how many years went by, she always felt that same impotent rage whenever she thought of the woman who'd birthed her.

"What of your sire?" Vasil asked in a low, tight voice.

"Who knows? Knocked my mom up and bailed." She tilted her head and swept her hair in front of one shoulder, fiddling with the strands. "He was probably a junkie just like her, but I hate not *knowing*. Because he could've been a decent guy. A decent dad. He could've been the one to take me away and save me from all that shit."

The remaining tension faded from Vasil's face, leaving behind a deep, troubled frown.

"You know what's funny?" Theo asked, but didn't wait for Vasil to respond. "My name wasn't even Theodora. She never really gave me a name. I was always *brat*, or *you little shit*, or *you fucking kid*. Once in a while, usually right after she took a hit, I was just *girl*. That was the best I had to hope for. I didn't think things could get worse, not that I knew any different back then.

But then she died of an overdose when I was around eight, and I got thrown into the system."

She didn't realize how tightly she'd been pulling on her hair until she felt a sharp pain on her scalp; she forced her fingers to relax.

"I don't want to talk about this anymore," she said quietly. For almost twenty years, she'd tried to keep those memories at bay, but they constantly reached out to grasp at her with icy claws and drag her into the darkness. To remind her that she was frightened and alone, that she always would be.

No, not alone. There was someone else in those memories, someone with putrid breath and sweaty palms...

Vasil's hand, its skin soft over firm muscle, settled lightly on her forearm. "You do not have to, Theodora."

"Don't touch me," she snapped, flinching away from him. The pounding of her heart sent bursts of pain through her chest, and, for a terrifying moment, she couldn't catch her breath. "Just...don't touch me right now, okay?"

Without another word, she pushed herself to her feet and fled. She hauled herself into the pod, crumpling to the floor the instant her feet touched down. It felt like a vise was closing over her ribs. Her constricted throat limited the air she could take in, making her breaths short and ragged. The walls of the pod spun around her, teetering wildly, and she knew they'd crush her any second.

"Theodora, I need you to breathe." Kane's voice was commanding, projected directly into her mind. *"Don't think about anything else. Please, just take some slow, even breaths."*

Pressing her forehead against the cool floor, Theo closed her eyes. She focused on Kane's voice and the movement of air in and out of her lungs, pushing through the tightness in her throat.

"Good. One at a time, slow and deep. You're here, *Theo. And as long as you have me, here is always the best place to be, right?"*

Theo released a raspy laugh even as tears gathered behind her eyelids. "Yeah. It is."

Drawing in deep, burning lungfuls of air, Theo blindly crawled to her toolbox and curled around it. She rested her cheek on its lid and brushed her fingertips over the etched letters there. "I miss him, Kane. I miss him so damn much."

"You carry him with you everywhere you go, Theo. Not in that toolbox, but in yourself. You didn't become the person you are because of the woman who gave birth to you. It was Malcolm's guidance and your *determination to be better than what you were shown as a kid."*

"I know," she said, releasing a shaky sigh. She hated that her past still affected her like this, that it *still* had control over her. It didn't hit her like this often, but...

She'd lowered the walls around her heart for a few moments to give Vasil a glimpse of her true self, of the Theo she never let anyone else see. That had been more than enough time for her memories to take advantage of her brief vulnerability.

Time crept on around her, unheeded, as she lay on the floor, clutching the only meaningful thing she owned. It was the only thing she had left of Malcolm. The only thing she had left of the one person who'd cared about her.

Tension drained from her body, and eventually sleep tugged at the edges of her consciousness.

"You know I love you, too, don't you, Kane?" she asked quietly.

"I know. Get some rest, Theo. I'll keep watch."

Just before sleep claimed her, she felt a comforting hum pulse gently through her body; it was the closest Kane could come to physical touch.

Vasil stared at the pod. His chest and throat burned, and the air scorched his insides like fire when he sucked in a shuddering breath.

She'd recoiled from him and fled. It hadn't been the sort of off-balance, uncertain reaction she'd had when he'd said he wanted her as his mate. This had been what Randall sometimes called a *gut reaction* — an almost instinctual reflex. But she hadn't stopped herself even after the point at which reason would've kicked in to tell her she'd overreacted.

He'd reached out to comfort Theo, and she'd withdrawn in disgust.

He rose from the ground, straightening his tentacles to lift his torso upright. His body felt oddly unstable, somehow too light and too heavy at once. Moving slowly, he dragged himself toward the pod, keeping his gaze fixed upon it. The droning of the ocean seemed far-off, though he was close enough to feel sea mist on the breeze.

Theo's voice drifted to him, too low and too distorted by the faint echo created by the pod's interior for Vasil to make out what she was saying. But he didn't need to know her words to understand their raw anguish and sorrow in them.

He halted halfway between the fire and the pod, clenching his fists. The tips of his claws sank into his flesh, producing numerous points of stabbing pain, but that pain afforded him no clarity, no focus.

What was she thinking, what was she feeling? Was she disgusted by him, or did he only assume she was because of the undeniable differences in their anatomies? For a little while, he'd felt the connection between them like it was a physical bond; she had been open, had been vulnerable, and he'd somehow ruined it. Whether he'd said the wrong thing, had failed to say the right thing, or she'd realized suddenly who — *what* — he was, *this* was the outcome. This loneliness despite her nearness.

Conflicting urges raged inside him. He wanted to go and take Theo in his arms, to make her understand he was here with her, *for* her, that she was safe. He wanted to have strength enough to let her be, to give her the space she needed until she felt ready to speak to him. But he also wanted to break something, to roar at the sky, to collapse into the sand in despair or swim away from here, wanted to carry Theo anywhere in the universe she wished to go.

Rather than release control to any of those urges, he held himself in place, close enough to hear her voice, to pick up a hint of her scent on the wind, and yet separated by an impossible distance.

Pursue your desires.

The choice belongs to the female.

He could not reconcile those concepts with each other in those long moments of uncertainty. They seemed at once in conflict with each other and somehow irreversibly interwoven.

The pod went silent. Vasil's chest constricted anew; a cold hand clamped over each of his hearts and squeezed. The sounds of wind and sea increased in prominence without her words to hold his focus. He counted the dull thumps of his heartbeats; three, nine, eighteen, faster and faster.

Theo's voice floated to him, little more than a murmur, a ghostly whisper claimed by the wind. She spoke only a few words before falling silent again; he couldn't make out any of them.

Vasil held his breath and listened.

Seconds passed, bleeding into minutes. The wind and sea sighed together, creating an airy, haunting song. Behind Vasil, the fire popped and crackled. Unseen creatures made their night calls from within the jungle's rustling leaves.

But no sound emerged from the pod.

Soon, his body was too hot, his skin itchy, his breath ragged. He knew too little about this situation — about *Theo* — to put himself at ease without checking on her. He had to know for sure.

"Theo?" he called, dragging himself closer to the pod.

When she didn't answer, he moved closer still, struggling to ignore his rapidly beating hearts. He called her name again; again, she made no answer.

She does not want me near her. I am the last person she wants to see.

Vasil thrust that thought aside. It didn't matter what she thought of him, didn't matter whether she wanted him close or not — her safety was his priority. He had risked himself to stay with her pod through the storm and again to rescue her from the snatcher. He would risk himself time and again to keep Theo safe.

He just needed to *know*, even if it sparked more of her ire.

Without further internal debate, he climbed onto the pod. It swayed gently atop the sand as it accepted his weight.

"Theo?" he said as he raised his torso to look into the hatch opening.

The console lit up, casting a soft glow over the pod's interior.

"What are you doing, kraken?" Kane asked quietly through the console.

Vasil's gaze fell upon Theo. She lay on the floor, curled around a metal box with her head resting on the lid. Her eyes were closed, her expression relaxed, her breathing slow and even.

A wave of relief swept through Vasil. "She is asleep."

"Yes, she is," said Kane, "and you need to scurry off before you wake her."

The computer was right. Theo must have been exhausted, and Vasil did not want to disturb her much-needed rest. And why would she be anything but angry if she woke only to find him staring at her?

"That means you need to *leave*," Kane said.

Without realizing his own intentions, Vasil did move — he

grasped frame around the hatch opening and drew his upper half into the pod.

"What the hell are you doing?" Kane demanded, console light flaring red.

Though the pod's interior was roomier than he'd expected, Vasil was fully aware of the walls around him. They were too close, too tight, and the air was suddenly thin. He breathed in deeply, desperately, but his lungs were empty, and the building pressure in his chest would not allow them to fill.

He forced his attention to Theo as he slipped his tentacles into the pod. This was for her; he could endure a little discomfort. Kane spoke again, but Vasil ignored the computer. The kraken took in another breath, forcing air into his lungs, and reached down with his arms and his two frontmost tentacles.

"She doesn't want to be touched," Kane said.

"Quiet," Vasil whispered. He carefully slipped his hands and tentacles beneath her, carefully distributing her weight to disturb her as little as possible. The bare skin of her arms and midsection was warm and soft against his.

He lifted Theo from the floor. Her breathing faltered, and she moaned. Vasil stilled. His hearts thumped as powerfully as they might have were he facing down a charging razorback. The pod's interior, stained crimson in the console's light, seemed to close in on the edges of his vision.

This is not that cell, he told himself. *That cell is buried at the bottom of the sea.*

Theo's breathing evened out again.

Keeping his jaw clenched, Vasil turned her in his hold and eased her onto one of the pod's two seats. The cushioning gave slightly beneath her weight, cradling her body in what *had* to be a more comfortable position than what she'd been in a moment before. With great reluctance, he withdrew his hands and tentacles, daring to draw breath only after physical contact between them had been broken. The console's light shifted to a soft, pale blue. Vasil picked up the blanket from the other seat and draped it over Theo's body; nights sometimes grew chilly during the wet season, and humans weren't as capable as kraken at handling the cold.

"Now leave her to rest," Kane said.

Vasil nodded, but his gaze lingered on Theo. He frowned at the slight indentation on her cheek. It had undoubtedly been caused by the box upon which she'd been resting. He wanted nothing more at that moment than to touch her again, to caress away all her sorrow, fear, and pain.

He hauled himself out of the pod and slid down to the sand, turning toward the fire.

"Thank you."

Vasil paused and twisted to look back; Kane's voice had come from the pod's exterior, but there were no visible speakers on its surface. He didn't waste much time contemplating it — human technology was beyond his understanding.

"I am the reason she is in this state," Vasil said.

"What state? A *living* state?" Kane asked. "Yes, you're right. She *is* alive because of you."

"She is distraught because of me."

"What did you say to her, kraken?"

A heavy weight sank in Vasil's stomach, formed of guilt, regret, and shame. "Very little. *Too* little. She was telling me about her past, and I—"

"*What?*" Kane interrupted.

Vasil furrowed his brow, frown deepening. "She was telling me about her time on Old Earth. About her mother."

Kane sighed; the naturalness of the sound was so great that it served as a reminder to Vasil — Kane was far more advanced than any computer on Halora.

"I've been with Theo for over seven years," Kane said. "In all that time...she's never told anyone but me about her past. Not even the few men she's had brief relationships with."

"And I did not provide her what she needed. I—"

"Enough, kraken. This time, *you* be quiet and listen to *me*. Theo had things rough in her youth. She's never really healed from it, but she's always been smart enough to avoid raising any red flags on her psych evaluations. If she told you even a *little* about her past, that means she trusts you, which means…" The computer released a frustrated grumble. "Which means *I* have to trust you, too.

"Thank you for helping her, Vasil."

Vasil was unsure of what to say; there'd been more emotion in the computer's words than many kraken expressed in their entire lives, and Vasil's time among humans hadn't taught him how to properly respond to it. He turned back toward the fire and nodded. "From the moment I first saw her face during the storm, I knew I would do anything to protect her."

"You kraken *do* move fast," Kane muttered. "I feel the same way about her. It was coded into my programming, of course, but it's become more than that over the years. *Much* more. Hell, it's even allowed me to override some of my core IDC programming."

Closing his eyes, Vasil bowed his head and released a long breath. "You love her?" He didn't know how it would be possible — Kane possessed no body, no physical form — but love remained a largely mysterious force to Vasil. He didn't fully understand it, though he'd witnessed its power many times.

"Yes," Kane replied softly.

Vasil's chest tightened, a fire sparked in his blood.

"But not in the way you would," Kane continued. "Theo is my family."

The pressure within Vasil only seemed to grow, though the newly ignited flames diminished. "I understand."

"Good. I don't know what will develop between you two, but I want you to understand this, too: if you hurt her in any way, even a little, I will find some way to obtain a body — no matter how many natural laws or codes of ethics and morality I have to break to do so — just so I can kill you with my own hands. She is a sister to me."

Despite everything, Vasil smiled. He would never have believed he'd one day be threatened by a computer. How could the possibility even have occurred to him? More than that, he knew Kane would make every effort to fulfill his promise should he come to believe Vasil had harmed Theo.

"Understood," Vasil said, pulling himself forward. "Call me if she requires anything more."

Kane made no response.

Vasil returned to the fireside, spread his tentacles, and eased himself down onto the sand. His awareness of his surroundings slowly expanded. He'd shut out the song of wind and sea for too long today already.

But as he stared at the dancing flames, calmer and yet no less confused than he'd been before, he found no peace. Instead, his memory summoned another seaside fire from only a few nights ago, though it felt like years had passed since then — the fire at which his suspicions had finally been confirmed.

Melaina was his youngling. He'd sired her.

And he'd missed so many years of her life already.

He could not help but recall Theo's story and relate it to his own experiences. Though he knew kraken society was different, though he knew they'd always handled younglings in their own way, he couldn't help the comparison. Theo's father had not been in her life, and she'd never let go of her anger, her resentment. Did Melaina feel the same way toward Vasil? Was there a relationship to be formed with his daughter, or was he too late?

He looked back at the pod.

Was there a relationship to be formed between himself and Theo?

CHAPTER 7

TIME LOST MUCH OF ITS MEANING TO THEO OVER THE FIVE DAYS following her freak-out. She kept herself busy almost without fail. She explored the surrounding jungle with Kane's assistance, foraging for more fruit and keeping her water supply topped off, always keeping an eye out for new dangers. When no pressing tasks presented themselves, she tinkered with the escape pod's internal systems on the off-chance she'd accidentally restore the comms by tweaking the right component in just the right way.

Of course, she had no such luck. The comms were fried. Even a scrapper would hesitate in taking them off her hands.

She swam in the stream and the shallow ocean waters. Playing in the waves proved an unexpected delight, even if Kane called her childish for it; the amusement in his voice diminished the effect of his admonishments.

Vasil went out early each day to scout the ocean for any familiar landmarks — or was *seamark* the word? — that could direct him home. He returned each evening with a frown. But however low his spirits appeared, he always seemed to cheer up when his eyes met Theo's. He'd flash her a sharp-toothed-yet-charming smile and bring his latest catch into their little camp. They chatted as they shared their evening meals, growing more comfortable with one another with each passing day.

She worried for the first day or two that he'd ask about her near-breakdown, but he never brought it up. In fact, her childhood *never* came up during their conversations, even when they talked well into the night.

Theo had more fun over those five days than she had in as long as she could remember. There were no lectures, no schedules, no stuck-up officers or barking sergeants — just total freedom in a tropical paradise with a male kraken for company.

And *boy* did she notice just how male he was.

She often stole glances at Vasil when he wasn't looking, admiring the muscles of his arms as he worked, the flexing of his abs with each undulation of his tentacles, and the subtle play of his jaw muscles while he spoke. She *might* even have *accidentally* brushed her fingers over his skin on a few occasions. When she'd first seen him, she'd assumed his skin was rubbery or slimy — perhaps both.

She'd been dead wrong.

His skin was the softest velvet, suede over hard muscle. Those stolen touches weren't enough. She yearned to feel more of him, to rub her bare flesh over his and learn what it *really* felt like, to explore his body and appease her ever-growing curiosity.

Most nights, she lay awake in the pod, wondering what it would be like to have *him* touch *her*. Even his tentacles didn't bother her. She'd come to see them as just another part of his body, not all that different from her legs. That wasn't to say she never noticed them — how could she not? — but they certainly weren't distasteful. If she were honest with herself, she found them intriguing. In fact, they only seemed to heighten her desire.

She *might* have fantasized about them a few times by the fifth day.

Her thoughts were occupied with recollections of those blissful days — and, perhaps, a few naughty tentacles — as she knelt beside the stream while that fifth afternoon burned away into evening.

Kane's voice blared through the neural link. *"Are you sleeping with your eyes open right now, Theodora?"*

Theo started, nearly dropping the water container she was refilling in the stream. "What?"

"The jug has been full for over a minute," Kane said. *"Are you still planet-side with me, or are you drifting somewhere in space?"*

"I'm here," Theo muttered with a frown. She lifted the container out of the water, stood it on the ground beside her, and screwed on the cap.

"Physically."

"My mind is allowed to wander from time to time."

"Yeah, maybe. But that time is not *when we're in the middle of the jungle. What if a killer leaf dropped on you from above?"*

"Then I guess you would have failed at keeping watch, huh?"

Kane scoffed. *"You're not going to blame your hypothetical death on* me, *Theodora Velenti. We both know my scanner range is limited."*

Theo laughed. "You got one job, Kane. One job."

"One job? One job?" he demanded.

His tone only made her laugh harder.

"I am performing hundreds of trillions of operations per second, I'll have you know!" Kane's frustration pulsed through the neural link, but the discomfort was tolerable. *"All* you *had to do was fill a damned bottle."*

"A job well done, if I do say so myself," she said, tapping the top of the container.

"Yes, you certainly went above and beyond — if we're talking about the rim of the container."

Theo shook her head. *"That's* what you came back with? You should stick to your day job. You know, keeping watch."

"Too bad I can't command you to go to sleep..."

"Don't tempt me. You're lucky I need you to watch my back while my mind wanders aimlessly."

"We both know it's not aimlessly, Theo."

Theo's cheeks warmed, and an image of Vasil flashed through her retinal display. "Sometimes, Kane, I hate that you can monitor my vitals."

"Yeah, well, you're not the—"

"Shh!"

Theo ducked down as a yellow bird-like creature fluttered down from the canopy several meters away. Its length was difficult to judge, but she guessed it would be nearly a meter long from beak to behind if it were stretched out. It had a long neck with blue and green plumes on its backside, and a short, curved beak. It turned its head back and forth, surveying the area with large, dark eyes before scooting closer to the stream, pecking at the ground as it went.

"You don't need to shush me, Theo. No one else can hear me."

She narrowed her eyes as though she could somehow glare at Kane.

But you are *distracting,* she sent through the link, *and I can't hear myself think when you blabber on and on.*

She slowly lowered her hand and curled her fingers around the pistol's grip. Without taking her eyes off the bird, she tugged the weapon free.

"What are you doing, Theo?"

What's it look like? Hunting.

Raising the pistol, she gripped it with both hands — just like they'd taught in basic training — and aimed at the bird. Seemingly oblivious, the creature pecked at the ground, hopped forward to gulp down some water, and backed away to drop its beak to the dirt again.

Did you learn to cook at some point after we crashed here? You don't even know—"

Shh!

Though the neural link went silent, she swore she *felt* Kane grumbling.

Gently, she used her thumb to turn down the power setting on the pistol. Sighting the bird down the barrel, she took in a deep breath, steadied her arms, and pulled the trigger as soon as she exhaled. The bird released a short, startled squawk as a cloud of yellow feathers burst into the air and rained to the ground around it.

Theo leapt to her feet. "I got it!"

"Great. Looks like there are enough feathers left for arts and crafts afterwards."

"Quit being a downer." Theo refused to let Kane sour her success. She holstered the pistol and strode to the carcass. Countless feathers littered the ground, bright against the green grass, gray stones, and brown mud. "Check it out! I'm surviving!"

"As I was trying *to say before, you don't even know if it's safe to eat."*

Theo's brows furrowed. "It's a bird, Kane."

"It is an alien organism, Theo, regardless of how familiar it may appear."

"Well, it's worth it to have something to eat besides fish. And this time, *I* am the one providing dinner." Lips pursed to one side, she crouched beside the bird and studied its body. "So… you wouldn't happen to have any instructions on prepping and cooking a bird, would you?"

"Let me check."

Theo tapped her fingers against her knee and waited. "Kaaaaane."

He remained silent.

"Kane!" she said out loud and through the neural link.

"Sorry, I forgot I'm not connected to the IDC network anymore. No decent recipes on file, unless you're in the mood for engine grease to garnish your supper. I suppose cooking wasn't deemed necessary for your rank and position."

"Man, they screwed us in the survival department. Cheap asses." She sighed. "Well, all Vasil does is cut heads off the fish, skin them, and jam them onto sticks. Can't be that hard, right?"

"I want you to know that in my imagination, I am staring at you incredulously right now."

"Oh, ye of little faith."

"I have plenty of faith that this is going to be entertaining — at least for me."

Theo rolled her eyes. Reaching out, she grabbed the bird and pulled it closer. Though the body was slight in weight, its limpness was unsettling. She drew her knife. "Well, here it goes."

Within seconds of cutting off the head — the thin neck had proven disproportionately tough — Theo had spun back to the stream, retching as she scrubbed blood from her hands.

"Oh that was—" she turned her head and gagged "—so gross!" Pressing the back of a hand to her mouth, she somehow held down the contents of her stomach as it heaved again.

"I think I'm going to maintain all this footage," Kane said with a snicker. *"Complete records are important in these survival situations, you know?"*

"You're such an ass, you know that?" She glanced back at the headless carcass and gagged again. "Ugh!"

Looking at it as little as possible, she grabbed the bird by the leg and held it upside down to let its blood drain into the nearby grass. Once the flow seemed about done, she plucked off its feathers by the fistful, trying to ignore the brief resistance each one offered. Once she'd successfully slit open its gut, dumped out the innards, cleaned up the carcass and impaled it on a stick — all miraculously without vomiting — she picked up her water container and hurried back to camp.

She was sure to hold the bird as far away from her field of vision as possible along the way.

The sun was low over the horizon when she reached the pod, casting the ocean in orange and gold. It would be dark within the next hour or so. There was no sign of Vasil at the camp, so set the bird aside, careful not to let it touch the sand, and went to work starting a fire like he'd taught her. Fortunately, they'd collected a sizeable store of relatively dry wood and animal dung.

Once the fire was burning high enough, she positioned the impaled bird over it, using a stone to hold the stick in place.

"There," she said, stepping back with her fists on her hips.

"So...now what?"

"Hell if I know." Theo laughed. "I've been eating food out of vacuum sealed bags and machines for nearly twenty years. This cooking stuff might as well be magic to me."

Returning to the pod, she changed into her under suit so more of her skin could be cooled by the breeze. She walked toward the ocean at a leisurely pace. Wind whipped her hair, and the sound of breaking waves filled her ears as she gazed over the blazing-gold water. She thrummed with anticipation.

"Vasil should be back soon," she said. He always returned before dark.

"Your heart rate picked up speed there, Theo."

"So?" With a disgruntled huff, she plopped her ass down on the ground, idly digging holes with her fingers in the wet sand.

"Just an observation," Kane said. He went quiet for several seconds. *"May I make a suggestion?"*

"As though I could stop you short of putting you to sleep," she said, tilting her head. Turning her torso to one side, she propped herself on one hand and scooped handfuls of damp sand out of the hole. A bit of water pooled at its bottom.

"I know I overstep most of the time, Theo, and I don't want to do that in this case. This situation isn't like anything we've faced before.

I'm out of my element, and that is...unsettling. The last thing I want is for the only person I have in my existence to be genuinely upset with me."

Theo paused, a slow smile curling her lips. "You should know by now that I could never be mad at you for long. And *I* know you'd never do anything to intentionally hurt me. We'll get through this. It's...a different way of life, but hey, I'm learning."

She resumed digging, glancing over her shoulder toward the cooking bird. A shudder ran down her back; killing and preparing the creature hadn't been easy — or pretty — but she was damned proud of herself.

"So, what's your suggestion?" she asked.

"Don't be afraid to give the alien a chance."

Theo stilled. "Okay, I guess I thought you were going to say something about our *living* situation."

"It kind of is *about that, isn't it? You're clearly interested, Theo. I'm not telling you to rush into anything, but...why deny your curiosity any longer?"*

Brows lowering, she frowned. "You've never liked any other guy I was interested in."

"Because all they wanted from you was sex."

"That's all I had ever wanted, too." Or had it been? She rarely sought men out for pleasure, and it was only when her loneliness had reached its limits. That she needed — *craved* — human touch.

"If that were true, I'd accept it. It's okay for you *to have shallow wants — you're my friend. But we both know you're lying to yourself about it."*

She dropped her gaze to the hole and clawed out more sand, adding to the growing pile beside her. She should've known he'd see through her lie; she'd rarely sought out men for pleasure, and when she did, it had only been when her loneliness had reached its peak. In those moments, she'd craved human touch. She'd *needed* it.

"And you don't think sex is all Vasil wants?"

"*I* know *he wants it.*"

Theo flushed, feeling the warmth from the roots of her hair down to her chest.

"*But I think you know that's not all he wants,*" Kane continued. "*Otherwise you wouldn't be fawning over him like you have been.*"

His voice had taken on a gentle tone that seemed to only come through in the neural link; it was in such moments that Theo felt most connected to him, though she'd never be foolish enough to tell him that. His ego was big enough already.

"Hey, I am *not* fawning. I don't fawn."

"*Fair enough, Theo. I will amend: you've been* drooling *over him.*"

"I don't drool!"

"*Oh really? Who's been the one keeping watch while you sleep?*"

Rolling her eyes, Theo shifted position, stretching her legs to either side of the sand pile. "Even if that were true, it doesn't count while I'm sleeping."

"*Why not? You're probably dreaming of him at night.*"

That was too close to the truth for her comfort.

"Ugh, why am I even discussing this with you?" She flattened her palms against the sand and compacted it into a harder mound. She used her fingers to smooth the sides and corners, slowly giving the pile a new shape.

"*Who else are you going to discuss it with? I mean, I'm sure* Vasil *would talk to you about it if you approached him, but you don't want to do that, right?*"

She scowled down at her work. "I can't talk to him about it."

"*Why not?*"

"Because he wants more than sex. He wants...a mate. A life partner."

"*Is that a bad thing?*"

"If I accept that, I accept *this* as my fate. It means...that this is where I'll spend the rest of my life. That there's really no going back…"

"Back to where?" he asked in her mind. *"Home? That ship wasn't your home, Theo. Even I understand that."*

He'd spoken the truth — she knew it in her heart. The *CSC Agamemnon* had been just another place she happened to live in for a while; it had never been her home, and neither had the ship before it or the one before that. The only time she'd ever felt like she had a home was with Malcolm.

Theo brushed the hair away from her face with her wrist, but a few grains of sand still scratched her cheek. "Vasil makes me feel too exposed. It…scares me."

"What about that scares you, Theo? You had a hard life, but you've always persevered. People close to you have failed you in the past, but if you never let yourself move on, if you never open yourself up again, you're going to feel isolated and alone until you die."

"Wow, thanks for the uplifting words, buddy. Can I ask you a question?"

"Of course."

"How is it you have all this…psychology crap in there, but cooking a bird is too complicated for your processors?"

"Ouch. I'll make note to use softer language in the future so as not to upset your delicate sensibilities. Really though, Theo. What do you want?"

She let out a puff of air. "I don't know, Kane."

"Well, whatever it is you want, I think what you need is…someone."

Movement ahead caught Theo's attention. She looked up to see Vasil rising from the waves. Her heart leapt at the sight of him, and a warm, exhilarating sensation flooded her.

With the fiery sunset behind him, Vasil's form was shadowed and mysterious, but light made the moisture clinging to his skin shine like glittering gold. She absently dug her fingers into the sand, and a different sort of heat swept through her as he drew nearer and his features — including his sculpted muscles — came into view.

"Theo, your vitals—"

"Nice talk, Kane," she said quietly, smiling up at Vasil. "Hey."

Vasil stopped a couple meters away from her and smiled. "Hello, Theo." His eyes dipped to the sand piled near her legs, and his brow furrowed. "What are you doing?"

"Building sand castles. That's a thing, right?" She looked down at the crumbled sand beneath her hands. "I mean I *was* building a castle."

Before I up and destroyed it the moment I saw you.

"I have seen younglings make little buildings out of sand," he said, lifting his gaze to her, "and Arkon, another kraken, has done it with them. But I do not know what a *castle* is."

"Oh, well, it's a building from the old times. Like, *really* old Old Earth times. It was a huge building made of stone and— You know, never mind."

"Why do you call it *Old Earth*? Is Earth not simply the planet from which your people came?"

"Yeah, it is," she replied. "There's this other planet the IDC colonized early on called Tau Ceti Three. I guess they sold it pretty hard as a second Earth to get settlers to go, and it was so popular that it became the IDC capital planet a couple hundred years ago. I saw some of the old ads after I enlisted — *Why live on Old Earth when you could live on the new one? Go to Tau Ceti Three and claim your piece of a new world!* I think they kept them around when I was in training to instill us with a sense of IDC history, but they were kind of a joke for all the soldiers."

"Your people just…abandoned their old home for a new one?" Vasil asked.

"A lot of them, yeah. Probably because even then Earth was pretty run down and worn out. It's not a very nice place, at least in my experience." She pushed herself to her feet and brushed the sand from her backside, catching Vasil's eyes straying to follow her hands. "Anyway, did you have any luck?"

"Only in obtaining food," he replied, raising a tentacle. A large, hard-shelled creature dangled in his hold. It looked like a giant bug.

Theo wrinkled her nose, glad that, if nothing else, the creature wasn't moving. "I'm not sure I want to know what that is." She moved past him to the water and rinsed her hands in the surf. "And tonight, dinner is on me."

"What do you mean?"

Grinning, she turned back to Vasil. "*I* went hunting today."

The light came on at her wrist. "She stumbled across a bird by accident and blasted it near to pieces. It *wasn't* hunting," Kane said aloud.

"Way to steal my thunder, Kane," Theo muttered.

"That's what I'm here for, Theo."

Brows lifting, Vasil moved toward their camp. Theo watched him, transfixed by the gracefulness of his tentacles as they flowed over the sand, by the muscles of his sides and back, by his powerful shoulders. He paused about halfway between the water and the camp and looked back at her.

"Do you have it propped near the fire right now?" he asked.

Theo blinked and straightened, dragging her eyes away from his well-defined muscles to meet his gaze. "Um, yes?"

"How long have you been building *castles*?"

"Not too long," she said, closing the distance between them. "Why?"

"It is not going to cook evenly that way."

"But I've seen you do the same with the fish."

He continued forward. "You have to watch it. Have to turn it so both sides are cooked."

"Oh."

As he reached the fire, he sank down — she still found it fascinating that he could raise and lower his torso so smoothly, even after seeing it so many times — and picked up the stick by its bottom end. The side of the bird facing away from the fire still looked pink and raw. He twisted the stick in his palm to show the other side.

Theo stopped and cringed at the blackened, charred mess he'd revealed.

For a moment, her mind was blank; she simply stared at the bird, unable to make sense of what she was seeing. Then the dam burst inside her. Despair and defeat rushed out to flood her from head to toe. She'd been so damn proud of herself…

Her eyes filled with tears, and, no matter how hard she tried to stop it, her lower lip trembled. She hadn't any shed tears since she was a little kid — Theodora Velenti was *not* a crier. What the hell was *wrong* with her?

"I guess I should have watched it, huh?" she said, voice thick and broken.

Vasil kept his gaze on her for a time; its weight was crushing. Finally, he set the charred meat aside and turned his body to face her fully.

"Have you ever done anything like this before?" he asked softly.

"No, but I've watched you do it and figured it couldn't be that hard. But I…I ruined it, didn't I?" she asked, glancing at the bird. Tears spilled from her eyes when she blinked. "How the hell am I going to survive out here if I can't even feed myself? I'm useless. A-All I know how t-to do is-is fix machines, and half the time K-Kane gives m-me instructions on that."

He closed the distance between them, and, despite her tears, she didn't miss his hesitance as he reached for her. Even having just come from the sea, his hands were warm and solid when he settled them on her upper arms.

"Look at me and listen, human," he said, keeping his voice soft but firm.

Theo sniffed and looked up at him with tear-blurred eyes.

"You were able to kill this animal, clean it, build a suitable fire, and start cooking it, all without ever having done so before. You made a mistake, Theo, but this is more than most could accomplish simply by watching."

His palms slid down the backs of her arms, over her elbows, and along her forearms, until he took both her hands in his. He led her closer to the fire and guided her down onto her knees. Releasing one of her hands, picked up the stick and held the charred meat toward her.

"Draw your knife," he said.

With a small frown, she did as he instructed.

He dipped his chin toward the bird. "Remove the burned portions."

She nodded and drew in a deep breath before setting to work. She removed the ruined meat, carefully cutting away burned chunks and scraping off flakes of char until only raw meat remained.

"I only learned these things over the last two years," he said when she was done. "Fire was not a part of my upbringing."

"What do you mean? Don't the other humans here cook this way?"

"Our peoples only truly began living together two years ago. Before that, we knew little of each other." He twisted toward the fire and sank the butt of the stick into the sand outside the ring of stones. "Do not put the meat directly in the flames. It only needs the heat, not the fire."

"Oh. Okay."

"Theo?"

"Hmm?" She kept her gaze on the fire, which flared and danced wildly as her tears refracted its light.

He brought up a hand, cradling her chin in the crook between his forefinger and thumb; his fingertips brushed over one cheek, the pad of his thumb the other. He turned her face to look at him.

Her eyes widened; she could feel the strength in his fingers, and the points of his hard claws were against her skin, but he was somehow so gentle, so delicate in his hold.

"You did *well*, Theo," he said. "Very well."

Warmth blossomed in her chest. "I did?"

He nodded. "Yes."

She smiled. "Good. Because cleaning that thing was *disgusting*."

Vasil's smile — which should have frightened her, were she sane — was wide, warm, and oddly charming. And he even had *dimples*! They were sexy as hell, too.

She caught her lower lip between her teeth as she stared at that smile. His nearness and touch did funny things to her body. The warmth that had begun in her chest had spread through the rest of her body, swirling low in her belly, to flood her core with liquid heat. Her nipples hardened to aching buds, and her sex clenched with sudden need.

Something brushed against her knee. She glanced down to see the tip of his tentacle slowly sliding up toward her thigh. The suction cups along its underside kissed her flesh as they moved, their touch both tickling and tantalizing, sending shivers through her. Still, the unfamiliar feel of it was enough to startle her. She scooted back, breaking all physical contact between them.

"So, um, you didn't find anything?" she asked, averting her gaze.

From the corner of her eye, she saw his hand linger in the air where it had held her face a moment before. His posture seemed to sag as he slowly lowered his hand and withdrew his tentacle.

"Nothing but this hardshell," he replied, shifting the creature into his hands.

Before she could get a good look at the numerous legs on the hardshell's underside — he was holding it upside down — Vasil turned away from her. He leaned down, his torso blocking her view, and set to work.

A series of wet cracks and snaps were her only indication of what he was doing; she cringed at each sound.

Gah, I do not *have the stomach for this life.*

"Are you unsettled by my appearance?" Vasil asked without looking back at her.

"What?" Theo asked, startled by his blunt question.

"You have recoiled from me several times after I touched you."

Frowning, Theo chewed on the inside of her cheek. Over the last few days, she'd come to appreciate Vasil's forwardness; it possessed a sort of innocence that made it endearing rather than annoying. He didn't skirt around the questions he wanted to ask or waste time trying to gently work toward the answers he sought, he just went right for it.

And in this case, she couldn't help the shame his question roused in her; there'd been hurt layered deep within his tone.

"I just... I'm not...*un*attracted to you..." She ran her palm over her face and groaned. Why was it so hard to answer?

Because I don't want *to hurt him.*

She cared about his feelings, cared about what he thought. Though she wasn't ready to commit to the *forever relationship* he wanted, she was interested in him — more interested than she'd admitted to herself. She *was* attracted to him. But she didn't know how to explain her simultaneous desire and trepidation without potentially hurting his feelings.

"You're different, Vasil," she said, looking at his back.

"So are you." He turned his head slightly but didn't quite look over his shoulder.

"Yeah, but you've had a couple years to get used to humans. I've had, what, a week to get used to you?" She absently fidgeted her fingers in her lap.

Unable to stand the anxiousness she was feeling, she moved

a little closer to him, grabbed the end of one of his tentacles and drew it over her lap. The muscles beneath its skin contracted, reminding her of a tube being squeezed. She wrapped her hand around the tentacle and held it in place.

He twisted his torso to stare at her with wide, confused eyes. "I do not under—"

"Just shut up and let me, okay?" she said, dropping her gaze to his tentacle. Though he kept it still, it remained tense in her hold.

Tentatively, she ran her hands along it in petting motions, brushing away the bits of sand clinging to his skin. Though his tentacle seemed to have a bit more give than the rest of his body, its skin felt the same — velvet over steel. His suction cups resumed their soft kisses on her legs, sending repeated thrills through her.

Slowly, she slid one of her hands to the underside of his tentacle. The flesh there was different; smoother and softer, it was closer to the feel of human skin. She pressed a fingertip to one of his suction cups and traced its edges. A shudder coursed through the limb.

"Theo," he rasped.

She didn't meet his gaze until he covered her hand with his own, halting her fingers. His features were strained — jaw tight, brows low, pupils dilated.

"What?" she asked.

"It is best you stop before I extrude."

"Ex...trude?" Her eyes dipped to his pelvis, where the slit she'd noticed the day he watched her bathe was once again partially open. It widened more the longer she stared.

Her eyes rounded with sudden realization, and she squeezed the tentacle in her hands. "Ooooh."

Vasil offered a smile, the expression somehow forced and genuine simultaneously, and gently tugged on his tentacle. She let go of it, but he did not release her hand.

"I appreciate your efforts," he said, "but I do not think you are ready for things to move that quickly between us."

"Uh, yeah. I mean, no! I'm not. Not..."

Yet.

"As smooth as polished granite, Theo," Kane whispered in her mind.

You better have been sleeping during all that, she sent back through the link

"I don't recall any command being given..."

Boundaries, Kane! Learn them.

"Humans like to take things slow, correct?" Vasil asked.

"Um, yes," Theo said, cheeks heating. "That's part of the whole dating thing, you know?"

He gave her hand a soft squeeze. "I am willing to go slow, if that is what you need."

Theo smiled up at him. That was...sweet. "Thank you."

Vasil leaned closer to her; the sea scent of his skin mingled with the smells of burning wood and roasting meat to create an oddly sweet, intoxicating aroma. His eyes locked with hers as he caressed the side of her face with the back of one of his claws. "But know this, Theo: you *will* be mine."

CHAPTER 8

Vasil fanned out his tentacles, slowing his forward momentum. He'd been swimming throughout the morning, keeping careful watch both for potential dangers and any features on the seafloor even vaguely familiar to him.

Five days had passed since Theo willingly touched his tentacle; it seemed a silly thing to mark the time by, so minor an occurrence, but it stood in his memory as a turning point. Every morning since, he'd gone out in search of clues to point him homeward, and every evening he'd returned to share a meal with her and deliver the same news — they were still as lost as they'd been on the first day.

Part of him embraced his failure; living with Theo on that beach was a life of contentment. He'd grown comfortable with their daily rhythms, and his want for her had only increased as days passed. He was skilled and knowledgeable enough to keep them alive and fed, and they'd both learn more over time. Vasil had no doubt they could survive there indefinitely — their camp was situated near the sea, with access to bountiful food and fresh water. The pod provided adequate shelter, and he was certain they could expand it as necessary given Theo's expertise, her collection of advanced tools, and the jungle's ample resources.

But he refused to accept that failure. Theo deserved far more than just *survival*; she deserved to *live*, to know joy, comfort, and freedom from worry. The Watch wouldn't offer a return to the life she'd known before, but it would provide security and potential companionship. All the humans he'd known, Theo included, seemed drawn to social interaction. Food and water nourished their bodies, but conversation and friendship fed their hearts and minds. He understood that well after the last two years — and had realized just how starved he'd been for most of his life.

And he could not forget Melaina. If he chose to remain on the beach with Theo, he would *never* have the chance to approach his daughter; he'd throw away any possibility of knowing her before ever trying.

He frowned as he scanned the water, which grew murkier with each passing beat of his hearts. Strong currents flowed around him, and sea creatures darted through the gloom with rarely-witnessed urgency and disregard for caution. The sea was restless.

A glance upward provided another clue —no sunlight beamed through the wavering surface.

Vasil angled himself upward and swam. Traversing open water alone was an undertaking to be avoided whenever possible; even kraken were vulnerable to other predators without strength in numbers. It was best to remain close to the bottom, where they could take better advantage of irregularities on the sea floor for cover and camouflage.

In this case, he considered the risk worthwhile — he had to be sure.

His suspicions were confirmed the moment he broke the surface. The sky was overcast and dreary. A thin strip of blue remained visible on the horizon in the direction from which he'd come, but the opposite horizon presented a dark mass of gathering clouds. Based on the direction of the wind sweeping over his head, the storm was moving toward him — toward Theo.

Halora's storms sometimes lasted for days, and the most violent of them could alter the underwater landscape — his only reliable means of navigation — enough to make it unrecognizable. If that happened, he risked never finding their beach again. He risked losing Theo forever.

Vasil plunged below again. He wouldn't accept losing his female; he had to get back to her.

He pushed himself harder, faster, riding every favorable current he encountered. The murky water — clouded by sediment, debris, and algae that had been stirred up by the agitated sea — surrounded him like fog would have on land, limiting his range of view.

Though he wasn't eager to return with more bad news — this time without a fresh kill to present — he could not deny his excitement at the thought of seeing Theo again much sooner than he'd anticipated. He wanted to find the Facility or The Watch, wanted to return to his people, his friends, but he also wanted Theo, and a secluded life with her just simpler. Easier. More fulfilling.

How easy would it have been to cast off the duties he'd performed for his people for most of his life, to take what he wanted, to pursue his desires at the expense of all else?

No. That is not me. That is not my way.

He would protect Theo, provide for her, do anything she required, now and after he found his way home and brought her to The Watch to share his den. She'd be his mate; she'd be *his*. Everything he did thereafter — whether for kraken, human, or both — would also be for her. He'd abandon neither his people nor Theodora.

His newfound resolve granted him a fresh burst of speed. He darted forward.

And a monster surged out of the murk.

In all his years of hunting the waters, he'd never seen anything like the creature before him. Its body was cylindrical, covered in long, dull brown plates that tapered at either end. Bumps atop its segmented shell reminded him of the rocks so common across much of the seafloor. Long, jointed appendages, each ending in a wicked point, extended from the creature's face, surrounding a set of four mandibles that parted to reveal a wide mouth possessing not teeth but strange, hair-like growths. Eye stalks jutted from either side of its head, tipped with fist-sized clusters comprised of dozens of dark, scintillating eyes.

Small flippers paddled water along its pale underside. At least a dozen long, thin tentacles stretched from the monster's back end, wriggling to propel it forward. From end to end, it was more than twice Vasil's length.

Vasil registered those details, despite the gloom, in the space of a heartbeat. His hearts stilled an instant later when he realized the creature was coming at him. He flailed his arms frantically and spread his tentacles to halt himself, snapping his torso backward.

The monster's pointed appendages — its mouth-fingers — lashed out as it sped through the water in front of Vasil. Two of the fingers clamped down on his forearm, piercing his flesh. He growled at the burst of pain as his torso collided with the creature's armored body. The other mouth-fingers clawed at his arm. He clenched his fist as tight as he could to flex the muscles of his forearm; another point sank into his skin, but it barely penetrated the bunched muscle.

Instinct seized control of Vasil's mind. He wrapped his tentacles around the creature's shell and raised his free hand to grasp one of the mouth appendages near its base. The creature's tentacles thrashed; kraken and monster tumbled and spun through the water, and the gloom made it difficult to tell the surface from the sea floor.

Vasil did not ease his hold. He wrenched the appendage to the side; it broke off with a *snap* strong enough to resonate in Vasil's bones. Dark blood misted from the wound. The remaining appendages flailed wildly, and Vasil caught another, repeating the process. His suction cups latched onto the creature's shell, and he tightened his tentacles around the creature, squeezing. The shell bucked under the pressure.

The monster's tentacles whipped through the water in all directions, slapping Vasil's back and arms with startling force. Its mouth-fingers released their hold on his arm, adding his blood to the hazy cloud.

He thrust away from the creature, withdrawing his tentacles. The monster darted away immediately, trailing wisps of blood, and disappeared into the murk.

Hearts pounding, Vasil swept his gaze over his surroundings. The range of his vision was greatly limited, and he wondered briefly if this was how humans saw the world beneath the waves — one small, fuzzy-edged portion at a time.

He shook his head sharply, willing himself to focus. Though his arm throbbed, the pain was distant; he knew the reprieve would only last until the excitement of the attack had faded. He clamped his right hand over the wounds, staunching the blood flow. It would affect his ability to swim, but not as much as if he'd used a tentacle to stop the bleeding. Better to swim a bit slower than leave a trail of blood in the water for other predators to follow.

I am still racing the storm. No more time to waste.

The mysterious creature had been wounded; it wasn't likely to come back. He had to go.

Tucking both arms against his midsection, he slowly spun in place, seeking anything familiar by which to orient himself. The loose sediments and algae clouding the water made every object

Vasil saw indistinct and indistinguishable from one another; his world was reduced to shapeless shadows looming in the murk.

He couldn't begin to guess how far he was from the pod. He could ride the swells on the surface, hoping to catch sight of land, but he doubted they were yet high enough for him to see their beach — he'd traveled a long way that morning. If only he'd been—

There!

A rock formation stood on the sea floor to his right, perhaps five body lengths away — three large stones in a row, the middle one taller than the other two, each ending in a jagged point. Maintaining his hold on his wounds, Vasil swam to the formation. He held himself aloft immediately over it and sought the next marker. He found it a moment later — a crevice in the sea floor marked now only by a depression in the cloud of sand blanketing the bottom.

He was going in the right direction.

As Vasil pressed onward, the water steadily cleared, and his awareness of his wounds increased. The throbbing in his forearm became a deep, piercing ache, and it was echoed, if only faintly, across his back. He had no doubt that his pain would've been several times worse had he been using his arms to swim.

Fortunately, he encountered no other predators, and eventually emerged in the shallows of the beach he shared with Theo. Both the sky and sea were darker than before, but he wasn't sure if it was due to the approaching storm, an unseen sunset, or a combination of both.

A chilled wind swept over his sea-dampened skin, blowing from behind him. It amplified the foamy white crests crashing onto the beach around him. The vegetation beyond the sand shimmered as that wind blasted through the leaves, making them twist and sway.

Theo entered his view as he approached the pod; she was on

her knees beside it, packing piles of sand under its rounded bottom.

Vasil called her name, but the roar of wind and sea swallowed his voice. He hurried across the beach to stop beside her.

"Theo," he repeated.

She started, whipping her head toward him. The wind blew her hair into her face. She yanked it back, spitting strands out of her mouth. "Fuck, you scared the crap out of me! I didn't—" Her eyes widened. "Is that *blood?*"

He glanced down at his right hand, which still covered his wounds. Watery blood trickled from beneath his fingers. "Yes."

"Get in the pod," she commanded as she pushed herself to her feet.

"What are you doing with the sand?" he asked.

"Stabilizing the pod. Now get in. I'll be right back." She ran past him toward the sea.

Vasil twisted to watch her. She stopped when the surf was around her ankles and crouched, dipping her arms into the water to scrub the sand from her skin.

After a quick glance toward the black storm clouds roiling over the ocean, Vasil rounded to the front of the pod. He grasped the rim with both hands. Fresh blood oozed from his wounds, and sharp pain radiated along his arm, but it was not the pain that gave him pause as he hauled himself up — it was the sight of the relatively dark, confined space.

His hearts, which had finally slowed to a normal rate not long before, sped up again. The pod trembled in the wind, its movement startlingly reminiscent of a ship rocking on the sea.

"Do you intend to bleed to death?" Theo said from behind him. "Get your ass in there, kraken!"

"I will not bleed to death," he replied, remaining in place. His skin was suddenly cold, and it had nothing to do with the weather. How had he brought himself to enter the pod before?

Because it was for her, *not for me.*

Something warm touched one of his tentacles. "Vasil?"

That warmth blossomed and spread across his flesh, all the way down to the tip of his tentacle. The pod rocked gently as Theo climbed up beside him. Her concerned eyes met his gaze.

"You okay?" she asked.

He drew in a deep breath, filling his lungs with air that smelled of brine and rain. "Yes. I am fine."

"Well, come on," she urged, "cause if you collapse, there's no way I can haul you in myself."

"I will not collapse. I am *not* seriously injured, Theodora."

"Then what are you waiting for, kraken? Get in so I can take care of it." She climbed higher, swung her legs over the side, and dropped into the pod.

Gritting his teeth, Vasil followed her inside. Theo stood to one side, bent over as she removed her pants and brushed sand off her ankles and feet.

"Sit down," she said as she rose, wadding the pants into a ball and tossing them aside. Her top followed, leaving only her body suit.

Despite his discomfort in the tight space, he could not keep his eyes off Theo after she bared her legs. He longed to run his hands over her skin, to press his lips to her every bit of her, to pull her against him and hold her like nothing else in the world mattered.

He managed to pry away his gaze before she caught him staring, turning his attention to the pair of seats nearby. They were designed for humans, but that didn't mean they couldn't work for kraken. Of course, sitting here would almost be like sitting on the floor of that cell, and—

No. This is different. Everything *is different.*

Vasil moved to one of the seats, bunched his tentacles together, and lowered himself onto it.

The pod continued to sway in the wind. The motion was subtle but could not be ignored.

Theo set a small box on the open seat and held her hand out to him, palm up. "Give me your arm."

Thunder boomed outside the pod.

Memories of dark, damp cells and rumbling thunder flashed through Vasil's mind; they were memories of pain, of blood, of Neo's angry yelling and Dracchus's unshakeable calm. His chest constricted as he drew in a shuddering breath.

The rain started a moment later, falling in fat drops that drummed atop the pod and splashed in through the open hatch.

"Damnit." Theo turned away from him, reached up, pulled the hatch down with a grunt. Wind whistled through the narrowing gap until she sealed the opening completely.

The interior went dark. Vasil squeezed his eyes shut and sought something, *anything*, upon which to focus — the pain in his arm, the pain in his back, the way Theo's scent filled the space. This was a new place. A safe place. But even with his eyes closed, he *felt* the walls and floor around him, felt them moving closer and closer.

"Kane, get the interior lights on, please," Theo said. "Vasil, your arm."

Vasil raised his injured arm; his other hand gripped the armrest of the seat tightly enough to make his knuckles ache.

He felt her hand on his arm, followed by pressure as she covered his wounds with something.

"Vasil, what's wrong?"

"Nothing."

"You're lying," Theo said gently. "You're paler than normal, you're tense, and if you squeeze that armrest any tighter, you're likely to break it. It's okay if you're in pain. I'm going to fix it."

"I have suffered far worse pain," he replied, willing his muscles to ease; they did not obey. "I will heal well enough without aid."

"Doesn't mean you shouldn't receive it." He felt her shift

closer, felt the warmth of her skin where her legs touched his tentacles. "Vasil, open your eyes."

Releasing a shaky breath, he did as she asked.

White light filled the interior of the pod, purer than even the best lights in the Facility. The walls — despite how he'd felt a few moments before — hadn't moved. He knew at his core that they hadn't, but the sensation had been so insistent, so real, that he'd been unable to reject it at the time.

With the hatch closed, only the round window offered a view of the outside — the same window through which he'd first seen Theodora.

The tightness in his chest eased just enough to allow him to breathe; it was a small improvement, but important, nonetheless.

Theo watched him for many moments, features drawn with concern, holding a wet cloth over his wounds. "You okay?"

"I will be fine."

"Yeah, I'm sure you will. But I know a freak-out when I see one, and that was *definitely* a freak-out." Her brows fell, and she bit her bottom lip. "Look, I'm not one to talk, and I don't want to pry, but…if you want to talk about it, I'm here to listen."

Nostrils flaring, he drew in another ragged breath. She was right; he'd *freaked out*, and the reason for it was so trivial that he couldn't help feeling foolish. He'd never spoken to anyone about it — not a word in the two years since it had happened. Perhaps that burden had become too much.

Perhaps it had always been too much.

"The walls are…too close," he said. "This space is too small."

"You're claustrophobic?" she asked. "I guess that's not too surprising considering you live in the ocean. Doesn't get too much more wide-open than that, unless you head out into space."

"I live in a house built by humans," he replied, "and I do not know that word."

"I stand corrected," she said, offering a gentle smile. "*Claustrophobic* means you're afraid of small spaces."

He frowned, keeping his eyes on her; he refused to look at the walls, even if he could *feel* them nearby. "I am not *afraid*."

"Okay then, you just *really* don't like them."

"Let's call it *anxiety*, shall we?" Kane said through the console speaker.

"Either way, we can fix that." She dipped her chin toward the cloth. "Put pressure on this."

Vasil settled his right hand over the cloth as Theo pulled hers away. She moved to the console, swiping her fingers over the symbols on the projected display. He recognized many of the characters from the Computer in the Facility, and even knew some of their names, though he'd never learned how to put them together to create words and sounds.

"I'm glad this stuff is still functional," she said. "And… There."

Before he could ask what she meant, the pod faded away.

His tentacles twisted around each other as he stared, wide-eyed, at the world *outside* the pod. The console, seats, floor, and storage door remained in place, but the walls and roof were *gone*. He could see the beach, the ring of stones where they made their fires, the angry waves lashing the shore, the jungle vegetation waving in the wind. He tilted his head back and watched with wonder as raindrops spattered on the invisible dome overhead, running off to the sides to create a transparent shell of water.

"Better?" Theo asked.

He tentatively reached toward the sheen of water but stopped himself before his hand touched anything. It was best not to know for certain because…this *was* better. Much better. He shifted his attention back to her, meeting her green-eyed gaze, and smiled.

"Yes."

"Good." She returned to his side. "Now, let's get this arm fixed up."

She opened the case she'd placed on the open seat and removed several objects from within, including a gun-like device similar to the tools he'd seen Aymee and Arkon use to seal wounds. This one was sleeker and longer with a wide front end.

"I've interfaced with it," Kane said. "Aim and fire, Theo."

"What does he mean *aim and fire?*" Vasil asked, brows falling low.

"He's just being dramatic," she replied, removing the wet cloth from his arm. She grimaced and dabbed blood off his skin. "You're gonna have to tell me what happened."

He watched warily as she aimed the device at one of his wounds. "I was attacked by a sea creature that I have never seen before."

"Relax, okay?" she said.

"Yeah, this won't be the *most* agonizing pain of your life. Probably," Kane added.

Vasil frowned, keeping his focus on Theo.

She sighed. "Please, don't listen to him. This will feel weird, but it doesn't really hurt. Trust me?"

Vasil nodded.

She pressed down the trigger, and a soft blue glow appeared over his skin just above the wound. A more solid-looking beam of light formed at the center, and within moments it was accompanied by several smaller beams that spun and twirled around it. His arm thrummed, and there was a hint of cold, but no pain.

The silence between them was filled by the drumming of raindrops atop the pod. Having the beach and thrashing sea in his peripheral vision was of great comfort, but he didn't let his eyes drift from Theo. His earlier fear — his *anxiety* — seemed even more foolish now.

"I did not have problems with small spaces before," he said without meaning to.

Her eyes flicked up to meet his briefly. Her brow knitted. "It's something new?"

"I was tortured by hunters a little more than two years ago."

Theo flinched, lifting the device away from his arm. "*What?*"

"They held me in a small cell on a boat, arms and tentacles bound, with my neck anchored to the wall. For three days they beat myself and my companions and denied us water." Just the mention of it made images flash through his mind, but he did his best to cast them aside. It was the past; he *needed* to move on.

Theo's grip tightened on the device. "When you say hunters…you're talking about…humans?"

"Yes."

"Why?"

"Because they viewed my kind as monsters to be eliminated for their safety. And because their leader thought we had taken his son."

She turned his arm to situate the device over the next wound, depressing the trigger again. "Did you?"

"Yes," he replied as the cold, thrumming sensation returned. "We saved his life after he was betrayed by his own, but we could not allow him the chance to reveal our home."

"How…did you get free?"

"A human released us when the ship caught fire."

"And since then, you haven't been able to stand enclosed spaces?" she asked, moving to the final wound.

"I have been all right in familiar places," he replied, "but even the home the humans built for me was difficult to adjust to. I left the windows open for weeks, even in rainstorms, before it stopped bothering me."

"Because you felt trapped."

Vasil nodded, dropping his gaze to the floor. "It makes me feel…weak."

Theo turned off the device and set it aside. Placing her fingers back on his arm, she lightly ran them over the now-healed wounds. His skin tingled beneath her touch, warmth spreading over its surface.

"I know the feeling," she said quietly, "but you're not weak, Vasil. If anything, that experience has made you stronger."

His gaze shifted to her fingers. "I do not *feel* stronger for it. I have been battered and wounded more times than I can count. Why should those few days affect me so much when all the rest do not?"

Her fingers slowed for a moment. "Because that was the one time you couldn't fight back. But no matter how helpless you might have felt, you remained strong." She placed a hand on the center of his chest. "In here. You wouldn't be here right now if that wasn't true."

For the second time since he'd entered the pod, it was difficult to breathe, but it wasn't anxiety now. The tenderness of her touch was overwhelming, amplified by her understanding. Though her circumstances had been different, she knew how he felt.

"Your heartbeat is so…*different,*" she said, staring at his chest.

"Kraken have three hearts." And Vasil felt like all three of his were beating for Theo alone.

Eyes wide, she briefly met his gaze before looking down again. "That's amazing."

You are amazing, Theodora.

Her teeth caught her lower lip as she tilted her head, and a lock of her hair brushed his arm. She cleared her throat softly and pulled her hand away. Her mouth dipped into a slight frown. "You'll have moments of…relapse, and they might make you feel powerless, but you're not. You can overcome them." Twisting away from him, she returned the device to its case. "I do."

Though she'd removed her hand, the once-gentle pressure

on his chest built to something uncomfortable. He felt the connection between them closing, felt her erecting barricades around her heart, and he wanted to roar in protest. He longed to draw her against him, to hold her, protect her, and tear apart anyone or anything that sought to do her harm — because she was *his*. He'd accept no walls between them.

He and Theo would quiet the ghosts of each other's pasts.

She replaced the other supplies she'd taken out of the box, closed the lid, and stood up. When she turned to move away from him, he caught her wrist.

Halting, Theo stared at him in surprise.

"Do not close me out, Theodora." He stroked the tender skin of her wrist with the pad of his thumb. "Not when you *just* let me in."

Her eyes fell to the hand on her wrist, her inner conflict written upon her face. After several moments, she tugged her arm, and Vasil released her with great reluctance. Silence stretched between them as she returned the case to the storage area.

Vasil clenched his hands and gritted his teeth, shifting his gaze to look outside.

Twilight had settled over land and sea, dragging the world toward full night, and the storm had only intensified with the growing darkness. Soon, the vegetation would be reduced to thrashing shadows, the angry ocean to roiling, impenetrable black.

"Kane, turn off the lights," Theo said.

Her voice called Vasil's attention back to her as she moved to the seat beside him. She plucked the blanket off the back of the chair, wrapped it around her shoulders, and sat down, all without looking at him. The lights dimmed as she moved until all that remained was the faint gray of the darkening sky.

"After my mom died, I was placed in my aunt's care," Theo said, staring up at the sky. "She wasn't an addict, but she wasn't much different from my mother. Didn't want any kids around that weren't hers. She had enough mouths to feed and no time for more, especially not her deadbeat, druggy sister's brat."

For a few moments, Vasil's jaw was slack; he hadn't intended to push her for more information, hadn't expected her to volunteer it. He respected her reluctance to share the painful parts of her past despite his longing to learn more about her. Sharing emotions — especially pain or fear — was something he'd never done until he started living among humans, and even then, those moments had been so rare and brief that they hardly counted for anything. But *this*...

This was important. This was *everything*.

"You were eight years old, correct?" he asked. "You said you were thrown into the *system*. Is that what your aunt's home was called?"

A smirk played upon her lips. "No. We just use that term for a lot of things. Anything that seems to treat people like...like something less than human, I guess. I was put in the government foster care system. They take orphaned children and place them in homes where they can be nourished with love and care." Those last few words contained a note of bitterness.

She ran a hand through her hair and pulled it over her shoulder in a bundle. "Anyway, yeah, I was eight. It was miserable. I had some food, more than what I usually got from my mom, but my cousins were mean little shits. They called me names, picked on me, and hit me all the time. The only time my aunt ever seemed to be looking was when I hit them back. I was always a scrawny kid, but I knew how to throw a punch, and at least I know I paid them back a little before their mom whopped my ass.

"Her and my uncle fought all the time, especially when it came to me. I was back in the system within a year. After that, I was moved around to a different few group homes — that's where they have a bunch of kids living together — to await *suitable placement*. But the last place…"

Frowning deeply, Vasil dropped his gaze to her right hand, which rested atop her thigh. He yearned to touch her, to reassure her. The move would be risky, but he didn't have the right words to express what he wanted her to know — he was *there* for her. He only hoped the risk was worth it. Every other time he'd touched her, she'd pulled away from him within a short while and closed herself off.

He drew in a deep breath and settled his hand over hers, giving it a gentle squeeze.

She started and looked down at his hand but didn't look away. To Vasil's surprise, she flipped her hand over, lacing their fingers together as far as his webbing would allow.

"Continue, Theo," he urged softly.

She tipped her head back against the headrest, keeping her eyes on their intertwined hands. "I was eleven when they sent me to my last group home. It was a nice place. Really clean, which kind of blew my mind. The kids were quiet, but they were friendly, too, and some were my age. We always had full bellies, and we each had our own rooms with all kinds of things. Things that we could call our own. It felt…nice. I even made a friend, the first one I remember ever having. Her name was Tess.

"I should've known something that good couldn't last, that it couldn't have been real, but I was so damned naïve. I gave in to hope, even though I should've known better."

Theo gathered the ends of the blanket with her free hand and held them together. Vasil would've loved to put his arms around her, draw her body against his, and hold her through the night, but he knew it would've been too much.

"I was having trouble sleeping one night and was just lying in bed. I heard a noise in the hall coming from Tess's room, which was across from mine. It sounded like crying. So, I got up and went to check on her. When I opened my door, I saw the man who owned the house coming out of her room. It's frustrating, but I can't remember what his name was. I'll never forget his damned face, but his name is just…lost. Anyway, I think I scared him, because he jumped when he saw me, but then he smiled.

"He told me to get back into bed, so I did, but he followed me into my room. I didn't think anything of it. A lot of the kids got tucked in at night, and like I said, it was nice to finally have someone who seemed like they cared, you know?" She squeezed Vasil's hand. "But…he didn't tuck me in."

Emotion loomed on the edges of Vasil's mind, but he held it at bay; he wouldn't allow himself to react until she'd said all she meant to say. He didn't know enough about humans to guess at what she'd say next, didn't know enough to guess what had happened to her. The only thing he knew was that it hadn't been anything good.

He leaned closer to Theo. Her scent perfumed the air, mixing with the briny smell clinging to him to create a new, sweet, maddening scent. He took her chin between the pads of his thumb and forefinger and guided her face toward his, meeting her gaze. "I am here for you. Tell me what he did, Theo."

She nodded slightly. "I remember the bed dipping as he sat beside me, and his breath. It stank. It always stank, but I never said anything about it because he'd been so nice. But I remember that smell as he leaned over me. He kissed my cheek, my nose. I remember feeling odd, like I *knew* it wasn't right but couldn't understand *why*. Then he kissed my mouth.

"I cringed away from him, but he followed, and kissed me again. Then he slipped his hand under my nightgown to grab my leg, and I knew, I *knew* what he was doing. What he'd done to Tess, what he was going to do to me. I'd seen it in other homes, heard from the other kids who'd been molested. And it was *wrong*."

The emotions that had been building in Vasil crashed into the temporary wall he'd erected in his mind, smashing it to pieces; they were held back temporarily by his disbelief. He understood what she was inferring, but it seemed unfathomable. Kraken, male and female alike, protected their young. That was the responsibility of *every* adult. *Protect, provide, and teach.* Everyone did their part to raise all the younglings. Not to take advantage of them, not to force them into situations they couldn't possibly understand.

Her story went against everything he'd learned in his life, and yet there wasn't a trace of deception or exaggeration in her voice or expression. She was sincere.

Vasil's skin took on a reddish hue as anger boiled up from his gut and filled his chest. He focused all his will on keeping his body still; he didn't want to risk causing her any harm in his rising fury.

"And did he?" he growled through clenched teeth.

"No," Theo rasped, shaking her head. "No. Even in that place, I always kept something on hand to protect myself. I don't know if it was habit, or paranoia, or a suspicion I never fully acknowledged, but I just felt safer that way, even when it wouldn't have made a difference. So when he touched me, I reached for it under my pillow, where I was hiding a fork from the kitchen…and I stabbed him in the throat."

She pulled her hand from his and looked at it. "I remember the heat of his blood on my skin and the choking, gurgling sound he made, but I didn't stay. *Couldn't* stay. So I ran. I just ran, and ran, and ran."

Vasil shifted his hand to rest atop his bunched tentacles, squeezing it into a tight fist. He released a shaky breath through his nostrils. "Did you kill him?"

Theo reached for him and took his hand, tugging gently until he allowed her to pull it closer. She eased his fingers open and rubbed the spots where his claws had pricked his palm.

"I don't know," she said. "I hope I did, because it would have meant he couldn't hurt anyone ever again, but...I don't know."

"I hope the same." He glanced down at her fingers as they continued to soothe his hand. What she'd described had happened long ago, when she was a child. He could not blame himself for his anger, but it would do neither of them any good. "What happened after you fled?"

"The home must've been close to a spaceport, because that's where I wound up. Somehow, I made it past all the security and to the launch pads. I really don't remember how, it's all fuzzy, but when I think about it now it seems impossible. I wasn't caught until I'd already snuck onto one of the ships. And that's...that's when I met Malcolm."

"Who was Malcolm?"

Theo smiled, but the expression was tinged with sorrow. "He was this gruff old man with black-stained hands and a big scar on one side of his face. And he scared the shit out of me when he found me in the parts storage room of that ship. He grabbed me by the wrist, and his hand was so strong that I knew he could crush my bones to paste if he wanted to. He looked me up and down, saw the blood staining my hands, and for a moment I thought I'd run away from one bad man into another. By the look of him, I was convinced he'd chop me up and eat me or something."

She chuckled softly. "And then he said *you look too scrawny to even lift a screwdriver, but I guess I got work for ya.* He tugged me over to some lockers against the wall, opened one up, and took out a shirt that was too big for me. Told me to get changed and get to work.

"When the ship's captain came down for inspection a little while later, I thought for sure I was caught. They'd turn me in to the police, and I'd go to prison… But Malcolm said I was his granddaughter, and that he'd taken me on as his apprentice. That was enough, I guess. I worked with him for eleven years on at least a dozen ships. We went wherever there was work, and he taught me almost everything I know about spacecraft, engines, and machinery."

Tears welled in her eyes and tumbled over her cheeks. She quickly wiped them away. "He was everything to me. He became my friend, my mentor, my mother and my father…and I can still picture the look he would've given me if he heard me say that. Hell, he was the one who gave me my name."

Vasil's brow furrowed. "You did not have a name for eleven years? Even after your mother died?"

"I made one up when I was young. When Malcolm found out that my mom never gave me one, he decided to because… Well, I was the daughter he never had." She flattened her palm against Vasil's, lining up their fingers. "What about the ones that hurt you? Are they dead?"

"A few of them died when the ship caught fire and sank," he replied; though he did not know all their names, he too remembered each of their faces. "The rest survived. My people chose peace."

"Did you?"

"I did not intend to as we fled the burning ship. I would have ended all the hunters then to ensure the safety of my people. Peace came at great cost to us." He looked down at their hands; hers was small and delicate-looking compared to his own, but he knew it was strong and sure. "The kraken clashed with each other, and many died. There is blood on my hands, too…but I think the cause was just. By the time we made contact with the humans again, we had had our fill of bloodshed and death."

"Have you told anyone else about the torture, or about the anxiety you've been suffering?" she asked.

"No one."

"Only me?"

There was something in her voice that called his attention back to her face, where he found something new in her eyes — vulnerability, perhaps? Hope?

"Only you, Theo."

"Besides Malcolm and Kane, you're the only one I've told about my past." Raising her other hand, she brushed her fingers over his siphon, smiling when it twitched. "Maybe it's time to let go of the past. To bury it here. It can't hurt us anymore. *They* can't."

Vasil shifted his gaze toward the sky, which had gone black. The console was the only remaining source of light, but its gentle glow did not extend beyond the invisible walls of the pod.

Was it really that simple? Just...*let go*, and be free? She'd said earlier that there would always be relapses — flashbacks to those moments that haunted him — but he *was* stronger than those memories, just as Theo was stronger than hers.

He nodded. "They cannot control us anymore."

Theo smiled. "Right."

Lightning flashed through the tumultuous clouds, lighting up their surroundings and displaying, for a few fleeting instants, the intensity of the storm. The nearby vegetation thrashed wildly, and the dark sea churned. Theo jumped and turned her wide eyes skyward. She nearly pulled her hand away, but Vasil laced his fingers with hers before she could.

Thunder vibrated the pod, beginning just before the world went dark again and lingering for several moments afterward, but its sound was greatly muted from what he'd expected.

"I've never seen a storm before," she said, staring at the sky. "Not like this."

"Did it not rain on your homeworld?"

"Not nearly this much, and not very often. It was usually pretty dry where I lived. Kane, could you turn the exterior audio up a little more?"

"Of course," Kane replied through the console speaker.

Vasil had forgotten about the computer's presence; he wouldn't have believed it possible for Kane to remain so quiet for so long. His mind was quickly turned away from those thoughts when the sound of wind and rain grew louder, heightening the immediacy of the storm.

His mind couldn't quite wrap itself around the situation — he was in the middle of the storm, witnessing it, hearing it, feeling the thunder rumble, yet was somehow so far separated from its touch.

He turned his head toward Theo. She was still looking skyward, her face bathed in the soft light of the console. The next pulse of lightning made her jump again. She squeezed his fingers, body tensing for a few moments.

Dipping his gaze to her bare legs, he stroked her knee with one of his tentacles. She drew in a sharp breath and glanced down but didn't break the contact between them. Emboldened by her acceptance, he coiled the tentacle around her calf, brushing its tip along her shin while he simultaneously brushed the top of her hand with his thumb.

The storm raged around them, but he wasn't aware of any of it — not the lightning and thunder, not the torrential rain, not the violent ocean or rolling clouds, not the invisible walls upon which the falling water shattered. All his attention, all his awareness, was directed toward Theo — toward the taste and feel of her skin against his, toward her nearness. Toward the fragrance of her arousal, which permeated the air.

He inhaled deeply, and his body heated in response to her scent. His cock ached behind his slit, and he tensed to keep from extruding, unwilling to spoil the moment. He wanted her. *Needed* her. From the first time he'd seen Theo, he'd felt an undeniable pull toward her, and he knew he wouldn't be able to resist it for much longer. She was meant to be his — Vasil's body knew the truth of it, even if the words had not been spoken. Fate had dropped her from the sky for him to find.

All he needed to do was make her understand that, too.

CHAPTER 9

THE STORM RAGED, AND THE HOWLING WIND, ROARING SEA, AND pounding rain were so loud and clear it was as if Theo and Vasil were standing in the middle of it, exposed. But it was the thunder and lightning that fascinated Theo as much as it frightened her, making the hairs on her arms and the back of her neck stand on end. It electrified her senses, increasing her awareness of Vasil — of his touch, especially, as he slowly, sensually stroked her skin and sent little thrills straight to her core.

With every arc of lightning that lit up the heavens, with every boom of thunder that rattled the pod, her body grew tenser with anticipation, fear, and...*arousal*. She stared at the sky through the blur of water hitting the pod as another forking bolt of lightning streaked across the dark clouds, but most of her attention remained on Vasil. His touch soothed her worries and heightened her desire.

She was out of her element here; every time she'd had sex in the past, it had been a passing thing, a moment of weakness, the mere scratching of an itch. There'd never really been words involved, and, despite what she'd wanted in her heart, there'd never been expectations established beyond a quick screw.

But Vasil wanted more. He wanted it all. He wanted *her*.

And I want him.

She wanted him here, now, at the peak of this storm. She wasn't concerned with tomorrow, she just *wanted*.

She sent a thought through the neural link. *Kane?*

Kane released a soft sigh in her mind. *"Go to sleep, right?"*

Yes. Good night, Kane.

"Good night, Theodora."

Theo slipped her right hand out of Vasil's grasp and turned toward him, lying on her side against the seat. She briefly met his eyes before lowering her gaze to his chest. Extending her left arm, she settled her palm on his abdomen. His muscles twitched, but he didn't pull away from her. His skin was warm and velvety, so different from her own. Slowly, she smoothed her hand down, absorbing his heat, relishing the feel of his flesh. When she reached the slight bulge at his pelvis, she paused, catching the inside of her lip with her teeth.

His breath hitched, and his tentacle tightened around her leg. Theo knew the faint tremor that ran through him had nothing to do with the rumbling thunder and wailing wind.

Trepidation clashed with her curiosity, but both were in the shadow of her excitement. Alien or not, this was *Vasil*. And, for a little while, he belonged to her.

She slid her hand farther down until her fingers met his slit. She lightly traced it, down and back up; it parted beneath her fingertips.

"Theo," Vasil groaned as he was wracked by a shudder.

His slit parted wide, and his cock, glistening with secretions, emerged to slide into her hand. Without hesitation, she wrapped her fingers around it.

Vasil squeezed his eyes shut and arched his back, pressing his cock further into her grasp. Her sex clenched at the feel and sight of him. He was hard and thick, her fingers not quite reaching all the way around him. Theo squeezed her thighs together against the surge of lust that filled her as she imagined him inside her, filling her, stretching her.

She pumped her hand up and down his length, relishing his every twitch and shudder, delighting in his soft groans. He tilted his head back and bared his teeth as he clutched the armrests. There was something empowering about having a strong, dangerous being at her mercy, about seeing him lose himself at her touch.

Lightning flashed overhead, illuminating Vasil and granting Theo a glimpse of his cock in her hand; it was pale gray like the rest of him, not pink and eel-like. But the light revealed something more, something at the base of his shaft she couldn't quite make out before the shadows returned. Thunder rattled the pod a moment later. The vibrations coursed through her to intensify her desire.

Sliding her fist down, she opened her fingers and felt around his base. Her fingers met several thin tendrils, perhaps five centimeters long, that seemed to seek her touch; they curled and pulsed around her fingertips with surprising strength. Theo knew exactly what they would touch when he was inside her. His alien body didn't repulse her, didn't frighten her — it *intrigued* her.

No more waiting.

Releasing him, Theo drew back and disentangled his tentacle from her leg.

One of his arms darted out, and his fingers slipped into her hair, halting her before she moved any farther.

Vasil's silver eyes gleamed in the console light as he met her gaze. "I need you, Theo. *Now.*" His voice was a deep rumble, matching the thunder.

Liquid heat flooded her sex.

"I know," she said, taking his hand and gently guiding it from her hair down to her body. She lay back against the seat, trailing his hand down her stomach, and opened her legs wide. With her coaxing, he slipped his fingers between her thighs, beneath the under suit, to dip in her essence. "I need you, too."

The pad of his finger brushed along her folds before he withdrew his hand. She tensed, desperate for more, but he was too strong. She released her hold on him as he raised his hand to his mouth, extended his tongue, and licked her wetness off his finger. The sight of it sent a fresh rush of heat through her.

Nostrils flaring, Vasil closed his eyes and growled. For a few moments, he was still — terribly, frustratingly still.

In a burst of speed, he was off his seat and in front of her. Her breath hitched as his claws shredded her under suit, somehow avoiding her skin. He shoved the pieces aside to expose her chest and pelvis to his hungry stare. Before she could react, he slipped his hands under her ass, lifted her off the seat, and lowered his mouth to her sex.

Theo gasped at the feel of his tongue against her folds. Her hands flew to his head, anchoring her in place, and she caught her bottom lip between her teeth. She moaned deeply. Vasil's head between her thighs was the most erotic thing she'd ever seen, and *nothing* had ever felt this good.

His tongue stroked upward to flick over her clit, and she released a cry, hips bucking against his mouth.

Correction. Nothing ever felt that *good.*

Vasil paused and tilted his head, seeming to consider her reaction. He repeated the same stroke with his tongue, pressing a little harder around her clit. Theo moaned louder, draping her legs over his shoulders and digging her heels into his back to spur him on. He didn't seem to need any encouragement. His tongue glided over her again and again, swirling around her clit, lapping at her essence as though he were a man starved and only she could provide him sustenance. Her fingers curled, nails grazing his scalp.

The storm faded from Theo's awareness; the pleasure coalescing within her chased away everything but Vasil and the sensations she was experiencing. He drove her unrelentingly higher and higher.

"Oh, fuck," Theo groaned, grinding her pelvis against his mouth. It was too much. *Too much.* "Vasil…"

Vasil opened his eyes and met her gaze. He growled against her, latched onto her clit, and sucked.

Everything inside Theo shattered.

She screamed, and her body went taut with overwhelming pleasure. She squeezed her eyes shut and dropped her head back against the headrest as wave after wave of sensation crashed through her body.

Vasil clutched her ass tighter, pulling her closer as he fed from her release. The tips of his claws dug into her flesh, but she didn't care; all that mattered was that he didn't stop.

He eased his hold on her only when her body, limp and weak, sagged against the seat. He lowered her bottom onto the cushion but didn't pull away, continuing to leisurely lap at her as though he were powerless but to consume every drop of her essence.

"I have never tasted anything so sweet," Vasil said against her. He pulled his hands out from beneath her and ran his palms over her outer thighs.

She lazily caressed his head as he continued to unhurriedly move his tongue against her sex, sending another rush of pleasure through her. She savored the feeling.

But she wanted *more.*

She pushed his face away from her.

"Get back in the seat," she commanded.

If there'd been any confusion in his expression when he first withdrew from her sex, it vanished the instant their eyes met. Hunger gleamed in his gaze, unsatisfied despite what he'd already done, and Theo was glad for it.

She hungered, too.

Vasil moved with startling speed once again, placing his hands on her hips, lifting her off the chair, and spinning to sit on the other seat. He settled her atop him with her legs to either side of his middle. His cock brushed her ass, hard and slick with his secretions.

Looking down at him, Theo placed her hands on his shoulders to brace herself. Her hair fell forward and brushed over his chest. She held his gaze as she sat up and wiggled her shoulders, shrugging off the tattered remains of her under suit. She dropped a hand to take hold of his wrist, lifting his arm. She kissed one of his fingers and smiled at him before playfully biting down.

He tensed. The heat in his eyes intensified as he tugged his finger free and caught her jaw in his hand. She gasped as he pulled her face lower, smashing his lips against hers.

The kiss was clumsy, but he made up for it with unbridled passion. Theo wrapped her arms around his neck and reined in the kiss, turning it into a subtle, teasing brush of her mouth against his. She nipped at his lips before increasing the pressure, and he followed her lead, molding his lips to hers. Then she added her tongue, sliding it across the seam of his mouth and delving in to touch his pointed teeth.

His fingers flexed on her waist, and he groaned, leaning closer to her. His tongue slipped out to stroke hers.

"Touch me, Vasil," she whispered. "Anywhere. *Everywhere.*"

THEO'S WORDS roused something deep and ravenous within Vasil. Her taste lingered on his tongue, her scent pervaded his every breath, his lips tingled in the wake of their kiss, and he craved more. He'd never *kissed* before, had never pleasured a female with his mouth, but he intended to do both over and over again with Theo.

Vasil released her jaw and returned his hand to her waist. He slid his palms upward, along her sides and back, delighting in her soft skin. Two of his tentacles rose to stroke her outer thighs and backside. He could taste the salty sweetness of her skin through his suction cups as he greedily moved them over Theo, wanting to drown himself in all that was her.

She leaned into him and deepened the kiss, shivering with his every caress. The hard peaks of her nipples brushed against his chest. He slid his hands between their bodies and cupped her breasts; even there, she was tantalizingly soft. She moaned against his mouth as he stroked her nipples, pinching and rolling them between the pads of his thumbs and forefingers.

Breaking the kiss, she brought her mouth close to his siphon. Her warm panting breath tickled his skin.

"Do you want me, kraken?" she asked, running a hand over his shoulder to cradle the back of his head. She undulated her hips, stroking his cock with her backside. He stiffened and hissed as pleasure pulsed through him.

"Need you," he grated.

"Then take me." Her tongue darted out, licking his siphon. "Show me how much you want me, Vasil. Let go."

He'd always done his best to honor his people and their ways, to temper his actions based on what would be best for the kraken, to prevent emotions from clouding his judgment. Those years of deliberate self-control shattered in that instant. He was through denying himself.

He would take what he wanted — *Theo.*

Vasil dropped his hands to her hips, dug his fingers into her tender flesh, and lifted her, angling his pelvis to press the head of his cock to her wet slit. She clutched his shoulders, her pink tongue slipping out briefly to wet her kiss-swollen lips. Without hesitation, he pulled her down and thrust his cock up at the same time, slamming into her.

Theo's blunt claws bit into his skin as she threw her head

back and released a choked cry. Her inner walls clamped around his shaft, hot, slick, and tight, creating pressure he wasn't sure he could resist. A tremor coursed down his spine and dispersed to the tips of his tentacles.

"*Theo*," he growled.

Theo lifted her head and met his gaze. She slowly rose over him on her knees, and the slide of her retreating sex stole his breath. Raising one hand, he grasped a fistful of the hair at the back of her head, forcing her gaze to remain upon him, and pulled her back down on him. Her lips parted with a gasp, and her eyelids drooped.

He coiled a tentacle around each of her thighs and a third around her waist, using them to guide her in a rapid, relentless rhythm; up and down, up and down, their bodies meeting forcefully in the middle, each thrust nearly breaking him.

Her moans and his grunts mixed with the sounds of falling rain and howling wind — fitting ambiance for their coupling, which raged as wild as the storm outside.

Breathing raggedly through clenched teeth, he raised one of his free tentacles and slipped its tip between their bodies to run along the top of her dripping sex. He lifted it farther, keeping his eyes locked with hers, and slipped it into his mouth to suck her glistening essence from it.

Her sex clenched, and her body quivered.

"Vasil," Theo rasped, squeezing his shoulders. "Oh, deeper. Faster. *Please.*"

He pulled her legs forward, forcing her off her knees. She sat on his pelvis, taking his shaft deep, and cried out. Still clutching her hair, he forced her head back. She arched into his touch as he moved his hand off her hip and squeezed her breast, presenting himself her nipple. He caught it between his lips, lavished it with his tongue, and slammed her up and down upon him with his tentacles, using her weight to drive himself ever deeper, ever faster. Intense pleasure swirled through him.

Her entire body tensed as her sex rippled and tightened around his cock. Her throaty cries increased in volume with each of his continued thrusts.

Clutching her body against his, he slammed her down again, and the pressure in him was suddenly too much. For an instant, he felt as though it would tear him asunder. All his muscles locked at once, and he finally burst. He threw back his head and roared as his cock pumped seed into Theo. The pressure diminished slightly with each gyration of his hips, rocking him with successive waves of pleasure that curled the tips of his tentacles.

Theo shuddered, moaning softly. Delicious heat radiated from her body. Vasil groaned and turned his face into her hair, breathing deep her scent and the aroma of their coupling. She undulated upon him, pushing herself to another quick climax, and produced a soft cry as her sex pulled him deeper still.

Skin slick with sweat, she sagged in his embrace. Her breath was warm on his neck. The tiny tentacles around the base of his cock stroked her lazily, offering him a hint of her sweet, enticing taste. It was enough to satisfy him — for now.

Vasil lay back against the seat, drawing Theo atop him without pulling out of her body. She inhaled deeply and released a satisfied hum. He gently combed his fingers through her hair, lightly grazing the tips of his claws over her scalp, her neck, and finally her back. Soon, her breathing evened out in sleep.

The storm filled in the quiet created by the silencing of their ragged breaths and pleasured cries, its chaotic mingling of sounds oddly steady and comforting. Even the random peals of thunder seemed somehow *right*.

Theo's body was warm, her flesh soft and smooth, and now that he had his arms around her, Vasil knew he could never let her go.

His experiences amongst his people told him this didn't necessarily mean anything; the act of mating did not create any obligations between those involved, did not imply any sort of relationship. But didn't humans hold a different view?

He and Theo had shared so much of themselves tonight, beneath the stormy sky — hearts and bodies alike. *That* was meaningful. That signified *something*.

But did it mean the same thing to both of them? When she woke in the morning, would she hurriedly pull away from him, realizing what she'd done while mesmerized by the power and fury of the storm? He could not deny her that right, but he also didn't think he could bear it.

Frowning, he held her a little closer, smoothing his palm over her hair.

She was *his*, and he'd do everything in his power to keep her.

CHAPTER 10

THEO'S EYES FLUTTERED OPEN AS SHE SLOWLY WOKE. ONCE THE blurriness cleared from her vision, she found herself looking out across the beach and watched the foamy waves rolling onto the sand for a few moments before shifting her gaze skyward. Large, puffy clouds filled the sky, giving a gray cast to the morning light. No rain fell.

Was this just a brief reprieve, or had the storm moved on?

As her awareness expanded, she realized she wasn't laying on a seat, but on a *body*. Vasil's body. And *laying* didn't quite describe her posture; she was *draped* over him. Her arms and legs were to either side of him, and her head was tucked beneath his chin, her cheek resting on his chest. The strange rhythm of his hearts was clear to her now — their pace was slow enough for her to make out each heart's individual *thump-thump*, though they still came in rapid succession.

Oh, and she was naked apart from what felt like a blanket covering her backside.

Theo's cheeks warmed, and she grinned.

I had sex with an alien.

As though her leisurely sprawl wasn't enough, Vasil had one

arm banded around her waist and a tentacle wrapped around one of her legs.

"Is it safe for me to be awake, or are you about to go at it again?" Kane asked through the neural link.

Theo pressed her lips together to hold back a chuckle.

I don't know. I think he's still sleeping, so it's safe. For now.

"I'd rather not see anything more than I already have. We should establish a safe word, so I know when to cut out."

What word should it be? Theo's brow furrowed. *And how do you even know about safe words?*

"There's a lot hidden on the IDCs networks that command doesn't know about. Soldiers get bored."

She smirked.

So do you, apparently.

"It's not like I have anyone in my life who can keep up with me," he replied. *"How do you feel about* tentacular penetration *as a safe word?"*

Laughter burst out of Theo before she could stop it. She quickly covered her mouth, but it was too late. The tightening of Vasil's arm and tentacle signaled that he'd woken.

That's a horrible safe word, she sent through the link.

"Too on the nose?"

There was no *penetration with tentacles! Not that it's any of your business.*

"Are you awake?" Vasil asked, his voice rumbling from his chest. He lifted a hand to her hair and lightly ran his claws through it.

"Mhmm." Theo rubbed her cheek against his skin. "Sorry I woke you. I was just talking to Kane."

She felt his head turn and his shoulders shift as though he were stretching, but he made no move to rise. "I do not normally sleep this late."

"Me neither."

"What were you talking about?"

Theo snickered. "Sure you wanna know?"

He hummed thoughtfully. "Only if you are willing to tell me."

"It had to do with a certain limb and…penetration."

"Penetration of what?"

Theo wiggled her toes, brushing them against one of his tentacles.

"Your toes penetrating my tentacle?"

Theo lifted her head and looked down at him with an arched brow. "What? No." She laughed. "Tentacle penetration."

"Penetration of *what*, Theo?"

Theo's shoulders shook with laughter as she ran a fingertip along his jaw. "Do you remember the conversation we had with Kane about octopuses?"

Vasil frowned. "I understand now why Dracchus and Kronus always complain about humans refusing to speak plainly."

"She means your tentacle entering her vaginal canal," Kane said cheerily through the console speaker.

"Kane!" Theo groaned, dropping her head to rest on Vasil's chest again. "Tentacle penetration."

"*Tentacular*, Theo. Tentacular. You have to say it right if you mean to use it," Kane replied. "And considering what the two of you did last night, I cannot possibly understand why you'd be so—"

"Just go!" Theo snapped.

"Fine," Kane grumbled, "but I just might not wake up the next time you call me. Think about *that!*"

Theo snickered.

One of Vasil's tentacles brushed Theo's inner thigh. Her breath hitched.

"I would not be opposed to trying," he said.

Lifting her head, she met his gaze. "Oh?"

The tip of his tentacle slipped a little higher. "It is only right that we attempt it at least once, would you not say?"

Heat flooded her core in response to both his words and the teasing stroke of his tentacle. Keeping her eyes on his, she raised one knee, spreading her thighs wider.

"At least once," she agreed.

His tentacle traveled higher, slipping between the folds of her sex until it covered her entire mound. She started when a suction cup pressed over her clit.

Vasil's mouth curled into a slow, sensual smile. "Kraken females do not possess this." The suction cup caressed the little nub before closing around it and sucking, creating surprisingly delicate, precise pressure.

Pleasure rippled through Theo, and she moaned, grinding her pelvis against his tentacle. "It's called a clit."

His grin widened. "I like it."

Another tentacle made its way upward, moving along her thigh to her sex. The tip slipped between her wet folds and pressed into her. Theo gasped and bore down on it, fingers curling against Vasil's chest. His tentacle sank deep before withdrawing almost all the way, only to slide in again; his other tentacle continued to kiss and stroke her clit throughout.

"Do *you* like *this*?" he asked, voice husky.

Though it was a struggle to keep her eyes open in her building pleasure, Theo forced herself to hold Vasil's gaze. Even in the light of day, she wasn't repulsed by Vasil or what he was. His tentacle inside her was a new, strange, erotic experience unlike any she'd ever had, his suction cups adding tantalizing texture as they slid along her sensitive inner flesh. It felt...good. *So* good. But it wasn't enough.

"*Yes*," she hissed, rocking her hips. Her hair brushed over his chest. Sitting up, she braced a hand on his shoulder and trailed the other down his body, over the rippling muscles of his abdomen, to stop at his already parted slit. Her fingers delved inside to stroke him.

A groan vibrated through his chest as he raised his hips into her touch. His cock, already slick, slid out into her palm. Theo took firm hold of it; she felt his pulse throbbing in her hand.

"But I would prefer this," she said.

"Kiss me, human, and it is yours," he growled, offering a glimpse of his pointed teeth as he cupped the back of her head with one large hand.

Theo lowered her face and brushed her lips over his. When she moved to pull away, his arm stiffened. He guided her back down and kissed her again, his passion bolstered by confidence he'd not possessed the night before. His lips, though soft, were unyielding in their message — she was his, and he'd take whatever he wanted from her.

At that moment, she realized that she was fine with him taking — because she trusted him completely to give equally of himself. This wasn't a simple *give-take*; it was a partnership, a *relationship*. That realization rocked her to her core — and fanned the flames of her desire to new heights.

He withdrew from her sex, leaving her feeling hollow, and coiled his tentacles around her thighs to spread them wide. Tugging her pelvis back and down, he pressed the head of his cock to her entrance. He breached her slowly, pumping into her a little at a time, a bit deeper with each upward stroke.

Theo closed her eyes and panted as excitement flared at her core, traveling throughout her entire body in a tingling wave of pleasure that was only amplified by the slight burn as he stretched her.

"Open your eyes, Theo," Vasil said, tightening his grip in her hair and ceasing all other movement.

She forced her heavy lids open to look at him. "Please don't stop."

"Say you are mine," he commanded, his eyes like swirling mercury, "and that I am yours."

Theo attempted to press herself down upon him, to take him as deep as her body allowed, but his tentacles held her still. She growled and undulated her hips, managing only a teasingly infinitesimal slide of her inner walls along his shaft.

"*Vasil!*" she groaned.

"Say it," he said, lowering his pelvis back to partially withdraw from her.

Her nails dug into his shoulders, and she squeezed her legs together as tightly as she could, desperate to keep him inside her. "Damn it! Yes! Now *fuck me!*"

"Say the words, Theodora."

Consuming need ravaged her from within, and frustration flowed in close behind. "I said it!"

"Say. The. Words," Vasil demanded, capturing her jaw and forcing her eyes to his. "Even if you do not mean them, I *need* to hear them aloud."

Something within his gaze struck her like a blow; it stole her breath and stilled her heart.

The lump in her throat was undoubtedly a tangled mass of emotion, but she was in no state to examine it. "I'm yours," she whispered, moving a hand to his face to caress his jaw. "And you are *mine.*"

The pads of his fingers brushed over her cheek as he searched her gaze for several moments. Then, without another word, he drew her face down and kissed her, at the same time thrusting his hips upward. She gasped against his mouth as he filled her, but he allowed no time for Theo to catch her breath. He drew back and slammed into her repeatedly, pushing as deep as he could go, his tentacles pulling her down to meet his thrusts. She was a puppet, and he held the strings, manipulating her as he willed.

It was *sublime.*

Theo kissed him, giving back as much as she took. She craved more of his touch, his scent, his heat, his *everything*. With Vasil, she didn't feel alone. She felt...*complete*. Desired.

Loved?

As crazy as it seemed, it was true. She'd never known love until Malcolm, but he and Kane had shown Theo enough for her to recognize it. This was built on the same base, but it was so much more — so much deeper, so much stronger, so much more uncertain. And that was as exciting as it was frightening.

Vasil's hands trekked down her sides to grasp her hips, and his movements became more feral. Guttural sounds escaped him to mix with her cries.

Her body quivered, the delicious pleasure permeating her growing with each stroke of his cock until, finally, she broke apart in rapture. Torrents of ecstasy blasted through her as heat flooded her core. Her inner walls fluttered and clamped around his shaft, drawing him deeper.

The fingers on her hips flexed, and his tentacles coiled tighter around her thighs as his thrusts grew suddenly erratic. His body turned to stone beneath her as he roared her name. His hold on her hips strengthened further, claws pricking her flesh, and he pulled her down one final time as he released his seed within her.

Theo fell limp upon his chest, panting hard with the resonating effects of her climax. It didn't help that those clever little tendrils at the base of his shaft continued stroking her.

Vasil relaxed beneath her, releasing a long, steady breath. He gently massaged her hips; she'd be surprised if she didn't have bruises in the shapes of his fingers there. But she didn't mind. The idea that he'd let go so much that he'd marked her was an arousing one.

"Now I can see why human women get down with kraken," Theo said with a grin.

"Now you see why it is worth your while to *get down* with *me*."

Theo chuckled and raised her head, wiggling her eyebrows. "Maybe I'll have to show you what it'd be like to *go* down *on* you."

He tilted his head, brow furrowing. "I do not understand."

She patted his cheek. "You will."

THE DULL GRAY clouds were several shades lighter than the choppy waters over which they stretched, but they darkened along the horizon to blur the line between sea and sky. A steady wind, tolerable but carrying the hint of a chill, blew tirelessly off the ocean. Vasil frowned as he surveyed the scene; though the storm had relented some time during the previous night, the weather hadn't given up. All signs pointed toward another storm before day's end.

He'd decided after their morning meal hours before not to go to sea today. It was too dangerous to risk going out; better to lose a day of searching to caution than to lose Theo to reck-lessness.

Vasil swung his gaze landward and settled it upon her. He watched as, eyes downcast, she carefully walked through the shallow tide pool. The wonder and curiosity on her face warmed his chest, but it wasn't quite enough to stop his atten-tion from wandering.

His eyes dipped to study her body. Though he knew what was hidden beneath her jumpsuit, the sight of the fabric pulling taught over her curves as she moved stirred his blood. Her rounded backside, in particular, caught his eye; he'd have to be sure to focus on it next time.

He smiled. It would've been a lie had he claimed their couplings last night and earlier that morning hadn't played a significant role in his choice to forgo his search. Vasil had never known sex could be so pleasurable. He'd never known he could want someone so much.

He and Theo had gone to the stream together after break-fast, bathed one another, and refilled her water containers before returning to the beach to begin their current trek along the coastline. They were perhaps two hours away from the pod now, by measure of their leisurely pace. Close enough for emergencies, far enough for everything to be new, exciting, and a touch mysterious.

Vasil lowered himself into the tide pool and moved toward her, his tentacles unhindered by the slick rocks and soft sand. Patches of color dotted the pool all over — small sea creatures and clumped plants that thrived in the shallow water.

"Is all this stuff really alive?" Theo asked, glancing at him over her shoulder.

"Most of it, yes," he replied as he closed the remaining distance between them. He followed her gaze with his own to a school of tiny fish moving just below the surface.

Theo laughed when several of the fish swam toward her boot and attempted to nibble on it. Her laughter was high and light, unburdened by the troubles that seemed to have weighed her down over the last few days. The urgency of his search for The Watch could be set aside for a little while. He wanted to bring Theo there so she could live in relative comfort and security, he wanted to return to attempt to form a relationship with his child, but for today, he just wanted to enjoy Theo's company.

This was an opportunity to learn about her, to grow closer to her, to have more of the shared experiences upon which their bond was being built. Though his people had never come together as mates based on conversation or something as fleeting as shared *fun*, things had changed. A lasting coupling required a deeper connection.

Theo skimmed her palm over the water's surface. The tiny fish scattered away from the disturbance. "Does it look like this farther in?"

"In some places, it looks similar," Vasil replied, "but mostly it looks very different. The sea is vast and varied."

"Everything in space seemed to blend together. Just blackness stretching on into eternity, broken by these little points of cold, distant light. If you get lost out there, you don't ever get found again. It's so…lonely."

Before Vasil could consider her words, Theo turned away from him, lifted her foot onto a rock, and climbed out of the pool. She walked away, rounded a larger stone outcropping, and disappeared from his view.

"Vasil!" she called a few moments later, voice brimming with excitement.

He moved to the edge of the pool and hauled himself out of the water to follow her path around the outcropping. She was only a body length or two past it, turned toward the cliffs that bordered the beach's inland side.

"What is it?" he asked.

"There's an opening there," she said, glancing back at him and pointing toward the cliffs. She grinned and ran toward it. "Let's check it out!"

"Slow down!" he called, hurrying to catch up with her. Once he was close enough, he reached out and caught her arm, tugging her back against his chest.

She came to him without a fight, laughing and smiling, and threw her arms around him. "Damn, you're fast for someone who doesn't have legs."

He couldn't keep his lips from curling into a smile. "Perhaps you are slow for someone who does."

Theo snorted, playfully smacking his arm.

"Caves like that can be dangerous, Theo," he said, forcing his tone to solemnity. "The tide can rise quickly, especially during storms, and many seaside caves flood because of it."

"Oh." She looked away sheepishly. "Guess I let myself get caught up in the excitement. This is just all…so new." Her eyes met his again.

"Well, it's a good thing no one will ever mistake you for a trained soldier," Kane said aloud.

Vasil glanced at the gentle glow on her wrist and shook his head. He understood sarcasm to a degree thanks to Randall and Arkon, even if he didn't fully understand the *why* of it. With few exceptions, he was used to kraken speaking plainly, and the subtleties and nuances of human communication were still lost on him from time to time.

"I never said I was perfect," Theo said.

Vasil brushed loose strands of hair back from Theo's face, using the tip of his claw to tuck them behind her ear. "You are to me."

Cheeks reddening, Theo smiled. "Vasil's definitely at the top of my favorite person list right now, Kane."

"Oh no," Kane cried in an exaggerated whine, "bottom fifty percent? How will I go on?"

Theo snickered. "Actually, you're in the bottom third. *I'm* my second favorite, at the moment."

"I would call you cold-hearted were I not well aware that your body temperature is perfectly normal."

"If you want to explore the cave, Theo" Vasil said, "we can. We just need to be quick."

"Yes!" Theo stepped away from Vasil. "Let's go exploring!"

He didn't release his hold on her arm. "You need to remain near me, understood?"

"Yes, sir."

"For the record, the technical term is *spelunking*," Kane said.

Theo smirked. "That sounds like a dirty word, Kane."

"It sounds like a made-up word," said Vasil as they moved toward the cave's entrance, side-by-side.

"*All* words are made up by someone at some point," Kane replied. "The ones that catch on become an official part of the language, and the rest, thankfully, are forgotten with history. I can only imagine how many words would—I *know* you're rolling your eyes, Theodora."

Theo bought her wrist up and crooned to Kane's blue light, "You know me so well."

"I'm connected to your nervous system," Kane said. "I know every move you make, no matter how small. It's *exhausting*. You have a tendency to fidget when you're bored."

"Guilty as charged." She tilted her head back as they neared the opening of the cave. "Now enough about me. Keep watch, okay?"

The cave's mouth stood nearly twice as tall as Vasil was long, wide enough for him to fit his shoulders through with a little room to spare on either side. Water ran from the entrance, cutting a shallow channel through the sand on its journey to the sea, its flow not quite strong enough to be considered a stream. He couldn't be sure if it was drainage from the last time the tide had flooded the cave or if there was a source of fresh water within.

The dreary daylight didn't reach very far inside before succumbing to darkness.

Exposed, uneven rock comprised the entrance's floor. Vasil moved in front of Theo as they crossed the stone. After less than a body's length of distance — a few meters — the rock gave away to standing water, the surface of which reflected the gray sky behind Vasil up until the point where the shadows claimed their dominion.

He entered the shallow water; it was cooler than the tidal pool had been. Theo stepped in behind him, the gentle splashes of her boots magnified by the stone walls all around. As they passed into the darkness, Vasil made his stripes glow to cast soft blue light on the walls and water.

"You can *glow?*" Theo asked, her astonished whisper echoing throughout the cave.

He paused when her hands settled on his arm. Turning his head, he watched with a furrowed brow as she ran her fingers over his glowing stripes, back and forth, up and down, her eyes rounded.

"This is sexy. I'm definitely going to have you do this later while you're—"

"Tentacular Penetration!" Kane said.

Theo stilled for an instant before bursting into laughter. "We *so* need a new safe word."

"How about *shut up?*"

"Works for now." Theo looked at Vasil, smiled, and brushed a kiss over one of his stripes before stepping away to trail her fingertips along the damp cave wall.

When Vasil continued onward, Theo followed. The air cooled as they moved deeper into the cave. The sound of the waves became a low, pervasive rumbling, felt more than heard. A familiar tightness threatened to grip Vasil's chest, and his skin tingled with the first hints of a coming itch; this place was isolated, dark, oppressive.

As if she knew what he was experiencing, Theo reached out, brushing her fingers over his back. "It's okay."

He squeezed his eyes closed and drew in a long, slow breath. The air smelled of stone and sea — a familiar enough blend to soothe him.

You'll have moments of...relapse, Theo had said. *You can overcome them.*

Vasil released the breath and opened his eyes. The walls were in the same place they'd been before — no closer, no more menacing.

"I know," he said. "Thank you."

Theo stopped several times to gaze at the rock formations, but she never lingered too far behind; her hands occasionally settled on his arms, her fingertips glided over his skin, reminding him he wasn't alone.

"There's a strange...buzz," Theo said, scratching behind her ear. "Do you feel it?"

Halting, Vasil dropped his gaze, focusing on his hearing and the feel of the air against his skin. There was a faint current both in the air and in the water, and he still sensed the muted rumbling of the ocean, but that was all.

"I do not feel anything out of the ordinary."

"Hmm. Must just be me, then." She reached out and ran her fingers over the wall.

"I'm picking up a strange energy signature, but it is very faint," said Kane. "It doesn't have a match in my database."

Theo's exploration slowed their progress, but Vasil was unbothered. She was like a youngling, curious and unashamed, finding wonder in everything she saw. He couldn't help but smile when she drew her knife to pry free a colorful shell that had been embedded in the wall. She called it a *souvenir*.

"This is pretty," she said, staring at the shell as though there weren't dozens more just like it lodged in the stone all around. She turned and took a few steps deeper into the cave only to stagger to a halt. She swayed forward and raised a hand to her head.

Vasil moved closer to her. "What is wrong, Theo?"

"That buzzing. I can feel it vibrating in my head. It's strange… It's like a headache, but it's making this weird pinch." She lowered her hand and looked up. "Is something glowing up ahead?"

"Theo, those readings are strengthening," Kane said, his voice oddly distorted.

Brows falling low, Vasil followed Theo's gaze with his own. The cave narrowed up ahead and curved to the left. A patch of impenetrable darkness waited beyond Vasil's soft glow, and beyond that shone another gentle light, cast from around the bend.

Vasil frowned. "It is halorium."

"That's what the IDC came here for, isn't it?" she asked. "What your people were forced to harvest?"

"Yes." He glanced behind them; only more darkness lurked beyond the light of his stripes. They weren't terribly far into the cave, but the sea was fickle. This place could flood in moments if the tide came in, and he'd have trouble protecting even himself from being slammed into the stone walls when that happened. "We should go back now."

"Hold up. We'll leave in a second, but I need to see this first." She ran ahead, water splashing around her legs.

"Theo!" Vasil turned to follow her. Dread coalesced in his gut, threatening to climb into his chest and throat.

"Theo, you ca—" Kane's words were lost in a jarring, staticky hiss.

As she reached the bend, Theo lifted a hand to her head again. Her torso dipped forward, and she stumbled, throwing out an arm as though to catch her balance. It was only when her hand found the nearby wall that she steadied herself and staggered forward a few more steps. She vanished around the corner.

Vasil's hearts quickened, and he pushed his body ahead to match their pace. Theo's cry — fraught with pain and fear — preceded a heavy splash just before he rounded the bend.

He looked down; for an instant, his hearts seized, and so much pressure built up in his chest that it felt near to exploding. Theo lay face-down in the water. Though it only reached her mid-shin while standing, it was deep enough to almost fully submerge her in her prone position.

Darting to her, he slipped his arms beneath Theo and snatched her out of the water. Her body was stiff — legs straight, arms clutched against her torso, and head tilted back. Though her eyes were open, they displayed on their whites. The blood trickling from her nostrils glistened in the glow of the large halorium shards jutting from the wall nearby.

Did the halorium somehow cause this?

There was no time to consider the question; he had to

assume the answer was *yes*. She shuddered in his arms, muscles remaining taut, and produced a choked, gurgling sound. Foamy spit oozed from the corners of her mouth.

Vasil gave over to instinct. He turned her sideways in his hold so the liquid flowed out of her mouth rather than gathering within and shifted his arm to support her head and neck. He rose and, moving as quickly as he could without jarring Theo, carried her toward the cave's entrance.

The light on her wrist flickered and flared, accompanied by a distorted, inhuman voice.

"Kane?" Vasil asked.

Theo continued to convulse, her body straining against his hold.

The computer spoke, but his voice was garbled and indecipherable, made worse by its reverberation off the cave walls.

Water sloshed around Vasil's tentacles as he pushed on faster. Panic clawed at the edges of his mind, but he would not allow it entry; panic could not help Theo.

"Stay with me," he said, tightening his grasp on her. "*Stay*, Theodora."

When the opening came into view, Vasil's hearts skipped. The sound of the waves washed over him but provided none of the comfort and relief it normally would have.

"She is having a seizure," Kane said, words finally understandable despite the lingering distortion. "Ease her down on her side in the sand and keep her head up off the ground."

Vasil lowered her to the sand the instant he crossed out of the cave, keeping a hand beneath her neck and head to maintain his support. Her convulsions continued, and foam poured from her mouth.

Kane's orb projected from Theo's wrist, hovering in the air over her. "Relax your hold on her, Vasil. If you try to restrain her, she may be injured."

Clenching his jaw, Vasil did as instructed. His limbs trembled; he wanted to clutch her against him so she knew he was there, so she knew she'd be all right, but that could do her harm.

He didn't know how to help her.

"What is wrong with her?" Vasil asked in a low voice.

"As I said, a seizure. My systems temporarily shorted out, causing electrical feedback in her nervous system."

"I do not understand, Kane," Vasil growled.

Theo shook harder for a moment, ejecting a spray of spit with a choked exhalation, before finally easing. Her eyelids fluttered shut as her body sagged in the sand.

"I am connected directly to her," Kane replied.

"You are on her wrist. How could that affect her like this?"

"My projector is at her wrist, Vasil. My systems are integrated with her. I am connected to her brain. I'm…part of her."

Vasil released a heavy breath, nostrils flaring. Questions swirled in his mind and gnawed at his gut, but none of them would help the situation. None of them would help her. He brushed wet hair out of her face and stared down at her. She was breathing, but otherwise unmoving.

"Theo?" he said softly.

"She's unconscious," Kane said. "And may be for some time. The strain on her body was immense. This sort of thing…it isn't supposed to happen."

"But it did," Vasil said. He skimmed the backs of his fingers over her cheek. "Will she be all right?"

"Her brain activity has normalized, so yes. I think so. We won't know for sure until she wakes up, but as far as I can tell… there's no permanent damage."

The sighing of wind and sea filled the ensuing silence. Vasil's fingers and tentacles tensed, but he didn't tighten his grip on her. He knew humans were fragile, but he didn't know something like *this* could happen; he still wasn't entirely sure what this was. Kane's explanation made some sense but remained largely beyond Vasil's understanding. Someone like Arkon might've understood and been able to explain it in clear, simple terms, but Vasil was not Arkon.

"You said there was halorium in that cave," Kane said. "That must've been the energy signature I was reading. Is that what caused this?"

Vasil's stomach sank as realization struck him. "I did not... *You* are the machine, not Theo. Why would it do this to *her?*"

"Because I am *part of her!*" Powerful fear and despair resonated in Kane's voice. "I should have told her to turn back."

"I should have *made* her turn back," Vasil said. He gathered Theo against his chest and rose from the sand. Her body was limp now, in such alarming contrast to the stiffness of minutes ago that it set his hearts to racing again. He started back toward their camp. "I...should have been able to *see.* I know the pieces, I should have been able to put them together."

Kane's orb swelled and brightened, only to dim and dwindle in size. "As much as I'd like to have someone to blame, I cannot hold you accountable for this. I should have recognized the energy as potentially harmful, and Theo should not have been so eager to plunge into the unknown. We *all* made mistakes today..."

Vasil dipped his gaze to Theo, his frown deepening. "I hope she does not pay any greater a price for those mistakes."

THEO WOKE WITH A GROAN. Pain pulsed in her skull, and every muscle in her body ached. She raised a hand and squeezed her temples between two fingers and a thumb as though the pressure could ease the pounding in her head, but even that slight movement was a strain on her weakened body.

"Theodora?" Kane said. "Can you hear me?"

Large, strong fingers settled over her free hand, grasping it gently.

She furrowed her brow and opened her eyes — only to snap them shut against the blinding light, which added a delightful stabbing sensation to her already monumental headache.

"What the fuck?" she said, turning her head to the side. "Turn off the damned lights."

"They aren't on," Kane replied. "You may be overly sensitive to light, at the moment. It should pass soon."

"Why are you talking so loud?"

"I'm not," he said at a lower volume. "Again, you are likely just experiencing some—"

"Sensitivity. Okay, got it." Theo lowered her hand from her forehead to rub her eyes. She couldn't remember ever waking up to feeling this shitty — and she'd gone drinking with IDC marines on more than one occasion. She turned her hand in Vasil's loose grip and laced her fingers with his. "What happened?"

"Halorium," Vasil said.

"And lo, for all your questions have been answered," said Kane.

"Wanna be a bit more specific?" She lowered her hand and slitted her eyes open. The light blasted her, jabbing another knife into her brain, but she blinked the brightness away until her vision cleared, and everything came into focus.

Vasil stood to her left, staring down at her with concern. The light that had so blinded her streamed in through the open pod hatch, cast by a clouded sky that looked to be dimming with approaching evening. She glanced down to find herself sitting in one of the chairs, blanket draped over her legs and torso.

She couldn't remember much from after she'd run toward the glow — toward the halorium. All she could recall was a sense of adventure and excitement, her eagerness to see what had pushed the IDC to break so many rules all those years ago, and then pain. She'd blacked out.

Her memory held a big black patch of nothing afterward — zip, *nada*, zilch — until she'd woken a few minutes ago.

Vasil grunted. "He must explain. I still do not understand."

"The halorium in that cave shorted me out," Kane said. "It emits a powerful energy, almost like a form of radiation, and it was more than enough to short me out. Vasil did not exaggerate the effects — if anything, the vague explanation he gave us was an understatement. You suffered a prolonged seizure due to the electrical feedback from my failing system."

"And that stuff — the halorium — was why your people were made, right?" Theo asked, looking at Vasil. "And if I didn't have Kane, I could have just walked up to it and touched it."

"Yes, it was, and yes, you could have," Vasil replied. "From what I know, it is usually found in the sea. Below depths at which humans would die before they ever got close enough without diving suits or underwater craft."

"And those things wouldn't work because they fail when they get close to halorium," she said.

Vasil nodded. His deep frown hadn't eased since she woke.

"Hey." She reached up and smoothed her fingers over his brow. "It's okay. I'm still alive, right?"

"You are, but what if it had been worse? What if I — *we* — had lost you?"

"You didn't."

"The possibility of it was…jarring, to say the least," Kane said.

Vasil lifted his hand to cup her cheek, brushing the pads of his fingers over her skin. "We were frightened, Theodora."

Theo turned her head and kissed the center of his palm. "I'm sorry. I should have paid more attention to the signs. It felt like something was off, but I kept pushing forward. You may not believe this, but I have a bit of a stubborn streak."

Vasil smiled, though the expression was still tinged with

sorrow. "I understand the want for exploration and adventure, but we must maintain some caution."

"All of this is new to me, and I let myself get swept up in that." She covered his hand with her own and closed her eyes. "I threw my training out the window and acted like a child. I won't let it happen again."

"You have...opened up since we first met," Vasil said. "You seem *freer*. I do not want you to give that up. As Kane said to me before, we *all* made mistakes today. Do not hold yourself solely responsible. None of us could have known what was going to happen with any certainty. I just...do not want to lose you, Theo."

Vasil's words, spoken with such sincerity, such depth and emotion, produced a flutter in her stomach and a warmth in her chest. She opened her eyes, ignoring the lingering discomfort from the light, and met his gaze. Slipping a hand to the back of his neck, she tugged him down. He came willingly. She kissed him softly, and he returned it, wrapping an arm around her to draw her body closer.

"You won't," she said against his mouth. Tilting her head back, she brushed the tip of her nose against his.

"Never," he growled. The promise and power he instilled that simple word send a thrill down her spine.

"*I like him,*" Kane said through the neural link.

Me too.

Though she had a feeling the word *like* wasn't adequate to describe what she felt for the kraken.

CHAPTER 11

V ASIL WONDERED IF HIS EYES WERE DECEIVING HIM WHEN THE lights on the sea floor, reduced to a ghostly glow by distance, first came into view. He knew the surrounding seascape well — he'd followed its familiar features to this spot, the beating of his hearts echoing in his chest like stones banging on a metal drum — but it had been so long since he'd been here that it seemed a place existent only in his memory. A projection of his own imagination.

The Facility took shape in the gloom as he neared it — several large buildings, defined by clashing light and shadow, gathered upon the sea floor, each older than the kraken people; the place of his birth. Relief eased his tension and dulled the ache in his muscles. The journey from the pod to this place had taken most of the day, but it was not yet completed.

He would allow himself rest only when Theo was beside him again.

Was she all right? She'd managed to keep herself safe every other time he'd gone searching, but he'd normally return to the pod at about this time of day to share their evening meal, and the incident in the cave three days before had left him shaken.

He wasn't likely to return to her until nearly sunrise the next day if he moved as fast as possible. He'd never left her alone for that long.

Though she was intelligent, tough, and capable, he couldn't help his worry. Between her gun, her training, and Kane, she should've been fine, but that wasn't enough to ease his nerves. He needed to be with her, needed to be certain.

And how must she feel with me gone, not knowing whether I am safe, not knowing when, if ever, I will return?

Two posts topped with white lights materialized in the darkness ahead, set about half a body length apart in the sandy bottom. There was no net stretched between them, which meant there was no hunt in progress; he wasn't sure if that was a good thing or not — more of his people present meant more potential questions. The last thing he wanted as any further delay in returning to Theo, especially if that delay was unnecessary.

He continued forward, and the shadows on the main building receded with his nearness. He knew those walls instinctively. Ever since he'd been deemed old enough to be given into the care of the male kraken — the hunters — the sight of the Facility's exterior had held great meaning to Vasil. This had been *home*. It had meant safety, security, comfort, and community, even if that sense of community often felt strained. The kraken had always worked together for mutual survival, but socialization was limited before human influence had offered a different way of life.

Now...he wasn't entirely sure what the Facility meant to him. Perhaps it maintained much of its old meaning, though not in the same fashion. It was safety, security, comfort, and the possibility of community not for himself, but for Theodora.

Vasil swam to the entry door, where he tapped the buttons on the keypad — *081305* — and waited for the red light over the door to change. Once the light switched to green, the door slid open, and he entered the chamber beyond. The door closed when he pressed the button on the interior wall, and the room thrummed gently as the water drained. The sensation of his body gradually growing heavier was as jarring as always; he found it strange how the transition seemed normal when emerging onto the land from the sea but remained somehow unsettling when it was so slow and deliberate.

Not important, he reminded himself, spreading his tentacles to support his weight as the water dipped below his waist. *I am here* only *to help Theo.*

Though that wasn't entirely true — he missed his friends, human and kraken alike — it was his primary motivation. She might have died in that cave because of the halorium, and that was but one of many threats to her safety. A swelling tide; a violent storm; a roving predator; the place they'd been staying held more potential threats than he could count. The Facility and The Watch were the only places where many of those dangers were reduced and, in some cases, all but eliminated. Nowhere guaranteed safety, but Theo deserved better than she had on that beach.

"Pressurization complete," said a familiar feminine voice from overhead — the Computer. She sounded flat and dispassionate compared to Kane.

The door ahead of Vasil opened with a hiss. He moved through, entering a familiar corridor that was bathed in pure white light from overhead. Water dripped off his body and flowed through the grates on the floor beneath him. The place was cleaner than he remembered, undoubtedly a result of humans like Larkin and Aymee living here with their kraken mates for long periods of time. This main building had been used more in the four years since Jax had brought his human mate, Macy, to the Facility than it had in all Vasil's life prior; the kraken used to keep to the flooded buildings unless they had reason to meet with one another and speak.

Oddly, the cleanliness instilled the Facility with a lived-in feeling. It was being treated as a home in a way the kraken had never dreamed, and that gladdened Vasil.

But coming back had only confirmed his suspicion — this was no longer *his* home.

Grunting, he cast those thoughts aside. Only Theo mattered. She was alone, awaiting his return, and he was eager to share the news with her. Though he wanted her to see the Facility, to see where his people had been created, this place was only important to him now because it could provide a diving suit — which she required to travel to The Watch. He didn't trust the pod to endure another ocean journey.

Vasil moved down the corridor, using the various handles and recesses to pull himself along faster. He took the turns without thinking; well over a year had passed since he'd gone to live in The Watch permanently, but he knew this place as intimately as though he'd never left.

He encountered no one on his way to the Pool Room.

He entered the large chamber, which had been named because of the huge, rectangular, humanmade pool dominating it. Vasil glanced at the water as he hurried past it. Thousands of stones lay on the bottom, their colors and arrangement creating a series of intricate circular patterns. The effect was the illusion of motion, all of it leading to the center — a small, glowing shard of halorium.

Vasil halted and turned to frown down at the halorium. He wasn't sure how wide an area that little piece could affect — the lights at the base of the pool all seemed functional, but it was possible they were somehow shielded from its effects.

When Vasil brought Theo to The Watch, they'd have to stop in this building; the Facility was on the way and would provide a safe place to eat and rest. Otherwise, they'd be swimming from sunrise to well after sunset. He doubted Theo could make such a journey in a single day, especially as she'd spent much of her life in some sort of machine that traveled between the stars. Even the diving suits, which eased human movement through the water, would not be enough to combat the inevitable exhaustion she'd suffer during such a trip.

She'd want to explore the Facility during their stay, and he'd be happy to show her around...

But this room would be off-limits.

Turning away from the pool, he continued to the lockers and containers arranged along the far wall. They'd served as storage for the diving suits since long before Vasil's birth — all the way back to the time before the uprising, most likely. He searched them one-at-a-time, frown deepening with each locker searched; though he found several pieces of old human clothing in some, there were no diving suits or their accompanying masks. He growled as he closed the last locker. Theo *needed* one of those suits. Without it, her departure from that beach would be far more complicated and dangerous.

Sped on by necessity, he searched the other nearby containers. Most held equipment he could not identify — artifacts whose purposes had been lost to time. He doubted that even the humans in The Watch could have given names to all the varied and mysterious objects. His only guess was that most of them served some function under water.

There were no diving suits amidst the items.

Grasping the sides of the last container, he tensed, ready to hurl it into the pool. He was failing his mate during what should have been the moment of his success. Now that he knew the way, he should've been bringing her home. He should've been bringing her to his den, which he would ask her to share.

Vasil growled, tightening his hold on the container. It groaned under the pressure.

Rage will not help me. Will not help her.

He released a slow, heavy breath through his nostrils and returned the container to its place. He could not recall the last time he'd acted in anger. He couldn't recall the last time he'd acted out of *anything* but a sense of duty and obligation to his people — at least before he'd seen a falling star, *his* falling star, streak across the night sky. Since that night, he'd been driven by many emotions — curiosity, lust, compassion, fear, and...*love.*

That word — *love* — seemed strange to him. He'd heard the kraken and human couples exchange it so many times that he'd been foolish enough to believe he understood what it meant. But he'd never truly known. Despite his keen eye, his perceptiveness, and his ability to understand why people behaved the way they did, he'd never truly deciphered love. He knew now that it could not *be* deciphered, that it eluded understanding. He knew because of Theo.

He knew...because he loved her.

Though he could not fathom everything that meant, it was indisputable.

Vasil was here for her, and he would tear apart every room in the Facility if that was what it took to locate a diving suit. If there were none to be found, he would not rest until he reached another solution. But ripping this place apart room-by-room was not a reasonable next step. Clear thinking would see him further than giving in to frustration and despair.

He exited the Pool Room and hurtled through the corridors, his frenzied pace setting his hearts to a rapid, thunderous rhythm. He darted past more than a dozen doors leading into side chambers for which the kraken had no use — chambers that had long rested in darkness. Though he'd wondered about some of those rooms for many years, he'd never explored them. The urge had never overcome his desire to be a dutiful kraken; searching rooms that were likely empty or functionless would have been of no benefit to his people. His time was better off spent in productive endeavors.

But he would explore them soon — with Theo. He would find a way to bring her here, and they would discover those secrets together. Even if the Facility was somehow similar to the ships she'd lived on for so long, it would be new to her; maybe he'd see it with fresh wonder through her eyes.

He turned another corner and entered the corridor bridging the main building to the Cabins, where the kraken and human couples denned. Broad windows ran the length of the passage, offering a view into the world outside — the gray exterior walls of the buildings, cast in white light, and the ocean beyond darkening from deep blue to impenetrable black. He wasted no time taking in the sight; without slowing, he passed through the corridor and entered the Cabins building.

It was only as he turned into the hallway along which the human-kraken mates kept their dens that his momentum faltered. This section of the Facility had rarely been visited before humans came here again; in many ways, it had come to signify hope, change, and growth. But the last time he'd been in this hallway, it had been in the wake of tragedy.

Neo had led a group of exiled kraken into this hall meaning to slaughter all the humans who'd dwelled here and the kraken who loved them. The traitorous kraken and all his followers had been killed, several by Vasil's hand. Blood had bathed this corridor.

Now, it looked as it had before that night — clean, empty, unremarkable, and yet somehow warm.

Shrugging off those looming memories, he continued forward. He would not allow the ghosts of kraken who'd sought to harm females and younglings to weigh upon him.

The door of Dracchus's den was open. Vasil moved into the doorway. Dracchus — easily the largest of their kind in length and breadth — leaned over the table within, working with something on its surface.

Vasil knocked on the doorframe, producing a quick series of metallic clanks.

Dracchus paused his work and turned his head to Vasil. His

eyes widened in a rare display of shock, and he turned his entire body toward the doorway. "You are here."

Frowning, Vasil glanced down at himself as though it would grant insight into Dracchus's odd greeting. He found no answers there, nor when he returned his gaze to the other kraken. "I am."

After days of searching.

Dropping the corners of his mouth into a frown that made Vasil's look like a smile, Dracchus twisted his torso toward the table and carefully placed the objects in his hands atop it — scissors and an oddly-shaped, folded paper. Once they were down, he approached Vasil, stopping only an arm's length away. His skin remained its normal black; with any other kraken, the lack of color change would indicate a lack of strong emotion, but Dracchus, like Vasil, rarely betrayed his thoughts through such outward signs.

For the space of many heartbeats, silence stretched between the two kraken. Vasil stared up at the larger male, uncertain of what to anticipate.

Dracchus's amber eyes revealed nothing as they moved over Vasil, studying him from head to tentacle.

"You are well?" Dracchus finally asked.

"Yes." Vasil's weariness was not worth mention.

"You have been gone for two weeks."

"And a day."

Impossibly, Dracchus's frown deepened. "What happened?"

For a moment, Vasil's instinct was to withhold his answer. Some part of him — recently awoken and as-yet unfamiliar — was unwilling to reveal *anything* about Theo to another male. She was Vasil's, and no one else deserved to even know her name. *No one* would take her from him.

He cast that instinct aside; Dracchus had a mate to whom he was fiercely loyal. He would not betray Larkin. And Dracchus was a kraken of honor, regardless, who would not willingly seek to disrupt the bond between a mated couple. Most important of all was that Theo needed help to get here — to get to safety.

"Something fell from the sky the night I left. I chased it to sea," Vasil said.

"We were woken by its sound. The humans said it was a *meteor*. A rock fallen from beyond the sky."

Vasil shook his head, holding Dracchus's gaze. "It was an IDC pod. Humanmade, from space."

Dracchus's brows lowered; it was his only response.

Drawing in a deep breath, Vasil continued. "I discovered it floating on open water just as a storm struck. We were caught adrift and carried to an unfamiliar beach. Only today did I finally discover signs to lead me back here."

"We?" Dracchus asked.

"There was a female in the pod. A human."

Clenching his jaw, Dracchus dropped his gaze. "She is IDC, then?"

"She *was*. I need a diving suit for her."

Dracchus met Vasil's gaze again. "Where will you take her?"

"The Watch. But we will have to stop here on the way."

"No."

A fire sparked in Vasil's gut. He gritted his teeth, forcing the flames down. "Explain."

"You know the history, Vasil."

"She is stranded, Dracchus," Vasil said through his teeth, struggling to maintain an even tone. "She cannot contact the IDC, and they do not know where she is."

"And if they come in search?"

"They will not."

Dracchus shook his head slowly. "No. We cannot risk our people."

"She has a computer inside her, Dracchus, and it does not know our world. They have forgotten this place. Forgotten our people."

"And we should not remind them." Dracchus's firm tone offered no space for argument, but that wasn't what fanned the flames inside Vasil.

It was the coldness, the detachment, of Dracchus's expression that ignited Vasil's rage. The unwillingness to consider a change of position. The sense that he didn't care what Vasil had to say, that he was an unmovable object set in place against the entire universe.

Vasil drew in another breath, seeking balance and calmness to counter his roiling agitation. "I trust her, Dracchus."

"We cannot risk our people," the big kraken repeated.

The fires in Vasil's belly flared, blazing across his chest, up into his throat, and out to the tips of his fingers and tentacles. "And what did you do by bringing two hunters to this place?" he growled as crimson spread over his skin. "Your mate was one of those who captured us!"

"And the one who freed us," Dracchus roared, skin turning red as he advanced. "She *saved* us."

Vasil gave no ground. He raised himself higher and held Dracchus's gaze. "And I did not question your choices then. I trusted your judgment."

"You saw her," Dracchus said, "her kindness."

"And I see Theodora. So do *not* tell me you act for the good of our people now unless you are willing to say you acted *against* us when you brought Randall and Larkin here."

Dracchus clenched and relaxed his jaw. "I could not allow them back to their people, or we would have been further exposed. The IDC has capabilities the hunters did not. Bringing the female here will lead them directly to us."

"If they were to look, Dracchus, they would find us whether she is here or not. They are more advanced now than we can imagine."

"That is only more reason not to—"

"Would you leave your Larkin?" Vasil demanded, moving

closer to Dracchus. Tension crackled in the air between them, but he barely noticed; his entire body thrummed with anger, passion, and desperation. He would not settle for defeat, not when it came to Theo.

Dracchus pressed his lips into a tight line.

"I have ever followed," Vasil said. "I have always done my duty. And what have I *ever* asked of you, Dracchus? Even when things were at their worst, I trusted your leadership. I have trusted you for as long as I can remember, and that trust has never felt misplaced. Now you must trust me. I do not ask you to endanger the lives of our people. Only to help protect hers."

Vasil forced his skin back to its normal gray and released a heavy breath through his nostrils. "She is mine, Dracchus. My mate. Help me keep her safe, or I will find a way to do so without you."

The crimson slowly faded from Dracchus's skin, but his expression remained tight.

"I need a suit," Vasil continued. "If I must challenge you for it, I will. If I must search every room in the Facility, I will. If I must go to The Watch to obtain one, I *will*. But she is alone in a dangerous place, and I do not want to be away any longer than necessary. So help me, fight me, or stay out of my way, for I will *not* be stopped."

Dracchus made a sound that was at once a grunt and a groan and turned to move away from Vasil again. "Everyone comes to *me* for help."

"Because you are good. You have given everything for our people, and only with Larkin have you taken for your own happiness. Now it is time for me to take what is mine. Tell me where the spare diving suits are, and I will ask no more of you. I will go."

"They are in a room down the hall. We moved them so they can be easily accessed by our mates." Stopping beside the table,

Dracchus rested a hand on its surface, keeping his gaze downcast. "I will go with you, and we will escort her here together."

Some of the flames within Vasil snuffed out, leaving an odd, hollow sensation behind. "You do not need to come. The journey is mine to make."

"She is your mate, Vasil." Dracchus met Vasil's gaze. "That means she is one of us. We will be better able to protect her if there are two of us, should the need arise."

Vasil moved into the room, halting within arm's length of Dracchus. He extended his hand like he'd seen so many humans do. Like Theo had done.

Dracchus turned to face him slowly, glancing down. He took Vasil's hand, clasping firmly.

"Allow me a few moments to clean the mess," Dracchus said, gesturing to the table. Scraps of paper littered the table top, along with a few larger pieces cut into kraken-like shapes. Dracchus released Vasil's hand. "Aymee taught me to make chains of paper dolls in different shapes. The younglings always seem to enjoy them."

Despite everything — or perhaps *because* of everything — Vasil smiled. "I will help you clean, but then we must go."

Dracchus nodded. "I will tell Larkin before we leave. I am glad you are safe, Vasil."

"And I will be glad once Theo is safe, too."

CHAPTER 12

Sitting in the damp sand, Theo nibbled on the corner of a ration bar and watched the endless advance and retreat of the waves. The food was tasteless and dry, nothing like the fresh fruits, vegetables, and meat she'd been eating lately, but she barely paid attention to it. The brisk morning wind swept around her, tossing her hair about her shoulders, flowing into the gaps of her modified jumpsuit to chill her skin.

"He'll come back," Kane said in her mind.

"He didn't come back last night." Theo ran her gaze over the surf. "What if he was attacked by one of those creatures again?"

"He'll come back, Theodora."

"But what if he *doesn't?*" she asked, unable to keep her fear from slipping into her words. She'd hardly slept the night before, kept awake by worry after he hadn't returned with the setting sun, and her worry was only stronger now that he'd remained absent all night. She didn't want to lose him. *Couldn't* lose him.

"Then you will carry on. You'll survive. But he will *come back."*

"How can you be sure?"

"Because dealing with your human irrationality for so long has

damaged my capacity for logical thought." Somehow, Kane's tone deflated any insult his words might have held. *"He is a hunter, a survivor. And...he is* very *fond of you. That seems to be a driving force for which any calculations I might perform cannot accurately account."*

Theo glanced down at the sand between her feet. She knew Vasil was fond of her; he'd made no effort to hide his want since the beginning. But was she enough? She was a nobody, unwanted by most everyone she'd ever known. Why was he different? What could he possibly see in her that no one else did?

"Stop it," Kane said.

"Stop what?"

"I know what you're doing, Theodora Velenti. You're in your own head, telling yourself that you're not good enough, that he's not going to come back for you because everyone that was supposed to care for you abandoned you."

"I thought you couldn't read my mind."

"I don't have to. I know you. And it's bullshit. Malcolm didn't leave you, he died. What was he supposed to have done about it? The others — your mother and your aunt — were not worthy of having you in their lives. You lost nothing in them. And who the hell is here talking to you right now? They would've removed me against my will *when your term of service was up, but now you're stuck with me until you're dead, so stop the damned pity party!"*

Theo smiled despite herself. "Wow. Thanks, Kane. You know, you're not bad at this whole uplifting speech thing."

"If I could, I'd have just kicked you right in the ass, Theo. I don't have any other choice."

She chuckled, glanced at the dry ration bar, and tossed it away. The thought of taking another bite nauseated her.

For several moments, she was quiet, running her fingertips through the sand and listening to the waves.

"Would it have been against your will, Kane? Would you have missed me?"

"Of course it would've been against my will, Theo. And what's worse is they would've wiped my memory of all that after they extracted the information they wanted. I know us being stranded here isn't ideal, and there's still some underlying IDC protocol coding in me that says I should be helping you find a way off-planet, but...I'm glad for it. You are like an irritating and less-intelligent younger sister to me."

Theo smiled. "Losing you would have been like losing a limb. I'm...glad this happened, too. I don't think I could have gone through losing you. Not after Malcolm."

And I don't want to lose Vasil, either.

"Which limb?" he asked.

"Probably my head. I can't live without that."

"Good answer. I've taught you well."

Theo laughed. Running her fingers through her hair, she looked up and stilled.

The sun had not yet fully risen over the jungle behind her, leaving the ocean a bleak, dark gray, but the figure wading toward her in the surf was immediately identifiable — Vasil. He moved forward at a steady pace, swaying as the tide continued its endless back-and-forth between shore and sea. He held a large, chest-like container between his hands, but his movements seemed unhindered by either its size or its weight.

His smile was radiant when their eyes met, in total defiance of the gloom.

Leaping to her feet, Theo ran toward him, heart pounding so rapidly that she felt as though it might burst from her chest. Vasil dropped the container on the beach and held his arms out to her. She slammed into him, embracing him tightly, and he wrapped her in his arms to hold her close. She didn't care that he was soaking wet, or how cold his skin felt against hers because of it; all that mattered was he'd come back. He was safe.

"You scared the shit out of me," she said.

"I am sorry, Theo," he replied, tightening his hold on her. "I had little choice."

Kane's voice was soft through the neural link. *"Um, Theo... there's another one."*

Eyebrows falling low, Theo glanced up.

Another kraken stood in the surf not far behind Vasil. Theo's eyes widened as she took him in; he had to be nearly half again as large as Vasil, with impossibly broad shoulders and thick, powerful muscles. She wouldn't be surprised if he weighed more than three hundred and fifty kilograms. And, as though his size weren't enough, his piercing amber eyes shone with a predatory glint, in stark contrast to his black skin.

Theo drew back from Vasil, keeping her eyes on the larger kraken. "Holy shit..."

Without removing his arms from her, Vasil twisted to glance at the other kraken. "He is Dracchus. Dracchus, she is Theo." He turned his face back to her. "Did I perform the introduction correctly?"

"Huh?" Her understanding of his words came slowly. "Oh, uh, yeah. Vasil, he's very...large."

"Yes," Vasil said.

Dracchus grunted. He also held a container in his arms; Theo guessed it was the same size as Vasil's despite appearing smaller in Dracchus's hold.

"Um, Hi." Theo wiggled her fingers in greeting. She leaned closer to Vasil's ear and whispered, "Why does he look like he wants to rip off my arms and beat me with them?"

Vasil glanced at Dracchus again and tilted his head. "That is just how he looks. Randall suggested it is some sort of medical condition called *RBF*, but he would not elaborate on what it meant."

Theo pressed her lips together to hold in her laughter; she succeeded only in snorting.

Dracchus's brows fell low over his unsettling eyes. "I do not mean you harm, human." His voice was the deepest she'd ever heard — so deep that she wondered if it pained him to speak.

"Good. I wouldn't want to have to hurt *you*," Theo said, smirking. "There's an old saying where I come from: the bigger they are, the harder they fall. And you look like you'd make a crater when you hit the ground."

"I am not sure I like her," Dracchus said.

"She is showing her lack of fear. Is that not what your mate would do?" asked Vasil.

"Humans do not speak that way when they are unafraid," Dracchus replied.

"I'll be honest," said Theo, "you're *terrifying*. But that doesn't mean I wouldn't try getting a few shots in before you grind my bones to a fine dust."

Brow furrowed, Dracchus looked at Vasil for a moment before returning his gaze to Theo. "Why would I grind your bones to dust?"

"Just a saying. *Annnnd* since you don't plan to, we don't need to worry about it." Theo pointed to the container in Dracchus's hands. "What are those for?"

"For holding things," Vasil replied.

"Kane, I believe your sarcasm is rubbing off on Vasil, and I don't know how I feel about that."

"You should feel *thrilled*," Kane said aloud, causing Dracchus's eyes to widen infinitesimally. "He just became that much more interesting."

"That was the computer inside her?" asked Dracchus.

"*Computer* is such a diminishing, impersonal term. My name is Kane."

"It does not sound like Sam or the Computer in the Facility," Dracchus said.

"Unless *you* want to be referred to as *it*, kraken, I suggest you accept that I am not an object to be dehumanized by your lack of consideration."

Dracchus frowned deeply. "It speaks, but not our language."

Theo rolled her eyes. "*He* is not an *it*. It's not that hard to understand."

"It is easy to understand when you say it. Tell your computer to speak plainly, like you."

"I can *obviously* hear you, kraken," Kane said.

"Kane, this is Dracchus. Dracchus, this is Kane," Vasil said. "Are we done now?"

Once again, Dracchus grunted.

"We're *so* not starting off on the right foot — or tentacle," Theo said with a smirk. "Anyway, back to my original question: what are those containers for?"

Vasil removed his arm from Theo, turned to the container he'd set down, and opened it. He removed a small black suit from within. "This is so you can swim with us. The containers are to hold your belongings along the way."

Theo arched a brow. "Looks a little…undersized."

Taking the suit by the shoulders, Vasil held it up in front of her body. It looked perfectly sized — for a six-year-old. "It will accommodate you."

"If you say so," she said, eyeing the suit skeptically. "I assume you found your home, then?"

He nodded. "We will go to the Facility first. The journey to The Watch, where I keep my den, is too long to make in one day."

Turning, Theo looked back, running her gaze over the pod, the circle of stones that served as their fire pit and the wood piled nearby it, and the line she'd put up to hang-dry her clothing. The little camp had become special to her — the place she shared with Vasil, a place of healing.

In many ways, it had been more of a home than anywhere else she'd ever lived.

"We're leaving now?" she asked.

He took her chin between his fingers and guided her face back toward his. "We are not safe here, Theo. We will leave as soon as you are ready."

Theo searched his eyes. Vasil was right. While most of their needs were met here, it wasn't an ideal place to live, and it had been the company that made her time here memorable. The rest was just scrap and sand.

"Okay," she said.

"Is that the pod?" Dracchus asked.

Theo glanced at the big kraken to find him moving inland. Vasil released his gentle hold on her chin as they both turned to watch Dracchus slowly advance on the pod; it reminded Theo of a predatory beast creeping up behind its prey, and the thought of a fierce-looking being like Dracchus stalking an inanimate object nearly made her laugh again.

"So why is he here?" Theo asked.

"In part because he does not trust you," Vasil replied, "but primarily because he *does* trust me. It will be safer to travel with Dracchus along."

Dracchus dropped his container a few meters away from the pod without altering the speed of his cautious approach.

"Well, it could be worse." Theo stepped closer to Vasil and pressed a kiss to his lips. "You didn't trust me at first, either."

Vasil's mouth didn't seem certain whether it wanted to smile or frown. "That seems a lifetime ago."

"Not that long." She gestured at the container on the sand. "Come on, let's see how much we can fit into those."

With a nod, Vasil dropped the suit into the container, closed the lid, and stooped to lift the whole thing into his arms.

Dracchus was examining the exterior of the pod when Theo and Vasil neared him. As Vasil placed his container beside the other, Dracchus lifted one end of the pod up from the sand, revealing the extent of the damage it had suffered on its underside.

"That *is impressive. And rather unsettling,*" Kane said in her mind.

His strength? Theo asked.

"*Not just that, but how effortless it looks for him. Probably best to stay close to Vasil if this Dracchus doesn't fully trust you.*"

"Good idea," she muttered.

"What happened to this?" Dracchus asked, turning his head to look at Theo.

"Debris from the explosion."

"What explosion?"

"I was a crewmember of an IDC battlecruiser, the *CSC Agamemnon.* There was an evacuation alert. I boarded one of the maintenance-level escape pods and was jettisoned into space, and the ship blew up behind me." Theo folded her arms across her chest and held Dracchus's gaze. "You want my full name, rank, and serial number, too?"

Dracchus lowered the pod onto the sand and moved around to its front. "Do you have more than one name like the other humans?" He stopped at the open hatch and grasped the edge of the opening. Rather than pulling himself up, he pulled the whole pod down, angling it to see inside. Some of Theo's belongings clattered and clanked within.

She hurried toward him. "Hey! Be careful!"

Dracchus glanced at her over his shoulder, holding the pod in place — with one hand — for several seconds. Then he slowly released his grasp, returning it to its prior position. He turned to face Theo fully, his face a neutral but surprisingly intimidating mask — likely because she had to look so far up to meet his gaze.

"You have no contact with them?" he asked.

Theo rolled her eyes and looked at Vasil as though to say *really?*

Vasil's expression fell into something darker and more frustrated than she'd seen from him yet. "I already told you, Dracchus."

"I want to hear it from her."

Theo glared at Dracchus as she climbed into the pod. Once she was inside, she turned to face him, bracing her hands on the edge of the opening. "Since *Vasil's* word doesn't seem to be good enough for you, I'll give you mine. I have *no* contact with the IDC. If I did, I would have already called them for a rescue a long time ago. There are no satellites near this planet, and I don't have a signal strong enough to reach them. Happy?"

Dracchus held her gaze unflinchingly; he certainly didn't *look* happy.

Vasil moved up next to Dracchus and put a hand on his arm. "I trust her, Dracchus, as I have told you. She is my mate."

Theo turned her attention to Vasil, eyes flaring. Warmth spread through her chest at the sound of that word — *mate* — and were Dracchus not present, she would have leapt upon Vasil and had her way with him that very moment.

"You made her change color, Vasil," Dracchus said. Though his tone was as flat as ever, the corners of his mouth tipped slightly upward.

Theo chose to ignore his comment, as though that would somehow ease the heat reddening her cheeks. "Oh my God, you *can* smile! I was afraid your face was permanently stuck like that."

Dracchus grunted, and his mouth returned to its prior state. He turned to Vasil. "She is spirited. I have decided I do like her."

Vasil frowned. "I was not seeking your approval, Dracchus."

"And yet you have it," Dracchus replied.

Shaking his head, Vasil collected one of the containers and carried it to the pod, where he held it up for Theo to take. She set the container on the pod's floor, opened it, and pulled out the child-sized diving suit.

"You're wanting me to change into this, right?" she asked.

"Yes," Vasil replied as he raised his body to fill hatch opening. "You cannot wear any clothing beneath, or it will not function properly."

Theo grinned at him. "You just want to see me naked."

"Of course. And I want to make sure *he* does not see."

The possessiveness in his voice produced a flare of heat in her core.

"I have my own mate," Dracchus said from outside.

"That does not matter." Vasil drew himself into the pod and, without looking away from Theo, reached up to grasp the handles on the hatch and pull it closed. His position blocked the window with his back and made the space inside feel suddenly very, very small.

The intensity in his eyes only increased that feeling.

"I guess tight spaces don't bother you anymore, huh?" she asked.

"I have something to distract me."

Theo raised her hands and released the jumpsuit's seal. As the material loosened, she slowly lowered one sleeve to reveal her bare shoulder.

"Think we could squeeze in a quickie?" she teased.

His eyes dipped, gleaming with undisguised want, and his nostrils flared. "Yes. But Dracchus would know."

"So?"

Vasil grinned. "I have missed you, human."

He had no idea what those words did to her; no one had *ever* missed her. She smiled, the heat spreading from her core to consume her entire body, turning into something deeper, something more intense.

Two of his tentacles swept behind her back, drawing her against his body. He lowered his head and captured her mouth, kissing her fiercely, confidently — a far cry from the first, uncertain kiss he'd given her.

Dropping the diving suit, Theo took his face between her hands and returned the kiss with equal fervor. She nipped his lower lip before pulling back to meet his gaze.

A low, rumbling sound vibrated from his chest. "We have a long journey ahead, Theo. It is best we waste no daylight."

"Later then," she said, rubbing her body against his, "so we can take our time." She felt the hard press of his cock against his slit even through her clothing.

"You make an already difficult task nearly impossible, female." Releasing his hold on her, Vasil turned away, tension rippling through the muscles of his back.

Theo stepped forward and kissed between his shoulders. "The wait will be worth it. Besides, I'm sure you're exhausted."

"Never too tired for you," he said over his shoulder.

She laughed. "Keep saying things like that and see how I reward you."

Catching her lower lip in her teeth, she trailed the tip of a finger down his spine. His back arched, and a gentle tremor shook his shoulders. She smiled to herself as she removed her jumpsuit. Once she was naked, she snatched the diving suit off the floor and held it up in both hands.

A blue outline appeared around the suit, and an instant later, Kane highlighted the internal systems, revealing intricate networks of wiring within the material. It all connected to two sets of controls, one at the wrist and one on the chest. A series of model numbers and technical specs scrolled through the corner of her retinal display.

"It's a Tureon Industries Personal Diving System," Kane said aloud, "commissioned by the IDC three hundred and seventy-nine years ago. I'm displaying the model and specs, but I know you're not paying attention. All you need to know is that it will stretch to fit your body."

Theo's brows fell. "Let me get this straight, Kane — you can identify an obscure piece of equipment from four hundred years ago by sight, but you don't have *any* relevant information on survival in your database?"

"Well, it's not like *you* had much relevant information on survival, either," he replied.

Theo bent down and slipped her legs into the suit. The material stretched easily around her body as she tugged it up. Despite how much the material stretched, its fit was comfortable — she'd expected it to constrict her half to death. "Yeah, but you're supposed to be my AI. You know, my *intelligence*."

Kane grumbled. "You left yourself *so* wide open, but...*argh*, I can't be *that* mean to you!"

"Good," Vasil said, "because if you are mean to her, I will find a way to take you out of her body so I can throw you into the sea."

Theo snickered; she enjoyed what she felt in response to Vasil's protectiveness, and she knew he'd never do anything to Kane. Vasil was aware of how much the AI meant to her — not that there was much chance of Kane's systems being removed without killing her. The IDC used extremely sophisticated equipment to install and de-pair AIs.

She pushed her arms into the diving suit's sleeves and brushed her covered fingers over the round device on the chest. The suit immediately sealed, molding to her body like a second skin. "You can turn around now, kraken. Your innocence is safe."

Vasil turned to face her again, dipping his gaze down her body. She followed it with her own. The suit hugged her every curve, and yet somehow wasn't overly revealing.

The smooth wrist piece attached to the suit's arm glowed, and Theo raised her arm.

Kane's voice projected through the wrist piece. "The systems in this suit are almost obnoxiously primitive, but beggars can't be choosers. There should be an accompanying mask. It's required to seal the suit and make it fully operational."

"It is in the container," Vasil said. He stooped down and opened the lid, revealing a curved piece of glass inside.

Theo crouched and picked up the mask. Kane scanned it like it had the suit, displaying a series of connections within the glass that were invisible to her naked eye. Kane considered it primitive, but Theo found the device fascinating. Though it would be little more than a piece of glass to anyone else, she admired the intricacy of its inner workings — even if this sort of tech was outside her area of expertise.

"Is that glow in your eyes because of Kane?" Vasil asked.

"Yeah," she said, setting the mask on the seat. "He can overlay information in my vision."

Vasil's brow furrowed. "What does that mean?"

"Um...well, I guess it's like... He adds images to what I already see. Sometimes it's to point out something I didn't notice, sometimes to give me information on what I'm looking at. With this suit, he's showing me all the internal components that make it work."

"Interesting. I think the masks—"

Several heavy thumps on the outside of the pod interrupted Vasil. He glanced over his shoulder. "We are trying his patience."

Theo chuckled. "I'm sure it's safe to open the hatch now. My naughty bits are covered."

Vasil looked at her again, his eyes roving over her body slowly, down and up, until they met her gaze. "I do not want to share you with *anyone*."

Theo flattened her hand on his chest. Despite the suit covering her hand, she felt the rapid beating of his three hearts beneath her palm. "You're it for me, kraken."

He covered her hand with his own and held it for several moments, stroking her lightly with his fingers. Only when Dracchus banged on the pod again did Vasil release her and open the hatch.

"I know what it is like to desire your mate, Vasil, but we are wasting light," Dracchus said.

Vasil straightened. "We did not—"

"We're packing up," Theo said, placing a hand on Vasil's arm as she stepped forward to look down at Dracchus. "Shouldn't take very long. I want to make sure we bring as much as we can because I don't think we're going to find any replacements on this planet."

Vasil retrieved the other container and worked beside her to fill them with as many supplies as possible — the first aid kit, rations, blanket, clothing, blaster, water filtration containers, and, finally, her toolbox. Only a ration pack and a water-gel pouch remained.

"They're waterproof, right? Airtight?" she asked as they closed and sealed the chests.

"Yes," Vasil replied. "We use them often to transport items between The Watch and the Facility."

"I'd ask how you could haul these things over long distances," Theo said, flicking her gaze toward Dracchus, "but that'd be a dumb question."

"It is not enjoyable, especially on long journeys, but we will manage." Vasil lifted the first container onto the lip of the opening and passed it to Dracchus, who set it down on the sand. The second container followed a few moments later.

At Vasil's insistence, she ate the ration pack — it was a bit more flavorful than the bar, but not by much — and swallowed the water-gel. When she finished, it was time to leave. Theo picked up the diving glass mask and cast one last look around the pod. The memory of them sitting side-by-side with the storm raging outside rose to the forefront of her mind. They'd grown so close since that night — closer than she'd been to anyone. It had been the best night of her life.

She turned to Vasil and smiled. "I'm ready."

They made their way to the water, with Vasil remaining

nearby Theo. The tide came in, sweeping past her calves, but she felt none of its chill. After tugging the diving suit's hood into place and tucking her hair inside, she lifted the mask to her face. She heard — and felt — a faint hum as the mask attached, sealing with the material of the hood. The hum spread across her skin, creating the odd sensation that the suit wasn't actually touching her anymore.

"Hi!" said a cheerful, unfamiliar voice. "I'm Sam, your System—"

"Shut up," Kane muttered. His voice seemed to come from an audio system within the suit. "Sorry, Theodora. I was a bit slow in establishing control of the suit's systems."

"So that's the Sam Vasil was talking about," Theo said.

"Yes, the *system assistant and monitor*. An artificial intelligence so primitive and undeveloped that I cannot rightly attribute any *intelligence* to it."

"Come on, Kane, no need to be so rude. He's pretty much your great-great-great grandpa, isn't he?" Her eyes flicked to Vasil, who was staring at her with mild confusion on his face. "What?"

"Nothing," he replied, shaking his head. "I am sure if I ask what the two of you are talking about I will only become further confused."

Theo frowned. "You can't hear him in this?"

"It projects your voice while you are in the air, but he is not projecting his."

"Oh."

"See. Primitive," Kane remarked.

"You *just* spoke through the wrist piece a few minutes ago, Kane. I *know* you can do it again if you wanted," Theo said.

"Why go through unnecessary trouble?"

"I imagine Kane is simply being...Kane?" Vasil asked.

"You got that right," Theo said.

A faint smile touched his lips, but it faded a moment later.

He brushed a tentacle against her leg. "We will not be able to speak to one another when we are in the water. Dracchus will swim at the lead, and I will swim behind you. Watch for any signals from him."

Theo nodded. "Okay."

"It will be a long journey. If you tire, I will carry you so you may rest. Just signal to me."

Theo smiled and caressed his cheek. "I got this, kraken."

CHAPTER 13

"I so do *not got* this," Theo rasped as she pushed onward. Sweat trickled down her face, and every muscle in her body screamed in absolute agony. Everything was dark and distorted; all she could do was focus on the soft glow around Dracchus, who swam ahead of her, and force her arms and legs to move. She was flagging, and she knew he'd slowed his pace so she could keep up, but she couldn't allow herself to even consider stopping.

If she stopped, she wasn't sure she'd be able to move ever again.

"You're in peak physical condition, Theo. You can do this. I believe in you." Kane's total lack of enthusiasm was not lost on Theo.

"You suck at encouragement," she spat. "Peak physical condition? The most exercise I've had before this was carrying around my toolbox and crawling through access ducts."

"But you were *great* at those things. Shouldn't that apply to this, too?"

"Says the one who doesn't have a body."

"Attacking me over things I can't control, are you? You've stooped to a new low, Theodora Velenti."

"If I had the extra strength, I'd roll my eyes at you right—Ow! *Ow!*"

Sharp pain shot down the back of her right leg her hamstring and calf seized simultaneously. Tears stung her eyes as she reached down to grasp her thigh, halting her forward momentum.

"Oh, fuck! Oh, fuck! Fuck!" She sucked in rapid breaths as though they could alleviate the agony.

"I *could* be wrong, but my analysis indicates you may be suffering from a leg cramp," Kane said.

She dug her fingers into her leg. "No shit, you jerk."

Vasil was suddenly there with her, his stripes creating an aura of light around him in the dark water. He passed the container to his tentacles and moved his hands to her thigh. His strong fingers massaged her hamstring, gradually fighting back the stiffness and pain. He worked his hands lower and lower, frowning all the while, and when he reached her ankle, his fingers trailed back up again.

The pain wasn't completely gone, but it was far more tolerable thanks to his attention. She met his concerned gaze and thanked him; he nodded as though he'd understood, though she knew her voice hadn't been projected out of the suit.

Shifting the container back to his hands, he wrapped two of his tentacles around her waist and guided her behind him. She looped her arms around his neck and her legs around his middle gratefully, pressing herself against his back. Even after wriggling to find a position that didn't threaten to cause another cramp, the muscles of her left leg continued to throb and ache, refusing to relax.

Vasil removed his tentacles from her waist and dipped his chin to place a kiss on her arm before propelling himself forward.

Theo tightened her hold; he was like a space ship taking off, moving with a burst of speed she hadn't thought possible from an organic being under water. Each time his momentum faltered, he flared out his tentacles and snapped them together again, creating a fresh surge. The rhythm of it was odd but steady. That predictability gave her something to focus on besides her pain.

Theo rested her head against the back of Vasil's neck. The journey had been exciting when it started, even pleasant. If swimming in the stream had been enjoyable, swimming in the ocean — being able to stay below indefinitely and *see* everything — was on a whole new level. She'd never imagined there could be so many different creatures in the water, or that the sea floor could be so varied and interesting.

But time had chugged on, and Theo's body, unaccustomed to the motions of swimming, had protested the exertion with increasing vehemence. She wasn't sure now how long they'd been at it — hours and hours, at least, as the sun had gone down some time ago. Kane could have told her, but Theo didn't want to know; she guessed the information would only make her *more* tired.

Stopping had *already* made her more tired; once her muscles had received a taste of rest, they'd decided to rebel. They were on strike — no more swimming until they'd been compensated with at least a week of bedrest. She wasn't sure how she was maintaining her hold on Vasil, and that uncertainty was the only thing keeping her weary eyes open; she could imagine falling asleep, losing her grip, and drifting into the darkness to be swallowed up by the sea forevermore.

She realized that the light ahead had intensified. She lifted her head to look forward, and her eyes widened. Dark shapes lurked in the gloom — buildings on the sea floor. She could see two of them clearly, but there were more beyond, all connected by tube-like tunnels. Light glowed from some of the windows, and light fixtures on the exterior walls created cones of illumination at regular intervals.

"You seeing this, Kane?" she asked.

"Yes, I am."

Dracchus swam toward the nearest building, and Vasil followed. All Theo could do was hold on and stare in wonder — not because these structures were marvels of engineering, but because they *existed*. If she'd harbored any doubts about Vasil's story, this place would've crushed them. Humans had been to this planet, and they'd been serious about it. The IDC didn't build places like this for no reason.

They swam between a pair of light posts that stood on the ocean floor; in Theo's imagination, they were the end — or perhaps the beginning — of a long pathway of lights that led all the way back to land. This was the finish line of the race she hadn't realized she was running — or rather, *swimming*.

Dracchus led them to a door on the side of the building over which glowed a single red light. He shifted his container to one arm, supporting it from beneath with a tentacle.

"The transmission range of this place's systems is extremely limited, but I can access them from here, if you'd like," Kane said.

"Go ahead," Theo replied.

"Access granted."

Just as Dracchus was reaching for the keypad beside the doorframe, the red light turned green, and the door slid open. He pulled his arm back and turned his head toward Theo, frowning.

She shrugged and winced at the ache in her shoulders.

The trio entered the chamber beyond the doorway together, with Theo still clinging to Vasil's back. She felt his muscles tense once they were fully inside. She smoothed her hand over his chest, letting him know without words that she was there. The brush of a tentacle on her knee told her he understood.

"He's going to push the button to close the door," Kane said, calling Theo's attention to Dracchus, who was now behind them. "Should I beat him to it?"

Theo grinned. "Do it."

Dracchus extended his arm, moving his hand toward a button on the wall, but the door slid shut before he pressed the button. His hand stilled. Slowly, he turned his head to glare at Theo over his shoulder.

She barely held in her laughter as she mouthed *what?* to him.

A strange pulse swept through the water, and the entire room seemed to vibrate gently. It took Theo a few moments to realize that the water was draining. Her body felt a little heavier with each passing moment, steadily increasing the ache in her limbs.

When the water level dipped below Theo's chin, Vasil spread his tentacles over the floor, anchoring himself in place, and stooped to set down the container. He rose and took hold of her wrists, gently breaking her hold on his neck.

Her arms fell to her sides, dangling like clubs she was too weak to swing. Fortunately, she was still buoyant enough in the water that she didn't have to put weight on her aching legs. Vasil turned to face her and looped a steadying tentacle around her waist.

She patted his tentacle, smiled, and sagged toward him. "Thanks."

He caught her upper arms in his hands and stiffened the tentacle at her waist to stop her fall. Once she was stable, he cupped the back of her head with one hand. "Are you all right, Theo? Have you been injured?"

"Just completely exhausted. I don't even know if I can stand upright."

"I will help you. There are rooms inside with beds where you may rest."

Theo smirked. "Oh, I'll be crashing, that's for sure."

"Do you want me to release the seal on the mask?" Kane asked.

"God, yes. I am so ready to be out of this thing."

The faint tingling that had coursed over her skin for the entire trip subsided as the mask hissed softly and sagged away from the hood. Vasil removed his hand from the back of her head and caught the mask as it fell.

Theo took in several long, deep breaths. The air wasn't much better in here than it had been in the suit, but it was almost *familiar* to her, calling to mind the recycled air she'd breathed for more than half her life on board various interstellar ships.

Vasil carefully pulled back her hood, lightly combing the tips of his claws through her hair. The gesture soothed her, and she leaned her cheek against his chest, relishing the feel of his skin despite it being wet.

"Mmm, that feels good," she said, closing her eyes.

"Pressurization normalized," a feminine voice said once the water was completely drained. It was followed by the sound of a lock disengaging and the slide of a metal door.

"Who's that?" Theo asked, lifting her head and opening her eyes.

"The AI of this facility," Kane said through the suit's wrist piece. "A step up from Sam, but not by much."

Vasil followed Theo's gaze toward the ceiling with his own as his hand smoothed down her back. "*Computer* is the only name we have for her. She holds all the information in this place. She is the main reason our people have continued to speak your language."

"Interesting..." Theo said. Her mind raced, battling her weariness; how much information did this computer contain? How many files could Theo and Kane uncover about the IDC's operation here, about their goals, about the kraken?

"Come," Vasil said softly, moving to her side. He bent down and opened the container, tossing the mask inside. After sealing the lid, he picked the container up, holding it against his middle, and guided Theo toward the interior doorway.

His tentacle remained around her waist — it was the only thing keeping her on her feet. Her legs moved only out of muscle memory, powered by a reserve of strength she hadn't known she possessed.

They entered a long corridor. Some of the overhead lights along the hall flickered, but the place was in surprisingly good shape considering its age. Though it was somewhat dated aesthetically, this could be the interior of any ship in space, and there was something comforting about that. The only thing throwing off that feel was the slight curvature of the floor, which undoubtedly had been designed to allow any excess water to flow to the drainage grooves running on either side of the main walkway.

The strange, soft slithering sound of tentacles on the floor behind Theo signaled that Dracchus followed as they moved down the hall, but her neck was too sore for her to bother looking back.

"The accommodations here are quite luxurious, compared to a typical military base," Kane said through an unseen overhead speaker, his voice carrying through the hallway.

Vasil halted abruptly, tipping his head back to search the ceiling as though he'd see Kane crawling on it like a spider.

"I suppose it was because of the private interests involved," Kane continued. "When you have a staff of scientists and researchers working on what may be one of the most valuable resources available to man, I suppose you want to keep them comfortable."

Theo shook her head. "Someone couldn't wait to be nosey."

Dracchus stopped immediately behind Theo and growled.

Though he did not touch her, his presence was stifling. "How is he speaking through the Facility?"

Before Theo could react, Vasil had tossed his container down, spun to face Dracchus, and swept Theo behind him, placing himself between her and the bigger kraken. "Back away from her, Dracchus."

"She needs to answer, Vasil. This is our home. We cannot allow such things to happen without explanation."

Theo placed her hands on Vasil's back. His tense muscles twitched beneath her palms. "Vasil, it's okay. Calm down."

"She is *mine*," Vasil said, not looking away from Dracchus. "I will tolerate *no* threat to her, no matter how small."

A thrill swept through Theo at Vasil's words — his *claim*.

Dracchus grunted. "Then let her explain. How is your computer speaking through the Facility?"

Theo massaged Vasil's back in a vain attempt to ease his tension before stepping around him. She inserted herself between the two kraken. She wasn't threatened by Dracchus — if he'd meant to harm her, he would have, and Vasil would never have brought her into this situation if he truly feared for her safety.

Vasil tightened the tentacle around her waist and settled a hand upon her shoulder.

"Kane?" she prompted.

"It's quite simple, really," Kane said from above. "All implanted AI of my generation are equipped with wireless transmitters and receivers to broadcast and receive information, primarily through the networks used and maintained by the IDC. These networks are typically—"

"He can connect to other electronics through the air," Theo said. "Basically, he can talk to anything else that has a computer, as long as it has the capability to send and receive signals."

Dracchus's brows fell low. "And this is…all invisible?"

"To us, yes. Not to Kane."

"This Facility is quite outdated," Kane said. "All of its security is long expired under IDC regulations, even the protection on the top-secret data, meaning I do not require clearance to access any function of this Facility."

"Look," Theo said, lifting her hands to waist level, palms up, "I know you don't trust us, but we really wouldn't do anything to hurt you or the rest of the kraken. And Kane would never do *anything* that would endanger my life. If you have questions about anything the IDC did here, Kane can access that information for you."

"While we are here, we will help in whatever way we can," Kane said.

Dracchus's frown, which seemed to be a permanent fixture on his face, deepened slightly, and he studied Theo for a long while. Finally, he nodded.

Vasil lingered in place for another moment before guiding Theo to turn around. He collected the container and continued down the corridor alongside her, holding her a little tighter, a little closer, than before.

"Speaking of endangering," Kane said through the neural link, *"there are some concerning results to the preliminary diagnostics I've run."*

What's wrong? she asked.

"The most concerning matter is that there's something off with the air filtration and reclamation system. I'll need a little more time to run full tests. I don't want to alarm anyone yet, but there may be a component failure in the near future."

Are we safe?

"Yes. I will look into it, and we'll talk after you get some rest, if you want."

Thank you, Kane. Do what you need to do and let me know.

She trudged onward beside Vasil, forcing her legs to move; walking was no easier than it had been when she first arrived, but her body adjusted to the strain of it well enough to numb her to the pain. They wound through a few similar-looking corridors, passed several signs denoting different specialized rooms, and finally entered a tunnel with large windows looking out into the dark water. Seeing the metal walls of the next building, cast in white light amidst the darkness, made her think of space.

How many times had she seen views like this on starships and space stations? Just a bunch of metal set in a fathomless patch of nothingness, less than a speck in the eyes of the universe.

She suddenly found herself missing the little stretch of beach she'd shared with Vasil. It'd had its discomforts, its dangers, but it had been warm, alive, and beautiful — a little slice of paradise she'd never known she wanted.

The tunnel led them into the next building, designated the *CABINS* by the sign near the entry.

The difference was immediate when they turned down the first hallway; everything was a little smoother here, a little less rigid. The lines and contours of the walls were more pleasing, and even the coloring was subtly warmer. After a short trip down the hallway, that coloring became vibrant; countless paintings adorned the walls, ranging from intricate patterns to almost photo-realistic depictions of plants, the ocean, and strange animals the likes of which Theo had never seen.

"These were done by Arkon and Aymee," Vasil said.

Theo started and turned her head toward him. She hadn't realized she'd stopped to look at the paintings until he'd spoken. She *really* needed to get some sleep.

"They're beautiful," she said.

Dracchus moved past her and continued down the hall, stopping a few doors down. He glanced back at Theo. "My mate, Larkin, prepared this den for you." Shifting his container to one arm and a tentacle, he pressed a button on the wall, opening the door before him.

Theo and Vasil moved down the hall to join Dracchus.

She peered into the room, and her brows nearly touched her hairline. "This…is ours? All of this?"

"Yes," Vasil replied. "Ours."

His tentacle slipped away as Theo crossed the threshold and gazed around in awe. Though the room she'd had in that last orphanage had been furnished with fancier décor, this place was even better. It was larger than the apartment she'd lived in with her mother, and even if the furnishings weren't top-of-the-line, they looked practical. Either way, this was a far cry from the cramped bunks she'd shared with other IDC crewmen on-ship and the tiny, often dark rooms she'd slept in while living with Malcolm.

Hell, just this bed alone was awe-inspiring — it looked like it could fit two people comfortably, maybe four if they squeezed together. *And* there was another door in the corner leading to a *private* bathroom; she'd *never* had her own bathroom. She hurried over to it.

"Oh my God, is that a *shower*?" she asked, looking at Vasil over her shoulder.

He set the container on the floor at the foot of the bed and turned to her, smiling. "Yes. The other humans are fond of them."

"They enjoy the hot water," Dracchus said as he entered the room and placed his container beside the first. "I do not understand why it is so important, but I will not deny my mate her enjoyment of it."

"Oh, you *know* I'm about to enjoy the shit out of it," Theo said, running her fingers over the circular control at her chest. The diving suit sagged. "Right after I take a long-overdue piss."

She yanked her arms free and shoved the suit down her body as she hurried into the bathroom. It didn't matter how hungry and tired she was, or that her legs could collapse beneath her at any moment. There was *hot water,* and she *needed* to empty her abused bladder.

"Dracchus, out," Vasil shouted behind her.

Dracchus grunted in response, and a moment later, the door *whooshed* closed.

Vasil's hearts thumped, and his muscles were stiff with tension. He turned back toward the bathroom only after Dracchus had exited the room and the door was shut. For kraken, nudity had never been an issue — it was simply their natural state of being. Clothing could be a hindrance in water, and the usefulness of their innate camouflage far outweighed any benefits a piece of clothing could offer. Despite that, the thought of another male seeing his mate bared was unacceptable to Vasil. He'd not realized her lack of inhibition regarding her body could be problematic until now; she was for *him* only, and *he* cared about who saw her even if she did not.

Theo had already climbed into the shower stall and closed the glass door. She turned on the water and moaned in pleasure as it cascaded over her chest. Billowing steam filled the air, fogging the glass and, frustratingly, hindering his view of her.

He moved into the bathroom, hoping to see more, but the steam was too obscuring. It reduced Theo to a blurred image, hands on the wall beneath the shower nozzle and head bowed to let the spray run over her hair and body.

"Oh, this is *good.*" She moaned again; her throaty sounds were similar to those she sometimes made during sex.

Vasil's blood heated, but he allowed himself to move no closer to Theo. He was exhausted — he'd spent two days traveling between the pod and the Facility without rest, leaving his muscles rubbery and uncertain. More importantly, *she* was exhausted. She'd been leaning on him rather heavily after they entered the Facility, and he knew she'd pushed her body to its limits well before their arrival.

Caring for his mate went well beyond their couplings; she needed food, water, and rest.

He forced himself out of the bathroom, casting a last glance over his shoulder at her indistinct figure before turning his attention to more pressing matters.

A table with a pair of chairs stood against one wall in the main room, and Larkin had left a tray with fresh fruit, cheese, and several strips of smoked fish atop it. He would have to thank her and Dracchus for their thoughtfulness later.

He took one of the glasses from the table and filled it with cold water at the bathroom sink. If Theo noticed him enter again, she made no indication; she remained in the same position she'd been in when he left, hands pressed to the wall. The ventilation system had kicked on, sucking most of the steam out of the air through an opening on the ceiling.

After placing the glass of water beside the food tray, he went to the upright box of drawers — he believed the human term was *dresser* — and checked its contents. Clothing of varying colors and materials, all neatly packed and folded, filled the drawers. He hoped Theo would be happy having something to wear other than form-fitting body suits, even if *he* preferred to see all her delectable curves accentuated as often as possible.

Now that he thought about it more, perhaps it would be best if she wore baggy, ill-fitting clothing whenever there was a chance of anyone else seeing her.

No...she is beautiful, and everyone will know it. She should not be hidden.

"I am being a jealous male," he muttered as he turned away from the dresser.

"There's nothing wrong with a little jealousy," Kane said softly through an unseen speaker. "It means you will fight all the harder to protect her. So long as you keep in mind that she is not a *thing* for you to possess, I don't see a problem."

Vasil frowned, unable to keep himself from glancing up in search of the source of Kane's voice. For as long as he could remember, only the Computer had spoken through the Facility in such a fashion. There had been ghosts — *holograms* — summoned from time to time, all of which spoke with their own voices, but they were always isolated things, so real and immediate that it almost seemed as though they could be touched. Kane was disembodied and seemed to permeate the whole place. Did he see all, hear all?

"I know she is not a *thing*," Vasil replied. "We have chosen each other, given ourselves over to each other. She *is* mine as much as I am hers." He moved to the foot of the bed and spread his tentacles, easing himself down.

Kane did not immediately respond; the only sound in the room was that of running water from the shower — a steady spray accompanied by heavier splatters as it ran off Theo's body and hit the floor.

"Will she be safe here, kraken?" Kane asked.

"Why do you ask with that tone?"

"I have seen surveillance footage I find somewhat alarming."

"I do not know some of those words," Vasil said, furrowing his brow.

"Images captured by cameras in this facility. I've seen much of what's happened here between humans and kraken."

"That was from long ago," Vasil said. "She is safe."

"Some of it was not that long ago — about two years, to be exact. That's hardly a long time. It took place only a few corridors away from here. I'm sure you remember, as you were there."

Vasil's mind flashed back to the battle against Neo and the exiled kraken who'd come back to murder the humans; the hallway had already been a bloody mess by the time Vasil arrived, and he'd added more blood to it. "It was a long time ago for us. We have moved on since then. I will not be dishonest and tell you everything is perfect, but the hatred our people held for humans has passed. I fought to defend the humans who'd come to live with us."

"I only want her safe."

"Her safety is the main reason I brought her here, Kane."

The computer made a sighing sound. "I know you would not knowingly place Theo in danger. I just…worry for her."

The flow of water ceased, and Vasil listened as the shower door opened. Theo's feet padded across the floor. She emerged from the bathroom a few moments later, skin pinkened by the hot water and damp hair loose around her shoulders, clad only in a towel.

She smiled as she approached Vasil. "I'll be using *that* often."

When she reached him, she brushed her hand over his jaw. Her touch was warm, but before he could lean into it, she pulled away and sat on the edge of the bed. With a groan, she flopped onto her back.

Theo stretched her arms to the sides. "I don't think I'm going to be able to get back up."

"You should." Vasil's eyes dipped to her thighs; her towel had ridden up to reveal more of her soft, pale flesh, flooding him with desire. He clenched his jaw for a moment to swallow down that craving, well aware of how quickly it could consume him. "There is food and water; eat and drink before we sleep."

She grunted, forcing herself to sit up. "What kind of food?"

He met her gaze, and the sight of her face allowed him to quell his desire; though she was as beautiful as ever, the dark circles under her half-lidded eyes were a stark reminder of how tired they both were.

Vasil rose and moved to the table, collecting the food tray in one hand and the glass of water in the other before returning to her. He held the laden tray to her in offering. "This kind."

"I think I just orgasmed in my mouth."

His brows lifted, and Vasil opened his mouth to reply, but he found no words.

Theo plucked a piece of cheese from the tray. "Is this cheese? *Real* cheese?" She tossed it into her mouth before Vasil could answer and moaned, closing her eyes.

Once again, the sound *was* like those she made when she was climaxing. It only heightened his confusion, given what she'd just said. Was it possible for such a thing to happen in a human's mouth? Was *that* why they were so fond of kissing?

Theo opened her eyes and laughed. "You should see your face right now."

"I am far more content seeing yours." He tilted his head. "Can you really…?"

She laughed harder and shook her head. "No. It's just…so good. Think of it as…over-stimulation of the senses. Everything is just *more*. It's just an expression."

"I understand." He set the tray down on the bed beside her and passed her the glass. Once she'd accepted it, he plucked a strip of fish from the tray and took a bite.

Theo ate quickly, though her soft sighs and moans suggested she was enjoying the tastes despite her speed. Before long, she'd eaten most of the food and emptied her water.

Vasil took the tray and the empty glass back to the table. When he turned back toward Theo, she was already laying on her side with her head on a pillow, the covers drawn halfway down the bed with her feet tucked beneath them— as though she couldn't have been bothered to cover herself any further.

His eyes swept along her bare thighs and up to the markings on her arm before settling on her face. Her eyelids were shut.

Frowning, he moved to the other side of the bed and pulled the covers down the rest of the way. He climbed on beside her, wrapped her in his arms and tentacles, and drew her back against his chest. He released his hold on her only long enough to pull the bedding over their bodies.

She sighed softly and covered one of his arms with her own, curling her fingers over the webbing between his fingers.

"Will you be happy with a human mate?" she asked sleepily.

Vasil pressed a gentle kiss to the hair atop her head. It took him a moment to realize that she'd fallen asleep immediately after her question. He brushed his nose over her temple and laid his head down, inhaling her scent.

"I already am," he said softly, holding her tighter.

CHAPTER 14

THEO'S BODY FELT LIKE ONE BIG BRUISE WHEN SHE WOKE. SHE
stretched and groaned softly, only to still with the sudden realization that she wasn't reclining on a seat in the pod but lying
on a large, comfortable bed in the embrace of a large, cuddly
kraken.

Smiling, she opened her eyes. A small illuminated strip on
the wall over the bathroom doorway provided the only light in
the room, glowing just brightly enough for her to see the
furnishings in fuzzy shades of black and gray. She tilted her
head back and looked at Vasil's face. His eyes were closed, his
features relaxed in sleep. He didn't react when she lifted a hand
and brushed her fingers along his jaw.

Heat radiated from his body, and hers absorbed it greedily.
The towel she'd gone to bed wearing had come undone some-
time as she slept, allowing their bodies to touch without barriers. She loved the feel of his soft, velvety skin against hers, and
at that moment, she wanted nothing more than to run her
hands all over him.

She shifted, brushing her hardening nipples against his chest
while carefully disentangling one of his tentacles from around

her hips. Vasil stirred, inhaling deeply, and his tentacle curled on itself before sliding to the side. Unmoving, Theo watched him settle back into a restful sleep.

Theo ran a hand down his abdomen with the lightest of touches, drifting over ridges of muscle until she reached his pelvis. Her smiled widened; his slit was partially open. Dipping her fingertips inside to gather his natural lubrication, she danced her fingers along the edges of his slit and over the tip of his cock, caressing him and coaxing his slit to open wider.

Vasil groaned, his body tensing as his cock extruded into her waiting hand. She curled her fingers around it. He sucked in a sharp breath and moved to sit up.

"Theo?" His husky voice rumbled straight to her core.

"Shh." She slid her body down along his without releasing his shaft, pressing a hand to his chest to guide him back onto the mattress. "Let me love you."

Theo settled herself on the bed between his tentacles. They writhed to either side of her, a few coiling loosely around her calves and ankles. She held Vasil's gaze as she lowered her head and took his cock into her mouth. His hips jerked, sending him deeper, and she closed her lips around his shaft, sucking. He was too large to take in entirely, but she used her hand at his base, pumping along with the up-and-down glide of her mouth.

Vasil released a low moan and tipped his head back. One of his hands moved to her head, claws grazing her scalp as he slipped his fingers into her hair. The tendrils at the base of his shaft brushed her hand on each of its downward motions, growing a little stronger, a little more eager, with each passing moment. She settled her free hand on his pelvis, using her fingers and thumb to tease and caress the tendrils. His salty-sweet taste delighted her tongue, but she craved more.

One of his tentacles slipped between her legs, brushing over her inner thighs. A moment later, its tip brushed along her folds and dipped in. The tentacle moved back and forth, stroking her clit, and she hummed her pleasure around his cock.

Vasil's fingers flexed, but he didn't tighten his hold on her hair, nor did he scratch her scalp. He groaned again.

"My mate," he growled low. His hips gyrated in time with the movement of her mouth, and his tentacles writhed around her, giving little suction cup kisses to every centimeter of her skin.

Theo quickened her motions, sucking him harder, deeper. Her hips undulated against his tentacle, her exhalations coming out as soft moans.

His shaft swelled an instant before he came. She pulled back just enough to keep her mouth locked around his tip and swallowed his release while continuing pumping her fist, milking him for everything he had.

He removed his fingers from her hair, grasping a fistful of the bedding with each hand. The sound of fabric tearing only urged her on. His hips rose off the bed as his entire body tensed, and he released a harsh, guttural growl, raw with pleasure.

"*Theo!*"

She withdrew only when his tension ebbed, and his hips fell to the bed. She had time to offer him a smug smile before his hands fell to her waist and a pair of his tentacles wrapped around her thighs. Theo yelped as he lifted her, spreading her thighs to either side of his head and pressing his lips to her open sex.

His mouth and tongue took over where his tentacle had begun.

Theo gasped as an overwhelming blast of pleasure struck her, slamming palms against the wall for stability. "Oh, *fuck!*"

Ripples of excitement swept through her, each hitting a bit stronger than the last, lifter her closer and closer to that euphoric peak to which only Vasil could bring her. She bit her lip and tilted her head back, grinding against his talented tongue.

Vasil moaned beneath her. He squeezed her ass, his powerful hands pinning her in place against his mouth. His tongue stroked over her flesh, stroked *inside* her, spearing her repeatedly — just as she longed for his cock to do. She was teetering on the edge, desperately holding on, when he closed his lips over her clit and sucked.

Theo came hard and released a series of cries which steadily grew in volume. Liquid heat flooded her, and Vasil lapped it up, licking her core as though no other taste could satisfy his hunger.

Body quivering, she dropped a hand from the wall to caress his head. *"Vasil."*

Before she realized what was happening, Vasil flipped her, throwing her face down on the bedding. He grasped her hips and lifted her ass in the air, tentacles spreading her thighs to expose her sex, which still trembled with the aftermath of her last climax. Vasil thrust his cock into her, their combined secretions easing his entry.

Theo gasped, clenching the bedding in her hands as the air fled her lungs. His pelvis pressed against her backside, and his shaft filled her, stretched her near to bursting, touching every wonderful nerve ending inside her to send jolts of delight through her body. The tendrils at the base of his shaft only strengthened the sensation with their insistent stroking. Over her sex and ass.

"You are *mine*, Theo," he snarled as he drew his hips back and slammed into her again, beginning a powerful, frantic rhythm. His hands and tentacles guided her movements, pulling her backward to meet his every thrust, keeping her thighs parted, leaving her to focus on only the all-consuming bliss of their coupling. "You are *my* fallen star."

"*Yes,*" Theo breathed, shifting her knees and propping herself on her hands to push back against him and deepen his entry; she needed *more*. "Yours. All yours."

He didn't stop, didn't slow; his pace only increased, quickening their ragged breaths and the racing of Theo's heart. Vasil seemed to permeate her entire body. She felt him everywhere; over her, around her, within her.

One of his tentacles moved up the front of her thighs to settle over her mound. A suction cup caught her clit, sucking and massaging the swollen bud. That was all it took to rocket her to a new peak. Her sex clenched around him as the sensation blasted her through the stratosphere, leaving her to drift through stars of a million impossible colors. She came with a choked cry, arms giving out beneath her as pleasure took away any control she might once have claimed over her own body.

Vasil tightened his grip on her, and his thrusts became erratic. He slammed her against him one more time, burying himself as deep as he could go, and his seed filled her like liquid fire. His hips bucked against her ass as he roared through a release even more intense than his first.

He leaned over her, wrapping an arm around her middle. He settled a hand over her breast — the glide of his palm against her nipple sending another ripple of pleasure through her — and held her close. He continued to rock his hips as though unwilling to let the sensations fade.

They both came down gradually from the heights of their pleasure, their ragged, heavy breaths filling the room. His tentacles lazily caressed her legs and hips as the tendrils around his cock brushed over her sex, sending delightful little pulses through her.

Vasil hummed and pressed his lips to her shoulder, trailing kisses toward the crook of her neck.

"I would not object to being woken this way every morning," he murmured.

Theo laughed, which only enhanced the feel of him inside her; they simultaneously released low, throaty sounds.

"Me neither," she said.

The pad of his finger traced a circle around her nipple. "I will remember for next time."

Tentacles guiding her legs along with his movements, Vasil leaned upright, withdrew from her, and lay down on his back. As he did, he turned her around to face him and eased her down atop him, entering her once more — this time slowly. Once his shaft was buried deep, he wrapped Theo in his arms and drew her close, winding his tentacles around her legs.

Theo laid her cheek against his chest, listening to the beating of his hearts. He ran one hand gently up and down her back while the other smoothed over her hair.

For a moment, Theo was speechless. This was...*cuddling*. The narrow seats in the pod would have made this difficult, but this bed was *perfect*; too perfect. So perfect that her eyes misted with tears.

How much had she longed for this, for this closeness, for this sense of security? To have someone care about her? She'd gone without as a child, when she needed to feel those things the most, and had told herself as an adult that she didn't need them at all. And now...

She didn't know what she'd do if she lost him.

Theo sniffled, unable to keep the tears from falling.

Vasil's hands stilled.

"You are crying," he said softly.

"No, I'm not." Her traitorous voice was thick with emotion.

"You are. What is wrong?"

"I'm not crying."

"Then you are... What is the word? *Drooling*? All over me."

She gently smacked his side. "I am not!"

He moved a hand to her chin and made her look at him. Fresh tears flowed down onto his hand.

"Tell me what is wrong, Theo."

"I love you," she blurted.

His eyes gleamed their impossible, beautiful silver, and his lips slowly turned up into a smile; the way his face brightened reminded her of the radiance of a sunrise, but his expression was more captivating than anything she'd ever seen in the sky.

Vasil shifted his palm to her cheek and brushed away her tears with his thumb. "Then why do you cry?"

"Because I'm scared. I've only felt something vaguely like this once, but it wasn't…wasn't nearly as strong as what I feel for you, and I lost him."

He stared into her eyes, his smile softening a little. "I love you, too, Theo."

Her heart leapt, and her tears came in earnest. Vasil pulled her against him and stroked her back soothingly, but she could only cling to him and cry harder.

"I fear losing you constantly," he said. "I have always been aware of how dangerous Halora is, but it is all the more terrifying now that you are here. I will do *everything* in my power to keep you safe…and to be with you always."

Somehow, her love for him grew in that moment. She didn't know how this kraken, who'd declared her *his* from the moment he saw her, had forced his way into her heart so quickly, but she knew he was there to stay.

She sniffled again, rubbing her wet cheek against his velvety chest.

"No more crying, Theo."

She hiccupped. "I said I wasn't crying."

Vasil chuckled; the light shaking of his body reminded her that his cock, still quite erect, was inside her. The motion sent fresh ripples of pleasure through her.

"You do not need to feel shame with me, Theodora. You are mine, and I am yours. We are as one." His shaft pulsed inside her, and the tendrils around its base stroked her flesh. "Shall I provide you a distraction from your thoughts for a while longer?"

Vasil gyrated his hips slowly, creating just enough friction against her inner walls and her clit to rekindle the fire in her belly.

Theo pressed her lips together. "Mmm."

"Is everything all right, Theo?" Kane asked from the unseen speakers in the room. "I know you were…engaged, earlier, but you seem to be in distress."

She gasped, eyes rounding as she lifted her head. "Fine, Kane."

Vasil increased the pace of his thrusts, fingertips and tentacles caressing her from head to toe, lighting up her entire body.

"Are you sure?" Kane asked. "Because it seemed like you were—"

"*Tentacular penetration!*" Her words ended in a cry as Vasil's movements catapulted her toward another climax.

"Oh. I see. I suppose—"

"*Kane!*" Vasil growled.

"Right. Goodbye."

Vasil cupped the back of Theo's head and pulled her face close to his. "Your cries are for my ears only, Theodora." He captured her mouth in a deep, soul-searing kiss.

CHAPTER 15

Theo scowled as she skimmed through the hundreds — *thousands* — of files Kane had uncovered. There were holographic videos, audio logs, and more documents than she could read in her lifetime, all detailing the operations of this facility, which had once been called *Pontus Alpha*. All she was really interested in were the files revealing what the IDC had done to the kraken — and what the kraken had ultimately done to the soldiers and scientists who'd mistreated them.

She understood the kraken's hatred of the IDC. Hell, *she* was pissed off, and she'd barely scratched the surface of the available information. Theo had been subject to cruelty and degradation in her youth, but her experiences were nothing compared to what the kraken had endured.

"I should be lucky it was Vasil who found me," Theo muttered as she watched the holo being displayed at the central control console — a kraken being punished for refusing to work. Hatred and murderous rage blazed in the kraken's eyes as the IDC crewmen approached with long prods and electrocuted him. She couldn't help but think of Vasil in that place as the kraken's muscles convulsed and his tentacles curled on themselves.

"All right, Kane. I've seen more than enough." She flicked her wrist, dismissing the holographic recording.

She recalled her pride when she'd been accepted into the IDC; the first time she put on that uniform, she'd been so proud of herself, so amazed at how well it fit. Having a place to belong and put her skills to good use had delighted her.

But she couldn't help her shame now, even though she'd had no part in what happened here all those centuries before. Theo hadn't been so naïve as to believe the IDC had never committed any wrong-doings, but *this*? Who knew what else they had done — what they were *doing* — elsewhere in the universe?

"At the very least, it corroborates the story he told you," Kane said through the console.

"I didn't need proof. I already trusted his word."

"I know that, but he skimped on the severity of what his ancestors endured. The violations documented here would've destroyed the IDC as it existed back then, had this gone public. Tureon Industries, too. They had a large part in all this."

Theo rubbed the bridge of her nose, briefly squeezing her eyes shut. "And even if I wanted to reveal the IDC for what they've done, I couldn't without revealing *them*."

"Correct. And we've no way of knowing what the response would be. Even now, there's a small chance the IDC would simply exterminate the species."

A chill, icier than any she'd ever felt, ran down her spine. "All the more reason not to say a word. Not like I could, anyway."

"It wouldn't accomplish anything," Kane said. "Everyone involved is long dead. Who would they hold accountable for three-hundred-and-sixty-year-old crimes?"

"And they'd likely just make me *disappear* to keep the whole thing quiet."

"They'd most certainly remove me either way. And I don't

want to be put in another body, not when I've just grown comfortable in yours. For the record, I know how dirty that sounds, but I stand by the statement."

Theo chuckled. "You're not going anywhere."

She was browsing the Facility's plans and blueprints when the control room door slid open. Vasil entered with Dracchus close behind; the larger kraken had to turn to the side and duck to fit through the doorway.

"Oh good," Theo said, facing the console to select one of the diagrams Kane had shown her earlier, "you're here."

"One would think you've never been in this place before, as long as it took you," said Kane.

"Can you make it stop talking?" asked Dracchus.

"Kane has a mind of his own," Theo replied.

"I thought if you say *tentacular penetration* he turns off?" Vasil asked.

Theo grinned, looking at Vasil from the corner of her eye. "No, Vasil, that's only when we're having sex."

Maroon pulsed over Vasil's skin, there and gone in a flash.

Dracchus seemed to notice the color change; he eyed Vasil for a few moments before grunting, shaking his head, and turning his attention to Theo. "Why did you ask us to come?"

"Because I ran a series of diagnostic tests on this facility's systems," Kane said. The console's projected screen expanded to a three-dimensional hologram — a model of the facility. Its walls were displayed as transparent with faint outlines, revealing a myriad of internal components within. "Considering this place has received no maintenance for hundreds of years, much of it is in surprisingly good shape. That likely has a lot to do with the reactor."

The image zoomed in to display the reactor deep in the bowels of the main building; though might've guessed its purpose based on its appearance, many of its parts were unlike anything she'd seen — both during and before her time with the IDC.

"This place is powered by halorium," Kane continued, "and there is insufficient data to predict how long it can be run on the halorium stores currently within the reactor. Hundreds more years, it would seem."

Theo turned to face the two kraken. "It's no wonder the IDC wanted the stuff. Unlimited power source."

Vasil leaned closer, studying the display. "We knew about the halorium core already."

"Sorry, I was excited and digressed from the point," said Kane. The hologram's focus moved down nearby maintenance corridors to another room filled with machinery — just the sort of places where Theo had spent most of her life. A huge machine lit up orange. "This is the air reclamation and filtration unit. It is what keeps breathable air circulating in this facility. And it has a component on the brink of failure, relatively speaking."

"What does that mean?" Dracchus asked.

"It means," Theo swept her fingers outward from the center of the hologram, zooming in on the small piece Kane had high-lighted in red, "once this part fails, the air in this place is going to become poisonous."

Wearing matching frowns, Vasil and Dracchus exchanged a concerned look.

"How long before that happens?" Dracchus asked.

"Impossible to say for certain," replied Kane. "But it is going to happen soon. I would estimate another year, perhaps three at best."

"Or it could happen tomorrow," Theo said.

"It would trigger automated alarms. An evacuation alert. There'd be some time before things got dangerous, but this place would become uninhabitable," said Kane.

Vasil met Theo's gaze. A glimmer of fear shone in his silver eyes. "What do we do, Theodora?"

"There's a parts storage room on the lower level of this building. I need you to take me to it so I can see what's there to work with." She expanded the image further, displaying the part at its actual size.

Vasil moved to stand beside her. "That is the piece?" He lifted a hand and cupped his palm beneath the part. "It is so small. What is it?"

"It's a sensor control valve," she replied. "The tank that sits over it fills with water containing all the toxins and impurities filtered out of whatever comes through the interior and exterior intakes, and this valve is supposed to detect that load and open to dump the contaminants before they exceed a certain amount. It's on a sensor so it can maintain proper system pressure the majority of the time."

She manipulated the holo to show more of the filtration system. "But if that valve doesn't purge the tank when it's supposed to, the bad water will overflow to here." Theo pointed at the top of the tank, where the cleaned air flowed into the next component. "And it will contaminate that air and compromise the system. Once that happens, it's game over for this place."

Vasil lowered his hand and leaned forward, studying the valve, as Dracchus drew closer.

"That tiny thing determines our survival here?" Dracchus asked.

Theo nodded. "Sometimes the smallest things are the most important."

He grunted; it was an oddly thoughtful sound. She hadn't realized grunts could be so nuanced before meeting Dracchus. They were a language unto themselves coming from him.

"And if there is a replacement part, you can fix it," Vasil said.

"Yep."

"If there is not?" Dracchus asked.

Theo spread her hands out in front of her. "Then we just wait for the inevitable."

Kane made a throat-clearing sound. "I have found a potential alternative source for the part we need, should the storage room prove fruitless."

"There is no fruit in the storage room," said Dracchus. "We keep the food in the kitchen, as Macy told us."

Theo smirked, scratching the back of her neck. "It's a saying, Dracchus. He just means if we don't find what we're looking for."

"Why not just say that?"

"We did. Just in a different way."

Dracchus scoffed and shook his head.

"What is the alternate source?" asked Vasil.

"I cross-referenced all the records kept in the computer system here and discovered three submarines listed as having been used to transport supplies to and from this base. They are military-grade vessels, each one hundred meters long and able to accommodate over one hundred crewmen. One of them seems to have gone missing entirely — vanished without a trace — but I have locations for the other two. Locations from just before the communications here were cut off, anyway. According to the plans, all three submarines were equipped with filtration systems very similar to this one. Close enough that Theo would be able to make the piece work."

Theo clapped her hands together. "Great! Now we just need to figure out if the part is here, or if we'll need to go searching for a missing sub." She glanced between the Vasil and Dracchus. "Who's escorting me?"

Vasil offered a hand to Theo. "There is no need to ask."

Dracchus's brows lowered. "I will speak with Larkin. If we need to search for these *subs,* it will be best to do so in a hunting party."

"One of the submersibles is located in a sub bay in another building of this facility," Kane said.

Dracchus and Vasil exchanged another glance.

"That place is abandoned," Vasil said, looking back to Theo. "There is nothing but broken metal and debris there. Much of it has been claimed by sea life. The old stories say there was an explosion during the uprising."

"Even if that component had survived in those conditions after all this time, it wouldn't be usable," Theo said with a frown. "Guess that leaves the other one if we can't find what we need here."

"Go look in the Underneath," Dracchus said. "I will speak with Larkin and a few others to ensure we are ready to move if necessary."

Theo followed Vasil out of the control room and through the facility's corridors. He was silent, and she couldn't blame him for it; she'd have been speechless herself if she'd been told her home could become a deathtrap at any moment. Though the kraken could live in the flooded portions of the facility, which would not be affected by the failure, this was still their place. It was where their people came into existence, where they'd lived ever since — and that was without mentioning the humans who stayed here with their kraken mates.

They stopped at an overly-wide, sturdy-looking door. Vasil pressed a button on the wall. The door slid open with a light scraping sound, revealing a large service elevator. Theo entered just behind him. She'd used similar elevators on IDC cruisers more times that she could count to move parts between various decks.

Being closer to the control panel, Theo pressed the button marked *MAINTENANCE*. The door rumbled closed and, a few moments later, the elevator descended.

"So, you called this the Underneath?" Theo asked, rocking

on her heels with impatience. She hadn't realized how much she missed fixing things; it felt like it had been so long.

"Yes," Vasil said. "My people rarely come down here. Some of the rooms are filled with devices we do not understand. It has always seemed best to let most of it remain below."

The elevator rumbled to a stop, and the door opened. Countless pipes, ducts, and conduits ran along the walls and ceiling of the dimly-lit tunnel before Theo. The air itself hum with the whirring of unseen machinery.

Theo grinned; *this* was her element. "I see why your people don't come here. It's nice and creepy."

Vasil turned his gaze toward her, brow furrowed. "Creepy? No, we are not afraid of this place."

Kane's voice projected from Theo's wrist. "That's exactly what someone who is afraid of this place would say."

Theo clicked her tongue. "Hush, Kane."

"It has nothing of use to us," Vasil said, "and the air here is… uncomfortable. It makes my skin feel like it is…crawling."

Frowning, Theo swung her attention back to the corridor and exited the elevator. "Nothing to be frightened of here."

Vasil followed her without hesitation. "As I said, it is not fear."

"According to the records," Kane said, "his kind have skin that is particularly sensitive to changes in pressure, current, and temperature. It may be that they are also more sensitive to the electromagnetic fields that always permeate tunnels like this. They are known to instill a vague sense of unease in many organisms, including humans."

"We just need to check for that part then we'll be out of here before you know it." Theo offered Vasil a smile.

He returned the smile. "You know where we are going?"

"Kane does."

"Left at the first intersecting corridor, right at the next," said Kane.

Following Kane's directions, they moved through the tunnels at a brisk pace. But a familiar sensation struck Theo halfway down the second corridor.

She halted abruptly. "Kane?"

"The reactor is straight ahead." A hint of static crackled through his words. "Though it is shielded, the halorium's energy fields seem to be leaking very slightly. We won't get close enough for it to do any harm."

A tentacle looped around Theo's waist, drawing her back.

"I will go to the parts room," Vasil said. "You return to the elevator and await me. Just tell me what I need to look for."

Theo patted the tentacle before brushing her fingertips over his skin; she'd never tire of its feel. "I'll be fine. If it was dangerous, Kane would tell me."

Vasil moved in front of her, leaning his face close and staring into her eyes. "He did not tell you last time, Theo."

"We didn't understand what it was then. We do now. He knows what to look out for."

"Kane, you are *certain* she will come to no harm?"

"I cannot be certain of anything," Kane replied, eliciting a deep frown from Vasil, "but according to the readings I'm picking up, we will be turning away from the source well before the energy fields are concentrated enough to cause any problems."

Theo caught Vasil's face between her hands and brushed her thumbs over his cheeks. "I'll be fine. If anything happens, I trust you to get me out of here."

He gently combed the claws of one hand through her hair. "Why take the risk at all?"

"This is your people's home, right?" she asked, holding his gaze. "That means something, Vasil. I never really had a place to call home, so I know what it feels like to be without one. We're not just doing this for ourselves, we're doing it for *all* the kraken. I have the resources and the training to find this part and get this fixed before it becomes a serious issue."

His pupils expanded, darkening his eyes. "Under different circumstances, I would take you this very moment, female." His fingers flexed for a moment before he lowered his arm and withdrew his tentacle. "Let us go, then. Carefully."

Theo wiggled her brows and grinned. "I'll hold you to that later."

After pecking a quick kiss on his lips, Theo continued down the corridor; Vasil fell into place behind her. The humming in her head strengthened, making her feel slightly off-balance, until they turned into the next tunnel — once they'd rounded the corner, the sensation rapidly diminished.

"Three doors down, on the right," Kane said. A blue marker appeared in Theo's vision, set farther down the corridor. The distance on the marker — originally fifteen meters — decreased with each of her steps.

The marker vanished when she reached the door, which was similar in size to the elevator entry. It opened automatically onto impenetrable darkness. Lights flickered to life beyond the doorway, banishing that darkness in flashes and fits until they finally went solid.

The room was large, though its full size was difficult to estimate because of the neat rows of shelves arranged through much of it. Theo and Vasil moved inside. Several large carts with what powered controls were lined up along the walls to the left and right of the doorway, docked at recharging stations.

"All right, Kane," Theo said, raising her left arm. "Let's get looking."

Kane's orb appeared over her wrist, casting a soft blue glow around it.

Theo walked down one of the aisles, thrumming with excitement as her eyes swept over the containers on the shelves. "Is there an inventory list for this room?"

Her retinal implant displayed part numbers for each of the items Kane scanned, accompanied by superimposed images of the parts inside the various boxes and cases. Her fingers itched to open each one and explore the contents.

"Yes," Kane replied, "and it does not list the part we're looking for."

"So why are we searching here?" asked Vasil.

"Due to the nature of this facility, I suspect that a number of the records were falsified to divert suspicions. Many of the files contain evidence of tampering, even mundane ones like inventory requisitions and releases. Though the activities here were undoubtedly approved by certain commanding officers within the IDC, it is very likely this was carried out without the knowledge of most ranking officials."

"Can you explain that in a way I will understand?" Vasil asked.

"They were breaking the rules here," Theo said distractedly, "so they lied about the materials they kept in stock."

"I understand… But why would the part we need have been involved in that? Is it not essential to this place's function?"

"Not even I can understand the inner workings of military bureaucracy," Kane said. "They often reclass items based on cost to manipulate budgets and make the numbers line up properly. I've already found several parts on these shelves that are not listed in official documents."

Theo extended her right arm and picked up a small box from a nearby shelf — simple, ten-millimeter bolts — and hefted its weight on her palm appreciatively before setting it down. "Could be that they had another base elsewhere. Another place they could move materials through without leaving a trail directly to this facility — once it's planet-side, the IDC doesn't usually bother tracking the movement of goods like that. They leave it to the commanders on-world."

"The Watch was an IDC base long ago," said Vasil.

Kane's orb brightened. "The name makes sense now. I assume you're talking about Watch Point Echo, which is listed as the nearest military outpost to this facility. There are a great many trips logged between here and there for all three of the submarines."

"Yes, that is what the Computer said it was once called."

Theo continued to scan the shelves, frowning. "I'm mostly seeing common components. Some replacement parts for the subs, too. Any luck yet, Kane?"

"No," Kane replied. "This place was built with state-of-the-art parts and technology for its time."

"Which means they intended it to last. Cocky bastards."

"Yes. They were on a regular supply schedule, with equipment and parts being dropped every few months while this planet was an active IDC colony. It's likely that key components like our valve would have eventually been dropped, but this place was abandoned before then."

They moved down the final row of shelves; Kane had identified no matches by the time they reached its end.

Theo crossed her arms over her chest. "So our only option is now to find that sub."

"It would seem so," said Kane.

"How are we to do that?" Vasil asked.

Theo turned to face him; he was frowning, and she guessed that he was thinking of all the potential dangers they'd face out in the sea.

"We begin at its last recorded location," replied Kane. "I can guide us there based on the extensive maps I've downloaded from this facility's database. The expanded scanning capabilities of the diving suits should help from there."

Vasil nodded, though his expression didn't ease. "Very well. We should inform Dracchus that we will require a hunting party for the search."

CHAPTER 16

"The sub's last reported location is sixty meters ahead," Kane said through the diving suit's comms, "right in the middle of that trench."

Theo frowned; they were deep enough already that the sunlight from overhead was diffused and everything was a deep, oppressive blue, her range of vision limited to a thirty-meter radius. The trench they were swimming over was an impossibly black gash cutting across the ocean floor, a place where no light touched.

"It's so strange not hearing Sam," Larkin said, her voice also transmitting through the comm system.

Theo turned her head and glanced at the woman swimming alongside her. She'd been introduced to Larkin soon after she and Vasil had left the maintenance tunnels, and she'd taken an immediate liking to the woman. Larkin had a sense of humor akin to Theo's and seemed prone to lapse into the sort of colorful language to which Theo had grown accustomed after a lifetime aboard interstellar ships. But Larkin was also capable of focus, solemnity, and a certain professionalism when the situation called for it — as news of the failing control valve had demonstrated.

With no concern for her own safety — or for Dracchus's immensely disapproving look — Larkin had volunteered to accompany the search party. Her mate had offered no argument, which had told Theo as much about Larkin as it had about Dracchus.

"I can make myself sound like Sam, if you'd like," Kane replied, "though I don't see why you'd want to hear such a one-dimensional voice."

"No, you're good," Larkin said. "I prefer yours. It's nice not having to ask twenty questions to get Sam along to the one answer I need. This is like talking to an actual person."

"Careful. You might inflate his ego enough that he bursts out of my body. I can barely contain him as-is," said Theo.

"*You* should be careful, Theodora," Kane said. "I've finally found someone else who enjoys my company. Be jealous all you want."

"You can't *spy* on us…can you?" Larkin asked warily. "Since you can take over the Facility and all that."

"Surveillance in the cabins is limited primarily to the hallways. I can access the cameras in the consoles within each room, but I *do* have some standards. And if you should ever feel uncomfortable or uncertain, just say *tenta*—"

Theo laughed. "That's enough, Kane. And to put you at ease, Larkin, he may be an advanced AI with a totally unique, life-like personality, but he doesn't have any sexual desires. He's not going to watch you — especially not during any private moments. Believe me, I was so weirded out when he was first installed that I refused to look into any mirrors or down at my own body for the longest time for fear of what he'd see."

Kane snorted. "That's ridiculous. Thirty meters."

Larkin twisted around, swimming backward while she made a series of hand gestures to the kraken accompanying them —

Dracchus and Vasil to either side of Larkin and Theo and four other kraken in formation just behind. They were called Calix, Donis, Orin, and Pythas; Theo *thought* she could link the names to the right faces, but she wasn't one hundred percent certain. They each emitted a soft glow from their stripes, chasing away some of the darkness.

"What did you say to them?" Theo asked. Larkin had proven invaluable thus far for her ability to communicate with the kraken without words; Theo hadn't realized during her trip to the facility that Dracchus and Vasil had been using a sophisticated sign language to speak with one another as she swam.

Larkin twisted to face forward. "Just telling them we're close and to keep an eye out. They've got better eyesight under water than we do. The suits give us an advantage because of their high-tech scanners, but we can't count fully on that."

"Twenty meters," Kane said.

A layer of dull yellow light flowed through Theo's vision, settling over the seascape just below her and mapping every feature of the ocean floor out beyond her range of vision. It even extended down into the trench, though it didn't reach the bottom. She couldn't be certain if Kane was doing it through the suit's interior display or her retinal implants, but she was grateful for it.

"Were the sub still at its last coordinates, we would see it by now," said Kane. "We need to go lower."

"It would make sense," Larkin said. "Something that big can't just disappear." Turning to Dracchus, she moved her hands through several quick signs.

Dracchus nodded, swung his harpoon gun to hang over his shoulder, and passed the information on to the other kraken with hand and tentacle gestures — at least Theo assumed he did. Once he finished, he signed to Larkin and angled himself toward the trench. The rest of the party followed his example.

"What'd he say to you, Larkin?" Theo asked.

"That they've never been down there. He doesn't know what we're going to find."

The darkness deepened as they descended. Though the diving suits' external lights came on, cold fear slithered through Theo, making her heart race. Kane's read-outs set the trench at thirty-five meters average width, but all she could see were the yellow-orange scanner projections of the rock walls; it was too dark to see with her naked eye beyond the limited range of her light. She glanced at Vasil and found some comfort in his closeness. The glow from his stripes created a strange, indistinct blue aura around him — kraken bioluminescence was not enough to combat this darkness.

"Breathe, Theodora," Kane said. "I am watching for any danger. Just breathe and keep swimming. You are safe."

Theo inhaled deeply and nodded. She trusted Kane. And Vasil. She envied Larkin's bravery, confidence, and calm — the woman was a hunter, well adapted to high-stakes situations. Theo's training had focused almost exclusively on how to crawl through access tunnels and ducts of varying sizes and how to fix complex machinery. Sure, the work was important, but she'd never had to face the unknown like *this*.

"You can tap into Sam's ability to scan for lifeforms, right Kane?" Larkin asked.

"Absolutely. I've been running it in the background, checking against the records from Pontus Alpha on known dangerous sea life," Kane said. "Would you like the information added to your display?"

"Yeah, that'd be helpful." After a moment, Larkin made a low whistling sound. "That's some scary shit."

"Not helping," Theo sing-songed.

Larkin chuckled. "Sorry."

"There is a surprising abundance of life here," Kane said. "This planet is fascinating. The diversity of the native fauna and flora is unlike anything in my database."

"Your *limited* database," said Theo, smirking. "I'll pass on the lifeform scan, thanks. Just going to focus on finding that submarine."

They continued forward and down. Soon enough, the bottom of the trench — or rather Kane's overlaid image of it — came into view. Theo's readout marked their depth at five hundred and twelve meters. She tried not to think about just how much water was above her, or how far she'd have to swim to reach air and sunlight again.

I spent eighteen years in space. This is nothing... Right?

"The sub was following a set course that ran along a large section of this trench," said Kane, briefly displaying a faint line of forward-leading arrows at the top of Theo's vision. "It was an established route between Pontus Alpha and the Darrow Nautical Outpost, another military facility on the coast."

Theo returned her gaze to the trench floor. "Guess we just keep going this way, huh?"

"I've never seen creatures like these," Larkin said.

"Adapted to the unique conditions of this trench," Kane replied. "Some of these creatures give off strange readings. It must be some quirk of their unique biology."

"What do you mean by *strange*?" asked Theo.

Kane made a thoughtful humming sound. "Erratic. There are traces of what I can only assume is halorium in their signatures — much too faint to be of any concern to us, but present nonetheless."

Ahead, two small blue orbs appeared in the darkness. As Theo neared them, the source became apparent — a half-meter-long fish with large, pale eyes and two points of bioluminescence near its mouth. The fish's glow went out abruptly, and the creature vanished in the gloom. More creatures entered Theo's view as she swam onward; a few cast their own light, but most were revealed to her as fleeting, ghostly images in the glow from the diving suits and her kraken companions.

She had the sense that those phantoms were lured in by the light only to be scared off by what they saw upon drawing close.

I survived the streets pretty much on my own as a kid, she thought. *I got this.*

"There is an anomaly ahead," Kane said, drawing Theo's attention to the spot with a briefly flashing circle in her display.

At first glance, it seemed a natural feature of the trench floor — a large outcropping of rock, perhaps, blanketed with sediment and clumps of what Theo assumed was some sort of vegetation. What she was looking at became clearer as she neared — especially the size and shape of the *anomaly*. It was long and roughly cylindrical, though the bottom was mostly lost in the sand on the floor of the trench. The anomaly extended far beyond her field of view, which was limited to only five or ten meters.

Kane superimposed a wireframe model of the sub over the anomaly; though centuries of sediment and growth had obscured the shape, it was a near perfect match. The rises and dips followed the contours of the sub's design exactly, stretching one hundred meters from one end to the other.

"I think we found our sub," said Larkin.

Finally, they came close enough for the exterior lights of the diving suits to fall upon the anomaly directly. Even partially buried, it stood at least twelve meters high. Odd, pale vegetation, dirt, and strange shell-like growths covered its surface, but there was something more to be seen — *metal.* Though dulled and dingy, Theo knew those little patches breaking through the sediment were glimpses of the hull.

"We sure did," Theo agreed, "and it looks like it's in one piece."

Larkin followed Theo closer to the old submarine, swinging her harpoon gun off her back and into her hands. "It's been here a long time. There's a good chance it's not intact, despite how it might look. Most things from the colonization are broken down or worn away."

"As long as there was no significant damage to the hull, it should be almost as good as new," Theo said as she reached forward to place her hand on the metal. She smoothed her palm over it; despite the bumpy grime caked on its surface and her diminished sense of touch through the suit, it felt familiar. She was back in her element just like that. "According to the specs Kane pulled, they put a *lot* of money into this thing. They wanted the stuff here to last. The IDC considered this place a long-term investment."

"I hope you're right. So, how do we get in?" asked Larkin.

The sub's plans appeared superimposed over Theo's vision again.

"There is an airlock on the starboard side near the fore of the craft," said Kane. A soft pulse of light drew Theo's attention to her right, where Kane highlighted the airlock entry door, seventy-five meters away.

"Okay," Theo said, "Let's go check it out."

Letting her harpoon gun hang by its shoulder strap, Larkin signed to the kraken, who had spread out to keep watch. After she was done, Dracchus made a few more signs, using his tentacles as well as his hands.

The party moved along the hull of the submarine. Everything within their combined light was perfectly illuminated, but only impenetrable darkness loomed beyond. Though she was with a group, Theo couldn't help the feeling of loneliness and isolation lurking on the edges of her mind; if someone were to die down here, they'd just be *gone*, never to be found. Claimed by the sea for eternity.

"Here we are," Theo said as they finally reached the airlock door. Though it was positioned low on the submarine's exterior, the door was only partially blocked by sand thanks to the curve of the hull. But that blockage wasn't her primary concern

— the hardened buildup of shelled creatures and grime was more problematic.

Larkin gestured to the kraken, who fanned out in a semicircle around the door, weapons in hand. She kept near Theo, having shifted her harpoon gun back into her hands.

"We need to get this door cleared before we try to open it. Kane, have you been able to connect to the sub's computer?" asked Theo.

"Yes, but it has been in a low-power state for hundreds of years, and its remote functionality is extremely limited. Everything seems to be operating normally. The filtration system has kept the air clean, and the reactor is stable, but you'll need to use the manual controls to open the door."

"Okay. Let's get to work."

Theo caught Vasil's attention and pointed to the sand gathered at the bottom of the entry door. She curled the fingers of both hands and pantomimed digging, imagining a dog pawing through the dirt. She'd only seen a few mangy strays during her childhood, but she'd always been fascinated by the animals; there hadn't been much other wildlife to see apart from roaches and rats.

He probably doesn't even know what a dog is, she thought.

When they were done with all this, when they finally had some time to rest, she'd have to show him. Even if he never saw one in person, it was better to *know*, wasn't it?

Vasil nodded. He carefully placed the container he'd been carrying on the sea floor about a meter to the side of the door. Her personal tools were stored within, protected from the water. Once his hands were free, he swam closer to her, cupped the back of her head with one hand, and leaned in to press a kiss atop her hood.

Theo's body hummed, and it had nothing to do with the diving suit's internal energy field. She wanted nothing more at that moment than to feel his skin against hers, to feel his *heat,* to smash her lips to his and kiss him long, deep, and passionately.

He moved to the door, sank to the bottom, and plunged his hands into the loose sand. He scooped it away in large handfuls. Dracchus joined him as Theo tugged the straps of her backpack off her arms and swung it to her front. She opened it and rummaged through the tools within — she'd found them all in the Facility, and each was designed for underwater use. She removed a rock hammer.

Kane scanned the hull again and adjusted the projected outline of the door to match the bit of visible frame. Frowning, Theo swam closer to the hull and ran her fingers over the buildup caking its surface. A few loose bits crumbled away, but most of it remained intact. She scraped at it with the pick side of the hammer. A clump of grime fell away, and the hammer scratched the bare hull beneath, producing a metallic whine she felt vibrate through her arm.

"At least *some* of this stuff will come off," she muttered, turning the hammer around in her hand. She banged it against the door several times in rapid succession; the clanging impact resounded through the water, loud enough to be picked up by her suit's external audio receivers. Only a few chunks of sediment and debris fell from the door, leaving cloudy trails in their wakes. "This is going to need something with a little more power. I bet that sonic jackhammer would do the trick…"

"We may have a problem," said Kane. "Something *big*."

A ping at the edge of Theo's field of view prompted her to turn her head to the left. Kane highlighted something at the base of the submarine ten meters away — a head. It was in profile relative to Theo, with two huge, pale eyes staring toward her and a set of long, wicked teeth jutting out of its mouth.

Despite the diving suit's precise temperature regulation, Theo felt suddenly cold. She watched in horrified silence as the head pushed out from beneath the sub. The body that emerged behind it began as a hulking set of shoulders with three legs on the side facing Theo, ending in claw-tipped, paddle-shaped appendages that scrabbled over the soft sand to drag the monster's long, flat tail out into the open.

"Well, *that's* new," Larkin said. She swam in front of Theo, raising her harpoon gun.

Dracchus joined the other kraken, who tightened their defensive semicircle with spears and harpoon guns at the ready.

The creature shook itself. Sand particles rained from its body. For an instant, it stretched to its full length and parted its massive jaws; it had to be at least eight meters long from its teeth to the end of its tail.

Turning its head toward Theo and the others — revealing two more eyes and three more legs on the previously hidden side of its body — it darted forward with a burst of speed so immense that Theo's heart leapt into her throat.

Harpoon guns thumped. The creature let out a piercing cry and veered away, leaving a faint trail of dark blood behind. Within a second, its body was lost in the darkness beyond the hunting party's light, granting Theo a brief glimpse of a pair of reflective eyes glowing like moons in an otherwise empty night sky.

"Get that door open, Theo," Larkin yelled.

Theo's eyes widened as the huge creature charged out of the blackness. Though it had no pupils, she knew in her bones it was staring right at her. Its body flicked and undulated as the kraken attacked; they were fast, but the monster was faster.

A strong arm snaked around Theo's waist, and she was turned away suddenly and pressed against the hull of the ship. A large body covered her, solid and powerful but somehow gentle.

Vasil.

He held her in place as something zipped by overhead, displacing enough water for Theo to *feel* the movement even through her suit. Only after it had passed did he release her and back slightly away.

Theo turned to face him. His features were strained with tension and concern, and fear gleamed in his eyes. He glanced over his shoulder in the direction the creature had gone before meeting Theo's gaze again and gesturing to the door. Then he turned away, skin scintillating red as he scanned the water for signs of the terrifying monster.

Heart pounding, Theo looked at the door. This was a life-and-death situation, and she needed to move quickly; the sub would provide the only possible shelter from the monster. Her racing thoughts somehow outpaced her frantic heartbeat. The sounds in the water all around made her skin crawl; she wasn't familiar enough with the environment to know what each noise meant.

All she knew was that things were happening. Things were *moving*.

"Kane, can you predict this thing's movements or something?" asked Larkin, her voice ragged.

"I'll attempt to, but its movements are quite erratic. I can't guarantee much accuracy."

"Just show me!"

Theo clenched her jaw. The door, the submarine, the tools in her bag...she *knew* those things. Even if she'd never worked with them specifically, she'd worked with similar components for more than half her life. She wasn't a hunter, a warrior, or even much of a soldier, but this *was* her thing. *This* she could do. She wouldn't let fear prevent her from doing her job.

She opened her bag to find the sonic jackhammer.

Vasil's gaze followed the indistinct form moving on the fringes of the light. He longed to pull Theo into his arms and tell her it would be all right, that *she* would be all right, but he could not lower his guard. The creature attacking them was unfamiliar to him, but the danger it posed was apparent. It was big, had a mouthful of pointed teeth, and swam with startling speed.

That the kraken had essentially invaded the creature's territory had likely heightened its aggressiveness.

He spread his claws and eased a little closer to Theo as she worked. The best he could do now was defend her, which meant keeping himself between her and the creature. His own safety would ever be secondary to hers.

Something tapped his shoulder, drawing his attention to the side. It was the butt of a spear, offered by Dracchus. Vasil accepted the weapon with a nod.

Grasping the shaft in both hands, he thrust it out as the creature made another pass overhead. The monster swayed, its long body rippling like the surface of a puddle in a strong wind. The point of the spear grazed its flank, inflicting little more than a superficial wound.

The creature swung its head to the side, snapping its jaws at Dracchus. The big kraken propelled himself backward, narrowly avoiding the gnashing teeth. Larkin kicked her legs, rising above Dracchus, and fired her harpoon gun. The monster thrashed so quickly its body became a blur. A cloud of sand rose from the bottom, obscuring the hunting party as the creature vanished from sight again.

Vasil narrowed his eyes against the irritating sand and twisted to look back at Theo. She withdrew something from her bag — a stout cylindrical object with four leg-like pieces spaced evenly around its exterior and a handle on top. She pressed its bottom against the side of the submarine and twisted the device's handle. It latched onto the hull, legs locking into place.

The sound of moving water called his attention forward again just in time to see the creature emerge from the surrounding abyss to attack the group of kraken again. Vasil's companions fought back with harpoons and spears — Pythas and Donis attempted to flank it from one side, Calix and Orin from the other, while Dracchus faced it head-on — but the creature seemed unfazed even when the weapons struck. It bit at the kraken and swiped its claw-tipped appendages at them, adding more dark blood to the clouded water.

Its onslaught was too furious even for Dracchus to stand for long; he propelled himself away from it, catching it with a glancing blow from his spear.

Dipping to the trench floor, the creature scrambled forward along the hull, tail undulating behind it — straight toward Theo.

Fire flared in Vasil's chest, blasting him into the creature's path. For an instant, he saw Theo out of the corner of his eye; she was frantically manipulating the controls of the device she'd attached to the door.

He jabbed his spear at the monster. It shifted its trajectory suddenly, causing the spear to glance off its head; Vasil felt it connect with hard bone through the shaft, jolting his arm. Before he recovered from his strike, the creature clamped its teeth over one of his tentacles.

Pain lanced through him, crackling like lightning up and down the length of his tentacle. The creature whipped its head to the side, tearing Vasil's flesh. But he would not allow himself to be dragged into the darkness. Twisting his torso away from the creature, he slammed the spearhead into the seafloor as hard as he could, using it as an anchoring point to fight the creature's pull. The additional pressure in his wounded tentacle heightened his agony.

Though Larkin, Dracchus, and the other kraken were close by, the creature's thrashing tail held them at bay; they could not get close enough to help.

Vasil lifted his head to look at Theo. She stared at him with wide eyes, her lips pressed into a tight line. Without looking away from him, she pressed a button on the device. Its small display glowed green.

The sound began low — a powerful hum from Theo's device that pulsed through Vasil's body and rattled his bones. He tightened his hold on the spear and the sound somehow deepened while a second noise — more a high-pitched whistle or whine than a hum — joined in. The first resonated in Vasil's bones, but the second was like a knife plunging into his brain. The pain was too great; he clasped a hand over his forehead and squeezed as though it would keep his skull from splitting open.

The creature released its hold on his tentacle and flipped onto its back, writhing in the sand.

Neck straining, Vasil swept his gaze over his companions. The other kraken were in similar states of pain, holding their heads in their hands and curling their tentacles, Calix and Orin doubled over. But not Larkin and Theo; the humans' mouths were moving as though they were speaking, their expressions dominated by confusion and concern.

Vasil struggled to pull his spear out of the ground; this was the one chance they had to strike the creature while it wasn't darting through the water. The pain in his skull only intensified with his effort. Tiny, tingling bubbles filled the water, followed by a cloud of disturbed sand from the direction of the submarine. Vasil released the spear to cover both ears with his hands, squeezing his eyes shut.

He did not know how long he drifted just above the trench floor in that agonized darkness before something brushed over his arm; his pain said it had been a thousand years, but it could not have been more than a few seconds. He forced his eyes open to see Theo over him, holding the spear in both her hands. Larkin was higher up, above the monster, with a fresh harpoon loaded. She fired it into the underside of the creature's jaw, but it was not enough to cease its movement.

Teeth clenched so tightly they seemed likely to shatter, Vasil forced himself upright. Theo met his gaze as he grasped the shaft of the spear behind her hands. That shared look was all they needed.

She planted her feet in the sand, and he his tentacles, and they launched forward together, Vasil driven as much by his need to eliminate the threat to his mate as by his own pain. At any moment, his brain would surely explode, but he'd kill this monster first.

The sound ceased an instant before the head of the spear plunged into the largest of the creature's eyes. With Theo and Vasil's combined weight and momentum behind it, the weapon sank deep; half the shaft slid into the creature's head, pinning it to the trench floor.

For several moments, Vasil and Theo remained in place on either side of the spear's shaft. The creature stilled. Though the device's sounds had stopped, Vasil's head throbbed, and his body felt as though it were still vibrating. The pain in his tentacle had grown dull and distant, but he knew the reprieve was temporary.

Theo's eyes met his again; they glistened beneath her furrowed brow. Releasing the spear, she leapt at Vasil, wrapping her arms and legs around him. He returned her embrace and held her tightly, wishing he could feel her skin or run the tips of his claws through her hair.

By the time she drew back, the others had gathered close by. Vasil kept a hand on Theo, unwilling to let go, as he looked over their companions. All five kraken — Dracchus included — bore fresh cuts and wore disoriented expressions. Only Larkin and Theo seemed to have been unaffected by the harsh sounds that had come from the device.

Any serious wounds? Vasil signed.

Dracchus shook his head and gestured toward Vasil's tentacle, which had been shredded where the creature had bitten down.

I will be fine, Vasil signed. He saw Larkin's lips move.

Theo shifted to look down at his wounded tentacle and frowned. She spoke rapidly. Vasil looked to Larkin for explanation.

She is not happy you are hurt, Larkin signed with her hands; human signs had seemed far more limited by their anatomy when Vasil first learned of them, but he'd realized their depth as he'd grown familiar with them during hunts with Randall and Larkin.

Tell her I am fine. We need to go in, he replied, pointing to the sub for emphasis.

Theo remained in place, staring at him.

He cupped the side of her mask and offered her a smile. Her return smile seemed forced, but she swam toward the door, nonetheless.

Vasil followed, but his movement faltered when he saw the side of the sub; the cylindrical tool was attached to the metal in the same spot she'd placed it, but everything else was different. The buildup and dirt that had clung to it were gone, much of it piled on the trench floor below, leaving the hull fully visible. Theo grasped the device's handle and twisted it in the opposite direction from what she had before. It came loose, and she returned it to her bag.

The outline of the door was clear now, marked in some places by chipped, fading yellow paint.

Theo gestured to the fresh rubble at the base of the door. Vasil dropped to it and began scooping it away as she opened a hidden panel beside the door markings. Dracchus helped him; they made short work of the task.

Once they'd finished, Theo gestured for them to move back. They obeyed, and Vasil kept his eyes on her as she worked at the controls, his chest tight and skin hot despite the chill of the water. After all they'd been through, he couldn't bear the thought of her coming to harm, and he did not trust this *subma-*

rine any more than he trusted anything else in the fickle, dangerous sea.

He wished he could talk to her, wished he could know what she was thinking.

A deep rumble came from the submarine. Theo swam backward toward Vasil, eyes locked on the door, as loose sand drifted off the top of the vessel's hull. He took gentle hold of her arms and guided her away, shielding her with his body and giving the sub his back. She turned in his grasp to peer around him, and he looked over his shoulder to watch along with her. Unease pooled in his gut.

With a resonating *clang*, the door slid upward, opening a crack. A torrent of bubbles burst from the opening, temporarily obscuring the door. Vasil instinctively turned his face away and shifted his body to protect Theo.

There came no deafening boom, no searing pain across his back, no wave of super-heated displaced water. All he felt was a hand on his cheek. Theo's hand.

He looked down into her eyes. She smiled and dipped her head, indicating something behind him. Vasil turned to see the door rising. It opened on a brightly lit room similar to the entry chamber at the Facility, though smaller in scale. He stared in wonder as Theo slipped out of his arms and swam toward it.

She waved for him to follow.

Vasil clenched his jaw and obeyed, stooping to collect the container with her tools before following her inside.

He had a sense of what this sub was, what it meant — and what had happened to the humans on board. Thanks to holograms uncovered by Arkon and Aymee, Vasil knew the Facility hadn't been the only place where kraken had killed humans. This had to be the submarine from which fleeing IDC soldiers had sent a final, desperate distress call.

He only hoped the evidence of what had happened within had long since rotted away.

CHAPTER 17

The chamber's vibrations as the water inside drained were more pronounced than those of the pressurization chamber at the Facility. Though Theo knew the potential causes for the difference — the foremost being centuries of disuse and neglect — it was still disconcerting. Whatever Kane's analysis said, they were still entering the unknown here. Anything could go wrong.

"What about the others?" she asked. Vasil, Larkin, and Dracchus had accompanied her into the chamber, and once Dracchus had entered, there'd been no room for anyone else. "They're going to come in behind us, right?"

"Dracchus told them to wait and hide," Larkin replied. "They'll keep watch in case another one of those creatures shows up."

The kraken had survived the seas for over three hundred years, and their camouflage was amazing, but Theo couldn't help thinking about the monster that had attacked them. Would Calix, Donis, Orin, and Pythas be able to hold off another such beast on their own?

I just need to trust them to do their job and focus on doing mine.

She nodded and turned her attention to the information streaming through her retinal display. As Kane had mentioned earlier, the submarine seemed to be operating normally; there were no posted alerts save for a few blocked intakes, no recorded errors in any of its systems. The low power state it had shifted to after coming to rest here had kept everything in working order for centuries.

"At least we know the part we need is functioning," Theo said. "Just need to grab it and get back to the surface without getting eaten."

Larkin chuckled. "You killed one sea monster today, you should be good to take a few more."

Something brushed over Theo's calf, calling her attention to Vasil. Her eyes dropped to his ravaged tentacle. Blood oozed from the wound, misting the descending water. She clenched her jaw against the fresh wave of worry, fear, and fury that surged inside.

As though sensing her turbulent emotions, Vasil lifted a hand and cupped her jaw, turning her face up toward his. Once the water had fallen below her mask, he said, "I will be fine, Theo. It will heal."

"That *thing* almost tore your tentacle off! What would you have done then?"

He shrugged. "Grow a new one."

Theo glared at him. "Not funny."

"But it *is* accurate, according to the research data," said Kane through the comms.

"What?"

Larkin lifted her hands and removed her mask. "It is true. They can regrow limbs."

Theo pressed her lips together and glanced at Vasil's tentacle again. With the water almost fully drained, the wounded limb lay on the floor unmoving. "I'd still prefer they remain intact."

"It will be *fine*, Theo," Vasil repeated gently. "You need not worry."

Theo snorted, flicking through the holographic controls on the suit's wrist piece to release her mask. She yanked it away from her face once the seal broke. "Yeah, and had it been *my* leg shredded and bleeding, I'd totally tell you not to worry, too."

Vasil's pupils dilated for an instant before shrinking back down to horizontal slits. "But I would worry because you are not kraken. I will heal. Things could have been far worse than they were. I will happily put your worries at ease once we are safe at the Facility again."

"Are you trying to shut me up with the promise of sex?" she demanded, brows low.

He tilted his head, a thoughtful expression settling over his features. "Yes."

Theo raised a hand, pointing a finger at his face. "Well I… I… I'm going to hold you to it, damnit." She lowered her hand and shook her head. "Is there *anything* I can do for it?"

"The bleeding on all our wounds will have stopped by the time we leave." Dracchus's deep voice echoed in the small chamber, making it seem like he took up even more space. "What was that sound?"

"It was from a tool I brought along," Theo said.

"It is dangerous. It rendered six kraken useless in an instant."

"Yeah, well, it also *saved* six kraken, didn't it?"

"It's what stopped the creature, Dracchus," said Larkin.

Dracchus grunted, keeping his eyes on Theo. "Explain it, human. I need to understand what it is."

"It's called a sonic jackhammer," Theo replied. "It's used to clear buildup under water — the sound waves break up all that gunk and grime and basically shake them off."

"Why was the sound painful to us while Larkin and yourself seemed unaffected?"

"I may be able to answer that," Kane said through the diving suit's wrist piece. "The tool in question utilizes sound frequencies outside the range of human hearing. Many sea creatures are sensitive to the lowest frequencies because those sounds travel best through water, but kraken hearing range is increased on the other end of the spectrum as well."

Dracchus's brow furrowed; though the change was relatively tiny, it communicated his lack of understanding without question. "Speak pl—"

"There are very low and very high sounds humans cannot hear, but you can," Theo said. "It didn't harm us because we couldn't hear it."

"Next time, have him explain it that way."

Theo turned her face away from Dracchus to hide her smirk. Vasil leaned closer to her and placed a soft kiss on her lips, letting the contact linger for several seconds. For that brief time, everything that had happened outside the sub faded away, and it was just Theo and Vasil enjoying one another's nearness, relishing the feel of one another's lips.

When Vasil drew back, he shifted his attention to Dracchus. "I believe this is the underwater vessel Arkon spoke of. The one he and Aymee learned about in the Broken Cavern."

Dracchus frowned and glanced at the door that would allow them deeper into the sub. "You are certain?"

"Almost."

"Broken Cavern?" Theo asked. "What's that?"

"The Darrow Nautical Outpost," Larkin said. "That's what it used to be called, anyway. It's an old submarine pen on the coast."

"So, what's the story? Why did they mention this particular sub?"

"The humans on board were attacked by kraken during the uprising," Vasil said.

"Oh." Theo turned to face the door. Unease warred with her excitement — the two feelings spread outward from her chest slowly, a tingling and a chill of equal strength. This place was unknown to her; it was new, mysterious, and terrifying, but the thought of delving inside was as thrilling as it was frightening.

She drew in a steadying breath. "Okay, Kane. Open this door so we can get that part and get the hell out of here."

"Absolutely," Kane replied. "But…I must warn you, what you will find on the other side of this door is…*unpleasant*."

Dracchus shifted closer to the door and swept Larkin behind him. "What do you mean *unpleasant?*"

Vasil pressed closer to Theo, slipping a tentacle around her leg; his touch seemed more comforting than protective.

The light over the door frame turned green, and the interior door slid open, smooth and quiet. Theo peered around Dracchus's broad frame. The hallway beyond him looked pristine; the walls, floor, and ceiling, each a slightly different shade of gray, were free of blemishes and signs of aging.

The three bodies lying within the corridor were the only exceptions to the cleanliness — rather noticeable exceptions.

"Our ancestors made sure none of the humans from the Facility escaped to tell what had happened," Vasil said.

"I can see that," Theo replied. The powerful sensations that had been coursing through her only moments before were suddenly gone, leaving numbness in their wake.

Theo stepped around Dracchus and crouched beside the closest body. It lay on its belly, head turned at a sharp sideways angle, lower jaw unhinged in a huge, terrified scream. Only bones remained — bones in a stained and faded uniform with its back ripped to shreds. Black and brown stains marred the floor beneath the body, undoubtedly the result of the flesh rotting away over the long years.

Kane had shown her some of the holos — the mistreatment, the revolt, the brief-but-violent war on humans. The kraken had suffered, and this had been the retribution they delivered.

"Sometimes I wonder," Larkin said as she stepped into the

corridor, "if the locked rooms in the Facility have the same thing inside."

"Bodies, yes, but most of their ends were not quite so sudden or violent," Kane said. "There was communication between the survivors hiding inside those cabins for a few weeks after the kraken attacked, but eventually…lack of food took some. Suicide several more. Those rooms have been locked ever since."

"Can you open them?"

"Why would you want them opened?" Kane asked.

Dracchus held his gaze on the skeletal remains, his expression brimming with undisguised disapproval. "To give the dead to the sea, as has always been the way."

"We can do the same for these before we leave," Larkin said.

Dracchus nodded.

Vasil moved to Theo's side as she stood up.

"It was a different time," he said softly. "A different world… and different people. But we can do what little is in our power to make amends."

"I know." Theo gently patted his chest, offering him a smile, before drawing in a deep breath and turning her attention toward the end of the corridor. "All right, Kane. Show me the way."

"But of course," Kane said. Her retinal implant flashed on, presenting the overlaid blueprints of the sub in her field of view — displaying every pipe, vent, wire, and part hidden within the walls, ceiling, and floor. A faint pathway appeared before her, marked by arrows which slowly marched in the direction she was meant to follow. She walked along the markers, occasionally glancing to the side to examine the tech readouts Kane provided for various components. The wet, dragging sound behind her told Theo that Vasil followed.

They turned off the relatively short entry corridor after about ten meters, entering another that ran toward the aft of the submarine. Numerous doors lined the corridor on either side, some of them standing open to reveal knocked over furniture, scattered objects, trash, and more bodies. Theo knew Kane could tell her how many people had been on board when the slaughter occurred, could tell her where all their remains were located, could show her surveillance holos of the entire incident, but she had no interest in learning more.

She didn't need to see what had happened, didn't *want* to see; the evidence spoke for itself.

Theo couldn't imagine the fear the people aboard this vessel had felt in their final moments — trapped under so much water that they'd be crushed if they left the sub without specialized equipment, facing down human-octopus hybrids their own scientists had created. Human-octopus hybrids who were pissed off because of the way the IDC had treated them. And yet, she couldn't find it in herself to regret what the IDC had done.

It was because of their actions that Vasil was here now. With her.

The path led ever deeper into the sub; they passed through the control room, where a body that must've belonged to the vessel's former captain still sat in the command chair, though the skull had fallen away and now rested at the base of a nearby console.

After that room, things took on a surreal feel to Theo — just like the Facility, this place could easily have been mistaken for a space cruiser based on the appearance of its interior, but the immense sense of stillness here didn't seem to belong in a living, breathing world.

After a couple more turns, they finally arrived at the maintenance access floor-hatch. Despite a groan of protest, it opened itself smoothly when she tugged the lever.

Vasil leaned forward to peer into the opening. "Seems tight."

"They usually are," Theo said. "The people who design these things cram as much into the maintenance tunnels as they can so most of the vital systems can be accessed through them. It's just like in a space ship."

The corners of his lips dipped as he lowered his torso to place the container on the floor near the opening. "I will go first. Pass me the container once I am down."

"You don't need to go." Theo handed him her mask and removed her backpack, setting it on the floor. Turning her body, she grasped the handholds on the hatch lid and lowered her feet onto the uppermost ladder rungs. "Just hand me my tools when I get down and wait here. It shouldn't take me too long to get the valve."

Vasil's brows fell low. "I will not leave you alone."

She climbed down the ladder until she could comfortably grip the top rung. "Vasil, no one's here but us. I'll be fine."

"Anything can go wrong, and if I am not there to—"

"This is what I do. What I've been trained to do." She smiled and ran her fingers over his nearest tentacle. "Believe in my abilities."

The tentacle flexed beneath her fingers as the tip curled back to brush over her knuckles.

"Call for me if *anything* goes wrong." He twisted away from her, opened the container, and removed her toolbox.

Once she'd gone down the last few rungs and had her feet on the floor of the lower level, Vasil leaned forward and passed her toolbox to her.

He met her gaze and held it. "Be safe, Theodora."

Theo blew him a kiss and grinned. "I will. Besides, you promised me sex later."

Vasil grinned in response; his pointed teeth sent a thrill along her spine.

Stepping away from the ladder, Theo studied her surroundings. The tunnel was far more cramped than the corridors above, and many of the pipes, conduits, and ducts were fully exposed along the walls and ceiling. Even more were visible through the metal grating of the floor. The air was also noticeably warmer, pulsing with the familiar hum of machinery.

Kane's path led her a few meters toward the front of the sub and into a narrow passage; she had to swing her toolbox behind her and twist her shoulders sideways to fit through. It opened on a room — not that she could truly call it a room, it was more just a *space* — filled with various machines and electronic components, including an air filtration and reclamation system similar to the unit in the Facility. The steady machine hum was more pronounced here, strong enough that she could almost feel it on her skin.

Her retinal display pinpointed the valve. Theo stopped in front of its location and set her toolbox on the floor nearby. She studied the plans, noting what she'd have to remove to reach the part, and crouched to open the toolbox.

"How long will the air last once I take this out?" she asked.

"Given the size of the vessel and the number of people currently aboard, I would estimate several hours of clean air," Kane replied.

She dug through the tools to find what she needed. "Plenty of time. Could you tell Larkin and Dracchus to start removing the bodies now so we're out of here as quickly as possible after I'm done? Guide her to the locations as efficiently as possible."

"Yes. They will likely require some assistance in clearing the remains. They are rather…scattered."

Theo plucked out her all-wrench, rose, and set to the bolts securing the unit's cover plate. They gave a bit of resistance, but she hadn't met a bolt yet that could hold out against Malcolm's sturdy old all-wrench. It used a small energy field to clamp down on whatever needed to be fastened or unfastened, molding perfectly to every groove and crack.

Theo smiled to herself as she removed the final bolt; Malcolm used to say the all-wrench latched on to every damned atom.

Shifting her hold on the tool, she grasped the cover plate as it came loose and lowered it to the floor, leaning it against the base of the unit. The sound of whirring machinery was immediately louder. Kane provided readouts on every part within her field of view, but she paid no further attention to the information; if nothing else, she'd always had a firm grasp of what the parts of most machines did, and her few glimpses of the plans had been more than enough to decipher these.

"All right, Kane. Shut her down."

The filtration system stalled abruptly. It released a prolonged hiss — layered over a deep groan — and went silent, leaving only that old hum to fill the void.

She reached into the opening, flicked the valve's manual release switch, and watched the fill-level indicator for the tank above it. Once it showed empty, she crouched to retrieve another tool and set about removing the valve. Even with her advanced tools and their supposedly atomic-level grip and amped-up torque, she had to throw all her strength against both connectors for several seconds to get them to loosen. She froze the instant they moved, her heart thumping and breath suddenly ragged; the enormity of what she was doing crashed down upon her in that instant.

This wasn't about swapping a part, it was about saving the place Vasil's people called home. Too much pressure either while removing or installing the part could cause enough damage to prevent a good seal, which would hasten the deterioration of the system and render all this effort pointless.

This is what I do. Even on that ship, my job was keeping people safe — half the parts I touched could've affected critical systems. This is no different.

"Good news is I don't think that would've ever come apart on its own," she muttered.

"It *is* a vital component if you want living humans aboard,"

Kane said. "The IDC standards have always been high for such systems, even hundreds of years ago."

"*Living* humans? Don't you think that's a bit insensitive to our hosts, Kane?"

Theo gently loosened the connectors the rest of the way. Once they were unfastened, the individual pieces shifted freely. She put her tools away and pushed the connectors down, creating enough leeway to lift the valve out of place. The sensor array built into its side, though no larger than her thumb, was the difference between life and death for the people living in the Facility.

Bending down, she opened the small case built into her toolbox's top tray and laid the valve on the foam padding within. Once the case was closed, she picked up the all-wrench, turned back to the air unit, and replaced the cover plate — she knew there was no reason for it, but it was a habit she'd likely never shake.

"There is one more thing," Kane said.

Theo furrowed her brow as she closed her toolbox. "What? I thought this was all we needed."

An indicator in her retinal display turned her attention back toward the front of the sub. The overlay indicated another room ten meters away, this one filled primarily with electronic components.

"What do we need in there?" she asked.

"It's not something we *need*, but... I am compelled to mention it due to IDC coding." He highlighted a part inside the other room and expanded its image.

Theo's heart skipped a beat when she scanned the part's readout. "No way."

"Yes way," Kane replied. "That's a class A transmitter, capable of sending deep-space communications. It just needs an antenna."

"And we could totally build one. We just need the material."

"Which seems to be laying around this world in abundance."

Theo picked up her toolbox and returned to the maintenance tunnel, following it until she reached the entrance to the electronics room. She removed the transmitter with the same care she'd taken with the valve, though it was a bit more difficult — she had to stand on her toolbox to reach it, and it was a bit larger and heavier. She carefully rearranged her tools and settled the transmitter amongst them on the toolbox's top tray.

Before she closed the toolbox, she paused and looked at the part. While she was removing it, she hadn't even paused to think of the ramifications it could have, hadn't considered what she could lose if she built an antenna and managed to transmit a message. Her working mind had taken over — the part of her that recognized a challenge and was eager to tackle it. The inability to communicate with the IDC had been the first major problem she'd faced upon waking on Halora, and the thought of finally solving it had swept everything else away.

She'd not allowed her heart to weigh in on the matter. Frowning, she closed and latched the toolbox's lid.

Just in case, she thought.

When she returned to the open hatch, she looked up to find Vasil there, his eyes fixing on her immediately.

"Got it," she said, smiling and lifting the toolbox up to him.

The box seemed even heavier than the two parts she'd taken should've made it — the weight of her guilt, perhaps. None of the kraken would know what the transmitter was, what it was used for, but Theo knew. That felt like a betrayal of both Vasil and his people.

He took the toolbox and turned away, clearing the hatch for a moment before reappearing with his hands free. He watched intently as she climbed the ladder, offering a hand as she neared the top. Once she cleared the opening, he pulled her into his arms, coiling a tentacle around her leg.

"You'd think you missed me or something," she said, burying her face against his chest.

"Only a little," he said, his smile evident in his tone. His hold on her tightened. "I do not like the feel of this place."

Theo gently pulled away from him and met his gaze. "Yeah, it doesn't have the best vibes, does it?" She scooped her pack off the floor and slung it over her shoulders. "We're operating on borrowed time now, so we'd best help Larkin and Dracchus gather the remains and take them out to sea."

The concept wasn't as strange to her as it might once have been; for a long time, the IDC had held to the tradition of *burying* the dead in space; they'd launch the fallen into the stars to drift forever. It was kind of...peaceful.

Vasil nodded, picked up the toolbox, and placed it inside the waterproof container. A twinge of guilt shot through Theo's chest; he wouldn't think twice about the difference in the toolbox's weight, but she knew.

He sealed the container and lifted into his arms, extending a tentacle to pass Theo her diving mask. "I will follow your lead."

Though he was only talking about following her out of this place, she sensed deeper meaning to his words — they were rich with *trust*.

And she couldn't help but wonder if she was breaking it.

CHAPTER 18

Theo replaced the air filtration unit's cover plate and fastened its bolts. "Done!"

"They're going to love you at The Watch," Larkin said. She stood leaning against the wall, arms crossed over her chest and red hair hanging over her shoulder in a single braid. Her blue jumpsuit and thick belt — upon which were clipped a pistol and a knife — spoke of a woman ready to handle business.

Over the past few days, Theo had grown close to Larkin — it hadn't been hard to do. There were only so many places to go in the Facility, and the place was quiet and lonely when the males were out hunting, as they were now. Though Larkin usually went with the others to hunt, she'd chosen to stay behind and keep Theo company. She'd even proven to be a reliable and competent assistant, helping Theo manually seal the lines and ducts leading into the flooded portions of the Facility to prevent the possibility of further leakage into the air system. It had been two days of hard work — much of it under water — but the sense of accomplishment now that it was all done was worth the effort.

"It'll be nice to have a place," Theo said, returning her tools to the toolbox and shutting the lid.

Larkin had explained that everyone in the Watch had a job, a purpose, and they performed those jobs to keep their community afloat. Theo's jaw had nearly hit the floor when she realized there was no currency there — hell, Larkin hadn't even known the word *money* until Theo told her about it. The universe Theo knew revolved around the spending and accumulation of money.

The way Halora worked was more alien to Theo than the kraken. The idea that hard work and cooperation were enough to guarantee a place to live, food, clothing, all the necessities, might've been laughed at anywhere else. But here...so long as you did your part, so long as you supported your neighbors, you didn't have to worry about the dwindling credits in your account or whether your landlord would evict you for not paying rent.

"You have a place," came a familiar voice from the doorway, sending pleasurable chills down her spine. "Your place is with me, female."

A wide smile stretched across Theo's lips as she turned to find Vasil, skin glistening with seawater, in the doorway. "You're back!"

Vasil moved into the room and swept Theo into an embrace that lifted her off her feet. She laughed and threw her arms around his neck, pressing her lips to his. His fingers flexed against her backside as he held her close, deepening the kiss. Though he'd only been gone since early that morning — perhaps eight hours — she'd missed his closeness, his warmth, his touch, and the heat in his eyes when he looked at her. Even now, though her clothing was wet from the water clinging to his body, she burned inside and craved more of him.

Only after Vasil set her back down did she notice Dracchus had accompanied him; the big kraken had Larkin pressed up against the wall, locked in a kiss as passionate as the one Vasil and Theo had just shared.

"I guess you kraken males are always happy to see your mates, huh?" Theo asked, tilting her head back to grin up at Vasil.

Larkin laughed, giving Dracchus a playful shove away. "You have *no* idea."

Dracchus growled, dropped his hands to her hips, and attempted to draw her closer, but she flattened her palms on his chest and locked her elbows.

"Behave. Wait until we're in our room," Larkin said. "Then you can have me all to yourself."

He grunted and lowered his hands, but the fiery gleam in his eyes did not diminish.

Vasil cupped Theo's face and lowered his head to press his forehead against hers. "You have given me something worth coming home to."

A warm, tingling sensation spread outward from Theo's chest. She smiled, cupped the back of his head, and closed her eyes. *Home.* She hadn't realized just how much weight, how much meaning, that word could hold until Vasil became part of her life. Old Earth had never been her home, nor had the ships she'd lived on for so many years. Her home was with Vasil. *He* was where she belonged.

"I've missed you, too," she whispered, opening her eyes.

His nostrils flared with a slow, deep inhalation, and he simply held her for several seconds. "How are your repairs progressing?"

"All done for now," she said.

"The air cleaner is fixed?" Dracchus asked. "Our people are safe?"

"Yep. Good as new. Well, as good as it can get. But…it's not gonna forever. You know that, right?"

"We have always known. Our people will adapt as necessary.

But you have made our home safe for a little longer, and for that I am grateful."

"You have done well," Vasil said, calling Theo's attention back to him. He leaned closer to her again, simultaneously drawing her pelvis against his. "And now I wish to have *my* mate all to myself. Come, female."

"Don't bother saying it. I'll deactivate myself, thank you," Kane muttered in her mind.

Theo chuckled, shaking gently against Vasil.

Vasil groaned, tightening his hold on her and pressing the hard bump of his slit against her belly. "I will not wait any longer."

Before she could respond, he lifted Theo off the floor and settled her over his shoulder, clamping his arm around the back of her thighs with one hand on her ass as he ducked through the doorway.

"Vasil!" she half-screeched, half-laughed, her palms flat against his back.

He moved to her toolbox, sank down to collect it in his free hand — that thoughtfulness alone undid her — and darted into the corridor. Her hair fell around her face, obscuring her vision except for the fast-moving tentacles below her as he hurried toward the elevator.

If Dracchus and Larkin saw what he'd done, they made no comment; Theo guessed they were somewhat occupied themselves.

Vasil stopped his frantic rush only when they were in the elevator. Though he remained in place as it rumbled up to the main floor, his tentacles moved restlessly on the floor, and the hand settled on her ass kneaded her flesh through her jumpsuit.

Theo hummed, the anticipation of what was to come flooding her with desire. She smoothed her hands down his lower back and massaged his powerful muscles. Turning his face toward her, he inhaled deeply.

Vasil groaned again. "I smell your need."

The elevator came to a halt, and Vasil exited it the instant the door was wide enough to fit through. Doorways zipped by on either side, blurred by his speed as he raced through the corridors into the cabins. The sound of him slapping the button to open the door of their room was so pronounced that she was convinced he'd broken it.

Before the door was fully open, Vasil slipped through. He set down Theo's toolbox, and she caught a glimpse of one of his tentacles pressing the button to close the door before he carried her across the room toward the bed.

Her world tilted once again when he lifted her off his shoulder and laid her atop the covers. She laughed, wiping hair from her face to look up at Vasil towering over her. His eyes were intent, alight with unmasked passion, adoration, and hunger. Arousal heated her core.

He tore at her clothing, his claws shredding the fabric to be torn away from her body piece-by-piece until she lay bare before him. His need for her, unrestrained and all-consuming, left her breathless.

Tossing aside her tattered clothing, Vasil curled his fingers around her inner thighs and spread them wide. His gaze trailed down her body, forging a blazing path over her skin, and finally settled on her sex. The hunger in his eyes intensified. He lowered his head and breathed in her scent, closing his eyes.

"Ah, female. I will never have my fill of you," he growled before his mouth was upon her.

Theo gasped and tilted her head back as pure bliss swept through her. His tongue flicked first over her clit, then explored and teased the delicate folds around it. She clutched the bedding, desperate for something to hold on to, something to anchor her lest she float away on a cloud of pleasure. His lips nipped at her, and his sharp teeth grazed the sensitive flesh around her clit; the hint of danger those wicked points posed only increased her pleasure.

His tentacles coiled around her calves, twirling higher to lock her knees in place. He lifted a hand off her thigh.

Theo opened her eyes and looked down her body as Vasil raised his head, moved his hand to his mouth, and bit the claws off his index and middle fingers. He turned his head aside, spat the pieces away, and returned his eyes to hers. He held her gaze as he returned his mouth to her sex and lapped at her, slowly running his tongue from the bottom of her slit up to her clit. Her hips bucked, and a fresh wave of dew flowed from her.

Vasil flattened a hand over her pelvis to pin her to the bed and moaned as he drank from her. The vibrations from his chest only added the sensations building within her.

Panting, Theo kept her eyes on him. Her body was flushed with heat; she was so close. Her thighs trembled in her need, and every teasing flick of his tongue held her on the brink of release.

"Vasil," she breathed, undulating her hips against his mouth.

He slid a hand along her inner thigh to her sex. A moment later, one of his fingers slid into her, followed quickly by a second. Her body clamped around them greedily as they pumped in and out.

He bit off his claws so he could do this to me.

Latching onto her clit with his mouth, Vasil thrust his fingers into her as far as his webbing allowed. Theo squeezed her eyes shut and cried out as cascading waves of pleasure crashed over her. She twisted and writhed, her moans filling the room. Each flick of his tongue and thrust of his fingers prolonged her climax. The manacle-like grip of his tentacles held her open to him, leaving her at his mercy.

Eventually, he withdrew his fingers and resumed his leisurely licking, trailing his tongue up and down her sex as though he couldn't get enough of her taste. She eased down from the heights to which he'd lifted her. When she shifted her hips, he clamped his hands over them and growled possessively; the growl faded into a contented purr.

He seemed content to lap at her for hours, but she knew he *needed*.

Theo's hooded eyes met his hungry stare. She reached down to caress his face, tracing his cheekbone with her thumb. "Make love to me, Vasil."

Vasil rose over Theo, covering her body with his. She lifted her arms in welcome, wrapping them around his neck to draw him closer, but he stopped before their lips met and simply gazed into her beautiful, green eyes. Though his body ached with need for her, though his cock throbbed, and his blood flowed like fire through his veins, his frenzy had subsided.

Make love to me, Vasil.

Love.

He knew what that meant now, and he wanted it too. Wanted to enjoy her, *all* of her, to enjoy every moment they had together.

His mate. His.

Mine.

Vasil brought a hand up and threaded his fingers in her pale hair, cupping the back of her head. "You shine brighter than the sun, my fallen star." He guided his cock to her slit. "My radiant, beautiful star."

He pressed into her slowly, savoring her scent, the feel of her heat and softness. She cradled him with her legs, and her body welcomed him without restraint until she'd taken all of him in. Eyes locked with hers, he pulled back and thrust forward, again and again, rocking into her like waves rolling against the shore. He spread his rear tentacles to grasp the corners of the bed as his front tentacles drew her tighter against him, increasing the force of his thrusts, pushing him ever deeper.

Theo's eyelids drooped, and her lips parted with breathy sighs. She clung to him; her dull nails scratched his scalp, her sex clenched his cock, and his tendrils delighted in the taste of her essence. Her body quivered against him. She was close, but Vasil didn't increase his pace. He kept her there at the edge, relishing her reactions even as pleasure blossomed from his belly to spread through all his limbs.

This was his mate — more than worthy, more than he deserved, and he would do everything to keep her safe, to keep her happy, to keep her with him.

She'd saved the kraken's home.

She'd given him purpose.

One of his tendrils found her clit, stroking and caressing it each time his pelvis met hers. She gasped and tightened her hold on him as her body suddenly went taut.

"*I love you!*" Theo's rasped words were followed by moans of pleasure.

Heat flooded her core, and her inner walls contracted around his shaft. Vasil growled and slammed his mouth over hers, drinking in her cries as he ravaged her mouth. He quickened his pace, driving his cock deeper and faster into her body, pushing her to new heights, extending her release as his took hold of him.

With a final thrust, he drove into her as deep as he could go. The pressure inside him became too great at that moment; he burst. His seed filled her as his muscles tensed. He wrapped Theo in arms and tentacles, turning on the bed so he wouldn't crush her, and held her with their bodies entwined, connected. One.

Theo broke the kiss and pressed her face against his neck. Her rapid breaths were warm against his skin, which was dampened by her sweat. Vasil did not release her; he ground his cock inside her, tendrils caressing her slit, eliciting another moan from her.

The pounding of their hearts eased over time. Vasil ran the tips of his fingers and claws through her hair and down the curve of her spine. He breathed in their combined scents as his suction cups kissed her flesh, granting fresh tastes of her.

Never in his life had he felt more content.

They lay together for a long while, the room silent save for their soft breathing. Part of Vasil worried that to speak might spoil the moment; what words could encompass the feelings shared between them, the *experience*? But he knew it was a foolish notion. What he and Theo had was not this moment, it was *all* moments, each as precious as the last and the next.

"We should travel to The Watch tomorrow," he said.

She inhaled deeply and released the breath in a sleepy, soft, "Okay."

There was no question in her answer. She trusted him to take her, to protect her.

He knew no delicate way to tell her what he needed to say next. "I have a youngling there."

For a moment, she was quiet and still; the sudden tensing of her body told him when his words penetrated the pleasure-induced fog that must have settled over her mind.

"A what?" she asked.

"A youngling. A...child."

Theo's head bolted up, nearly clipping his chin as she propped herself over him with her palms on his chest. "A *child*? And you...we..." Her brows fell, and her eyes narrowed. "You had better not tell me you have another mate waiting for you in The Watch, or I swear I'll rip your god damned co—"

Vasil's eyes flared. "Theo—"

"I don't know what kind of lives you kraken live, but I don't share! Got it?"

Grasping her upper arms, Vasil flipped Theo onto her back

and rolled to position himself over her. He covered her mouth with one hand, unable to keep an amused smirk from his lips; her jealousy was oddly satisfying.

"Listen well, human," he said. "*You* are my mate. My *only* mate. Now and forever after. I only learned she is my daughter without a doubt just before I met you, but she is nine years old. My time with her mother was long ago and brief. It was the fulfillment of my duty to my people. Nothing more. Do you understand?"

The fire had gone out of Theo's eyes as he spoke. She nodded.

He removed his hand from her mouth and cupped her cheek. "You are the only one I have ever connected with, Theo. The only one I have ever been truly close to."

She searched his gaze and placed a hand on his forearm. "What's her name?"

"Melaina."

"How did you only just find out she's yours?"

"I have suspected for a time, but things were different before we made peace with the humans. Our kind was designed to have difficulty reproducing. Female kraken took many mates, rarely keeping one for long, in the hope of conceiving a youngling. We have been on the brink of dying off without human intervention for generations. Younglings were always raised by the females in isolation, where they could be safe until the males were old enough to learn from the hunters. We were never told who had sired the children."

Theo's brows furrowed. "What a shitty way to live."

"It was the only way for us to survive."

"But why the separation? Why not tell the males so they could be fathers? So you could have families?"

Vasil stroked her leg with the tip of his tentacle. "Because such was not our way, Theo. Younglings are rare and precious, females even more so. They needed to be protected, to be kept safe. We all took on that responsibility. It did not matter who sired a youngling, only that a youngling had been born."

"You said you only found out without a doubt recently, but how long have you suspected that Melaina was yours?"

He slid his cock out of Theo, rolled off her, and lay on his back, keeping his tentacle around her leg. She turned on her side to face him. His gaze wandered to the ceiling as he sifted through his memories, searching for that first suspicion, the first time he'd put the clues together.

The answer came far quicker than he'd anticipated — it had been the day Vasil and a party of kraken had been attacked by human hunters. They'd returned to the Facility and brought Kronus to the infirmary so his wounds could be tended only to discover several females and younglings sick; they'd been poisoned while the males were away.

Melaina had been one of those affected. She'd been much smaller than she was now, and the moment he laid eyes upon her — curled up in that big bed with her features contorted in pain — some part of him had known. Some part of him had recognized her as his blood, as his offspring. His hearts had stilled, and for an instant, the world had seemed to spin around him uncontrollably. But he'd shaken it off and said nothing because that was what had been expected of him. That was what a dutiful kraken did.

"More than two years," he replied, brows furrowing. He'd wasted so much time already.

"*What?*" Theo raised her head, hair tumbling over one shoulder, and glared down at him. "You knew for *two years* and did nothing? Said nothing?"

"I do not know what I am meant to have said, Theo."

She sat up, crossing her legs as much as his tentacle would allow. "Anything!"

Vasil met her gaze, refusing to release his hold on her. "She has a life. A family."

"Two years..." Theo shook her head. "At least she has you now. Better late than never, right?"

"She does not know."

The fire that flared in Theo's eyes at that moment burned hotter than anything Vasil had ever seen.

"You *still* haven't said anything, Vasil? *Done* anything? Do you have *any* idea what I would have given for my father to have known I existed? How many times I wondered if my life would have been different if he'd been in it, if he'd come to save me from that shithole? From *her*?"

Vasil wanted to tell her he understood, that he knew exactly the things she'd felt and experienced, that he'd felt the same way at some point, but he couldn't bring himself to lie to her. The way things had been could not be changed. Vasil had never known his sire and had never cared to know because it was never of any importance.

But *now*...

Everything was different. *Everything*. Though it didn't alter his past, it *could* alter his future.

"She has always had her mother. Rhea is fierce and devoted, and Melaina will be strong. And she has had a male in her life, as well. Randall. He is a good man, and she adores him. *He* is a father to her. What place is it of mine to disrupt what she has?"

Theo stared at him, her eyes glassy with tears; he couldn't tell if they were fueled by anger or sorrow. Perhaps both.

"She's *your* daughter, Vasil. *Yours*. She deserves to have *you* in her life, too. To know."

Randall's words from the beach on the night the star had fallen came back to Vasil.

You're just as much a father to her as I am.

It's not too late to be part of her life, Vasil. It'd do both of you some good.

For most of his life, Vasil had been focused on the concept of *place* — what was his place as a kraken, as a male, as a hunter?

How could he perform his duties and benefit his people? How could he avoid causing trouble, avoid violating the way things had been done? He'd been passive because that had seemed the best way to maintain the kraken way of life. Leave leadership to the more aggressive males, those who were driven to it. Ask no unnecessary questions.

Follow. Survive.

But none of that applied anymore. Working with the humans of The Watch, the kraken no longer needed to struggle for survival. They had abundant food. They had new lives, new *hope*, and a chance to explore the side of themselves they had so often denied — their *human* side.

Randall had been right.

Theo was right.

"I will speak with her when we return," he said. He slipped his arm around Theo's shoulders, drawing her down against his side. "I will give her the choice, as I should have long ago."

Theo cupped his cheek, turning his face toward her. She smiled. "You have made your mate proud."

He settled a hand on her face and stared into her eyes — eyes which seemed to hold unlimited depth and beauty, as boundless as the stars from which she'd fallen. "I will have earned that pride when I do as I have said."

She snuggled against him. He tangled his tentacles with her legs, craving the touch of her skin, needing as much contact with her as possible. She sighed, relaxing in his hold. Vasil closed his eyes.

Fear dwelled in the recesses of his mind — fear of rejection, fear that Melaina would denounce and resent him because he'd not gone to her sooner. Though he knew that fear was irrational and unwarranted, it persisted; Melaina was strong, but she was also kind, warm, and forgiving. She was old enough to know the traditions, even if she was not yet old enough to fully understand them.

But there was excitement within him, too. Anticipation. What had he longed for more than a true connection to other people? To have a family of his own, like Jax, Arkon, Dracchus, Rhea, and even Kronus had found? Vasil had Theo, and Theo would be forever enough, but he wanted a relationship with his daughter, as well. He wanted to know her because she was an amazing child. *His* child.

Melaina pursued her passions and curiosity. She was open to everything and questioned freely things she did not understand. She was bold, seemingly fearless, and had been a larger part of humans and kraken coming together peacefully than she might ever have realized.

She was everything Vasil hoped to become.

CHAPTER 19

"So... That went well, right?" Theo asked, swinging her foot to kick a rock off the dirt road they were following. The rock crashed into the nearby jungle foliage.

"If your goal was to have everyone stare at you like an alien, yes. A smashing success," replied Kane aloud, his light pulsing at her wrist.

"It went well, Theo," said Vasil. He settled a hand on the small of her back and continued to move beside her, matching her pace. "It has been hundreds of years since anything came here from beyond Halora. Some shock is expected."

"He *is* right," said Kane begrudgingly. "And they seemed to understand the value of your skills to this settlement."

They'd arrived in The Watch early that morning; thankfully, the journey from the Facility hadn't been as long as Theo had feared. Despite Vasil's assurances before they'd left, she'd been unable to shake the memory of her utter exhaustion when they swam from the pod to the Facility.

Though they'd stopped at Vasil's house — he called it their *den* — before anywhere else, they'd spent the rest of the day in town, meeting people and looking around. The day had been capped by a late-afternoon meeting with the town council, at which at least a hundred people had been present.

She smirked. "Damn right I'm valuable."

Vasil chuckled. "More so than you may ever understand, female."

Ahead, a natural archway created by the trees marked a break in the jungle through which pure sunlight, tinged red-orange by the coming sunset, shone. Though the swim from the Facility had been a cakewalk compared to her other underwater travels, Theo was exhausted. She couldn't wait to get back to the house — *their* house, Vasil had insisted — crawl into bed, and fall asleep in his arms.

"Their wonder at where you are from will pass," Vasil said, "and be replaced by their wonder at your capabilities. This place will be better for having you. Just remember, human — I will not share."

Theo grinned, glancing at Vasil from the corner of her eye. "I don't expect you to."

The work she'd take on in The Watch would be different from what she'd known. Based on what she'd seen today, there'd be a lot more engineering involved than repair — she doubted there were either the parts or the resources to make new ones for most of the old tech lying around, but with Kane's extensive collection of plans, her know-how, and the parts hoarded at the Facility, she was sure she could build new things to help make everyone's lives easier here.

That wasn't even the biggest difference — building or repairing, it all brought her the same satisfaction. For the first time in eighteen years, she'd be spending her days somewhere besides the bowels of a ship. There was a town here, with open air and fields of crops, pastures with farm animals, a jungle, and beaches. She'd never realized how greatly the dark, often cramped environments she'd lived in for most of her life had affected her mood until she crashed on Halora.

They broke through the trees, emerging onto a grassy rise overlooking the sea. The path cut through the grass, leading to the row of houses built along the rise, each a little different than the others. She'd only been here for a few minutes after their arrival, but seeing this place now, bathed in the light of the setting sun, it felt like coming home.

Home.

Warmth filled her. She had a home. With Vasil.

A tentacle brushed against her leg. She turned her face toward Vasil.

He was looking at her, his eyes soft and loving. Taking her hand in his, he led her toward the houses through the grass.

Shrieks of laughter caught her attention. Two children barreled through the long grass — *kraken* children, but there was something different about them…

Theo halted abruptly. "They have *hair.*"

Vasil stopped beside her. "They are half-human, half-kraken. Thus far such younglings seem to favor their kraken parentage."

Theo watched the children — a boy and a girl who seemed of similar age — as they played. In addition to the hair atop their heads, they had eyebrows and more prominent, human noses. Otherwise, they looked fully kraken.

"Sarina! Jace," someone called.

The new voice caught Theo's attention; she turned toward it to see another kraken — another female — emerge from one of the houses. The newcomer was taller than the children, though she didn't appear full-grown; she was slim and feminine with refined features and hairless, light gray skin. She seemed like a girl on the verge of womanhood, and though that didn't make sense given Melaina's age — nine — Theo knew it was her.

"It's time for dinner," Melaina said.

The two children paused to look back. While the little girl was distracted, the boy turned toward her and pounced, tackling her to the ground.

"Jace!" the girl cried, her tentacles thrashing as she fought to dislodge the boy.

Theo glanced up at Vasil to find him looking at Melaina. His expression was too confused to be readable, but she could hear the whisper of his tentacles restlessly flicking over the grass.

"She looks like you," Theo said.

"I…see more of her mother in her," he replied softly.

Theo couldn't help the stab of jealousy his words provoked. It was a reminder that he'd touched another woman, had made love to her. That he'd created a life, a child, with someone else. He'd told Theo it had been duty and not desire, but she still didn't want to think of him being with anyone else.

She quickly pushed those thoughts aside. His relationship with Melaina's mother was in the past, and that was where it belonged. Just like Theo's time with other men was part of her past.

Melaina, though…she was *here*, part of Vasil's present. Part of his future. And Theo would do everything she could to support him in that, to accept Melaina as part of her own little family.

They watched as Melaina approached the two younglings and, with some difficulty, broke them apart, before leading them back to the house from which she'd come. Once they were inside, Theo and Vasil continued along the path to their own dwelling.

Vasil entered ahead of Theo and moved aside to allow her through. As he closed the door behind her, she ran her gaze over the place again; it looked different with the evening light streaming in through the back windows than it had in the morning. The light made the place seem almost…magical.

Everything but the bathroom was contained in the single main room — a large bed rested in one corner, a table and chair stood in front of one of the sea-facing windows, and the cabinets, fireplace, and kitchen were in the corner to the immediate right of the entrance. An armoire and a storage chest rounded out the furniture.

It was small and simple.

It was perfect.

Everything was hand-made, displaying all the little faults that automated manufacturing had eliminated in the rest of the galaxy, and it granted the whole place an undeniable charm and character she'd loved from the first moment she'd stepped inside. Theo's life had been filled with bland, machine-constructed components — precise angles and maximum practicality even when constructed of the cheapest possible materials. Even the apartment building she'd lived in as a child had possessed that cold, inhuman aesthetic.

But this place felt *alive*.

Theo walked across the room, turned, and fell backward onto the bed. She sank into the soft covers and mattress with a groan. Though she was eager to take off the diving suit she'd been wearing all day, all she needed right now was to lie there unmoving — to enjoy some blessed stillness.

"Are you hungry?" Vasil asked.

"I'm practically withering away. My stomach is eating itself right now." Though Theo didn't lift her head to look at Vasil, she sensed his frown from across the room.

"Should I send for Aymee or her father to examine you? Or...is that another human *expression*?"

Theo chuckled. "An expression. Yes, I'm starving."

She turned her head to watch him as he moved into the kitchen. She smiled, letting her gaze roam over his broad shoulders, trek down his strong, muscled back, and settle on the curve of his spine, where his upper body met his faintly-darker lower half. The play of his muscles as he moved was exquisite. When she looked up at his face again, her smile faded.

His eyes were focused, but he appeared...distracted. There was a furrow in his brow, and the corners of his lips were downturned. Though he appeared calm, his tentacles curled and slid restlessly across the floor.

Theo pushed herself up on her elbows. "Vasil? What's wrong?"

He stilled his hand, in which he held a piece of winefruit. Frown deepening, he set the fruit down on the tray of feed he'd been preparing and turned his face toward Theo. "What if she does not want me in her life?"

Melaina.

Theo's heart hurt for him. It wasn't like Vasil to doubt — the kraken she'd come to know always charged ahead with purpose, with confidence. This was a side of him she'd not really seen before now, and she could relate to it.

She slid off the bed and walked across the room, stopping in front of him to cup his face between her palms. "Why wouldn't she?"

Vasil's hands settled on her hips; his fingers were firm and strong, even if the uncertainty in his expression remained.

"Before me, I see a worthy male," Theo said, staring up at him with love and pride in her eyes. "I see a man who wants nothing more than to connect with a daughter he's never known. A man who is wonderful and kind, strong and protective. A man who would go to the ends of this world to fight for those he cares for." She stood on her toes, tugged his face down, and kissed him. "She will love you, Vasil."

He pressed his forehead to hers and closed his eyes as he pulled her close. Theo slipped her arms around his neck.

"We had all gathered on the beach the night Randall told me I was Melaina's sire," he said. "Everyone else went home, one by one, until only I remained. I wrestled with my thoughts deep into the night. I did not know what to do. And then a star streaked overhead...and I gave chase.

"When I jumped into the sea to follow your pod, not knowing what I would find, *if* I would find anything...that was the first time I can remember acting at my own whim. Doing something because *I* wanted to, without considering everyone else. It was for me. I have learned that it is all right to take for myself sometimes. To take risks. Because it was a risk that gave me you."

Tears stung Theo's eyes as she drew back to look at him. He curled a finger beneath her chin and brushed his lips against hers. She returned the kiss.

"For all the dangers I have faced," he said when he finally broke the kiss, "I have been afraid of telling that girl who I am more than anything. At least until I had to face the thought of losing you."

Theo smiled and shifted one of her arms to cradle his jaw in her palm. "Meet with her tonight."

"I must speak with Randall and Rhea, first. They will want to be involved, as is their right." He smoothed back her hair and stared into her eyes. "But I *will* do so tonight. After we eat and you are comfortable."

"Don't worry about me. I'll be fine, and I will be waiting for you. Right here." She grinned. "In our *home*."

He returned the grin, flashing his sharp teeth; they'd gone from frightening to tantalizing to downright sexy.

"*Ours*," he agreed. "But I am *not* leaving until I have eaten. I am *withering away*."

Theo laughed and lowered her hand to the tray beside them, plucking up a piece of smoked fish. She brought it to his lips. "Then let your mate take care of your needs. *All* your needs."

Vasil's eyes heated with a different sort of hunger.

THE SKY WAS dark by the time Vasil made his way along the path toward Randall and Rhea's dwelling, with only the faintest sliver of orange blazing on the horizon beneath dusk-blackened clouds. He twisted briefly to glance behind. Soft light shone in the windows of his den, and it lent him more strength to push on. Theo would be waiting when this was done, no matter how it went.

He reminded himself that it would go well as he neared Randall's door. His nervousness and unease were holdouts from a bygone time, a time now lost to history, and all he needed to do was embrace the new world to move on from them.

Lamplight glowed in the dwelling's windows, spilling onto the ground outside to highlight the grass' gentle swaying in the ocean-kissed breeze. This place smelled of land and sea together; Vasil liked the mingled scents even more now that he had Theo.

Allowing himself no hesitation, he lifted a hand and knocked on the door.

Something large thumped inside, the sound followed by a soft chirruping. A moment later, there was a scratch at the inside of the door.

"Relax," Randall said from within, voice muffled.

The door swung open. Vasil's eyes widened, and he shifted aside as Ikaros, Randall's pet prixxir, bounded through the doorway. The creature was at least as long as Randall was tall, powerfully built, with sleek scales and a spiny fin along its back.

Ikaros darted into the long grass and out of sight.

"Son of a bitch," Randall muttered. "Sorry, Vasil. He'll uh… guess he'll come back when he's ready."

Vasil turned back to Randall, who was rubbing the back of his head. "It is all right. No harm done."

"Good." Randall nodded, eyes flicking up and down Vasil's body. "Good. Hey, I just wanted to say I'm glad you're back safe. We searched for you for days, but I guess from what I've heard you were carried out a lot farther than we realized was possible."

"Yes. A full day's swim from the Facility."

"Damn. We were worried that a razorback or something made a meal out of you. Wasn't long ago there were a bunch of them up and down the coast."

"I know." Vasil smiled despite his lingering anxiousness. "The only things that tried to eat me were certainly *not* razorbacks. I would say the change was a welcome one, but... I suppose I would choose the known over the unknown."

Randall chuckled. "I hear you. You'll have to tell me about it. I caught up with my sister earlier, and she mentioned some kind of monster you guys killed at the bottom of a trench. Scary shit."

"It was. Especially with my mate being in danger."

"That's right! She mentioned you have a woman." Randall slapped a hand onto Vasil's shoulder and leaned forward, peering out into the night. "Congratulations, man. You didn't bring her? We'd love to meet her."

Vasil's gaze flicked back toward his dwelling for an instant. "Not tonight. There is something we must address first."

Randall drew back and regarded Vasil with an arched brow. A few moments later, his eyes rounded, and his grip on Vasil's shoulder tightened. "Oh. Oh! You're ready? Right now?"

Vasil nodded. "I do not wish to waste any more time."

A bright, joyous grin spread across Randall's face — the sort of genuine display of happiness that Vasil might never have experienced had humans and kraken never reconnected in peace.

"Rhea and Melaina are over at Macy's. They ate dinner there, since I was out late. You want to wait here while I go get them?" Randall released his hold on Vasil and stepped back, moving aside. "I'm sure you don't want an audience or anything."

Despite all the time he'd spent with humans, despite the many occasions upon which he'd visited them within their dwellings, the experience of being invited into someone's den remained strange to Vasil. Of all the old kraken ways, that had seemed the most unshakeable; a kraken's den was a sanctuary, a private place, shared *only* with a mate — if at all. As usual, he shrugged off those feelings and moved inside.

Randall and Rhea's dwelling was larger than Vasil's, with two rooms — both intended solely for sleeping — built off the main chamber, not including the bathroom.

"Make yourself comfortable. I'll be right back." Randall stepped outside, closing the door quietly behind him.

Vasil crossed the main room and stopped at one of the wide, sturdy chairs. Arranging his tentacles, he eased himself onto the seat in the closest posture he could accomplish to sitting. Several other chairs stood nearby, some designed like this one — larger and more solidly built than their counterparts to accommodate kraken size and weight.

Settling his elbows on the armrests, he allowed his gaze to wander as he waited. All the dwellings that housed humans seemed to have something in common — decoration. No two dwellings were decorated in quite the same fashion, but he'd noticed that humans tended to adorn their dwellings with various trinkets and baubles which seemed to hold little purpose other than being pleasing to look upon. A few kraken had taken to doing the same.

The collection of items here was eclectic — much of it seemed to relate to Randall's hunting, but there were also interesting rocks, shells, dried plants and flowers, scraps of cloth in nearly every color Vasil could imagine, and dozens of other objects.

Would Theo do the same to their den? The corners of his lips rose at the thought. He couldn't guess how she'd decorate, but his imagination produced images of machine components and metal scraps on display throughout their home, so scattered and chaotic that guests would never know for certain if the items had been placed there as adornment or were parts for Theo's active projects.

Voices from outside called his attention to the door, which

opened only a few moments later. Randall muttered something and stumbled through the doorway as Ikaros shoved past him. The prixxir came to Vasil immediately, sniffed at him with twitching whiskers, and lay down atop his tentacles.

"No, Ikaros, that's fine," Randall said, "just do whatever the hell you want."

The prixxir lifted its head briefly to make a snorting sound before settling back down.

"You spoiled him, human," Rhea said, entering behind Randall.

Vasil's gaze dropped to Rhea's middle — her rounded middle. It had been some time since he last saw her, and there'd been no visible proof of the life growing inside her then.

Melaina followed immediately after her mother, closing the door once she was inside. She looked at Ikaros with a grin before her eyes shifted to Vasil. Her grin widened. "You're back! Where did you go?"

Vasil's hearts leapt at the excitement in her voice and expression. He'd thought he was just another adult to her, no one of consequence or importance. "I was carried off to a distant beach during a storm."

She moved closer and lowered herself down to the floor in front of Ikaros, absently brushing the prixxir's belly with a tentacle. "What did you see? What was it like? Did the beach look the same as it does here? What—"

"Melaina," Rhea said in a warning tone.

Randall chuckled and eased himself into one of the human chairs. "Let's give Vasil a chance to answer your first twenty questions before you ask twenty more, okay?"

Melaina ducked her head and peeked up at Vasil. "Sorry."

Vasil offered her a smile. He understood her curiosity, but he had denied himself its pursuit for all his life. "The sand felt the same, but it was a few shades lighter, and most of the beach was backed by jungle instead of rocks and cliffs. We found a sea cave there that was filled with halorium shards."

Her brows rose, and her siphons twitched. "Really? A cave? Halorium? Could you take me?"

"It is very far away." Vasil glanced at Rhea, whose hard gaze left no question as to her thought on the matter. "I do not think it would be a safe journey to make."

Melaina visibly deflated. "Nothing is *ever* safe."

Rhea frowned. "We have discussed this, Melaina."

Vasil wanted to tell Melaina he'd take her, that he'd find a group of kraken willing to make the journey and show her every part of that beach until she was content, but he knew better than to contradict Rhea.

"The ocean is dangerous," Vasil said, "especially for a lone kraken. Your mother wants only to keep you from harm, not from seeing the wonders of the world."

"I know." Melaina sighed. "I just…want to see it."

"Melaina… I… I didn't come here to talk about caves or my journey."

She looked up at him, brows furrowed. "You didn't?"

"There is something we have wanted to tell you," Rhea said. "The ways of our people have changed, and we believe it is time for you to know."

"I don't understand, Mom."

"Well, I've filled the role of a father to you," Randall said, leaning forward to rest his elbows on his knees. "And I love it; it's been great, and more fulfilling than I could have ever imagined. But I'm *not* your birth father, and… Well…"

"Vasil is your sire," said Rhea. "Your father by blood."

Melaina looked back and forth between Rhea and Randall until her gaze settled on Vasil. There was still confusion written upon her features. "And?"

"What do you mean, *and?*" asked Randall.

"I already knew that. Was there something else you wanted to tell me, or was that it?"

Vasil's lips parted, but no words came out. His mind was, for several heartbeats, empty. After all his deliberation, all his struggle…

"You *knew*?" Randall asked.

Rhea spoke at the same time. "How?"

Melaina gathered her tentacles beneath her and shifted closer to Vasil. She smiled at him and settled a hand over his. "We are alike. You hide it inside, but I've seen it. And we have the same eyes."

Vasil couldn't have stopped his laughter if he'd wanted to; it flowed from him freely, and it felt *good*. "How long have you known?"

"For many years. I saw you once when I snuck out of our den, while the males were gathering for a hunt, and I just knew. I knew you were my sire."

"I feel like a fool for having waited so long."

"It was not our way," Rhea said softly.

Her words made his smile fade; Rhea was right, but knowing what he did now, he could no longer look upon that tradition favorably.

"I did not know my sire," Vasil said. "I never followed my curiosity because it was not our way. But our ways have changed, and I know now what I have missed. If you would allow me, Melaina, I would like to be more than your sire. I would be a father to you."

She grinned and squeezed his hand. "I would like that very much."

They talked for a while longer; Melaina was quite animated as she rattled off stories and a seemingly endless string of questions. Eventually, she led him into her room to show him the various objects she'd collected over the years, both on land and in the sea, and told him stories of how she'd come by them. The items ranged from shells, driftwood, rocks, and dried flowers to paintings similar to those Aymee often created, carved toys, and bits of humanmade jewelry.

Melaina plucked something off the stand beside her bed and turned to Vasil, holding the object to him on her palms. It was a shell, its silvery interior surface reflecting the light in the room.

"You can have this one," she said. "I found it the day I first saw you. It made me think of you."

Vasil looked down at the little shell, a strange tightness spreading through his chest. "And you kept it all this while?"

"Of course. And now you can have it so you can think of me."

He lifted his hand, palm up, and she carefully laid the shell upon it. Slowly, he curled his fingers around the precious little bauble. "I will keep it always. I am sorry. I have no gift for you."

"You could bring me one. Tomorrow," she said, eyes bright and hopeful.

He nodded. "Tomorrow."

"Melaina," Rhea said from the doorway, "it has grown late. We should let Vasil return home to his mate."

"So soon?" she asked with a frown.

"This is just the first time," Vasil said. "Not at all the last. I have to bring a gift tomorrow, do I not?"

"Yes!"

Smiling, Vasil raised his hand — fingers still around the shell — to his chest. "I will find a safe place to keep this. Rest well, daughter."

Like a silver darter, Melaina threw herself at Vasil and wrapped her arms around him. "Thank you, father."

He embraced her, the sensation in his chest only intensifying. He'd never imagined it would be so simple — just a few exchanged words, and he had another piece added to his little family. "Thank *you*, Melaina."

"You are welcome in our den, Vasil," Rhea said.

Vasil bid the females, Randall, and Ikaros goodnight and exited their dwelling, feeling oddly light as he moved along the path. A few stars had broken through the clouds, and one of the two moons was visible over the water, casting silver light on the rolling waves. He entered his dwelling quietly; Theo was silent and still in bed, and he didn't want to risk disturbing her until he was alongside her.

He moved to the storage chest at the foot of the bed and lowered himself to open it but stopped before he put the shell inside. He wanted to keep the shell safe, but it held too much meaning to him to be locked away in a box. Rising, he turned to survey the room. Muted lamplight bathed it in a soft glow, but he'd lived here long enough that he would've known the place just as well in total darkness. After several moments, he went to the fireplace and propped the shell on the mantle, its reflective surface facing outward.

He backed up and assessed the placement, smiling to himself.

When the setting sun shone through the windows, it would hit the shell and set it aglow with reflected light.

He turned off the small electric lamp on the table and crossed the room to climb into bed beside Theo, gently slipping his arm beneath her and drawing her against him. She turned to face him, snuggling her arms and cheek against his chest.

"How'd it go?" she murmured.

Vasil twined his tentacles with her legs and settled his cheek atop her hair. "Good. You were right, Theo. You have made both myself and my daughter happy."

She hummed contentedly. Her breathing slowed.

He kissed the top of her head. "I love you, Theodora. You are the only star I need ever see shine again."

CHAPTER 20

"THANK YOU SO MUCH, THEO," JENNY SAID, THROWING HER ARMS around Theo in an unexpected embrace. "It took Camrin three days just to figure out the sink was broken, but you fixed it twenty minutes."

Theo awkwardly patted the woman's back. Since her arrival in The Watch a little over a week ago, she'd discovered that most everyone like to touch — handshakes, hugs, pats on the back, kisses on the cheek. It was a tight-knit community.

The townsfolk had done nothing but make Theo feel welcome, but it would take time for her to grow used to their demeanors. The lessons of her childhood — *no one gets close to you without trying to take something* — were still hard to shake all these years later.

"It didn't take me that long, Jenny," Camrin said, scowling with his arms crossed over his chest.

Jenny released Theo and stepped back to look at her husband. "You flooded the kitchen. Twice! You may be a fine fisherman, Camrin, but a repairman you are not."

"Aww, come on," he said, his tough-guy scowl giving way to a wounded frown beneath his short, red beard. "That was just run-off from my boots. You know I get splashed with seawater all day."

"From your boots? It covered the entire floor, Camrin! James was practically swimming in it."

He shrugged sheepishly. "Can't stop the kid from playing, right?"

Jenny pinched the bridge of her nose. She glanced at Theo, and her cheeks reddened as though she'd forgotten there was an audience present.

"Walter asked me to take a look at the lighthouse today," Theo said, jabbing her thumb over her shoulder. "So... I'm going to head over there. If you have any other issues, just let me know."

"Oh, I will," Jenny said. "*Before* Camrin breaks it more next time."

Camrin scoffed. "I *didn't* break it, Jen."

Theo chuckled as she put away her tools and closed her tool-box. "Have a great day."

"You too! And thank you again, Theo," Jenny said, smiling.

Theo picked up her toolbox and made her way toward the front door. Behind her, she heard Camrin's footsteps as he moved toward Jenny, followed by soft words and giggles. If Theo had guessed they were on the verge of a fight, she'd apparently guessed wrong.

She closed the front door firmly, but quietly.

"*If nothing else, I can say this life is markedly different than our old one,*" Kane said in her mind. "*Certainly more entertaining.*"

Theo breathed in the pleasant, salty air, and briefly closed her eyes to relish the refreshing breeze on her face. "Yeah, but it's a good kind of different. I don't feel so...alone. So trapped."

"*It makes me happy that you're so happy,*" he replied with none of his usual snark. "*This place lets you tackle problems you wouldn't have faced on that ship. I think it will only help you grow — there's going to be a lot of improvising in your future.*"

"There will be — in *our* future. And getting hot water for everyone, without having to light fires, is the top of my list right now. I'm tempted to have Vasil bring me back to the Facility just for a shower." She shuddered as she recalled the cold shower she'd taken on her first night in town while Vasil was meeting with Melaina. Calling it unexpected would've been the understatement of the millennium. Her scream had been so loud that she wouldn't have been surprised had the roof collapsed on her. The shock of that first blast of icy water had been more than enough to knock Theo on her ass.

Her short stay in the Facility had spoiled her.

"What about you, Kane?" Theo asked, shifting her toolbox from her left hand to her right as she walked through town toward the lighthouse. "Are you happy?"

"Of course I am," he replied. *"I get to live, Theo. If we weren't here, it'd only be a couple years before I was removed and wiped. We have meaningful work, we don't have to worry about getting blown out of space — at least not again — and the only person that matters to me is happy and healthy. All in all, it's more than I could've ever hoped for."*

She ran her free hand through her hair, tugging it back as she fought back stinging tears. "Thank you, Kane. I don't think I would have been the same after you were removed."

"I know I wouldn't have been the same."

"But at least you wouldn't have any memory of me to be sad about. I'd never forget you."

Aymee, who stood in front of the town hall with the town's bartender, Aiden, waved to Theo as she passed.

Theo offered a smile and a wave in return. Aymee was one of the town's doctors and a good friend of Larkin's. Theo had met her and her mate, the kraken called Arkon, soon after her arrival, along with the other human-kraken couples — Jax and Macy, Randall and Rhea, and Eva and Kronus. They'd all been friendly and welcoming.

Well, except for Kronus. He seemed to have a metal rod permanently shoved up his—

Theo quickly shoved the thought from her mind before her imagination ran with it and generated unwanted images.

Though the ochre kraken was a little rough around the edges, Theo had seen a light in his eyes when he looked upon his mate. She suspected, against all the instincts that she'd built during her early life, that he was a good guy deep inside.

Theo followed the main road up a steady incline that took her out onto the promontory. The buildings she passed were varied in their appearances; centuries of modifications, expansions, and repairs had turned each into a unique testament to human ingenuity and perseverance, but she could see the old bones hidden beneath many of them. Like so much else humans had made on this planet, the structures in The Watch had been built to last, and it showed.

The road ended at the lighthouse. The door squeaked open when she pressed the button, and she stepped inside and began her ascent, trudging up the winding steps. By the time she reached the top, her legs were burning, and she was covered in sweat.

"Fucking hell," Theo groaned and pressed her hand to the door that led into the upper chamber, taking in several deep breaths.

"I believe in you," Kane said cheerily. "You can make it!"

"I already have. Encouragement would have been nice about two hundred damned steps ago."

"We all have our limitations, Theodora. I've done my best."

"Ass." She slammed the heel of her hand into the button beside the door. It opened quietly, in sharp contrast to the entry door below.

I'll have to take a look at the door downstairs... After I rest for about two weeks.

The door closed behind Theo after she entered the chamber.

The air was immediately different — muffled, contained, *close*. The echoes of her footsteps, which had followed her up the entire staircase, were nonexistent here. Even the crashing of waves against the cliffs far below was silenced.

The room was circled completely by tall windows. Theo glanced through them as she walked to the central console beneath the beacon. The bright blue sky was filled with tufts of gentle white, a far cry from the dark rain clouds she'd seen so often since waking on Halora. The horizon seemed impossibly far away — from this high, the sea went on forever.

She set her toolbox down at her feet and turned her attention to the console. "All right, Let's see what we're dealing with. Walter said the light's been flickering when they use the manual turn-on, and the watchers have been having to kick the console to get it to work, right?"

"Essentially, yes. Likely some loose connections in the wiring," Kane replied.

"Exactly what I was thinking. Can you turn the light away from the sea? Don't want to bring the fishermen in early for no good reason."

"The system here is closed. I need you to make physical contact with the controls in order to gain access."

Theo placed her palm on the console. "Here ya go."

"Hmm. Strange."

"What?"

"I'm going to try something. You might feel a bit of... discomfort for a moment."

Theo's brows furrowed. "What do you—"

Electricity jolted up her arm, locking her muscles for an instant before it cut off and she yanked her hand back.

She rubbed her stinging hand, frowning. "What the fuck, Kane?"

The control console sparked to life, projecting a holographic control panel. A progress bar at the bottom stated the system was performing a background repair function.

"I just needed to give it a jumpstart," Kane said innocently. With a soft whir, the light above Theo turned to face inland. "I'm in. That's what counts, right?"

"A little warning next time, yeah?" she grumbled.

"I *did* give you a warning."

"*A bit of discomfort* is not the same as you trying to cook me from the inside out." She turned her attention to the holographic panel. "What's it repairing?"

"This system has been inactive for a long while, but it suffered several failures in the past. It has nothing to do with the light's functioning. There's a surprisingly complex computer system installed here… This was part of a military base, long ago."

"Well, we're not here to fix the computer, right?" She reached for the manual control switch and flipped it on, tilting her head back. The beacon flickered, struggling to come on fully. She banged her boot on the side of the console. The flickering intensified.

"Looks like you need to open that sucker up," Kane said.

Theo crouched down and felt for the panel's release along the bottom edge. Tugging the lever, she pulled the panel up and lifted it away from the console, setting it aside. Wires and circuit casings filled the opening. Kane inserted the purpose of each in her retinal display, flashing through them rapidly until he identified the most likely source of the issue.

She opened her toolbox, took out an old-fashioned screwdriver, and opened the connection box. Sure enough, several of the wires bridging the manual control switch to the beacon were loose. She had them tightened within half a minute. Placing a hand on the console, she pulled herself upright, positioned her finger at the on-off switch, and tested it.

The light went off and came back on four times without the faintest flickering.

"Easy," Theo said. "Don't know if I should be happy or disappointed." She crouched again to replace the lid of the connection box.

"So…interesting bit of information available, now that I'm able to access the data stored in this system," said Kane.

Theo slid the outer panel back into place. "And what interesting bit of information did you happen to find?"

"This lighthouse was also utilized as a control tower to communicate with ships. Space ships. They organized landings and supply drops from here."

"And?"

"The structure itself can act as an antenna. It just needs the proper transmitter to compensate for the lack of satellites in orbit…"

Theo stilled. A loud rushing sound filled her ears, reminiscent of space cruiser thrusters during takeoff. Her heart quickened as she glanced at the toolbox beside her. The transmitter was no longer inside, and she hadn't even thought about it since she'd arrived in The Watch and stowed it away in their home. But that didn't mean it didn't exist.

And this lighthouse was the key.

This was what she had needed since she arrived on this planet. Her way off.

"It works?" she asked numbly.

"Presumably. There's minimal structural damage, so far as I can tell."

She stared at the toolbox. If Kane was right — and she had no doubt he was — the installation would be a simple one. Remove the current transmitter and replace it with the one she'd taken from the sub. Worst case meant she'd need to find a power adaptor or different connectors, but even that would be relatively easy given the spare parts in the Facility.

Absently, she brushed her fingertips over the engraved letters on the toolbox's lid — *M. VELENTI.*

Theo knew what she needed to do.

VASIL WIPED a hand over his face, brushing away the water, as he lifted his torso out of the sea and made his way onto the beach. The other kraken who'd also assisted the human fishermen's work today — Jax, Charos, and Brexes — emerged around him. The evening sun cast the sand and cliffs in an orange-tinged, beautiful light that only seemed to exist at this time of day. It seemed fitting to return to Theo under that glow, almost as unique and captivating as her.

"You are different since claiming your mate," Jax said.

Vasil turned his head to find Jax smiling. "Am I?"

"Always quick to notice the changes in others, but not in yourself?"

Furrowing his brow, Vasil nodded. "I am...*more,* with her. More myself."

Jax looked toward the clifftop homes — toward his home. "Macy makes me feel the same way. More myself, truer to who I am."

"You were always true to yourself, Jax."

Chuckling, Jax shook his head. "I was always forced to choose between our people and who I am. Now I understand that there was no choice to be made — I am myself, and that is of benefit to our people. It does not mean I swim against the kraken."

"And I..." Vasil released a sharp breath through his nostrils. "I did everything I could to be what our people expected. To work toward good for all of us. I gave everything of myself until I had nothing left. Theo was what I needed to finally understand the error of that, to finally learn that I must act not only for others, but for myself, too. I suppose I might have learned that from you much sooner. Taking for myself from time to time does not mean taking *from* our people."

"Even the keenest-eyed amongst us cannot see all, Vasil," Jax said as they climbed the rocky path leading to the dwellings. "But you still see more than most. You are of great value to our people — kraken and human both."

Macy awaited her mate at the top of the path. Jax's smile widened when their eyes met. She crossed the distance separating them and leapt into his arms, wrapping her arms and legs around him as he caught her. She grinned, pressing a swift kiss to his lips.

Vasil's eyes dipped to her rounded stomach, in which another youngling grew. It was a sight that had been rare among the kraken in the past, but the humans had made it more common; they had given the kraken hope. There was a future for their people. Theo had explained to him that she was on *birth control*, a concept still foreign to him, but she'd also said it was temporary. He couldn't wait until his mate was carrying their child.

Macy's cheeks were flushed when she pulled away from Jax. "Hi, Vasil."

Vasil nodded. "Hello, Macy."

She turned her attention back to her mate. "Rhea and Randall took the kids into town." She brushed her fingers along the back of Jax's neck. "There was going to be music and dancing tonight. They...should be gone a while."

Jax's brow rose slowly, somehow tugging the corners of his mouth even higher along with it. "Rest well, Vasil. Until tomorrow," he said without looking away from Macy. He moved quickly toward their home, carrying his giggling mate the entire way.

Vasil watched them for a few moments; seeing Jax and Macy together only made him ache for Theo more. He did not regret doing his duty to provide for his people, but he missed his mate throughout the days, and his want for her company often made the hours drag.

He hurried along the path to his own dwelling, anticipation speeding his hearts; was she there yet? He'd beaten her home on a few days — the repairs she was performing for the townsfolk were not always quick or simple, and Theo was dedicated to finishing each task she undertook to her own satisfaction. According to Arkon, Theo's standards were high, and that made Vasil even prouder of her than he already was.

Without hesitation, he opened the front door and entered their shared den.

Theo was seated at the table, looking out the window. At the sound of the door, she turned her head to face him and smiled; the expression seemed oddly strained.

"Hey," she said softly.

Vasil's smile faded as he closed the door with a tentacle and approached her. "What is wrong, Theo?"

She rose from her seat, the corners of her mouth dropping. She looked away from him to stare down at a strange device laid on the table. "I want you to know what this is because I feel like I've been hiding it from you."

Vasil placed a hand on her arm when he reached her, his brow furrowed. He turned his gaze to the device. It was roughly cylindrical with several wires extending from one side.

"What is it?" He looked at her again. "I do not understand, Theo. What is *wrong*?"

She held his gaze. "When we went to that submarine, I took more than the valve."

"Speak plainly, human. Please."

"It's a transmitter, Vasil."

"A transmitter?" The term sounded familiar; he sorted through his limited knowledge of human technology, gained mostly through working alongside Arkon from time to time. But that was not what had sparked his recognition of the word. *Theo* had been the one to say it to Vasil, not Arkon. His voice was low when he spoke again, dragged down by the sinking feeling in his stomach. "The part you needed to contact the IDC."

She nodded. "And today, Kane told me the lighthouse is an antenna. That it could send a signal into deep space if I connect this transmitter to it."

Vasil couldn't tell what the sensation building inside of him was; hot or cold, dread or anger. It came out in a rush. *"No."*

"Vasil—"

He drew her into a desperate embrace, cupping the back of her head with one hand to keep her gaze locked with his. Tension stiffened his muscles as his tentacles wrapped around her legs, but he fought to keep from harming her. His every instinct screamed to hold her, to pull her close, to feel all of her at once and let her feel him.

"You cannot leave me," he rasped. "I will not allow you to go. You… I *need* you, Theo. I love you."

She settled her hands against his sides and brushed her thumbs over his skin. "Vasil, it's okay. I'm not going anywhere." She leaned her face closer to his, skimming the tip of her nose along his jaw. "Shh."

The thundering of his hearts almost made it impossible to hear her, to hear his own thoughts. "So why do you have it? Why did you take it?"

Theo laid her head on his shoulder, burying her face against his neck. Her breath was warm on his skin. He held her a little tighter, a little closer.

"I don't know, honestly. I just…did. After I took it, after we came here and I put it away, I didn't even think about it until today while I was in the lighthouse. When Kane told me about the transmitter on that submarine, everything inside me just stopped. It's what I needed, right? To leave. To go back to where I came from.

"But Vasil, I don't want to go back. I'm not a fallen star. Just a woman who's had a hard, lonely life. But you, Vasil, *you* changed that. You've given me a home. *You* are my home." She kissed his neck. "And I won't leave you. I need you, too."

The feelings inside him grew even more confused and tumultuous, but one was slowly overpowering the rest — love. It was a simple word for a complex emotion, so easy to say but so *big*, so impossibly powerful, that it could not be contained. His fingers flexed involuntarily, and his tentacles coiled a tighter before he eased his hold on her.

"Why show me?" he asked. "Why, when you could have… thrown it away, or left it hidden?"

"Because I hated the deception. It took me a while to realize that's what it was. By hiding it, by not telling you about it, I was basically lying to you. I needed to show you, so you know — and *I* know — that there are no secrets between us. But I also wanted to do this." She gently pushed away from Vasil, and he reluctantly released her.

Turning away, she crouched and opened her toolbox, which sat on the floor beside the table. She rose with something in her hand — a gun-shaped tool that reminded him a little of the heat guns from the Facility.

"I'm here to stay, Vasil," she said, lifting the transmitter in her free hand. She set the tip of the gun against the end of the transmitter and pulled the trigger.

In an instant, the end of the device was sheared off. It fell heavily to the floorboards.

"The people of Halora are my people," she continued, cutting off another piece. "My friends." A third piece fell to the floor. "And you, Vasil, are my family."

The transmitter dwindled with each cut until only the loose wires remained in her hand.

"You, kraken, are my *mate*." She opened her fingers and let the wires drop to the pile of sliced metal and electronics at her feet. She placed the tool on the table and stepped over the debris. "You are mine. You saved my life, and you own my *heart*, Vasil."

Theo looped her arms around his neck and pulled him down into a scalding kiss, pressing her body against his. Vasil groaned and gathered her in his arms. He lifted her off her feet, turned, and carried her toward the bed.

He knew the feeling inside him now; it was hot, it was *fire*, but it was not born of anger. It was the heat of a fallen star, *for* his fallen star, and he would gladly let it consume him again and again.

ALSO BY TIFFANY ROBERTS

THE INFINITE CITY

Entwined Fates

Silent Lucidity

Shielded Heart

Vengeful Heart

Untamed Hunger

Savage Desire

Tethered Souls

THE KRAKEN

Treasure of the Abyss

Jewel of the Sea

Hunter of the Tide

Heart of the Deep

Rising from the Depths

Fallen from the Stars

Lover from the Waves

THE SPIDER'S MATE TRILOGY

Ensnared

Enthralled

Bound

THE VRIX

The Weaver

The Delver

The Hunter

<u>THE CURSED ONES</u>

<u>His Darkest Craving</u>

His Darkest Desire

<u>ALIENS AMONG US</u>

<u>Taken by the Alien Next Door</u>

<u>Stalked by the Alien Assassin</u>

<u>Claimed by the Alien Bodyguard</u>

Saved by the Alien Crime Boss

<u>STANDALONE TITLES</u>

<u>Claimed by an Alien Warrior</u>

<u>Dustwalker</u>

<u>Escaping Wonderland</u>

<u>Yearning For Her</u>

<u>The Warlock's Kiss</u>

<u>Ice Bound: Short Story</u>

<u>ISLE OF THE FORGOTTEN</u>

<u>Make Me Burn</u>

<u>Make Me Hunger</u>

<u>Make Me Whole</u>

<u>Make Me Yours</u>

<u>VALOS OF SONHADRA COLLABORATION</u>

<u>Tiffany Roberts - Undying</u>

<u>Tiffany Roberts - Unleashed</u>

ABOUT THE AUTHOR

Tiffany Roberts is the pseudonym for Tiffany and Robert, a husband and wife writing duo. The two have always shared a passion for reading and writing, and it was their dream to combine their mighty powers to create the sorts of books they want to read. They write character driven sci-fi and fantasy romance, creating happily-ever-afters for the alien and unknown.

Sign up for our Newsletter!
Check out our social media sites and more!
http://www.authortiffanyroberts.com